SURVIVAL OF THE FITTEST

by
Robin Hawdon

Strategic Book Publishing and Rights Co.

Strategic Book Publishing and Rights Co.
12620 FM 1960, Suite A4-507
Houston TX 77065
www.sbpra.com

ISBN: 978-1-62516-617-3

Design: Dedicated Book Services (www.netdbs.com)

My researches for this book involved many sources, including of course Charles Darwin's own writings. But I should mention in particular Edna Healey's magnificent biography of Emma Darwin which partly inspired the whole project.

Valuable information about Klaus Fuchs also came from various sources, including biographies by Robert Chadwell Williams, and Russell Aiuto.

Some of the Darwin quotations have been edited for clarity and brevity.

R.H.

LOGIC (*Greek–'logos'*): The science that investigates the principles governing correct or reliable inference. Inexorable truth or persuasiveness.

PROLOGUE

Peculiarly, the thing that dominated his dreams was the smell. The sickly sweet odour of decaying flesh. Only after that came the image of the limbs—limbs that in youth had been so smooth and neatly formed, which he could have sketched all day had he been an artist—now scarred with festering wounds. And of course the hair, gathered in handfuls each morning from the pillow—grey, wispy, brittle, that had once been the luxurious brown into which he used to bury his face as if to smother himself. And lastly it was the eyes. Eyes that had always been so amused and knowing—that were now so faded and pain filled.

And it was always the same—the dreams were always a panic stricken rush down endless corridors to find the room and cover the awful wounds with dressings which were never large enough, feed the intravenous drips which never seemed to ease the pain, interpret the flashing lights which signalled a never ending emergency.

He had the dreams every night. He was resigned to the fact that there was no way of evading them. It was God's way of telling him. Of reminding him that he had failed her. He had allowed her to slip from his grasp, sending her on her way with all her questions unanswered, her doubts un-soothed, her remarkable love unmatched. He had failed her miserably, and God would punish him for evermore.

Except of course that there was no God. How could there be? She was the living and dying proof that he was not there.

CHAPTER ONE

January 1951. Wakefield Prison.

I have been sitting here staring at my dark stone wall for almost an hour and still I have no idea how to commence this treatise, memoir, chronicle—call it what you will. There is so much to tell and it is all so complex. I am truly angry at what has happened to me, yet I have to keep that anger at bay in order to rationally explain my purposes.

I have to jump in somewhere, so let me begin with the simple part.

My cell is roughly twelve feet by eight. The size, I suppose of a normal bedroom. In most prisons it would probably accommodate two people, but thankfully here at Wakefield we have our own individual cells, probably due to the violent proclivities of many of the inmates. I cannot imagine the anguish of having to share this space with some coarse hoodlum. I have a somewhat sagging metal and wire bed with a hard horsehair mattress, a wooden table and chair, a basin with a cold water tap (which I am told sometimes freezes up in the bitter Yorkshire winters), and an odd cork-backed board on the back wall which I suppose is for attaching letters, photos, the traditional half naked pin-up girls, or whatever else the occupant desires. I use it to pin up my mathematical calculations, which to me at least have their own beauty. It gives me some amusement to watch the wardens puzzle over them when they pay their visits. There is no toilet, merely a crude bucket with lid, which I empty twice a day in the vile slops room at the end of the building, an unpleasant task to my fastidious self. The cell door is solid, with a small observation window in it, and there is, joy of

2

joys, a high barred window through which I have a view of the sky, part of the opposite prison roof, and just a glimpse of the foliage of what must be quite a large tree beyond—a beech by the look of it, or possibly an ash—I must find out which. Occasionally I catch birds flying across my piece of sky—pigeons, sparrows, once or twice a hawk of some kind. Free spirits—I envy them. I must face east or south-east because the sun, when it is out, slants into my cell first thing in the morning, but by early afternoon it has gone, and by evening the opposite roof is bathed in its glow. I am fortunate with that position. It is good to wake to the sun. It starts the day with hope. It helps to keep my black demons of despair at bay, which are always worst at first wakening. I have lived with that first assault of negativity most of my life, but here without the challenge of a vocation to distract me the threat is worse. So I am glad of the sun, and especially of the tree. It is a friend. It will enable me to keep track of the seasons. It will tell me whether the wind is blowing, and how bright the sun or the moon is. It will remind me there is life.

I am told I am quite lucky to be at Wakefield. It is not the worst of British prisons, and not the harshest of prison regimes. And British prisons and regimes are a long way from rivaling the worst elsewhere, that is certain. This will be my home for the best part of the next fourteen years. A long time. A large proportion of anyone's life, let alone as a proportion spent in prison. I wonder how they arrive at such a maximum term? It seems a strange number until you realise that of course it is exactly one fifth of man's allotted threescore and ten. Yes, twenty per cent of one's lifetime as a penalty for betraying one's chosen country—I suppose that's a reasonable equation, though still a fairly arbitrary one. Of course it's better than the prospect of execution, which is what I anticipated. Perhaps I should be grateful to the moderate British legal system for not imposing the harsher sentence. However, contemplating such an infinity here in my claustrophobic space, I sometimes think that perhaps execution might have been a kinder alternative. Oh lord, such self-pity is ridiculous!

I have begun writing this during my third week at Wakefield. I have decided that, if I am to retain my sanity, I must establish a strict routine of mental exercise. I have my maths (or math as they call it in America) of course—a never ending source of challenge and fascination—but in addition to that I need something else, something to replace the intense routine of research and experiment, debate and argument, which has been at the core of my daily existence for most of my life until this point. This chronicle is my solution. And perhaps in the course of writing it I will be able to refute some of the slanders that have been cast upon me, and to disprove the more pernicious accusations. It might have considerable repercussions, not least from my original Russian paymasters (they never paid me anything but I don't know what else to call them), but nevertheless I feel honour bound to explain myself. The world has a right to know my reasons. Though why I should imagine the world will ever read it, I don't know.

I am fortunate that the regime here is so relatively relaxed. I have access to ink and paper (although even this is in short supply thanks to the post-war austerity measures), and also to the prison's surprisingly extensive library. I have this modest, but not hideously uncomfortable cell to myself, whilst at the same time a tolerable amount of contact with other inmates. There is quite a bit of banter between the cells, across the corridors, and amongst the duty orderlies. I rarely participate but I get considerable amusement listening to it. Many of my associates in crime are extremely colourful characters, some quite witty (not one of my own attributes), and a few surprisingly intelligent, despite their perverted mentalities. They are the kind of men whom I encountered all those years ago back home in my own country, the difference being that there they were the ones in command. They are the kind of men I suppose one needs to understand if one is to interpret the origins of war, which is—was—one of my aims.

I am allowed visitors, although I'm not sure how many of my former associates will deign to come here, since I appear now to be a total bete noire amongst the scientific fraternity. It is the thing that distresses me most about the whole business. I had grown to look on most of my fellow scientists with a good deal of fondness—even though I was by nature and circumstance unable to demonstrate it effectively. But then it would have been naive of me to expect them to react differently to my circumstance. They were all so certain of their loyalties and affiliations. So confident of what the great struggle was all about. Few of them had actually seen the terrible things I had seen. They had no cause to suffer the titanic ethical struggle with their consciences that I had. And of course, being in the position I was in, I could never communicate those thoughts to them. I know they respected my abilities as a physicist, but they must have found me a strangely enigmatic animal.

The plain fact is that I was in the unique position of being able to assess, perhaps better than anyone, the immense and fundamental issues that now lie so glaringly exposed in the aftermath of that appalling war. Presumptuous of me no doubt, but after all few people were as well qualified to do so. I may not have the reputation of Einstein or Niels Bohr, but few have been endowed with the intellectual and analytical capacity that I have. And few were able to observe the strategies of the contesting nations from such an elevated inside position. To that extent I was privileged.

Despite my acceptance of the charges against me, I still look back on the three days of my trial with resentment. I should by now, some nine months later, have come to terms with things, but I am still offended that my motives were so misunderstood. The judge, Lord Goddard, distinguished though no doubt he is, was clearly prejudiced against me right from the start. What was it he said in summing up? That I had 'betrayed the hospitality and protection given me with the grossest treachery.' That I had 'done incalculable harm both to this country and to the United States, merely for the purpose of furthering my political creed.' Such immoderate language shows that he had no idea of my real motives. He had not the remotest concept of what I was about. I certainly had no intention of betraying anyone, or of doing harm to any country, except perhaps temporarily the country of my birth. No—attempting to further the cause of humanity, is how I would describe my purpose. A touch portentous perhaps, but sincere. And in the light of the subsequent events it may appear to have been misguided, but in the cataclysmic circumstances of that time it was not an unreasonable assumption. An error in political calculation is the most one could accuse me of, and one which no-one could have predicted at the time. The judge called my crime, 'only thinly differentiated from high treason,' but I consider that grossly misinterpreted. I do not claim innocence but I am, I think, justified in feeling deeply wronged. The question is, can I prove to the rest of the world that I was wronged?

Good. I have begun. It has not been as difficult as I imagined. Writing is without doubt a therapy. I feel more optimistic already.

CHAPTER TWO

Lamarck was the first man whose conclusions on the subject excited much attention. He upholds the doctrine that species, including man, are descended from other species. He first did the eminent service of arousing attention to the probability of all change in the organic world being the result of law, not of miraculous interposition.

Preface to Origin of Species.

It was around eight o'clock in the morning when the telephone call came. It wasn't a dramatic call. It didn't seem hugely significant at the time. But as it turned out it changed the course of his life. Subtly at first, then more radically.

And let's face it, his life's course needed changing. His life was going down the pan.

It was the start of another working day. He had, as always, listened in bed to the seven o'clock headlines and the weather forecast, which, although both invariably gloomy, usually managed to distract him from the even gloomier blues which bedevilled him first thing. He had risen, cleaned his teeth, put on his underclothes, and was well into his morning workout. As always, he was talking to himself: 'Breathe in, breathe out. . . . *I will arise and go now. And go to Innisfree. . . .*' No, not strictly true. He was talking to his wife Alice, but since she had been dead these three years it would seem to an impartial observer that he was talking to himself. 'In, out, in out. . . . *Nine bean rows will I have there, a hive for the honey bee . . .*' Puffing a bit, since he was doing knee-bends by the open window and it was taking a while to work off the inevitable hangover from the night before. Knees creaking a little but managing his two dozen all right. 'One, two, three, four . . . *And live alone in the bee loud glade.*' He could see from the window the grey sky and jumbled roof tops of Primrose Hill, and as always he hoped the neighbours opposite weren't watching with secret hilarity from behind their own window. He was aware that he was a minor figure of fun in the street. 'Yes, we'd be quite happy in a bee loud glade, wouldn't we? As long as we had each other and the bean rows and the small cabin 'of mud and wattles made.'' Change from knees-bends to half push-ups on the window sill. 'Up, down, up, down. . . .' The neighbours were probably in convulsions. 'I don't suppose the glade would be bee loud always. Pretty foul weather I expect they get at Innisfree a lot of the time. But still, it's a seductive image, isn't it? The ultimate poet's poem I always think.'

Alice didn't answer, but he knew what she'd have said so it was almost as good. 'Yes dear, very poetic, but firstly you'd be bored silly within twenty four hours, and secondly I don't know how I'd manage with the laundry in a bee loud glade.' He smiled to himself. Trust women to think practically. But as usual she was right. The mechanics of life would go neglected without women to handle them. The world would come to a stop. Just as his world had almost done, without her to see everything was wound up and ticking along. On the surface he'd kept things going. Kept changing the sheets, and vacuuming the Wilton, and ironing his shirts just as she would have done. And just about kept the book shop going— a rare oasis of erudition in the centre of teeming London. But he had to admit it was all a pretty vacuous pretence. The sheets were worn, the dust was accumulating along the Wilton's edges, and even the book shop was in serious trouble now. And without that he would be totally lost. Floating in an Einsteinian void. Spinning into a Hawking black hole. Collapsing into a Lorenzian chaos.

Maurice knew his science. Scientific literature was one of his specialities.

It was at this point that his reflections were interrupted by the telephone. He stopped his exertions and frowned at it for a second. He was unused to getting calls at home at this time of the morning. Glanced at his watch, muttered, 'If this is a damned sales call I'll. . . .,' left the threat unfinished, and went to the instrument. One of the old fashioned kind, the hand-set still anchored to its resting place by a flex. Not many of those around these days. His spectacles sat beside it, and he put them on before answering, though for what reason he couldn't have said. Answered a little breathlessly. 'Hello?'

'Am I speaking to Maurice Aldridge?' The deep voice was precise, with one of those slightly drawling Bostonian accents that cultured Americans either possess or adopt.

'Yes, that's me.'

'The distinguished antiquarian book dealer?'

'Hardly distinguished, but I am a book dealer, yes.'

'My name is Donald Easterby.' The voice paused a moment as if to see if the name provoked a response. 'As you can probably surmise, I'm from the States.'

'How, er. . . . how did you get my private number?'

'Oh, forgive me. I can explain that. I do have your professional number also, but I wanted to catch you early. I hope I haven't called too soon, or perhaps interrupted your English breakfast?'

Maurice felt faintly piqued. Yes, the man was delaying his breakfast, and yes, of course it would be English. What did he expect—chopsticks? 'What can I do for you, Mr Easterby?'

'Well—maybe nothing, maybe a great deal.'

Maurice wiped the mild perspiration from his brow, hitched up his undershorts and waited for the other to get to his point.

'I'm looking for a specialist dealer. I'm particularly interested in original editions of scientific books and papers. I believe that may be your field?'

'One of them, certainly.'

'Then you might know who Klaus Fuchs was.'

Maurice frowned, searching his memory. This was going back a bit. 'Fuchs? You mean the spy? The, er. . . . atom scientist?'

'Correct. And you'll also know who Emma Darwin was.'

Maurice blinked irritably. This felt like Brain Of Britain. 'The wife of . . .?'

'Charles Darwin, yes.'

'I'm afraid I don't . . .'

'An extraordinary woman in her own right.'

'I don't know a great deal about either of them. What's the connection?'

The confidential tone increased. 'Yes, that's the question. But there is a connection. An obscure one, but an extremely significant one, which I won't explain just yet. Suffice to say that they were both rather remarkable people.'

'Yes, I er. . . .'

'What would you say if I told you that I have reason to believe they both kept journals? Quite different in style and purpose, but both equally private, and in fact clandestine. Fuchs's written during the nineteen fifties while he was in prison in this country. Emma Darwin's composed as a kind of secret commentary of her years with Charles.' Again Maurice was silent. 'Hello? Does that surprise you?'

'Not completely.'

'Ah. You've heard about them?'

'I think I've heard the odd rumour about Emma Darwin over the years. Not Fuchs though.'

The man's voice took on an added eagerness. 'Really? You knew about Emma Darwin?'

Oh dear—was he one of those irritating obsessives? 'Well just vaguely. The book world is always echoing with those sorts of rumours.'

'But you've never pursued them?'

Maurice couldn't keep the impatience from his voice. He was falling behind schedule. 'I haven't the time to follow up every clue about every paper and pamphlet that crosses my path, Mr Easterby.'

'No, no, I realise that.' The tone was placating. 'But I'm intrigued that it didn't come as a complete surprise to you.' The voice changed. 'Of course if such a thing came to light it could be one of the most important literary discoveries ever made.'

Maurice frowned. Surely a bit excessive. 'Really?' he said.

'Oh, yes. I can explain. Look, I can't talk more about it at the moment, Maurice—may I call you that?—but might such items be of interest to you?'

'Well, naturally, but . . .'

'I'm afraid I have to dash now. But are you by any chance free for lunch today?'

'Today?'

'It's short notice, I realise that. But I'm only in London on a flying visit. I'm leaving for France in two days so there's not much time. I have a proposition to put to you.'

Maurice's brain spun. He didn't think anything was happening this lunch time. 'Well, er. . . . well yes, I suppose I could. . . .'

'I'm staying at the Ritz. A bit obvious, I know, but it suits my purpose. Shall we say twelve thirty in the main restaurant? If we make it early we can avoid the rush. I will reserve a table, and you'll come as my guest of course.'

'That's very kind. But I, er. . . .'

'You won't regret it, Maurice. You might find it a useful meeting. If I may speculate a little about you, it could be the sort of encounter you might find valuable at this moment.'

Maurice said nothing, stunned into silence by the presumption, or was it prior knowledge, of the statement.

'Just ask for me at reception. Donald Easterby. I look forward to meeting you.'

And he rang off, leaving Maurice standing by his telephone in his undershorts, spectacles, and a state of bemusement. He shook his head. Who was this man? How could he presume to understand so much of Maurice's situation? The latter was an extremely private person, and was appalled at the idea of a complete stranger assuming intimate knowledge of his circumstances.

He abandoned the rest of his exercises and went to the bathroom to shave. As he lathered his face (still wet-shaved—he disdained the use of electric shavers) he pondered the conversation. He was used to approaches from out of the blue, seeking either to obtain rare publications or offering such for sale. But there was something extraordinary about this one. Not only about the man himself and his apparently psychic powers, but also about his purposes and the subjects of his interest. He did not sound like your usual book trader (the Ritz indeed!)—and the combination of historical characters mentioned seemed incongruous, the description of the material vague. Private journals were, in Maurice's experience, usually objects of contention. Not only over their provenance and ownership, but also over the reliability of their content.

He chatted on to Alice in the mirror as he shaved, speculating about the phone call. For once he could not imagine any response from her which might illuminate matters. He dressed even more precisely than usual in clean shirt, striped tie, best tweed suit (which was the nearest he could get to Ritz style attire), and traditional brown leather shoes bought at the Jermyn Street sales. Then polished his spectacles meticulously with a tissue, and went through to the bow-fronted living room for breakfast. Another tradition from his married days, and he stuck to it resolutely, resisting the temptation to simply grab a quick bite in the small en suite kitchen. '*A bachelor's life is a fine breakfast, a flat lunch, and a miserable dinner.*' Maurice had a quote for every occasion.

He checked the level on the whiskey bottle which still stood on the table from the night before, muttered a pointless self reproof, and put it back in the drinks cupboard before preparing the meal and sitting down. His very British breakfast consisted of an orange cut into quarters, bowl of All Bran and muesli, slice of wholemeal toast and Tiptree thick cut (he had long ago finished the stock of Alice's home-made marmalade—another small deprivation amongst so many to remind him), and a pot of tea—best Ceylon loose leaf with just a half spoon of Earl Grey to add that subtle flavour. As he sipped from the Wedgewood china cup he pondered further over the implications of the peculiar phone call, and his eyes turned inevitably towards the mahogany book shelves running the length of the room. Rank upon rank of leather and cloth bound volumes rising to the ceiling. His private collection. Prized editions discovered over the years—poetry mostly, from Keats to Kipling, Browning to Betjeman—diverted from the shop to his home because of their special and personal appeal. *'The proper study of mankind is books.'* Alice used to complain, saying they took up too much room, they were depriving them of essential income and so on, but he had always clung to them. They were the children he never had. They were the things he couldn't bring himself to trade.

Until now. Soon he might have no choice.

Snippets from the phone call came to him: '. . . . very remarkable people. . . . both kept journals. . . . both equally private, in fact clandestine. . . . one of the most important literary discoveries ever made. . . .' He frowned and absently cleaned his specs again on his napkin. Was the approach an indirect way of offering the works in question for sale? Was the Yank acting as someone's agent? Was he following some particular trail? Was he laying the ground for some ingenious scam? All these were possibilities that Maurice had encountered before, but he had no way of judging in this case. However, if the man was genuine, the articles he mentioned would certainly be of interest. Not your usual sort of dusty tome or obscure manuscript. Maurice began to feel more enthusiastic. At least lunch at the Ritz with an apparently wealthy, visionary, bibliophilic American was something that would enliven the working day.

He turned on the radio for the rest of the morning news. Well into an item about another misguided rocket attack in the Middle East, which had killed a large number of civilians including several school children. Followed by Thought For The Day, in which some well meaning prelate tied himself in intellectual knots trying to explain God's part in the atrocity. Maurice listened for a moment, sighed, and switched it off again with an irritable shake of the head. Another effect of his circumstances—the highlighting of all that was negative in the outside world. When Alice was alive and well the two of them had in an unspoken pact managed to repulse, or at any rate ignore, the more unattractive aspects of contemporary life. But now, on his own, those aspects seemed to be looming up, surrounding him, rushing in upon him like a tsunami of bad omens. Wherever he turned, to the live media, the newspapers, the conversation of his acquaintances, all he could glean was an overwhelming barrage of information or disinformation about everything that was wrong with the world, from wars and terrorism to natural disasters and political intrigue, or, at a more trivial level, from the problems of domestic and community life to an endless preoccupation with celebrity scandal and financial crises. The public at large were evidently fascinated by such manifestations, and Maurice supposed that his despair at it all made him either an unworldly recluse or more probably a grumpy middle aged man. A bit of both probably, since he now largely shunned their previous quite wide and eclectic circle of friends (who had mostly got the message and given up on him), and since he was given to sudden outbursts of ill temper at inopportune moments—at the supermarket check-out girl, the inoffensive bank clerk, the indecisive customer at the book shop—even, God help him, at his own bleary-eyed face in the mirror in the morning. He was usually contrite afterwards (which often made him appear still more of a fool), but again there seemed little he could do about it.

No, Alice's slow death from the dreaded C over those four terrible years of alternating remission and relapse had clouded his hitherto pretty optimistic outlook for ever, and made him doubt the fundamental tenets of his own philosophy and inner being. That and 7/7—the London bombs. Which had happened so soon after her diagnosis, and being another personal experience seemed to confirm his cynicism. *'Evil is easy, and has infinite forms.'*

He gazed around the wide living room which spanned the first floor of the terraced Victorian building. He had changed nothing since she had left him. Her presence was everywhere. In the decor, photos, nicknacks, paintings—even, he fondly liked to imagine, the scent. His glance moved back to his dominating shelves. Books. It was to them he always turned in adversity. Here and at the shop his rows of ancient sagging shelves with their priceless cargo of thumbed, yellowing parchment and leather—these were his companions in adversity. They contained the immense accumulation of human knowledge and wisdom which gave the lie to all his pessimistic conclusions. They were the works and thoughts of serious minds, the near infinite record of individual mental effort that had driven civilisation onwards and brought the world to its present brilliant, appalling, sublime, anarchic, and utterly unpredictable state. Lorenzian chaos.

'And I shall have some peace there,' he murmured. *'For peace comes dropping slow. Dropping from the veils of the morning to where the cricket sings . . .'* Yes, Yeats's escapist

vision seemed very attractive sometimes. At least they probably didn't have terrorist bombs at Innisfree. Maybe not even cancer.

Maurice put his tea cup down, missing the edge of the saucer and slopping tea onto the table cloth. He cursed beneath his breath and mopped at the spill with his napkin. His very real problem was that the books too were under serious threat now. 'What should I do, Alice? What shall I do about the shop?' he mumbled at the tea stain. She would surely have had a suggestion when she was alive, but this time there was no answer. His accountant had been warning him for two years that the once moderately thriving business wasn't profitable any longer, and he was having to admit that the growth of internet trading and the impact of other entertainment media were having a serious effect on his trade. Alice would have known that he'd find it impossible to contemplate a life that did not include either her or the books. How would he survive without either to commune with? How fill the days without his daily bus ride (he avoided the tube whenever possible—it always caused him mild claustrophobia) through some of the pleasanter parts of London, to his musty premises right in the heart of the capital? Without his encounters with the last surviving members of the cultured classes who came there for similar escape and enlightenment? What on earth would he do? Go for endless walks on Hampstead Heath? Take up crosswords, golf, bridge? No, such a life was not to be contemplated.

He banished the thoughts from his mind and considered his various appointments for the morning. He was expecting a visit from one of his auction hounds who usually had something interesting to offer; he anticipated acquiring a rare Blackwood collected works of George Eliot from an old dealer colleague; he hoped to dispose of a signed first edition of Evelyn Waugh's *Vile Bodies* to a regular customer for a tidy profit. And all before his mystifying lunch appointment. Well at least today held a few things to anticipate.

He suddenly realised that, what with phone calls and pessimistic reflections, he was falling seriously behind schedule. 'Chop, chop, chum,' he muttered, drained his cup of Ceylon and Earl Grey, swallowed his last bite of toast, then donned his tweed overcoat and brown trilby and checked his appearance in the long mirror in the hallway. The figure that stared back at him would not perhaps have impressed others, but it satisfied him. Not far short of average height; hair receding a little perhaps but not showing many signs of grey; form a touch portly but pretty trim considering; legs not exactly long but sturdy and straight. And quite fit too, thanks to the daily exercises, and despite his pathetic reliance on scotch to get him to sleep. There were as yet only minor signs that his mental state and the whiskey were beginning to take their toll.

'Watch out, Dorian Gray,' he grunted at the mirror. Then confirmed that he had his wallet, small purse for loose cash, keys, crucial note-book, specs case, and half-full hip flask of Bells—which had lasted through yesterday and might just last today if he was strong—and went out of his originally quite cheap but now mercifully valuable Primrose Hill apartment, to brave the chill March breeze. If the neighbours were watching there was no sign, and as he left the building he resisted the temptation he always felt to stick two fingers up in their direction. He strode towards his bus stop appearing for all the world like a confident country gentleman from another era.

Given his true background and history that was quite an achievement.

CHAPTER THREE

Foreword

I have decided, against her own expressed wishes, to publish this abbreviated edition of my mother's personal journal, because it seems to me that such a record of the most significant twenty years of our family life, and such a commentary on the most crucial period of my father's work, should not be lost, at least to their descendants. I have excluded some of the extensive scientific material, which is of limited interest to the majority and is anyway covered more fully in my father's writings, and I have added notes of information where I deemed necessary.

I hope my mother will forgive me from wherever she is in the heaven she so fervently believed in.

F.D. 1898

September 28th 1842. Down House

This is a bold step indeed for me to take, and I confess I am apprehensive. Should any of my family happen, despite my wishes, to read it in the future I trust they will understand my motives.

I have purchased my own private volume of plain foolscap pages, with the intention of writing down my current thoughts and experiences. This is such a momentous time for me, and for my family, that I feel strongly the need to give my feelings expression, if only to relieve myself of their burden. Acquaintances of mine keep records, I know, and pride themselves on their reflections concerning domestic and national proceedings, but I have never been a literary person so this is a truly personal journal for my own benefit. It is my way of finding release for a heart that is too full of feelings.

Dramatic events began the moment we decided to move to the country, after nearly four years in noisy, dirty, odorous, clattering London. Both Charles and I had dreamt of such a moment almost since the day we were wed, but he was shackled to the capital by his work and his responsibilities, and it was not until a few months ago that I (and his doctors) prevailed upon him to take this step for the sake of both his health and his work. It came at a timely moment for the Chartist mobs were threatening riot in the City, with noisy masses of workers out on strike, clamouring against the poor laws and wage cuts and unemployment, and I know not what. The Government was forced to call out battalions of Guards against the rabble, which even had us penned in our house in Upper Gower Street—shouting crowds and police and soldiers with fixed bayonets everywhere. It was truly terrifying, and felt at times as if the whole of society was on the edge of destruction. I cannot help sympathising with the poor, especially the large numbers in the North, where they say the slums in such cities as Manchester and Glasgow are like hell-holes, where the workers have no prospect of employment and the children are used as little better than slave labour. One's sense of justice demands a better existence for them. Even so, such riotous behaviour in the capital cannot be tolerated in this peaceable country, and one has to hope the politicians can keep a firm control of the situation.

Nevertheless we finally arrived here at Down House, our new home in the country, and have exchanged one grievous situation for another. This time of a far more personal and sorrowful nature. I still cannot accept that the joy of this move, added to in so timely a way by the birth of our third child, little Mary, would be shattered by her death in my arms barely a month after our arrival. I cannot comprehend how

fate can play such malicious tricks. How can honestly earned
joy be turned on its head in such a cruel fashion? It is a frequent enough case I know, and she was sickly from the start,
but her loss when only three weeks old, after nine months
of expectancy and nurturing within one's body seems too
cruel and unjust an event. Her sweet face was so composed
in death, as if she knew she had simply gone to God, but I
have never before known such despair in my heart. I am confident He has His reasons and His purposes for the human
race, but I confess I sometimes find them hard to understand.
I know that Charles feels the same, yet I wonder in my secret
thoughts whether it might be that the Almighty is punishing
us for my husband's explorations into matters which are not
perhaps for us to know, especially when they seem to bring
into question His holy plan and purpose. I could never mention this to Charles. I know without question that he is a truly
good man in his own fashion, and I cannot believe, when
I see the evil some men promote, that his concerns can be
comparably offensive to the Lord.

Herein however lies the cause of my deepest concern.
Charles's researches consume him to such an extent, his obsessions occupy so much of his waking (and probably sleeping) hours that I fear for his mental health as much as his
physical. I know enough of his work to understand that he is
struggling with mysteries that have concerned mankind since
the beginning of time, and he feels compelled to seek solu-
tions that have evaded the finest minds throughout history.
But why a man of such humble disposition should concern
himself with such mighty ambitions I cannot fathom, and
when I question him on the matter he can give me no answer.
He merely shrugs his shoulders and mutters, "There is so
much, Emma, so many things to understand," or sometimes,
"God has left us with so many questions, and it us up to us
to find the answers." Well indeed that may be so, but I do not
believe we have to spend our whole lives agonising over the
matter. God himself knows those answers, which ultimately

is all that <u>we</u> need to know. We can happily trust in His divine purpose without attempting to interpret it ourselves, and as I have said it seems to me that we risk his wrath if we do so. However it is not a wife's place to challenge her husband's purpose, and I am happy at least that C is so fulfilled in his work that he does not show the wantonness some other husbands display.

Which brings me to our material circumstances, Charles has proclaimed that he will not be making another move for the rest of his life—a somewhat rash promise I feel—so there is much obligation on this house and small community to take us to their hearts and make us at home. I have to allow, when I first saw the place, at 'the extreme verge of the world' as C describes it, I was not overwhelmed by its attributes. The house itself is not one that immediately appeals to my feminine senses—although spacious enough for our needs and for £2000 a fair bargain—and the village of some 40 households, though quite pretty, is hardly in the most picturesque setting, being backed by the bleak chalk Downs. But we have eighteen acres of land, and Charles is full of the improvements he will make to the place, and the village has the essential trades amenities (though lacking the theatres and concert halls which are the only attributes of London I shall miss), and a populace of what appears to be good hearted people, as well as some well-presented local gentry. Amongst these in particular is the squire Sir John Lubbock,[1] up at High Elms, who to Charles's delight is a brother philosopher[2] and Fellow of the Royal Society. And of course there is the church, St Mary's, dated from the 14th century, quite well attended, and the young curate, Revd John Willot, is earnest enough, though perhaps a little pompous in his administrations.

---

[1] *City banker, land owner and High Sheriff of Kent.*
[2] *Meaning scientist (which word was not yet in common use).*

The children, Willy & Annie, appear to have recovered well from their own grief at losing their little sister, and now spend much time running around our few acres, and exploring the village, and soon enough they will be in need of a governess to begin their education. They seem to be already benefiting from the space and country air and are, to my great consolation, growing into the most sweet natured of young people. Charley's sisters, when they come to visit, are always exhorting me to keep a stricter rein on them and to have the servants order their routine, but my own instincts are that they should have the freedom to roam and be their natural selves at this tender age. Time enough for discipline later.

As for Charles himself, his own precarious health does not as yet appear to be similarly well affected, but he is greatly energised by the prospect of creating his longed-for rural haven, and he spends much of the day in his new study organising shelves and cupboards and cabinets for his myriad of specimens. I myself can never understand the significance of such an enormous collection of rocks and fossils, plants and seeds, beetles and bugs, fishes and feathers from around the world, but my extraordinary husband has a name and a category and a function for every one, and as each day brings more and more by post and courier from his following of like-minded enthusiasts, his involvement seems to increase further and his pain at our sad loss healed.

Would that I had such distraction. However I do have a different one—the distraction of our finances. I have the suspicion that I would not be so concerned were it not for C's concerns on the matter. It seems to me that, with the generous allowance from his father, and the marriage settlement from my own father, we are not as impecunious as Charles would have me believe. Nevertheless I concede that this is not going to be an inexpensive household to run, and C insists that I keep exact record of every penny earned and spent, an onerous task for such a scatterbrain as myself.

The major expenditure is of course the servants. We will be employing some half dozen at least—our butler of course, the invaluable Joseph Parslow come with us from London, who is almost one of the family; and a footman to aid him at table and door; together with Eliza, my own maid. Then there is Jessie Brodie, the children's nurse, newly moved to us from the Thakerays,[3] a dear woman and much adored by the children. She is aided by a local lass, Bessy, extremely good-hearted and kind with them, though sometimes at odds with Jessie, at which moments I have to threaten horse-whips and thumb screws; and we are trying various cooks, although finding one to suit is difficult in these rural parts. We also of course need a coachman for C's new carriage (his pride and joy, but costing 100 guineas!) which must take us on our social rounds of the neighbourhood—not, I trust, too frequent—and bear C to the station for his train journeys to London and his meetings—ditto.

Such a household is not excessive by some standards but it is large enough, and would not perhaps be necessary were we to be leading the reclusive country life we had hoped for. However it would seem from our early indications that this is not to be. If the days are not taken up with relatives then they are occupied with academic visitors from the capital, or passing migrants from the Continent, all seeking my dear Charles's counsel and opinions. He claims to be as unenthusiastic about this as I am myself (his fragile constitution always suffers from too much social exertion and the after effects of copious dinners) but I think secretly he delights in their attentions, for his gravest concern about moving down here was that he would find himself excluded from all that was happening in the hurly-burly worlds of botany and science. It is evident that will be far from the case. I am

---

[3] *William Thakeray, novelist, 1811–63, who had to release Jessie for financial reasons.*

constantly astonished at the consequences of his long ago voyage around the world, about which he still talks so much, and which of course was the inspiration for his present obsessions.[4] Admittedly five years is a long time to spend afloat (or afoot as he insists was often the case), and wondrous were the far off places he visited. Yet to an untutored brain such as mine the furore over the collection he carried home with him, of rocks and fossils and plants and skeletons, seems exaggerated to say the least. Again I reflect that we are all the products of the Almighty's great design, and we know enough of the marvellous diversity of fauna and flora within our own beautiful land to understand that He must have extended that diversity to suit other terrains and climes, so why the hullabaloo? But then I dare not enquire too deeply into the speculations of C's associates and fellow minds, for I rather fear the implications of their replies. I hear enough at the dinner table to sometimes wonder if a divine thunderbolt might not strike the house there and then, but amongst such company I would not dream of giving voice to my thoughts. I know from his occasional sidelong glances in my direction that C is well aware of them.

Ah, well, I feel I have written enough for my first attempt at journal keeping. Despite my lack of aspiration to literary achievement I have found the experiment quite therapeutic. In a strange way I feel it provides some sort of epitaph for my little Mary. My problem now is where to keep this volume safe from prying eyes. If I am to enter my innermost personal thoughts here it is perhaps best that the members of my dear family (not to mention the servants) do not become privy to them. There are some things which should, I think, always be kept to one's own confidence and shared only with one's Maker. Even to the exclusion of spouses.

---

[4]*Voyage aboard the Beagle sloop under Captain Robert Fitzroy, 1831–6.*

CHAPTER FOUR

Is it possible that an animal having, for instance, the structure and habits of a bat, could have been formed by the modification of some animal with wholly different habits? Can we believe that natural selection could produce on the one hand organs of trifling importance, such as the tail of a giraffe which serves as a fly-flapper, and on the other hand organs of such wonderful structure as the eye, of which we hardly as yet fully understand the inimitable perfection?

Origin of Species

Maurice had a relatively satisfactory morning at the book shop. The George Eliot edition made its appearance in remarkably good condition—collected works invariably spend most of their lives untouched on the least accessible library shelves—and he acquired it for a reasonable sum; he sold *Vile Bodies* for a wholly unreasonable sum, but wasn't too conscience stricken about it as the client was indecently rich and anyway delighted at his purchase; he made one or two other transactions; and he received a brief second phone call from Donald Easterby, who apologised profusely for his earlier haste, and confirmed the lunch appointment.

For some irrational reason the nearer that appointment approached the more uneasy Maurice felt about it. He did not these days usually go out for lunch. He had of necessity, both economic and digestive, forced himself to stop going to the pub in the middle of the day, the crunch coming one afternoon when he had returned late and fairly drunk and made a fool of himself with a valued client. He was now resigned to collecting a sandwich from the local Covent Garden snack bar, whilst his assistant—a rather nerdy but relatively well-read youth called Rupert who was escaping from an unsatisfactory course at the London School of Economics—kept shop for a moment or two. However Maurice did not pay him enough to entrust him with responsibility over long periods, so on this occasion he decided to close up and give the grateful youth a couple of hours off, before setting off on the half mile walk to Leicester Square and along Piccadilly to The Ritz.

A brisk spring morning and even at this time of year the heart of the capital was thronged with tourists, mostly foreign with a smattering of natives. He had to weave an erratic path between them and the various vendors plying their tatty trade along the pavements, but for once Maurice didn't mind too much. Good to be out of the shop in such weather, and his old self responded to the vibrant beat of the huge city with which he was so familiar and which was like that of no other that he knew. Paris may be more romantic, Rome and Venice more ancient, New York more startling, Sydney and Rio and Cape Town more spectacularly sited (he had been to them all in his time)—but London had for him an air of simple greatness that no other could match, despite the advance of squalid contemporary manifestations. It was to do with the space and the variation. The numerous individual village centres that comprised the whole, the tranquil tree-framed parks, the graceful period terraces, the endless architectural variety flaunted in churches, palaces, museums, theatres, the teeming populace from practically every race on earth (too many, some would say), the underlying aura of sheer historic permanence. '*When a man is tired of London, he is tired of life.*' Even the weather was not so bad as tradition had it, he reflected as he took off his jacket in the sunshine and slung it over his shoulder.

He was feeling more confident as he reached the Ritz, donned his jacket again, straightened his tie, and entered the famous portals. At which point the confidence immediately evaporated. He had only been there two or three times in his lifetime, and though not completely unfamiliar with the do-mains of the rich, he found this particular palace, with all its historical associations and its flamboyantly exuberant decor, especially daunting. There had been a time during his spell of relative prosperity in the publishing business when he had himself entertained the odd eminent writer or agent at such places, but those days were long gone and he didn't miss them.

He enquired as instructed at the reception desk, and was pointed with unctuous servility in the direction of the main restaurant. There, under the crystal chandeliers and past the gilded mirrors, he was ushered to a discreet table on one side of the room beside a huge window with its splendid views over Green Park. An intimidatingly tall, smooth skinned man with an almost bald head, and wearing a bright red cashmere jacket that could only have been tailored in America, half rose from his seat and proffered a sinewy hand.

'Mr Aldrige? Donald Easterby. Extremely good of you to come.' He had that slightly over effusive manner that Ameri-cans often affect—and that Englishmen often find threaten-ing. 'I know how busy you must be.'

'Not at all.' Maurice negotiated the tricky business of sit-ting at the same time as the waiter manoeuvred his chair, and remembered just in time not to pre-empt the man's job of placing his vast napkin.

'A drink to start with?'

'Oh—just a glass of mineral water, thank you.'

'Oh come on, you must do better than that. They have a very nice New Zealand Sauvignon by the glass here. Try that.'

(New Zealand? At the Ritz? Times had changed.) 'Very well, just one glass.' It surely couldn't do any harm.

Easterby nodded to the waiter, who handed Maurice a menu and glided away like a pilot boat that had fulfilled its task of docking a luxury yacht.

Easterby smiled a lopsided but seductive smile. 'Let's get the important business out of the way first. What'll you have to eat? I'm going to have the sole meunière.' The unlined features hinted at regular skin treatments, perhaps even occasional attention from the plastic surgeons. Maurice guessed that he was perhaps a year or two older than himself. There was an intensity about the pale, wrinkle-free eyes which was disconcerting. They were a touch too direct for comfort.

Maurice contemplated the menu briefly through his spectacles. Too daunting for him to study seriously. 'Oh yes, the sole will do me fine,' he said pushing it aside.

As a way of avoiding the other's stare he glanced around the large room. Its exotic Louis XVI styled confines were already filling up with affluent diners—dark suited businessmen intent on manipulating markets, modishly dressed women intent on manipulating their men. The murmur of muted conversation and the refined clinking of cutlery on bone china permeated the background. At the next table a large man in a pale grey city suit sat alone reading *The Times*. Maurice barely noticed him.

'This is a good place to talk,' said Easterby, 'but I don't actually eat here very often.'

'Oh?' said Maurice.

The other shrugged dismissively. 'I get too much of discreet hotel dining rooms. I prefer to have noise and bustle around me at meals, so I usually wander out and choose more popular places.' His tone was even more precise and delicate than on the phone. 'I live alone you see, so at home I don't get much social activity.'

'Ah,' said Maurice, not sure quite what to make of that.

The waiter reappeared with the wine on a tray. 'Two glasses of the Gravitas Sauvignon, sir.'

Easterby rotated his glass, sniffed, took a sip, and savoured it critically. Someone who likes his prandial experiences, thought Maurice. The other nodded to the waiter, put the glass down on the table and sat back. 'There are some distinguished vineyards around my area of France, but they had better look to their laurels. The New World is rapidly outclassing Europe at modern wine production, don't you find.'

'I, er. . . . well I'm no connoisseur but . . .' Maurice tailed off, refraining from adding that he *was* quite a connoisseur of malt whiskeys but didn't get much chance to drink them these days.

'Well that's incidental.' The grey eyes were direct across the table. 'You're a connoisseur of manuscripts and that's what I'm interested in.' The American inclined his bald head in an indication of sincerity. 'I'm grateful to you for coming to meet a stranger at such short notice, Maurice. You're probably used to these sorts of approaches, but I would like to think this is a bit different from the usual approach, and I'm a bit different from your usual customers.'

Maurice confirmed all those suppositions with a nod. No doubt about that.

'I think you'll find this worthwhile even if nothing, um. . . . concrete comes of it. I hope you will forgive me but I have made a few enquiries about you, and you seem to be the sort of professional expert I'm looking for.'

'Enquiries?'

'It's the way I work. I have to be careful in my choice of associates. For all sorts of reasons.'

'Ah.' That explained a few things. But it didn't lessen Maurice's suspicion.

'So what are your thoughts about the items I mentioned? In particular the Darwin chronicle?'

Maurice hesitated. 'Well naturally, Mr Easterby. . . .'

'Call me Donald, please.'

'Naturally that would be of great interest. However I'm not quite sure of the circumstances and grounds for your, er . . . interest, or why you wish to, er. . . .'

'You said you already knew of its existence?'

'No. I said I knew of *rumours* that it existed. That's not quite the same thing.'

Easterby contemplated him for a second, increasing his sense of awkwardness. 'Well, supposing I told you I'm fairly certain it does exist. Or at any rate did. Whether any copies still survive is not so certain.'

'Ah,' said Maurice.

'However what is darned certain is that if any came to light it would cause quite a furore in the scientific—not to say literary—worlds.'

Maurice, as was his way when ill at ease, cleaned his spectacles on the end of his tie. 'Well, yes, I'm sure that's true. If any became available and it, er. . . . turned out to be a work of substance.'

Easterby's lips parted showing the immaculate work of his orthodontist. 'It's supposed to be of considerable substance. And to contain personal revelations which might have quite an impact . . . which might cause a small sensation in fact.'

'Well then, there's no doubt the discovery would be important.' Maurice put his specs on again and frowned a genuine frown. 'But, forgive me, I don't quite see where I come in.'

'You come in because I need a specialist in the field to help me in what is in effect a difficult detection job. A quest if you like. And you've been highly recommended.'

'By whom?'

'Another customer of yours. Tommy Houseman from Michigan. He's bought quite a bit of stuff from you in the past, I believe.'

'Oh yes. Specialises in early twentieth century European literature.'

'Amongst other things.'

Maurice remembered an intense, humourless American with a somewhat graceless attitude and a relentless passion for his collection. He had tracked down a number of volumes and manuscripts for the man in the past, not without a good deal of obsessive harassment from across the Atlantic which at times had made him wonder whether the commissions were worth it. 'Quite a. . . . dedicated collector.'

'You could say that. He's an old associate of mine—I won't say friend. We were at Harvard together.'

Well naturally, thought Maurice. Where else?

'Except that I left after a year. Harvard is an extremely conservative institution under the veneer of sophistication. I didn't fit in.'

No, well that too was believable.

Easterby's jaw jutted an inch. 'Tommy and I have competed for various items in the past, and he doesn't lose gladly. He made a fortune as an investment banker and he's not afraid to spend as much money as necessary to get what he wants.' He sniffed disdainfully, then spoke in a lighter tone. 'Anyway I told him I had need of an expert, preferably in England, and after some persuasion he recommended you. Strongly.'

'I'm flattered.'

The other sat back. 'Let me begin at the beginning. . . .' Except that he didn't immediately. He paused as if distracted by some inner preoccupation. A look of ancient weariness crossed his features. Then he pulled himself back and directed his crooked smile again at Maurice. 'I'm a rich man, Maurice.' With a wry intonation, 'I'm a ridiculously rich man. That's not a boast. I did very little off my own baseball bat to get it. Just luck of the draw. I happen to belong to one of the wealthiest families in America.'

'Really.' Maurice felt he should comment. 'Based on what?'

Easterby waved a vague hand. 'Based on anything the world finds essential. If you Google the Easterbys you'll find countless entries mentioning Texas oil, coal, wineries, real estate, et cetera, et cetera. An empire founded by my grandfather, expanded by my father, and when he died ten years ago inherited by his three children.' He stared reflectively at the table cloth. 'My father even managed to avoid the pitfalls of several wives and murderous alimony payments which deplete so many fortunes. Just.' The word held a depth of meaning. 'Anyway I own a third of the business, but not being inclined to spend my days in a Manhattan office I have left the running of it all to my brother and sister, and now go my own way content to spend my inheritance as I choose. I'm considered the black sheep of the family, if you know what I mean.'

Maurice blinked behind his spectacles and waited.

'I like to fill my time with travel, with my charitable foundations, and above all with my collection.'

'What collection is that?'

'My collection of manuscripts and first editions.' The eyes held Maurice's. 'Which is where you come in.'

'You have a large collection?'

He didn't directly answer the question. 'It's not particularly famous because I try to avoid publicity or hassle, but it's one of the world's finest.'

Of course, thought Maurice with a jolt of recognition—the Easterby collection. Why hadn't he made the connection earlier? Feeling a little foolish he didn't remark on the sudden revelation. 'You keep it in the States?' he asked innocently.

'Yes. I know you Europeans sometimes resent our acquiring of your cultural heritage, but . . . well, I guess you benefit from that too.'

'Oh yes, we do indeed.' Maurice's business would be totally unviable if it wasn't for the transatlantic input.

'Anyway it's kept in various locations. In a custom built library at my home in Vermont, in vaults, or on loan to various universities and museums.' Easterby turned his head to gaze out at the wide arena of Green Park. 'I have Mozart manuscripts, Shakespeare folios, King James Bibles, first editions of Bunyan, Dante, Pascal, Payne, Milton. . . .' He looked back with a half smile. 'I have stuff, Maurice, that would make your mouth water.'

Maurice's mouth was indeed watering, at least metaphorically. He would give a great deal just to gaze on such an array.

'You will know what I mean when I say that I get the most extraordinary thrill out of old books and documents,' went on Easterby. 'It's an aesthetic thing, almost a sexual thing.'

Well that was a new slant on it. But in a way Maurice knew what the man meant.

'It's not the contents so much. I haven't even read a lot of the stuff in my collection. It's the *history* behind them. It's the thought, the labour, the genius. The fact that owning them brings me as close as one can get to those remarkable people who fashioned our thinking and laws and philosophies all those years ago in some different era. You know what I'm saying?'

Maurice's heart responded. He nodded and took another sip of the Sauvignon, a rather bigger one than before. It was a *very* nice wine.

'Seems to me we could perhaps do with a bit more of that kind of reflection in today's world.'

Yeats whispered in Maurice's mind again: '. . . *There midnight's all aglimmer, and noon a purple glow, and evening full of the linnet's wings . . .*' He put down his glass. 'Yes, yes, I do know. Absolutely.'

'I'm also especially interested in science and scientific works. I'm intrigued by how man solves his practical problems, how he is beginning to affect the planet, the cosmos with his extraordinary ingenuity.' Maurice nodded again. 'So you see, I also have a considerable collection of original scientific papers and books. Einstein, Popper, Hubble, Niels Bohr, Heisenberg. You name the boffin, I've got him.'

'Remarkable,' said Maurice, transfixed.

'I have a whole network of people around the world who keep a look-out for stuff I might be interested in. Dealers, auction houses, university librarians—you know the sort of thing. I expect you have them too.'

'Well, er . . . yes, but not quite on your scale, Mr Easterby.'

'I thought we were on Christian names.'

'Sorry, yes. Donald. I do have a network as you call it, but I deal in rather more humble stuff than you do.'

'Yes, but from what I've heard it's quite a large network, and you're a genius at tracking down anything a person might be seeking. You were described to me as. . . . what was it?—a literary bloodhound with the tenacity of Sherlock Holmes.'

'That's very flattering. Funnily enough I have an early Conan Doyle edition in stock at the moment. Unusually good condition.'

'No interest to me, I'm afraid. With literature I rarely go for anything later than the early nineteenth century.'

'Oh no, I wasn't suggesting . . . I just meant . . .' Maurice got flustered and picked up his glass again. The waiter appeared with their meal, and there was a pause as he served them with flamboyant expertise. Easterby waited until he had departed, then waved his fish knife as if conducting a string quartet and continued.

'This is how it all began, Maurice. Now forgive me—this is quite a long and involved story, but I think you'll find it intriguing.' He waited, apparently for some sign of affirmation, but receiving nothing obvious continued. 'A year or so ago I was having lunch in New York with one of my contacts—an occasion not unlike this really. He's a dealer who specialises in scientific stuff, and he's found me some really good items in the past. He's a bastard at the negotiations, but he knows my limits and we usually part friends.' He neatly separated a fillet from the backbone of his fish, and said, 'Hey, this sole isn't bad. They've gotten so small recently, it's hard to find good ones.'

Maurice nodded and said dourly, 'We soon won't get fish unless it's purpose bred in tanks and tasting of nothing.'

Easterby squeezed more lemon onto his and said, 'Still, if the Ritz can't find 'em nobody can.' He continued, 'Anyway this fellow had brought me one or two things—among them a hand-written notebook of Fermat's mathematical scribblings, would you believe? I couldn't make head or tail of them, but I bought it out of sheer fascination. Then at the end of the meal, almost as an afterthought, he asked me if I had any interest in Charles Darwin. You bet I have, I said. Most important scientific mind ever. More so than Newton, Einstein, the whole bunch.' Easterby smiled with pleasurable recollection. 'That kind of floored him. Like most people he just saw Darwin as a sort of super zoologist who hit the headlines with a controversial theory about monkeys.' He took a sip of his wine, savoured it again, and, like an actor having satisfactorily stretched out the suspense, went on. 'So I had to explain to him that all those other geniuses made their names in specific areas of science. They progressed knowledge by individual discoveries, like adding links to the various chains. Darwin was bigger than that. He came up with the answer as to how the entire caboodle operates. The machinery by which the whole of life. . . . in fact the whole universe evolves. In which all the other discoveries are just cogs. Understand?' The grey eyes were unrelenting again as they watched Maurice.

Maurice frowned for a moment, then nodded. 'Yes, I think so. I'd never really thought of it in those terms, but . . .'

'That's the trouble. People don't. They still haven't grasped the implications. They're still tied up with their arguments about creationism and intelligent design and all that stuff. They can't separate their inherited superstitions from the logic.'

'No. Well . . .' He had to admit that, whenever he thought about evolution, which wasn't very often, Maurice did find there was some puzzling contradiction between its implications and his—and Alice's—original spiritual beliefs. '*There is only one religion, though there are a hundred versions of it.*'

'Anyway, now we're getting to the point. My contact went on to say that he'd been to a dinner party recently, and quite by chance found himself sitting next to a woman who had married into the Wedgewood family. Does that mean anything to you?'

Maurice inclined his head. 'Wedgewood china?'

'Yes, but a great deal more than the famous china. They were among the founders of the Industrial Revolution here in England—a highly influential and wealthy family.'

'Well of course I know who you mean, but I don't quite . . .'

'And Charles Darwin's wife, Emma, was a Wedgewood.'

'Ah.'

'She was the youngest child of Josiah Wedgewood, head of the dynasty. And as it happened he was also uncle to Charles Darwin. The two families were closely connected. Both based in the Midlands, both distinguished in their own ways, and both linked by various inter-family marriages. Emma and Charles were in fact first cousins. Wouldn't be advised to wed nowadays.'

'Interesting,' said Maurice, and picked absent-mindedly at his fish.

'Apparently this woman at the dinner party had married into a minor offshoot line of the Wedgewoods which had moved to the States in the early twentieth century and were settled now in New England. Pretty well heeled, but only spasmodically in touch with the British side of the family.'

'So . . .?'

'So . . .' Easterby pulled a bone from his mouth and placed it delicately on the side of his plate. '. . . my dealer friend became quite interested because, being active in that field he actually knew about the Wedgewoods' connection with the Darwin family. So he questioned the lady about it. I don't know word for word how the conversation went, but she did tell him the one thing that brought him to me. And subsequently sent me on to you.' He paused, his delicate lips pursed in a suspenseful manner.

Maurice waited, eyebrows raised to show his continued interest.

'She told him that it was common talk around the family circles whenever they discussed their illustrious forebears—which was naturally quite often—that Emma Darwin may have kept a private journal much of the time she was married to Charles.'

'Ah, right.'

Easterby tilted his head. 'So tell me what you know about the thing.'

Maurice shrugged. 'I don't know anything. As I said, I had heard over the years that it might exist, but then many people have kept journals and I didn't pay any particular attention to rumours about this one. . . .'

'Well let me fill you in. This is supposed to be a private memoir type thing, quite separate from her ordinary household diaries. She kept those of course—they were published some years ago—but they were small simple things, listing daily events and so on. This is apparently a much more comprehensive effort, written spasmodically when she felt the urge to record matters of importance. It was concerned with personal and family affairs, but it also involved Charles's work, with which she had quite a lot to do—commenting, editing, assisting with his experiments, all that kind of stuff.' A wave of the fork. 'The journal was never intended for publication. In fact during her life she kept it secret from everyone, even the family. It was just for her personal satisfaction. I suppose, being married to an important man involved with significant discoveries, she wanted to keep a memento of those times, like women do.'

Maurice nodded. He was so grateful for Alice's sometimes irritating habit of taking photographs wherever they went. He now had several volumes of snapshots of their life together, a great comfort to him whenever he got especially morose. 'This woman told your dealer acquaintance all this?' he asked.

'That's right.' Easterby went on. 'So naturally my friend asked what was supposed to have become of the journal. Apparently nobody knew for sure, but it was rumoured that after Emma's death—she lived well into her eighties, considerably longer than Charles who suffered from bad health all his life—the thing surfaced. Must have been pretty thick as it covered several decades. The story goes that one of her sons decided it was too important to leave lying about in the family attic, edited it down to a workable size, and then had a private printing of it done. Just half a dozen copies, which he passed around the direct family members to keep as an interesting record of the great man's domestic life.' Easterby paused and wiped his mouth fastidiously with his napkin. 'Now the strange thing is that for a long time nobody except the family had ever seen one of these copies, and nobody knew if any still existed. It's said that Emma very much wanted it to be kept private—it wasn't the thing in those days for a woman to go publicising her intimate personal thoughts.' His tone changed. 'Also—and this intrigued me—it was supposed to have contained some extremely personal revelations about her marriage. Consequently none of the descendants had ever allowed a copy to circulate. They probably didn't even think it was of particular interest, since, from a scientific point of view, it wouldn't seem to add much to the huge amount of stuff already written and published by Darwin himself.' Easterby twinkled wryly at Maurice. 'But you and I know different, eh Maurice?'

Maurice was feeling a slight shortness of breath—something that occasionally happened when a discovery of exceptional interest crossed his vision. 'Yes.'

'And that's not all.' Easterby's lips tightened again in that effete way they had and he sat back with his wine, deliberately keeping Maurice in suspense. 'How much do you know about 'The Origin of the Species'?'

Maurice hesitated. 'I, er . . . I've handled a few editions in the past. Can't say I've actually read it all. And it's 'On the Origin of Species' by the way. Not '*the* Species'. A common mistake.'

'Oh, sure. I knew that. Just doesn't seem to sound so good.'

'No.'

'Well of course it's Darwin's major oeuvre. The principle account and description of his whole theory of evolution. Caused quite a furore when it came out, and it's been the source of all the argument and controversy ever since.'

'Yes.'

'Not least in my country. The debate over how much of it should be taught in schools is still raging, a century and a half after its publication.'

'Our schools too—though perhaps not quite as heatedly.'

'But there's an interesting thing about that work.'

'What's that?'

The American leaned forward slightly and his voice lowered. 'He himself was so fearful about the reaction it might provoke, so aware of the huge philosophical and religious implications, that he didn't dare publish it for several years after his theory was developed. And furthermore, he didn't put into the book any of his own thoughts and deductions on that aspect. He just laid out the details of his various biological researches and their evolutionary conclusions, but refrained from making much in the way of deeper comment.' Easterby's face showed frustration. 'You see, Darwin was a secretive old bugger. Either through fear or just modesty he largely kept his philosophical thoughts to himself. He didn't want to stir the pot too much, if you know what I mean.' He lowered his voice further. 'He refrained even from including his deductions about *man's* precise place in the evolutionary pattern. He knew that would *really* put the cat among the pigeons!' He gave a brief chuckle. 'Or should I say the monkey amongst the humanoids. No, he left that part of it until his next book, 'The Descent Of Man', which again he didn't dare publish for a decade or more after 'Origin of Species.' He sat back. 'But it's pretty clear he knew his own mind when it came to the religious aspects to it all.'

'What was his own mind, do you think?'

'That there aren't any.'

'Religious aspects?'

'Impossible to reconcile evolution with conventional religion if you take it to its logical conclusion. He called himself an agnostic, but he almost certainly ended his days as a convinced atheist. Though as I say he kept this largely to himself. Hinted at it in his writings, and admitted it further in his personal memoirs—but he never expounded on the scientific basis for it. That was not the era to go about proclaiming such convictions.'

'No. Quite.'

'However . . .' Easterby swirled the wine in his glass as he paused again provocatively. Maurice sat with a forkful of pomme sauté motionless on his plate. 'However this woman then told my friend that there was another family rumour to add to the whole story. And I've confirmed this in my subsequent researches.' His eyes were unblinking as he stared at Maurice. The latter remained motionless in suspense. 'The rumour was to the effect that Darwin *did* in fact write down his explicit conclusions, and that Emma, who edited all his stuff, hinted at it in her journal. She is supposed to have intimated that he put them into a postscript to 'Origin of the . . .' sorry, 'Origin of Species', or possibly to 'Descent of Man', but at the last moment chickened out and didn't include it for publication in either book because it was so contentious. The story went that this postscript—the summary of his whole philosophic judgement if you like—was probably hidden away until his death and is still drifting around somewhere, most likely in one of the family attics or archives.'

Maurice frowned. 'If no-one has found her journal, how do you know all this?'

'I'm coming to that.' Easterby raised a neatly groomed eyebrow at him and lowered his voice again, 'Now, can you imagine what the effect would be if such a thing came to light? Can you imagine its significance?'

Maurice's frown deepened. 'I'm not sure. I. . . . Doesn't everyone know by now what Darwin thought?'

'Yes, Maurice, but the point is he never publicly *announced* his beliefs. He never *explained* them in scientific terms. That's what's so frustrating about the old war horse. Here are all these people squabbling about the existence of God, and he comes up with what might be the ultimate answer to the puzzle, yet he refuses to expound on it.'

'Ah. Yes.'

'Yet now suddenly, here are his specific thoughts. Here are the ultimate doctrinal deductions of the man who revealed the evolutionary process! Can you imagine the stir it would cause around the world? Can you imagine the furore amongst all the religious communities?' Easterby's eyes were alive with the anticipation of it all. 'Can you conceive its *worth*?'

Maurice could not. He abandoned the forkful of pomme sauté which had yet to reach his mouth. 'No, I can't. If you mean money, then a lot.'

Easterby waved a dismissive hand. 'No, I'm not really talking of money, though certainly it would be worth a pile of that too. Millions.'

'Possibly. I wouldn't like to say.'

'Oh, yes. If it was a single manuscript, written in his own hand, then I know several collectors like me who would pay the earth—some who would kill for such a find. Not to mention of course its value to every museum and scientific institution on the planet.' He pointed his fork again. 'No, I'm talking about its intellectual worth. Its effect on the academic and philosophical community. Yes I know, the arguments have been fought over ad infinitum ever since, but the point is nobody can yet agree on any final conclusion. In fact they still go to war over it!' The fork made patterns in the air. 'But if we know what *his* final conclusions were, then just imagine its impact on the great debate!'

'Yes. Yes, I can see it would be significant.'

The American's eyes sparkled with amusement. 'Significant? I'd call it volcanic!' He chuckled delightedly. 'Imagine it being read to the Pope in the Vatican! Or your Archbishop of Canterbury in his palace! Even better—I'd love to see the apoplexy amongst the Bible thumpers and Jesus freaks in my country!'

Maurice allowed himself his own half smile. 'I gather you're of the same persuasion as Darwin.'

Easterby sobered. 'Ah, I didn't say that. That's a whole other story.' He did not elaborate further. '*I am a millionaire—that is my religion,*' thought Maurice smiling to himself. Easterby raised a theatrical finger. 'However. . . . Now we come to Klaus Fuchs's part in it all.'

Maurice had forgotten the atom spy. This was becoming more intriguing by the minute. Easterby signalled to the waiter to fill up their wine glasses and Maurice didn't refuse. There were times when good resolutions took second place.

'This anecdote from my dealer friend stirred something in my memory. Several years previously—eight or ten—I had bought at auction the original hand-written treatise of Fuchs, which he had made whilst he was in prison for treason. It had resided with some family member after his death in the nineteen eighties, and they then decided they needed the money so sent it for auction.' Easterby cocked a thumb. 'Here in London actually. It sold for a pretty modest sum— not many people were interested in the private musings of a weird boffin whose main claim to fame was that he had passed a lot of scientific data to Russia half a century previously.' He wiped his lips and glinted at Maurice with that odd stare of his. 'However the thing about Fuchs is that he was without doubt the most successful spy of the Second World War. No-one else came near to transmitting the amount of crucial intelligence that he did. He succeeded partly because he was such a strange man. Social misfit, egotist, bit of a recluse, but a brilliant scientist. He was right at the heart of the Allies' race to invent the atom bomb during the last years of the war, and subsequently to create a nuclear missile system during the Cold War. Because of his solitary ways none of his fellow scientists got to know much about his private life. Astoundingly it transpired that during that entire period he was passing on to Russia all his own information and any other technical data he had access to. He wasn't arrested until nineteen fifty-five.' Easterby pointed his knife again. 'The extraordinary thing about him was that he didn't do this for money, or because of blackmail, or for any other reason than pure idealism. Fuchs was a victim of the Third Reich's oppression in Germany before the war, and he was obsessed with trying to understand the origins of evil in humankind. Hitler was his devil, and of course at the time of the war the Russians were considered one of the main hopes of defeating the monster.' He paused as if distracted from his thread.

Maurice prompted, 'So what was Fuchs's connection with Darwin?'

'Yes—well, this talk of Emma Darwin's writing is what jogged my memory. I hadn't studied his thing too closely. It was a kind of polemic, written mainly as a vindication of his espionage activities. I skimmed through it when I bought it, but then moved on to other things and it languished somewhere in my collection awaiting its moment.' He put down his knife and fork and raised both forefingers. 'But I did remember that Fuchs had written about his fascination with Darwin and evolutionary theory. It apparently had a big effect on his thinking. And I also remembered that somewhere in his piece he had alluded to some stuff by Emma Darwin. I didn't pay too much attention at the time—the connection seemed too ambiguous and I was preoccupied elsewhere—but now I realised the possible significance.'

'Ah.'

'So of course I went back to his document and searched through it. And. . . .' Easterby lent down and picked up from the floor beside the table a slim leather brief case which Maurice had not noticed before. The American opened it and pulled out a file of perhaps a couple of hundred pages, ring-bound and enclosed in dark blue covers.

'I'm not going to tell you any more about that aspect at the moment. This is a transcript of the Fuchs piece which I had my secretary scan and print out. I'm just going to ask you to read it and discover for yourself. That is if you're interested in the story of course.'

He handed it across the table. Maurice took it and flicked through the neatly printed pages. He was by now definitely interested. 'I'd love to read it.'

'Good. You'll find it intriguing on its own merits actually. There are various parallels with Darwin's reflections on humanity.' Easterby reached for his glass. 'I don't need to tell you to take good care of it, and to keep the substance to yourself.'

'Of course.'

Easterby sat back in his chair, his story told, his performance for the moment finished. 'So you can guess what I'm after, Maurice. You can guess what I want you to do.'

Maurice peered over his spectacles and waited for the specifics.

'I want you to read the Fuchs record, and if you're convinced as I am that the Darwin things exist and are around somewhere, then I want you to put out feelers—discreetly needless to say—get in touch with your contacts, see what you can discover. I want to find out how *much* truth there is in all of this—Emma's diary first of all, and if that then leads to Charles Darwin's postscript, well and good.'

'And if I was successful?'

'I want first pick at the cherry.' Easterby's countenance softened. 'Emma's writings would be of utter fascination to me. And the postscript itself—well that would be like finding the Holy Grail or the original Ten Commandments.' He reflected for a moment. 'I'll say it again—Darwin is the key to everything. Once people realise that they'll start thinking straight about things. Especially in my country. Religious bigotry distorts everything in the USA, from domestic life to politics. It's a long haul, but once the real inferences of evolutionary science are universally understood we can get on with organising this little planet in a more satisfactory way.'

Nothing like ambition, thought Maurice.

'And above all. . . .' Easterby's expression was intense again. 'Above all I want to know for myself what he said. I want to read that postscript myself. I want to know what's in it.'

Maurice was for a second mesmerised by the man's fervour. Then Easterby shook his head in an odd impatient manner and became businesslike again. 'I'll pay you an ongoing fee and all your expenses of course, and if you come up with the goods, a commission which could well provide your pension for the rest of your life.' The gaze was direct as ever. 'I think you're rather in need of that kind of security at the moment, no?'

Maurice stared back. 'Exactly how much do you know about me, Donald?'

The American smiled and sat back. 'Don't worry, I'm not the CIA. But it's easy to find out simple facts these days. I happen to know that your business is financially stretched at present.'

Maurice was silent for a long moment, fighting the ambivalence in his head. Indignation at the intrusion into his private world, curiosity over the proposition, and temptation over the financial aspects. Finally he said, 'Well of course, Donald, either would be a fascinating discovery. But I'm not sure I . . . I mean, don't you need a detective agency or a university researcher or someone, rather than me? I'm just a book dealer.'

Easterby shook his head. 'I've been down that route. I've had people track down the direct descendants of the Darwins—quite a few of them with American blood incidentally—I've followed up leads, I've scoured the internet, I've written dozens of letters. I got some polite replies, but nothing of much help. There's a stone wall around this whole thing. Either people don't have anything, or they're obeying Emma's wishes and keeping it confidential.' He gestured. 'However the one unspoken message I got from the exercise was that many of the family at least know about the work. None of them have denied that copies may still exist. The impression I get over and over again is that quite simply nobody *wants* the thing to surface.'

'Then shouldn't we obey their wishes?'

Easterby stared at him gravely for a moment, then his features broke into a broad smile. 'Oh, Maurice, Maurice—don't tell me you're an idealist?'

'Well, no, but surely. . . .'

'Which is more important—the general enlightenment or ancient inhibitions?'

Maurice thought about that for a moment, then said, 'I still don't see how I can do better than all your other people.'

'Well, maybe you can't. But knowing what I know about you. . . . well if anyone can do this I believe you can. I believe the way to find this thing is through the book world. It's well over a century since Emma Darwin would have finished it, and as we've said, it would have had such a fascination for bibliophiles and collectors, not to mention scientific groupies, that I can't believe someone somewhere isn't sitting on a copy and just quivering with the desire to let it loose on the world. You know yourself, Maurice, you can't keep something like this secret for ever. It will have to come to light at some stage. And just imagine if you were the one to bring it to light!'

Maurice did try to imagine. His ambivalence did not diminish. 'If I did take on this, er, task, could you let me have that list of descendants?'

'Of course. I'll give you everything I've got. The family are quite a distinguished bunch. A number of scientists and botanists, following the tradition. You should also pay a visit to the Darwin home down in Kent. Down House. It's preserved as a museum by your, um. . . . by English Heritage. Ugly great place, but fascinating in its way, and full of original family stuff and memorabilia. I've been there. Couldn't find anything relevant to the quest, but you never know, you might.' Easterby took a breath. 'My feeling, you see, Maurice, is that Emma's journal could be the key to finding Charles's postscript, if such a thing exists. It would have been so controversial—particularly to her, as she was a devout Christian—that I can't believe she wouldn't have mentioned it.' He reached across and tapped the blue folder. 'Read what Fuchs says about it.' He leaned back again. 'She might even have left a clue as to where it went.' He twisted his lips. 'Let's just hope she didn't burn it!'

Maurice sat in silent contemplation, the remains of his fish abandoned on his plate, his wine glass half emptied in his hand. There was something unnaturally compulsive about this American and his quest.

'Look,' said the other, sensing his hesitation. 'Let's you and I take a stroll back to your shop, and on the way I'll give you some more details. Then I'll leave you to think about it for twenty four hours. What do you say?'

'Yes,' said Maurice, relieved. 'That sounds a good idea.'

'I will need an answer before I leave for France in a couple of days though.'

'Of course.'

'Coffee? Desert?'

'Not for me, thank you.' Easterby waved at a waiter for the tab. To fill in the pause Maurice asked, 'Are you going to France on business or pleasure?'

'Both. I have a house down at Cap Ferrat on the Cote d'Azur. It's staffed, and I spend quite a bit of time there. Different world to the States. I do a lot of my work from there.' He gazed out at the park again. 'Of course that part of the world's a playground for rich bastards like me, but it still holds its magic.'

'I can imagine,' said Maurice. 'I've been there a couple of times with my wife. It's beautiful.'

'The earth has its delights, despite everything. You must come and visit me. You'd enjoy it.'

Maurice blinked, and stuttered his thanks. The tab arrived, Easterby scribbled a signature and rose to go. As he stood it became apparent just how very tall he was—at least six and a half feet—and like many tall men he stooped slightly as if to hide the fact. The pair passed the lone man at the next table who was also gesturing for his bill, and they left the restaurant. They stood for a moment at the hotel reception whilst the American enquired if there were any messages for him. He was handed a note which he glanced at briefly.

'Hm,' he grunted. 'I mustn't be too long. Meeting this afternoon. I have a foundation for the advancement of scientific understanding with an office in London.' He turned, looking down at the smaller man from his great height. There was a mournful look about him again which was vaguely comical, in the way the sad look of the great comedians—Buster Keaton, Chaplin, Stan Laurel—was comical. 'You know, Maurice, civilised cities like London and beautiful places like the

Cote d'Azur notwithstanding, this planet's in a pretty shitty state.'

His guest nodded his slightly puzzled concurrence. Was this the moment to discuss the faecal condition of planet earth?

'We humans have reached a stage of technological advancement, combined with philosophical confusion, that for the first time ever has us in danger of destroying it.'

Maurice inevitably thought back to the occasion of 7/7, and before that of 9/11. It had certainly seemed that the planet was in danger of imploding at such moments. 'Yes,' he said, 'you're probably right.'

Easterby was gazing out through the entrance doors in the direction of the nearby stream of Piccadilly traffic as if it was to blame for all the world's ills. 'Well I believe evolutionary theory is part of the key to solving the problem. And like most well-off people I'd like to put my wealth to some good before I depart the place. . . . so it's another reason for finding this thing.'

He suddenly smiled with a flash of warmth, took Maurice's arm in an oddly intimate gesture, and led the way out of the hotel and down the street towards Piccadilly Circus.

They were retracing the steps Maurice had taken less than two hours previously, but this time he felt a different response. He didn't know if it was a reaction to the cultured urbanity of the American's world, but as they passed the throngs on the pavement and the roaring queues of traffic Yeats whispered his final lines in his ear, '. . . . *and always night and day, I hear lake water lapping with low sounds by the shore. When I stand on the roadway, or on the pavement grey, I hear it in the deep heart's core.*' As always Maurice wondered whether the lines denoted simply the poet's desire for peace, or his desire for death.

Neither of them glanced back at the large man in the grey suit who was walking some fifty yards behind them.

CHAPTER FIVE

February 4th, 1951. Wakefield.

My book is proving an interesting experiment. Nine months have passed since my trial, and by writing about it I find I can look back on the ordeal with a little more objectivity. It was one of the shortest ever treason trials, they tell me, partly because I accepted all the charges against me without argument. Why should I argue?—the facts themselves were beyond dispute. But despite that the nine months have passed in a blur of shock and bewilderment and disorientation. I spent the first three at Wormwood Scrubs, which was so unspeakable I have blotted most of the experience from my memory, and the next six at Stafford, where all I can recall is endless hours spent sewing mail bags. (What do they <u>do</u> with all those mail bags? I can't believe the British postal system has need of such an unending supply.) Then the authorities finally decided on my ultimate destination here at Wakefield, which is a prison specifically for long-term offenders. There is a quite different atmosphere here. Since the inmates all have sentences stretching over the years they are resigned to their futures, so the mood is far more acquiescent than at the other places. Furthermore, since under British law good behaviour can result in a reduction of one third of one's sentence, the incentive to conform over a long period is considerable. Despite the fact that many of them are here for extremely ruthless and violent crimes the general attitude is calm and ordered. This permits a relatively tolerant system, fostered by an apparently liberal minded management. This is my saving grace. Sparse conditions I can endure, but I'm not sure how long I could have survived the inhuman practices one hears about at other places. And I shudder to think what my plight would be had I been arrested in America, or if their determined extradition attempts had succeeded.

A large proportion of the inmates here are of course moronic, but I have encountered several who have quite distinguished intellectual accomplishments (it is an evolutionary fact that brain power does not always entail a corresponding moral awareness—witness the Third Reich). I have already shared serious conversations with some of them. They all seem to know who I am—my case was apparently quite a notorious one even in this company—and I have a reputation within the prison of some standing. Spies apparently have a ranking somewhere between first degree murderers and major fraudsters. I have acquired the nickname 'Doc', which amuses me, and I am frequently made fun of for my academic skills, which I am assured is a sign of respect. I am expected to have authoritative opinions on all matters political and economic, which sometimes has me at a loss. I have also joined an informal chess club boasting a number of quite good players, and we have regular games which is a welcome diversion. I have taken to removing my queen at the start so as to even up the challenge, but with that arrangement we have had some engaging contests.

Another source of pleasure is my acquaintance with Gordon Hawkins, one of the assistant governors and an interesting personality. He sent for me when I arrived, ostensibly to advise me of the rules and regulations at the prison (of which I had already been fully informed by the head warden of my section), but privately I think to satisfy his curiosity about me. He turned out to be a highly intelligent man, with a degree in history no less, and quite how he came to enter such a bizarre profession as prison administration I haven't yet discovered. We have already had challenging discussions on world politics and philosophy, we have exchanged some books, and he has promised to assign me to special work in the library, for which I am extremely grateful. Remarkably he is especially interested in the two subjects which, outside of physics, I suppose have been the most influential in my life—Marxism and Darwinism. He knows almost as much as I do about the former, and a great deal more than I about the latter, so it is indeed a lucky acquaintance. He it was who pointed out to me that, not only does the prison library contain a copy of Marx's *Das Kapital* (which species of prisoner reads <u>that</u> I wonder?), but also of Darwin's *Origin Of Species*, which, despite my long term peripheral interest in the implications of evolution, and my chance encounters with Darwin descendants, I have strangely never read. It's an omission I now have plenty of time to correct. I feel instinctively that the answer to the huge conundrum which has always confronted me, and which has in a way led me to take the actions I have, lies somewhere within the boundaries of those two great and apparently conflicting hypotheses. Between the logical attempt to organise society along rational lines, and the inherent compulsion for it to develop through natural evolutionary forces. Gordon Hawkins agrees with me, though as is his wont he inevitably turns the whole thing into a joke and calls it 'revolution versus evolution,' adding with that dry twinkle in his eye, 'and it's debatable which is which.'

He also, once we got to know each other a little, showed some discreet inquisitiveness about the motives which drove me to my actions. I was unable to answer him satisfactorily, just as I have been unable to answer anyone since my arrest. It all seemed too complex at the time. But if these musings are to have any significance then I suppose I have to explain what brought me to this prison cell. The psychological path, that is, not the physical one. The world knows all about the latter already, thanks to the endless publicity and press speculation which followed me during my detention and exhaustive interrogations and eventual trial. The world however knows very little about the psychological path. It understands nothing at all about my justifications and purposes. It simply branded me 'traitor', heaped its opprobrium upon me, locked me away and then forgot about me.

It began of course, as most such paths do, with my childhood.

I think I had a happy childhood. I say 'think' because, strangely, I cannot remember much about it. I have a remarkably good memory for most things—photographic in some departments—but as to my early years they are just a vague blur on my consciousness. I have often wondered why. I suspect it may have something to do with the fact that, although I class myself as having been happy, other members of my family were evidently not. I was not consciously aware of this at the time, but since in later years both my mother and my sister Elisabeth committed suicide, as had my grandmother before them, and since my other sister, Kristel, was eventually diagnosed as schizophrenic, I have to conclude that there must have been turbulent subconscious undercurrents swirling around me during my childhood, which caused me subsequently to delete much from my memory. Why we should have been so prone to mental instability as a family I cannot say. To all outward appearances we were a very normal, fulfilled and reasonably prosperous unit. My father in particular was a much admired pillar of society. I had, and still have, a huge admiration for him. He is everything I would have wished for myself. A kind and well respected man, firm in his philosophy—he is a Quaker and Lutheran pastor; eminent in his career—he became a professor of theology at Kiel; and dutiful as a parent—he was ever considerate of all our well-beings, and wisely solicitous in the advice he gave us. I am none of those things. I have never achieved my own family (a huge regret but inevitable given my character and circumstances), I have always had to wrestle with my beliefs, and even my career, although originally set on a distinguished trajectory, is now irretrievably tarnished. This is my greatest tragedy. Considering the immense risks and gigantic obstacles I had to overcome en route to achieving that career, it pains me beyond measure that I now appear to have lost all that I had won.

That said, I have frequently heard it mentioned that I have changed the course of history. That is something my father cannot claim. Or indeed few others.

The outward reasons for doing what I did were simple. When I came to manhood that course of history was on a fairly disastrous spiral. The economy of the entire civilised world was on the brink of collapse. My own homeland Germany in particular was devastated by the financial crisis after the ending of the Great War. Millions were out of work or in extreme poverty. The national psyche had suffered a blow to its pride that seemed terminal. The belief in capitalism as the path to unlimited affluence and glory lay in tatters. Faith in religion, in politics, in the leaders, in the systems—all had evaporated in the mud of Flanders and the ruined institutions of Wall Street. And to cap everything the once noble and principled German nation was in thrall to an appalling little man, to an ethic and a regime so patently fiendish that I felt the planet had fallen out of orbit.

I saw things in my late teens which no-one should have seen. I saw people reviled and beaten in the streets simply because of the clothes they wore, or the shape of their mouth or nose. I saw an old professor forced to crawl in the gutter cleaning up dog dirt with his hands by jeering youths wielding sticks. I saw a young girl stripped naked in front of her sobbing parents and led away to suffer God knows what abominations. I heard of so many disappearances and tortures and murders that I lost count, and it seemed to me that the brutal faces of the Nazis parading the streets belonged to some alien species that had arrived from nowhere. Furthermore it appeared that the majority of my countrymen were in complicity with it all. I could not conceive how a nation could have changed character so radically. Was it simply the herd instinct? Were we Germans so weak in character that we could en masse revert to our primeval brutish state at the mere behest of a ranting maniac?

It is a fact that constant exposure to extremes can eventually make one immune to shock, insensitive to tragedy. I almost reached that point, as I suppose did most of my family and acquaintances. We were living in a state of permanent numbness. We were anaesthetised against the barbarism. Until eventually, even though I was not Jewish, I became a victim of it myself.

The development of my political philosophy had its origins in my time at Leipzig and at Kiel universities, where I went to study mathematics and physics. It was already becoming clear to me that the world was going astray, and a new doctrine was required. A completely new method of doing things. And the way that presented itself was communism. The writings of Karl Marx came as a revelation to me, as to so many others. The idea that the evolution of successful societies depends first and foremost on the creation of successful economic conditions rather than on dominant ideologies; that all sections of society must have access to the basic necessities of life before society as a whole can function efficiently; that the 'surplus' value produced by the mass of the world's workers cannot be the property of the few who happen by descent or by chance to be in positions of power—all these tenets struck me as being so self evident, so utterly relevant to the circumstances of the period, that I knew I had to devote as much of my energy to their propagation as possible. One must remember that this was well before the gross abuses of the Lenin/Stalin regimes came to light. It was causing me great distress that so few of the German people, even amongst the political and intellectual classes, were prepared to speak out against the ascent of the Nazis. The communists were the only group so far as I could see who presented any sort of active opposition.

That said, I only joined the party at Kiel after a great deal of soul searching and argument as to their own methods. But having done so I quickly began to make a name for myself as a political agitator. Which of course put me high on the list of suspect persons and brought me to the notice of Hitler's brownshirts.

That was when I awoke to the reality. That was when I realised that I was not simply living in a bad dream, but in a live situation in which my own life was at stake. I had already been threatened verbally several times within the university itself. I did not take these approaches too seriously, but then one night as I was walking back to my lodgings along the river path I was accosted by a gang of half a dozen brownshirts. They said little except to call me a 'Kommunistische drecksack', and then set about beating me up with sticks, fists and boots. I was quite badly hurt, but fortunately was able to break free temporarily and leap over the railings onto the river bank. They then cut off any further line of escape and attacked me over the fence so fiercely that I was sent flying down the bank and into the freezing river itself. I was swept away with their jeers and laughter ringing in my ears, and I feared that my last moments had come. It was only by a small miracle that I was brought inshore some way downstream, and was able to cling to something and eventually pull myself out, bruised, frozen and exhausted.

The message was clear. My days as an open communist activist were numbered. I decided to put my studies on hold and go to Berlin to discuss my future with the heads of the student communist organisation there. I took the train to the capital. But then whilst on the journey I read in the newspaper about a national sensation. The Reichstag government building had been burned to the ground, supposedly, the paper said, by communist sympathisers. I immediately realised the significance of the accusation. The fire had almost certainly been started at Hitler's own instigation (he probably wanted a grander headquarters in any case)—providing justification for the addition of communists to his long list of species to be persecuted. I hastily took the hammer and sickle badge off my jacket, watched I may say with some suspicion by the other occupants of my compartment. On arrival at Berlin I hurried to the meeting with some trepidation. It was a secretive but well attended gathering of like minded students. The air of apprehension amongst them was palpable. When my turn came to speak I briefly recounted the situation at Kiel. I was praised for my activities but warned that it was now too dangerous for me to return there. I was told I should remain in hiding in Berlin, and when the chance came go abroad. There I could join all the other fugitives in foreign lands who were preparing for the future revolution which inevitably had to come.

A girl student member of the party bravely gave me hiding place in her Berlin apartment. She was almost the only human being I had contact with during several terrible months, although I should report that nothing romantic happened between us. I was unable to venture out or contact any of my family for fear of exposure or of compromising them. Each day I feared discovery and arrest. Then came the event that finally and for ever altered my view of mankind and set me on the road to what I suppose would be called my radicalism. I find it hard to recount this, but I feel I must.

The girl, whose name I will not mention even now, herself had a girl friend who occasionally used to visit with food parcels and other essentials, and who was the only other person who knew of my existence there. This girl was a shy and sweet natured person for whom I knew those gestures were an act of great bravery. She was engaged to be married to a young man whom I never saw, but whom I gathered also had, if not communist, at least anti fascist views, and who belonged to one of the many secret factions operating in Berlin. She was very much in love with this boy—whenever she spoke of him her eyes shone with adoration, and I could only envy the recipient of such worship. They planned to marry as soon as matters improved in Germany, which at the time we all still believed must surely happen soon. Then, one dreadful afternoon when I and my protector were alone in the flat, there came a clattering on the stairs and a desperate banging on the door, and the girl tumbled into our tiny apartment in a state of utter desperation. Her fiancé had been arrested and taken away by the Gestapo. She was out of her mind with worry, and there was nowhere she could go for help except to us. She lived with her parents and did not dare go home in case she was caught herself, or incriminated her family. For three days we kept her there trying to calm her despair and anguish. I lay awake at night listening to her stifled weeping and there was nothing I could say or do to comfort her. During the day my protector made what discreet enquiries she could as to the fiancé's fate.

We eventually discovered what had happened to him. They had taken him to the infamous headquarters in Prinz Albrecht Street. There they stripped him and hung him from the ceiling. Two of the Gestapo then took up iron bars, and, starting at his feet and working upwards, they methodically broke every bone in his body. They ended by smashing his skull.

When I heard the story I vomited in the sink. One week later the girl hung herself at her parents' home.

From that moment on what little faith I had in the ability of the human race, or at any rate the Teutonic section if it, to redeem itself evaporated. All my philosophical theories and conjectures lay in pieces at my feet. I knew I had to leave Germany as urgently as possible, and then to take stock of my life and of what role I would play in the ungodly cesspit that the world had become.

The party was able to arrange my escape to Paris. I went with nothing but a few clothes and papers to my name, and only the names of one or two distant contacts of the family as glimmers of light in my darkness.

CHAPTER SIX

The inhabitants of each successive period in the world's history have beaten their predecessors in the race for life, and are higher in the scale of nature; and this may account for that vague yet ill-defined sentiment, felt by many. . . . that organisation on the whole has progressed.

Origin of Species

'Oh, Maurice, what a place! What a wonderful place!' Easterby's voice floated at regular intervals from the depths of the shop. The moment they entered he had exclaimed at the Dickensian atmosphere, sniffed at the unique grassy odour that emanates from old books, and dived down the maze of narrow passageways between the shelves. 'My God, do you know everything you've got here?' he called as he skimmed titles, flicked pages.

'Oh, well this is just run-of-the-mill stuff in here,' Maurice answered as he followed along the foot-worn lines on the ancient linoleum which he had vowed to replace a thousand times (did they *make* linoleum any more?). 'Anything valuable I keep in the back room locked away.'

'Well I must come back! I must spend some time here,' Easterby exclaimed, checking the publication date on a Cambridge edition of Newton's *Principia Mathematica.*

'Anytime, of course. Though I doubt whether I have anything of real interest to a collector such as yourself.'

'You never know, Maurice. You just never know. That's the wonder of this business. You can never be certain what little gem can spring out on you from the most unexpected places.'

'No. Quite. Absolutely.' Maurice was warming to this man. Despite the vast gulf in backgrounds he was something of a kindred spirit. Maurice had always resisted the temptation to expand the shop, in spite of the financial pressures. The thought of gradually mutating into an ordinary book store—piled high with all the current trashy best-selling authors, screaming aloud their 3 for 2 offers, adorned with grinning images of the latest celebrity to produce a sensational kiss-and-tell 'autobiography'—appalled him. And here was the type of client who gave purpose to his determination.

The shop door bell pinged as Maurice's assistant, Rupert, returned from his lunch break, still chewing on a Mars bar. He glanced towards the shelves, noted that Maurice was with a customer, and went behind the big oak counter to peer at the computer screen. Self-effacement and ability to immerse himself in the minutiae of the administration were his chief merits. Easterby replaced the book and reluctantly abandoned his exploration. There were no other customers in at the moment, but he indicated Rupert. 'Is there anywhere we can go. . . .?'

'Oh, yes of course,' said Maurice, and led the way to the back office. It had the same air of dated scholastic industry about it, but everything from the old mahogany filing cabinets to the big leather-topped desk was neatly ordered in Maurice's fastidious fashion. Only the heavy steel safe at the back and a modern photocopier contrasted with the period atmosphere.

'Do sit down,' he said, indicating the library chair opposite the desk, its leather seat polished by a thousand bottoms. But Easterby was already prowling the glass fronted shelves filling three sides of the room where Maurice kept his more valuable stock.

'Oh, yes, yes—I must *definitely* return here!' he exclaimed, stooping to peer at titles through the glass. Maurice sat behind the desk and waited patiently. The American straightened again, deftly avoided hitting his head on the ancient brass chandelier hanging from the ceiling, and sat opposite, saying, 'Well, first things first.' He crossed his giraffe-like legs. Maurice wondered idly how he found trousers to fit. 'The big thing is this, Maurice. If you take this on. . . .' A moment's hesitation. 'I don't want to seem melodramatic here. . . . but no-one must get wind of what you're looking for.'

Maurice raised his eyebrows. Easterby went on. 'I don't know if anyone else is out there searching for the same things—they most likely are—but we mustn't give away more than we have to.' He sniffed distastefully and fixed Maurice with his pale, sharp gaze. 'You must know as well as I do, people in the rare manuscript business—like in the art world—can be pretty fanatical.'

Maurice nodded. He hadn't been on the end of any extreme examples of collectors' compulsions, but he knew of numerous incidents. He wondered vaguely how ruthless Easterby himself could get. 'Does your friend Tommy Houseman know what you're looking for?' he asked.

'Good God no!' Easterby's chin jutted. 'And he's no friend, just a fellow collector. I wouldn't let that bastard know about something like this. He'd be after it like a ferret.'

'You must have told him something, for him to recommend me.'

'Well just the vague nature of the quest, but none of the details.' He waved the subject away. 'Anyway, I suggest that when you're asking around you say nothing specific. Simply that you're interested in Darwinian memorabilia and does anyone know of anything? We mustn't give anything away. I know people who would literally murder for something like this.'

Maurice blinked. 'A bit of an exaggeration surely.'

The other's gaze was even more intense. 'Oh no, Maurice. I'm not trying to scare you, but everyone is capable of murder under certain circumstances.' He paused and his eyebrows rose a fraction. 'Even you for instance?'

The question hung in the air, pregnant with unexplained meanings. Maurice was speechless, not for the first time.

Easterby smiled, a brief knowing smile. 'I see that struck home. I wondered as much.' He waved a placatory hand. 'Pay no heed to me. I shouldn't have gone there.' He leaned forward. 'However I just want you to understand. You are practically my last chance at finding this thing. I've exhausted all other avenues. And this quest might be as important to you as it is to me.'

Maurice's head was spinning with unformulated questions. But he just asked, 'Why is this so crucial to you? It can't just be a matter of your collection.'

Easterby sat back and gazed for a moment at the ceiling. 'No, you're right, it's more than that. Let's simply say that I am seeking explanations. What are the causes of evil? Why the necessity for tragedy?' He looked back at Maurice. 'One day I'll explain more to you.' Then his expression abruptly changed and he clapped his hands together. 'That's enough of solemn matters. This should be a celebratory occasion. I have a good feel about our association.'

'Well, yes indeed,' replied Maurice, less demonstratively. His mind was still not functioning properly. 'But, er . . . I still think I must take a bit of time to decide.'

'Of course, of course. Circumspection in all things.'

'And please don't hold out too much hope. You seem to have covered most obvious avenues, and I'm not certain I'd be able to. . . .'

'Oh, I'm sure you could come up with something, even if it's simply that the whole thing is a myth. But I think not. Read the Fuchs piece.' Easterby reached into his inside pocket, took out a wallet and extracted a printed card. 'This has all my relevant addresses, emails, telephone numbers on it—including France. Take it now on the assumption that we'll have an agreement. You can always contact me via one of those.' Maurice put the card away in his own wallet and

Easterby waved his hands in a more businesslike gesture. 'OK, let's talk finances. I like to have those cut and dried at the outset, then everyone knows where they stand. If you took this on what do you think your weekly expenses might be?'

'Oh dear,' thought Maurice. He had a horror of discussing such subjects. 'It all depends on how much time I would have to give to it. How much travelling I would have to do. . . .'

'O.K., well look. How about we set a figure for now, and if it turns out not enough, you just tell me and we'll up it?'

He mentioned a sum which seemed more than generous to Maurice. For a rare grateful moment he felt the sensation of having financial headaches ease. He gave his attention to the string of details and sources that Easterby imparted concerning his searches to date. Then he sat back studying his notes.

'I'll have my secretary send you the list of descendants we've compiled,' said the other. 'It's quite long.'

Having apparently decided he had done all he could with regard to that topic, he abruptly switched his attention. Rose and again started wandering along the book shelves. 'Got any first editions that may be of interest to me? Early American literature for instance?'

Maurice pondered. 'I have a Webster first edition of *Huckleberry Finn* somewhere there,' he said. 'Dated 1885, I think.'

Easterby's head swung round. 'Not signed by any chance?'

Maurice smiled. 'That would be too much to hope for.' He too rose and went to the fiction shelves. Found the green morocco bound volume and took it down, showing the gilt embossed cover. 'Pretty good condition.'

Easterby grabbed it and ruffled through the pages. 'Much better than my copy. How much is it?'

'Er. . . .' Maurice had to go to his ledger to find out. He had held the book for some time. 'Three thousand, seven hundred pounds.'

'Very reasonable. I'll take it.'

Maurice blinked. He was not used to such fast major sales. If all his customers were like this one he wouldn't have any financial worries. 'Well, if you're sure. . . .'

'Absolutely.'

'I'll have my assistant wrap it for you.'

'Don't bother. I'll take it as it is.' Easterby stared at the book reflectively. 'I first read this as a teenager. I remember being enthralled that people could lead such adventurous lives.'

'Yes', replied Maurice, 'certainly action packed.'

'Then later I encountered a few adventures of my own, and found it wasn't so entertaining.' He didn't elaborate, but carefully put the book away in his brief case. 'Can we add this to your first expenses cheque?' He saw the hesitant look in Maurice's eyes and laughed. 'Of course not—that could be the cleverest con trick you've ever come across.' Fished for his wallet. 'I presume you'll take a credit card?'

Maurice rode home on the bus that evening in a highly disturbed mood. He did not take his usual pleasure in observing the thronged streets and freshly budding parks as he sailed serenely by on the top deck. He was too confused by the visitor who seemed to know more than was seemly about his personal circumstances. Too disturbed by threats of malevolent deeds performed in pursuit of rare items. And too preoccupied with the decision he had to make. If he said yes to the mission, would he find himself riskily involved in another man's personal obsessions? Would he be committing himself to a wild goose chase? To weeks of fruitless hunting, pointless phone calls, endless letter writing? To exhausting journeys around the country following false trails? And supposing he did come up with the goods. Would they really be as significant as this eccentric American claimed? Would the journal be anything more than a Victorian housewife's trifling account of her domestic concerns? Would Darwin's postscript reveal any more than his copious writings had already revealed? In any case was there any more to be said about the theory of evolution that the legions of scientists, philosophers, and ecclesiastical pundits who had raged over the subject during the intervening century and a half since he published his seminal work, hadn't already said?

He absently polished his spectacles as he stared unseeing out of the bus window. On the other hand, he had to admit his antiquarian's instinct was stirred at the idea of such a discovery. His historian's curiosity was fired at the idea of new revelations of the great man's lifestyle. And, beyond all that, the concept of Darwin's hypothetical postscript aroused his interest in a way that very few literary discoveries had done throughout his career. As Easterby had hinted it seemed to have relevance to his own quest. His lifelong search for some method in what had been since childhood an anarchic world. If it was true that the man who had proposed the most likely explanation for that method had actually put his ultimate conclusions into words, then Maurice—like Easterby—would dearly like to read them.

He opened his ancient leather briefcase with difficulty in the narrow space between the bus seats, took out the Fuchs journal and stared at it. Then there was this. This was not hypothetical—it *did* exist. And now it was his political instincts which were aroused, his detective's curiosity which stirred. In its different way this was equally fascinating. What did it have to reveal about the state of the world in one of its most endangered eras? What were its unlikely connections with Darwin and his thinking?

Maurice stared again out of the window at the broad swathe of traffic winding its way with much growling of engines and hooting of horns around Marble Arch. 'What do you think, Alice?' he mentally asked. 'What do you think I should do?'

And he imagined her turning her face to him, and contemplating him with those eyes which harboured so much feminine shrewdness in their depths. 'You must do what your instinct tells you, dear,' she would have said. 'Life is all about opportunities, isn't it? And it's high time you found something to distract you. You've been far too maudlin for far too long.' Then she would almost certainly have added a barbed afterthought, such as, 'Careful though—do you want to get involved in all that religious squabbling? Haven't we enough of that in the world already?'

He sighed as the bus ploughed its way up Park Lane, between the stately hotels on the one side and the equally stately plane trees of Hyde Park on the other, like some giant insect following the trail laid down by all the other insects preceding it. He was reminded, as so often, of the other fateful occasion when he had been riding on the top of a bus over six years previously. The incident which was forever linked in his mind with the diagnosis of Alice's condition, two months prior. The two events had heralded the start of his downward spiral. They seemed the confirmation of his ultimate defeat in the struggle of life. He shook his head and banished the memory from his mind. Too many negative images. We are all Darwin's children, thought Maurice. All just wayward atoms struggling along the evolutionary road towards some vague, unspecified and unimaginable destination. He himself was a microbe riding a genetically engineered vehicle numbered 13, which he trusted was going to take him home, but for all he knew might dump him in hell, or in an alternative universe, or in some obscure cul de sac of this universe, from whence he might never find his way back.

It didn't deposit him in any of those places of course. Merely dropped him as it always did some three hundred yards from the front door of his home, and continued on to regions north which he had rarely explored or conjectured about.

Well, he knew what he would do this evening, he thought as he walked the three hundred yards. A long hot bath, with just one glass of scotch on the side and some good music on Radio Three; a Marks and Sparks Chicken Tikka from the freezer; a beer with it but no more scotch (seriously, seriously no more scotch); then settle down to look at Fuchs's writings. Perhaps they would cast some light on the matter. Maybe even provide him with inspiration as to what to do about it. At least they'd give him nuclear explosions to dream about, instead of the usual.

Yes, good. Course of action decided for another lonely evening. He reached home, glanced up and down the street, but seeing no strangers lurking, no movements in the shadows, no threatening shapes on the horizon, he put his key in the lock with a lighter heart.

CHAPTER SEVEN

August 16th, 1843, Down House

My darling father[5] has left us. It is less than a year since the loss of our little Mary, and now death has visited us once more. I cannot grieve in the same way, since Father's time was come after a fruitful life, and these last years he has been but a shadow of his former self. In some ways it is a welcome relief, since his once fine figure was reduced to little more than a skeleton, and my dear sister Lizzie,[6] who has cared for both my parents for so long and with such selfless dedication, tells me that these last months he has been like a ghost, trembling and muttering between the sheets. Nevertheless, to watch his grave, lined face now so calm and still upon the pillow brought back the memories of all those years when brothers and sisters, uncles and aunts, cousins and friends of our three great entangled families[7] were gathered together in his quiet and magnanimous patronage, and his going leaves a void in my heart that can never be filled. The dear old house and park,[8] which I for so long shared with Lizzie the responsibility of running before my marriage took me away, holds a lifetime of such images for me, and to see it now silent and empty of his great spirit is a sadness scarcely to be born.

---

[5]*Josiah Wedgewood, potter, industrialist and Whig statesman. 1769–1843.*
[6]*Elizabeth Wedgewood, 1793–1880. Crippled spinster sister of Emma.*
[7]*Wedgewoods, Darwins, and Emma's mother's family, the Allens of Tenby in Pembrokeshire, all of whose various members inter-married with some frequency through the generations.*
[8]*Maer Hall, nr Shrewsbury, seat of the Wedgewoods-Elizabethan country house with Capability Brown gardens.*

My mother[9] too is a complete invalid and barely in sufficient mind to realise that he has gone. She cannot be far behind. The service at the church was crammed with family and associates and workers on the estate, and of course staff from the potteries. It was an army, it seemed to me, of ancients from the past, and though the vicar spoke well of Father's great legacy to industry and of his noble spirit, there was a tangible concern amongst the devout that his confessed disbelief in the workings of God might not have ensured him his deserved place in heaven.

Charles too was much moved by the event, for he has of course lost an uncle and a wise mentor who has aided him much in his endeavours (In fact I believe that, were it not for my father's intervention on his behalf, he would never have gained his own father's permission for his expedition aboard the Beagle).

However we have our consolations. I am seven months on with child again, which pray God will compensate for the loss of Mary, and Charley is now engrossed in his improvements to the house and grounds. We have had since the spring a squad of workmen sawing and hammering and digging and delving, and a more practical, not to say handsome residence is beginning to take shape here. The bedroom accommodation is much improved, essential for our growing family; there is a pleasant new schoolroom for the children and their governess; the kitchen and pantry are extended; and, most important of all to dear C, he has a new study, with large windows to light his work and experiments, and room for all his endless collections of jetsam and flotsam. The grounds too are greatly altered, with a larger walled kitchen garden, and a complete new earth bank to the front of the house to give privacy and shelter from the south-westerly gales. I have inherited a gardener's instinct from my Uncle

_____

[9]_Elizabeth 'Bessy' Wedgewood, nee Allen. 1764–1846._

John,[10] and have found much joy in planting the copses with shrubs and wild flowers (which of course C insists on scrutinising and classifying as is his wont), and the sound of the larks and nightingales is a constant background to our walks there. I feel truly at home here now, and am growing to love this house more and more.

Charles as usual is immersed in his work, and has commenced yet another new treatise, this time entitled 'Volcanic Islands'. I can only wonder at the industry of a man whose health is so permanently fragile. He has already published the journal of his great voyage, together with endless papers on zoology and biology and ornithology and geology and countless other 'ologies' of which I scarcely know the names, let alone the meanings.

Furthermore C has received a request from George Waterhouse,[11] for whom he has been quite instrumental in obtaining a senior post at the British Museum, for help with a vast new project. That of classifying all living species! This threw Charley into quite an agitation, and he has been muttering and shaking his head about the house like some irritable old cart horse. This morning I lost patience and confronted him, demanding to know what was the matter.

He huffed and puffed as is his way, and then said, "The matter is that George's request goes to the heart of my whole professional dilemma." I pressed him further and he tried to explain to me. If I understand correctly his argument went something like this: "The traditionalists see the entire question of classification as identifying the correct family or circle for each species, all revolving within their own spheres as originally devised by God. However I and my

---

[10]*John Wedgewood, founder of the Royal Horticultural Society. 1766–1844.*

[11]*George Waterhouse, architect, naturalist, and collector of specimens. 1810–88.*

fellow thinkers follow the conception of the controversial Frenchman, Lamarck,[12] which implies that the species have developed in linear sequence one from another over the generations, so that the mightiest have their origins in the lowliest, and it is merely a matter of which has best adapted to the environment which determines its success or failure."

I then had the courage to state my own opinion on that proposition. I could not see the logic. How can a horse for instance possibly have developed from the same origins as a crocodile, or a peacock from those of a flying bat?

C replied with that patient condescension which is both infuriating and utterly defeating: "One has to see it in the context of aeons of time and countless numbers of generations—something we humans find very difficult to do since the timescale of our own immediate generations is the normal boundary of our vision."

I was not convinced but as usual had to temporarily concede the argument. I had not the weapons to counter him. When I hear C and his friends debating in such infinite detail the structure of organisms I have to concede that they are vastly more knowledgeable on these matters than I. I am therefore resigned to letting them fight their obscure battles in their own way, provided the blood is spilled in the debating chamber or in the pages of the scientific journals, and not at home. That however is the difficulty. My dear obsessed Charley admitted it himself. "My convictions on the matter are absolute, dear Emma, but my predicament is that, if I make my opinions too public and openly disassociate myself from such as Waterhouse, then I could bring the wrath of the entire establishment—scientific, philosophical and ecclesiastical all together—down on my head, and therefore on yours and the family's too."

---

[12]*Jean-Baptiste de Lamark, French naturalist and philosopher. 1744–1829.*

Well yes, that is a certainty. However my concerns are rather that it is the wrath of God rather than the establishment he will bring down upon our heads!

These are indeed tumultuous times we live in, when the whole structure of accepted thought and wisdom appears to be under threat from so many different directions. It may be that these developments are necessary, and once more the Almighty's method of challenging our complacent ways with deeper thought and investigation, but it does not make for a comfortable existence. However it is the next existence that is my true concern, for if our struggles here are ever to achieve fulfilment and due reward, and if we are to live again in the next life with our nearest and dearest in God's presence, then it must surely be that we pay due homage to Him in this one.

Charles though has been wrestling with doubts about this whole conception for some years now, as he confided to me diffidently even before we were wed. This gave me great anxiety at the time, the only cloud over our betrothal. It gives me even more so now. I am secure in my own convictions and I cannot conceive of life without their reassurance, but I do not have the intellectual means to argue with him.

Even so I will continue to pray for him. It is the only way I know to counter his weakness of faith.

CHAPTER EIGHT

Nothing at first can appear more difficult to believe than that the more complex organs and instincts should have been perfected, not by means superior to human reason, but by the accumulation of innumerable slight variations, each good for the individual possessor. . . . The mind cannot possibly grasp the full meaning of the term of a hundred million years; it cannot add up and perceive the full effects of many slight variations, accumulated during an almost infinite number of generations.

Origin of Species

Several developments happened during the forty eight hours after the lunch at the Ritz. Maurice's resolution to lay off the scotch the previous evening had of course failed dismally and he was morose and fuzzy headed. The appropriate words came as they did so often: '*Drink today, and drown all sorrow. You shall perhaps not do't tomorrow.*' He had gone through his usual waking process of suicidal despair, followed by violent self-criticism, and then gradual recuperation as the routines of the day took over. However, having got to the shop he was scarcely prepared for the first event of the morning, which was a telephone call coming only minutes after he had opened up and got behind his desk. He immediately recognised the American voice at the other end, which was older and more guttural than Donald Easterby's.

'Maurice, it's Tommy Houseman here.'

'Hello, Mr Houseman.' He looked at his watch and frowned irritably. 'This is an unusual time for you to ring.'

'I'm in L.A. at the moment. It's eleven at night here.'

A carefully calculated call then. Maurice was wary. 'What can I do for you?'

'Have you heard from a friend of mine, Donald Easterby?'

Maurice hesitated. How much should he say? 'Easterby? Oh yes, I did get a call from him.'

'Hah! I thought you might. Well I put him on to you.'

'Ah. Yes, well he. . . .'

Houseman as usual was brusquely to the point. 'Thing is I'm not sure what he's after. Did he say?'

Again Maurice hesitated. 'Well it's all a bit vague.' He stretched the truth a little. 'We didn't have time to talk a great deal. I gather it's something that nobody seems to know much about.'

'He didn't say what precisely?'

Maurice stretched the truth further. 'Not precisely. Some hypothetical manuscript or other. He's going to send more details.'

'Yeah—trust Donald to keep it cagey. I know it's to do with biology or science. He told me that much. Which is why I recommended you.'

'That was kind of you.'

'I also know from the way he was so evasive about it that it could be something I'd be interested in.'

'Well, I. . . .'

'Now listen, Maurice, I'm a good client of yours, right?'

'Indeed.'

'If this guy's on the trail of something good I want to know about it, OK?'

'Well, I. . . .'

'He's a collector like me, and we have quite a rivalry going in some departments. I can tell when he's fired up about something. I don't want you to do anything unprofessional, but your first loyalty's with me and if this is something big then I want you to tell me about it.'

Oh dear. The complications were starting already. 'I have to respect client confidentiality, you know that, Tommy.'

'Sure, sure. But you can at least give me the chance to bid for it. The reason I recommended you was that I knew I could rely on you to keep me informed.'

Maurice bridled. A touch underhand one would think. 'Well, I know very little about it as yet, Tommy, and I'm not sure that I'm going to be of use in any case. However if it turns out to be something important it will probably be on the open market and, er. . . .'

The voice was harsh. 'Don't give me that bullshit, Maurice. If Donald gets a sniff of it there's no way it'll reach the open market. You and I both know that.'

'Well. . . .'

'All I'm saying is I want to be kept in the picture, all right? I know that son of a bitch, and I know he wouldn't be going out of his way after something petty.'

Maurice bristled further. 'Look, Mr Houseman, I haven't said I'm going to be involved yet, and if it's important I imagine a lot of other people will be after it too. I'm only a small time book dealer and I can't commit to promising anybody anything at this moment until I know a great deal more about it.'

'Sure, sure, Maurice—keep your hat on. I'm just reminding you that I'm an old client whose interests you're familiar with, and who you can always trust to pay good money for the right thing.'

'Yes, I'll remember that.'

After he had rung off Maurice sat for a moment reflecting, not for the first time, how extraordinary it was that people who had more wealth than they knew what to do with could get so fanatical about acquiring things—whether it was yachts, mansions, football teams, works of art, or manuscripts. It kept other people like himself in business, but it wasn't the most edifying of human characteristics.

However the call helped him to make up his mind, and he telephoned Donald Easterby at the hotel shortly afterwards. He thanked his host politely for the lunch and then said,

'I've been thinking about your proposition. I might say I've thought about little else since we parted. I've been in something of a quandary over it, but I have considered various avenues of exploration which I could possibly follow up.'

'That's great,' said Easterby encouragingly.

'I'll tell you what I'd like to do, if this is acceptable. I'd like to work on the project for a month, and see if it gets me anywhere. If after a month I don't feel I'm making any progress, then I would ask you to release me from the obligation. I can imagine it becoming quite a distraction, you see.'

'That's fine, Maurice. I understand completely. No obligation at all.'

'And I. . . .' How to put this? 'I would be obliged if you didn't look into my private affairs any further.'

'I understand, Maurice. I assure you I wasn't being prurient. I just have to be careful with how I go about things.'

'Right, well. . . . You are obviously going to be in France or back in America before I have any news at all. May I telephone or write to you there?'

'Sure. You have my card with all my details. Tell me, Maurice, I didn't see a computer in your office. Do you use email?'

'Yes of course,' replied Maurice with a touch of petulance. 'My wife installed a system some years ago. It's behind the shop counter.'

'Good, then. . . .'

Maurice felt immediately contrite and added, 'Sorry. It's just that we do a fair bit of internet trading these days, and of course emails are an excellent way of corresponding with clients around the world.'

'Then you'll be able to do the same with me wherever *I* am around the world. And if you come up with anything exciting I'll be ready to return to England at the drop of a hat.'

Well, dropping such hats was fine for some. 'Very good. That's agreed then.'

Maurice didn't mention the call from Tommy Houseman. No desire to be involved in billionaires' private rivalries. The conversation ended with Easterby apparently satisfied, and Maurice less so but relatively tranquil.

During the remainder of the day he found time to send off, either by email or conventional post, half a dozen messages to various contacts of his. The wording in all of them was more or less the same, and carefully crafted to convey the maximum casualness and minimum significance:-

'Dear—,
Just a quick note to ask if you might have access to any items pertaining to, or knowledge of any connections relating to, Charles Darwin or his works, other than the usual well known publications. I am doing a favour for someone who is engaged in researching the lesser known aspects of his lifestyle and scientific investigations, and who has the resources to pay for any such which might interest him.
Best wishes, Maurice Aldridge.'

The next development occurred the following morning. Maurice was in his back office again, engaged in everyday matters of administration when the shop doorbell pinged announcing a customer. He left it to his assistant to deal with whoever it was. A few moments passed, then Rupert knocked and stuck his unruly tangle of black hair round the door.

'There's a chap here wants a valuation on some books. Don't know if they're worth anything.' He tilted his head and lowered his voice. 'Bit of an odd character.'

Maurice nodded and got up from the desk. He was used to odd characters in his business. He went out and found a youngish man waiting with a couple of old books. Slimly built with fairish hair that curled about his ears. He would have been extremely good looking were it not for one small flaw. The blue-green eyes were minutely offset in what was not exactly a squint, more the slightest non-correlation. It gave him a vulnerable and vaguely myopic air, which however disappeared as soon as he smiled. The smile illuminated his face in an unusual way.

'Good morning,' said Maurice. 'You have some books you'd like valued?'

The fellow held out the books. Spoke in a voice which was not quite upper middle class—probably grammar school, surmised Maurice. 'Yes. I don't actually want to sell them. But they've been in the family for a bit, and I just wondered if they're of any, um . . . value.' He handed the two volumes across. They were leather bound, early editions of *The Idiot* and *Madame Bovary*.

Maurice skimmed the publisher's pages and checked the condition. 'Not greatly valuable,' he said. 'But nice books. You might get twenty or thirty pounds each from a dealer. Possibly a bit more at auction.'

'Oh, right. Yes, thanks,' said the other. The smile flitted diffidently across his face and he hovered uncertainly.

'You . . . don't wish to sell them though?' Maurice prompted.

The young man, whom Maurice reckoned was probably in his late twenties, looked down at the books and shook his head. 'No. There's um . . . quite a lot of old books like this in the family. My grandfather and my uncle collected them.' He tapped the two volumes. 'A lot of stuff like this. I just wondered what they would cost. I was thinking of . . . perhaps building up the collection, you see.'

Maurice frowned. 'Building it up?'

'Yes, well I like old books like that. I never really . . . I mean I only just got hold of them when my uncle died, you see.' His radiant smile flitted briefly again. 'I was wondering how easy it was to collect more.'

'You have others at home like that?'

The other hesitated. 'Yes. Things I've inherited. Nothing really valuable, you know. Nothing you'd be interested in. Just nice old books.' That was the joy of this business, thought Maurice—one never knew where interesting stuff would turn up. The young man ran a hand through his thick hair. 'I quite like having them around, and I just wondered what it would cost me to add to the collection, d'you know what I mean?'

'I see. Well, contrary to what you say, Mr, er . . .?'

'Hemingway. Roger Hemingway.'

'Ah. Illustrious name, Hemingway.'

The fellow looked at him and frowned. 'Sorry?'

'The writer.'

'Oh. Yes.' Came the half smile. 'No relation.'

Maurice gestured at the shelves. 'Well, contrary to what you say, I do deal in books such as yours. If you look around you'll find plenty in that price category. So, if you are seriously intending to increase your collection you would just have to search around here, or the stock of any similar dealer, and you could do so at modest cost.' Adding reluctantly, 'And of course there's always the internet.' Though why he should promote the source which had so depleted his and his fellow dealers' profits he couldn't think. He went on, 'But you would really need to decide what it is you wish to specialise in. The choice is so vast. Do you have a favourite genre?'

'Favourite. . . .?'

'Genre. Any particular era? Just novels, or non-fiction as well? And is it English books you prefer, or Continental, or . . .?'

'Oh, English, yes. English novels mostly. And older stuff, you know.'

'The classics.'

'Yes. Classics.' Hemingway shifted awkwardly and lowered his voice a touch. 'You see, the thing is, I don't actually know a great deal about . . . literature and so forth. I. . . . well I missed a lot of that at college.' He grinned seductively. 'Football and girls—you know.'

'Ah yes, well. . . .' Maurice's education had suffered different distractions, but he felt only a small pang of envy.

'Quite regret it now, but. . . . well, I'd rather like to learn a bit more. Try and catch up a little. And seeing as how I got all these books through the family, I thought it would be a good way to start. . . .' His myopic gaze was sincere. 'If it's not too late.'

'It's never too late, Mr Hemingway.' Maurice felt a touch of admiration. There was hope for the world yet. 'Yes, so er. . . . I wish you well in your endeavour. If ever you want advice on your collection, or you just want to come in and browse my own stock here, do feel welcome.'

'Thanks. That's very kind of you.' The young man turned away. Then on an afterthought he turned back, and held up *The Idiot*. 'You don't have any more books by this writer, do you by any chance?'

'Dostoyevsky? Yes, we have one or two. Would you like to see them?'

'Yes. I'd be interested. I rather like him.'

The last writer Maurice would wish to read in his present state of mind. However he was not one to deter a customer. Which is how the fellow left his establishment carrying not two, but three volumes, the addition being a cloth bound, nineteen thirties edition of *The Brothers Karamazov* which had cost him fifteen pounds, reduced by the book seller from twenty.

CHAPTER NINE

March 24th, 1951. Wakefield

I am grateful for my access to newspapers here, even if they are usually several days old. At present they are full of the cold war. The Allies are forever squabbling with Russia over the division of Germany. I agonise constantly about my homeland. I am not especially patriotic, but as always I puzzle that my nation, once so proud and so progressive, can have lost its way in so radical a fashion and be now suffering such repercussions. I find myself comparing the German mentality with the English. I have always had great respect for the English. Despite their outward arrogance and reserve they have always seemed as rational and forward looking a people as one might hope to find on this earth. Yet the English are not so radically different in nature from the Germans. Indeed they are partly descended from the same stock. Could they, I wonder, under the right circumstances revert to a similar despotic state?

I had an interesting discussion yesterday with the assistant governor, Gordon Hawkins. I asked him, as an Englishman what did he think the basis of the English character was. He gave me the standard reply, which was that it was moulded by the fortunate circumstances of their inhabiting a strategically placed and secure island, which in turn caused them to become such a dominant maritime nation, which then brought about their astonishingly widespread empire, and finally led to their initiating the industrial revolution. All of which earned for them both a relatively tranquil and effective political system and a relatively even spread of affluence.

However I then replied that many of those circumstances might be applied to the modern Germany—yet look what had happened there—and that gave him pause for thought.

After a silence he replied, "It probably all goes back to Magna Carta. Do you know what that was?"

I nodded. Of course I knew about the contract reached between King John and his feudal barons in the 13th century, although I was hazy on the detail.

"That was an extraordinarily far-seeing agreement," continued Gordon, "which guaranteed rights to ownership, access to the law, and individual freedom for every citizen. Of course it has often been abused throughout the centuries, but the overall effect I would say has had enormous influence, consciously and subconsciously, on the shaping of the English identity."

This gave me my opportunity, and I jumped in saying, "Ah, but the principles of communism sought to take this principle even further."

Gordon then smiled at me in that ironic way he has, and said, "Yes, but the trouble with creeds that try to <u>impose</u> systems on communities, instead of motivating them to come about naturally, is that they invariably lead to unforeseen consequences and abuses. Which is what has happened in Russia. Revolution versus evolution."

I had to concede his point. But I maintained my defence of Marx's original principles and we debated at some length.

He then asked me why I had chosen to come to England in the first place. I explained that England, or should I say Britain (for the Scots in particular have contributed their share) has always been a productive breeding ground for all the sciences—for the very reasons that he had advanced to explain her worldly success—and this was another incentive for me to make it my desired destination.

Looking back now and reflecting on the path which led to my present circumstances, I realise that it was the traumatic events that happened while I was in Berlin, followed by the weeks of recuperation and reflection spent in Paris before I was able to cross the Channel, that cemented my embryonic ideology. As I struggled with my youthful ideas and ambitions, as I wrestled with my bewilderment at the dire events which had overtaken my own country, I was gradually confirmed in my belief that the broad path of science was the best hope for this beleaguered planet. Man could thresh around in the cloudy waters of religion and politics as much as he liked, but all they ever seemed to produce was confusion, bigotry and conflict. Whereas it was the great discoveries of science and industry which in the end improved his lot, brought improvement for the masses, and the hope of progress against the forces of ignorance and poverty.

And the language of science is mathematics. And mathematics was my subject.

Thus it was that in the September of 1933 I found myself, with nothing but a few clothes in a canvas bag and scarcely a mark, franc or shilling to my name, sailing for England and an extremely tenuous connection with a family who lived in the rural South West of the country.

Mr and Mrs Gunn, who were the employers of the fiancée of one of my cousins (that is how tenuous was the connection!) turned out to be the epitome of the civilised and hospitable English couple. They had invited me to stay with them purely on the information that I needed sanctuary, that I was a budding scientist, and that I was also a communist (they were themselves communist sympathisers, as were many British opponents of Naziism at that time, believing that communism in general and Russia in particular could prove valuable allies against the threat). Fortune was truly on my side at last, since they proved to be well-to-do and generous hosts with a lovely home in the tranquil Somerset countryside, and also to have invaluable connections with the nearby Bristol University, one of the foremost British scientific learning establishments. They introduced me to Professor Nevill Mott, the head of the physics department there, who not only spoke German but was also a left-wing sympathiser, and he, presumably impressed by my mathematical qualifications, took me on as a research assistant in his laboratory. My scientific career had begun!

However I did not explain all this to Gordon Hawkins. Long habits of secrecy formed during my years in espionage still exerted their influence, even though there was now little reason to maintain them. That is my problem. I will by nature probably never be able to get truly close to my fellow beings. I am not sure why. I do not have the gift of intimacy. I don't know whether this is simply part of my inherited make-up or due to the conditioning of my childhood. I live inside my head. I do not have the desire to get inside the heads of many of my fellow creatures. Not unless they have interesting facts to communicate or theories to propose. I am interested only in the product of their intellects. Does that make me a psychotic? Or simply an introvert?

Gordon himself is neither of those things. He seems quite interested in learning what goes on in my head. Whether purely out of personal interest, or at the behest of the authorities I can't tell. However, as with all my previous interrogators, I do not divulge too much about myself.

CHAPTER TEN

Domestic races of the same species often have a somewhat monstrous character; by which I mean, that, although differing from each other and from the other species of the same genus in several trifling respects, they often differ in an extreme degree in some one part. . . . especially when compared with all the species in nature to which they are nearest allied.

Origin of Species

The absence of children was the biggest regret of Maurice's life. It was something he never admitted to anyone else, scarcely even to himself, but it was a large factor in his emptiness.

It had been the only serious flaw in the marriage. During the early years Alice and he had appeared something of a charmed couple. He a presentable, if not quite dashing, graduate from Cambridge with a reasonably good degree in literature and philosophy, and a responsible job with a large London publishing house—she a stunningly pretty producer's assistant at the Beeb (*'The fatal gift of beauty'*?), with a svelte figure and a host of male admirers whom he had by some miracle eclipsed in her affections. They had gone to bed together on their fourth date and discovered the true joys of sex in an abandoned fashion which astonished both of them, and the abandonment continued unabated for the first decade and more of the marriage. Without results however.

He could see her face as clearly as if it were yesterday, when he walked into the kitchen of their small Surrey cottage five years into their marriage and found her sitting at the table, the tears drying on her cheeks, the medical report open in front of her. After endless false alarms and tests and trials it had turned out that there was some obscure fault with her internal female workings and children were out of the question.

Of course they considered the possibility of adoption, but there was something in both of them that shied away from the option. It was perhaps connected with Maurice's subconscious feelings about his own abnormal upbringing, and her awareness of them. But whatever it was the decision was constantly deferred until it had faded from their consciousness. Now he regretted that deferment bitterly. But he had learnt to live with the ache as one learns to live with permanent arthritis or back pain. It was absorbed into his psyche as a fundamental component, for ever in the background, never quite forgotten.

All this added to the factors which drew Maurice to the persona of Roger Hemingway. The young man was more or less the age that in normal circumstances a son might have been. During the next couple of weeks he dropped in to the bookshop twice more—each time spending an hour or so browsing the shelves, even reading a chapter or two of whatever attracted his attention, and then leaving with a couple of cheap editions to add to his 'collection'. During the visits he would engage either Maurice or Rupert in innocuous conversation involving the merits of various classical authors whose names he had picked from the shelves. Maurice was happy to accommodate him in these exchanges, but Hemingway actually appeared more relaxed chatting to his younger assistant. The two even exchanged a few personal details such as where they both lived, which schools they went to, and so forth. Rupert was better educated than the other but humoured him in his questioning.

During one such exchange Maurice was in his office reading a letter which had arrived in the Saturday post. It read:-

   'Dear Maurice,
     Hail to thee blithe spirit! Nice to know you're still alive and kicking. Business is pretty grim out here

in the wilds of Shropshire, where even the local yo-kels now buy their reading matter at Tescos. I'm seri-ously thinking of packing it all in and retiring to my garden and my paint box—though what I'll live on I'm not quite sure. I keep hoping I'll finally stumble across a signed first edition of 'Canterbury Tales' or 'Pilgrim's Progress' in somebody's attic, but it hasn't happened yet.

As to your Darwin quest, I can't help you per-sonally, but I did notice something the other day which might be of interest. Hills, the auction house in Shrewsbury, whose catalogue I keep a beady eye on, has itemised in their latest list: 'Assortment of books and general historical trivia from the estate of George Weldon FRS.' Now he was a local science bof-fin who married a descendant of the Darwins—not sure which one—but he lived near Shrewsbury where Darwin was brought up, and kept up his connections with the naturalist world. Funny old boy. Came into my shop occasionally looking for good editions of John Gould and such. Always used to boast about his Darwin connection. You never know, you might find something relevant amongst his stuff if you can be bothered to venture all this way.

The auction is next Saturday—sorry for the short notice—but do call in if you come, and we'll sup Shi-raz or at least best Darjeeling together. High time we saw each other.

Love and kisses, Felicity.'

Maurice sat for a long moment after he had finished read-ing. He had half an ear on the conversation going on in the outer shop between the two young men, which involved the comparative merits of various Dickens novels. But squalid nineteenth century London was not a subject that concerned him at the moment. A trip to Shropshire, this was something different. Did it appeal? A weekend in the country? Escape from the all enveloping grasp of the capital? He had a fondness for that rather remote Mid Westerly corner of England, which had preserved its historical origins better than most, yet still hadn't been too ravaged by tourism. Problem was how to do it. Have to close the shop for the Saturday, even though it was the busiest day of the week. And would it be worth it? He could be pretty sure what he'd find at the auction. An assortment of old but valueless books, and a pile of personal and domestic junk that might give a clue to the owner's lifestyle but to little else. Still, you never knew what might come to light. Auctions did occasionally prove gold mines for such as himself.

Also, nothing much else had appeared so far from his enquiries, apart from a cursory email from an associate in Oxford. That had read simply: '*Maurice. Can't help much with your Darwin thing. There was only that odd incident I told you about a few years ago, but that's long gone and I've come across nothing else since. Trust all well with you, James Goodwright.*

Maurice couldn't remember what the odd incident had been, and Goodwright wasn't the sort of dealer he had much to do with, so he paid less attention to the message than perhaps he should have done. The other's letter seemed more fruitful. No, he decided, one shouldn't miss such a chance however remote. Especially when someone else was paying the expenses. Also he quite warmed to the idea of visiting the old friend who had written. She was an eccentric, but one of the few amongst his acquaintances who had both known Alice well, and with whom Maurice might feel at ease discussing personal matters. He was in need of someone like that to counter his growing psychotic tendencies.

He stared reflectively at his desk top and played with his spectacles. There was another reason to visit that part of the world also. A reason that had distantly occupied his thoughts for some time now. It took him back once again to the London bombs, and concerned an issue he had resolutely avoided facing for a long time, either out of cowardice or perhaps simple inadequacy. If he travelled north he would be forced to consider it.

However he didn't have to make the decision immediately. He pushed it to the back of his mind, put on his specs, and turned his thoughts to the Fuchs journal. Well into it now and becoming more and more engrossed in the musings of the scientist. Fuchs had taken a more tortuous route, but had been on the same mission as Darwin it seemed. The search for some sort of meaning to existence. But what the direct links between the two were, Maurice hadn't yet discovered.

He went through to the shop where the two young men were still talking. 'How is the book collection progressing?' he asked as they looked up.

Hemingway smiled his radiant smile. 'Oh, pretty well, Mr Aldridge.' He indicated a volume on the counter. 'Rupert here is trying to sell me your Dickens' complete works. What do you think?'

Maurice raised an eyebrow. 'Anyone would think he was on commission.' He glanced at his assistant. 'Don't be too pushy, Rupert.' Then to Hemingway, 'That's quite a big outlay for a large body of work, much of which you may not read. Why not just buy individual novels, and build the collection as you go along? There are a number of separate titles back there.'

'Yes, that's probably best.' Hemingway hesitated, looking at the sample volume. 'It's a nice looking edition though, isn't it?'

Ah, the seduction of leather and gold. 'Yes, Chapman and Hall, published in the nineteen twenties. Well it's up to you, Mr Hemingway.' Maurice hesitated. 'Tell me, what do your parents think of all this collecting? Do they read a lot? Have they had any influence on your selection?'

A shadow crossed Hemingway's features. 'Ah well. . . . my dad's not really into all that. Tell you the truth, he thinks I'm stupid spending so much on. . . .' He waved a hand. 'He says, once you've read a book what's the point of having it take up space.'

'Yes, but then you might say the same about a rare vase. Once the flowers have died, do you put it away in a cupboard or do you leave it to be seen for its own sake?'

The smile again. 'Exactly! That's how I feel. You can't talk to my father about stuff like vases though.'

Maurice's immediate reaction was that the boy was lucky to have a father of any kind to talk to, but he did not comment. He said instead, 'Well then, I suggest you take a day or so to decide about the complete works, and meanwhile we'll keep it on reserve for you.'

'Thank you.' The crooked eyes warmed. 'You're a nice man, Mr Aldridge.'

He left and Maurice turned to send an email in response to Felicity, the friend in Shropshire. His assistant said amiably, 'You always tell me to send people out with more than they came in for, boss.'

'Sometimes there are exceptions, Rupert. It depends on the customer.'

He realised that Felicity didn't have an email address and reached for the phone instead. A brusque female voice spoke at the other end. 'Hello?'

'Felicity, it's me, Maurice.'

'Hello, hello, lover!'

'Thanks for your message. I'm coming up to Shrewsbury for the auction. Thought I might drop by on the way back for that cup of tea.'

'Tea—nonsense. Come for lunch. I'll rustle up a snack, and if the weather's fine perhaps we can have dejeuner sur l'herbe.'

'Splendid. See you then.' He turned back to Rupert and smiled. 'That's my weekend sorted.'

'Good for you, boss. Mine's watching cricket.'

CHAPTER ELEVEN

October 2nd, 1844. Down House

C has handed me yet another essay to read and offer my comments on. I understand that it is a sign of faith in my judgement that he should seek my counsel before all others. However I tremble with apprehension each time, for I am never sure what new thoughts I will discover. Where are his conjectures eventually going to lead him? What unconventional direction is he going to explore next? And this treatise promised to be yet more controversial than the rest, for he said as he handed it to me, "You must read this with objectivity, Emma. You must put aside your own instincts and beliefs and judge it as a purely intellectual hypothesis. I wish to know whether the logic holds and is comprehensible to one such as yourself."

I tried not to show my trepidation as I took it, and I tried to obey his instructions as I read it. However my fears were confirmed about its contentiousness! The growing trend of his opinion seems now to be differing from the followers of Lamarck, who propounds the controversial enough theory that the species have developed one from another in ascending sequence through the generations. Lamarck at least concurs that this process occurs through each individual creature's lifelong struggle to improve themselves in body and mind, and to pass on such improvements via their progeny. This I might conditionally accept as being part of God's grand design for the advancement of the planet.

However, the more I read of my dear husband's painfully produced work, the more it appeared to me that he is approaching a quite different conclusion. Which is that the progression in the species happen by <u>chance</u>. That the changes in each generation propagate themselves purely as a result of being <u>fortuitously</u> more appropriate for survival, and through no design or effort on behalf of the organism itself. He calls the process 'natural selection', as if existence were decided by the mere spin of a roulette wheel!

This is indeed the most provocative and radical of propositions and, if I interpret him correctly, presents me with a great dilemma. For I cannot—I <u>cannot</u>—in my heart agree with such a thesis. It runs counter to all I have ever been taught, all that gives me assurance in this turbulent world.

When I handed the paper back to him I tried to be as conciliatory as possible, praising his language and the clarity of his exposition. But then I was forced to say, "However I do have a difficulty with your argument. This indicates to me that we are every one at the mercy of mere accident, and that the Lord has forsaken all responsibility for our development and abandoned us to anarchy and lawlessness. The implication has to be that His love and power is irrelevant, and He chooses not to employ His guiding hand for the eventual greater good. How can this be? It is the bleakest philosophy I could imagine."

Charley did not react to my outburst. He has endured them before. He merely nodded his great head and contemplated me with those large dark eyes which as always disarm me utterly. "I know, dear Emma, I know," he said. "It is a difficult concept to accept for a sincere believer such as yourself."

I pursued him further. "There are so many instances of the power of prayer. Does that not sway your thinking?"

He smiled benevolently and said, "For every prayer which has supposedly averted a tragedy or aided a circumstance, there must be a hundred where it has had no effect. Are you saying that God is selective?" Then in the face of my silence, he added, "I would not try to alter your faith, for that is something that can only come from within. I ask only that you keep an open mind, and perhaps one day you may be able to reconcile your beliefs with mine."

I cannot for the life of me see how that might come about, but I will as always try to keep an open mind. I do however shudder to think what an outcry this proposition would cause were it to become public. C's fame is ever on the ascendant and his opinions are broadcast far and wide. He is already being claimed as a champion by all those contentious persons who are challenging the Anglican state and calling the clergy complaisant and hypocritical and over-privileged (which I have to concede is often the case), and such a theme would link his name yet more strongly with their cause.

I cannot however add such anxieties to those of my husband, and must try in future to confine myself to comments on clarity of text and argument. He has invested so many years of effort in his work, he has studied and experimented and pondered so much and at such cost to his health that, were I to come out in open rebellion against his conclusions I think it would mean the complete collapse of his spirit. He depends on me, both physically and mentally, and he is so sick at present—writhing with his stomach cramps and vomiting every day, scarcely able to work two hours together—and I wonder at his determination and ability to continue year after year with his efforts. The doctors produce every theory possible, from inherited disorder, to congenital deformity of the organs, to rare contagions caught when he was in the tropics, but none of them has been able to alleviate his suffering. Natural selection does not appear to be working very well in his case!

My poor dear Charley. He is such a good man, such a diligent husband and loving father, and he does not deserve such torments. I wish he would forsake his irreverent quest, and then perhaps he would find both peace of mind and of body. But I know this is not in his nature. And that in itself gives me a puzzle. For if God made his nature, then how can it be working so contrary to God's own purpose?

There is at any rate one stand of his that I do wholeheartedly approve of. Charles abhors the attitude of those who are campaigning against the abolition of slavery, and he is considering an addendum to the latest edition of his 'Journal of Researches'—the chronicle of his voyage around the world. Whilst in the Americas he witnessed the real effects of the slave trade. He saw slaves being tortured and abused, he saw young children torn from their mothers and put to work where they are beaten with horse whips for trivial misdemeanours, he knew an old woman who kept screws to crush the fingers of her female slaves—the catalogue of evil is sickening, and he flies into a rage when he reads of the defence of this vile commerce by those who claim its abuses are exaggerated, and that the trade is necessary for the continuance of human prosperity and the education of the lesser races, and suchlike arguments. In his proposed proclamation, which I have seen, he denounces the hypocrisy of this business 'done and palliated by men who profess to love their neighbours as themselves, who believe in God and pray that his will be done on earth!' Yes, there I can have sympathy with his doubt of the Almighty's influence—in the hearts of some at any rate.

However it will no doubt make him the target of further censure. It would seem our lives are fated never to be free of controversy. I am so thankful for this journal. I write in it only spasmodically when the mood takes me, but at least I am able to impart my thoughts and fears to it, as if to a friend. I find the process therapeutic, and it helps a great deal to relieve my qualms.

CHAPTER TWELVE

Not a single domestic animal can be named which has not in some country drooping ears; and the view suggested by some authors, that the drooping is due to the disuse of the muscles of the ear, from the animals not being much alarmed by danger, seems probable.

Origin of Species

A couple of days after Maurice made his decision to take the trip to Shropshire—the Wednesday of that week in fact—he arrived at the shop as usual for his nine o'clock opening. As he pottered about drawing blinds, unlocking the till, arranging display books on the reception desk, the phone rang.

'Aldridge's Book Shop,' answered Maurice.

'Maurice, it's Rupert here.' His assistant sounded subdued, or was it apprehensive?

'Yes, Rupert? Are you all right?'

'Well, actually no. I've, er. . . . well I've had a bit of a family problem, and I'm afraid. . . . well, I won't be able to come in today.'

'Oh dear.' Maurice was mildly annoyed at the inconvenience, but he could probably manage all right for a day. 'What's the problem? Can I help?'

'No, no—it's just. . . . well I don't really want to go into it, but. . . . I may not be available for a while.'

This sounded more serious. 'A while? What do you mean?'

'Well I. . . . I'm not sure when I'll be able to get in again. It's a bit of a crisis, you see, and it may take a while to resolve.'

'Oh dear, Rupert. That's awkward. Is there nothing I can do?'

'Not really. I'm very sorry to put you out like this. It's just. . . . well it all happened rather quickly, and there was nothing I could do about it.'

Maurice was now seriously inconvenienced. Also mystified at the lack of information offered. He asked more questions, but received little satisfaction beyond a vague promise that Rupert would keep in touch and let him know if matters improved. Maurice rang off in a state of frustration and puzzlement. There were things unsaid behind the phone call, but he could not guess what they might be.

There were few customers during the morning and he handled them adequately. However his mind was distracted by thoughts of what to do next. Should he advertise for another assistant? Should he go to an agency for a temp in the hopes that Rupert would return eventually? It took time to train someone new in the ways of the business, never mind discover how much they knew about books. In a moment when the shop was empty he made himself a coffee and sat down at his desk, spilling some in his irritation (this was becoming a habit!). He grunted petulantly, 'Pull yourself together, man!' and mopped it up with a tissue as he contemplated the alternatives. No conclusion reached when the bell pinged again. He looked out from his office and saw the fair-haired figure of Roger Hemingway hovering at the desk. Damn— not the first person Maurice wished to see at this moment. He went out into the shop.

'Hello,' said Hemingway, half squinting, half smiling.

'Good morning, Mr Hemingway. Back on the Dickens trail again?'

'Well, no actually. I was wondering. . . . I mean I really enjoyed that book I bought from you a week or so ago—'Tom Jones'. . . .'

'Good,' prompted Maurice brusquely. 'A rollicking read.'

'Yes. Well I was wondering if you had any more by Henry, er. . . .'

'Fielding.'

'Yes. I'd like to read another by him.'

Maurice thought for a second. 'I don't think so. That's his most popular novel. 'Joseph Andrews' is probably the next one you should read, but I'm afraid I haven't got that.'

'Oh. Well I just thought I'd ask. I'll have another look around if I may.'

'By all means,' said Maurice, turning away. 'Try Samuel Richardson. He was a contemporary of Fielding's. I think there's something of his back there.'

'Yes, right.' As Maurice reached the office doorway he sensed that Hemingway had not moved, and he turned back. 'Um. . . . are you all right?' the young man asked politely. 'You look a bit. . . . hassled, if I might say so.'

Maurice cleaned his spectacles fussily. 'Yes, I am a bit.'

'What's the problem?'

'I, er. . . . I've lost my assistant, and I'm a bit short staffed until I find a new one.'

Hemingway looked sympathetic. 'Rupert? Oh dear.' He frowned. 'He seemed nice. Why did he leave?'

Maurice shrugged. 'I don't really know. He just phoned out of the blue and said he had to give in his notice for family reasons. It was rather sudden, and quite frankly inconsiderate.'

'That's tricky.'

'Yes. I'll have to advertise through the trade again, I suppose, and that takes time.' He shook his head irritably, and expounded a bit more than was his wont. 'It's not easy here on one's own. There's quite a lot to do in the office, you see— correspondence, accounts—as well as looking after customers off the street.'

'Yes. Well I hope you find someone,' said Hemingway. 'I won't bother you now then. I'll just go looking on my own.' And he wandered off to the shelves.

Half an hour later Maurice had more or less made up his mind to close the shop for a week whilst he sorted out his staffing problems, even though it might have a further impact on the financial situation. He was trying to assess this when he became aware that Hemingway was again hovering in the office doorway with the first volume of *Clarissa* in hand.

'I'll have this,' he said.

Maurice rose and took the book to the shop counter. 'Yes, you might enjoy that,' he said, taking the money. 'Not quite the classic that 'Tom Jones' is but an intriguing picture of the times, and several further volumes to read if you like it.'

As he wrapped the book the other made as if to speak, then hesitated. Maurice raised his eyebrows enquiringly.

'I was wondering . . .' Maurice waited patiently. Hemingway ran a hand through his hair as he did when feeling reticent. 'This may be a stupid idea. I mean it may be a *really* stupid idea because I don't know anything about the business or anything, but I'm out of a job at the moment, and books are something I'd really like to learn about, and, well . . . I was wondering if perhaps I could do that job you were talking about?' He stole a glance at Maurice, and the smile came and went. 'I mean, you'd have to teach me what to do and so on, but I'm quite a fast learner, and I think I'd quite like working here.'

Maurice was taken aback and could think of no response for several moments. 'What, er . . . what was your previous job, Mr, um . . . Hemingway?'

Hemingway spread his hands. 'Oh, well I've had various jobs. Motor trade, restaurant business. I was quite good at most of them but never really found the one that suited me, know what I mean? I didn't have the qualifications for a really good position, and those jobs didn't have the . . . the challenge to keep me interested. I somehow feel that books might have that.'

Maurice's brain ticked. 'Have you any references?'

'Oh, I could provide them, yes. No problem.'

'Well . . .' Maurice was at a loss. Hardly a candidate he would have considered under normal circumstances. But these weren't normal circumstances and the offer had come at a remarkably timely moment. 'I'm flattered you should be interested. The job doesn't pay very well, I'm afraid.'

'Oh, that's all right.' Hemingway smiled self-deprecatingly. 'It'd be more than the nothing I'm earning right now.'

'I'll tell you what. Let me think about it for twenty four hours, and I'll give you a call. Have you a phone number?'

'Yeh. Best to call me on my mobile. I'll write it down.'

'When might you be available to start?' Maurice asked, handing across a note pad.

'Oh, whenever you like. I'm free any time. I was thinking about going back to one of my previous employers—they're quite keen to have me—but I'd prefer this.'

'Right, well, thank you again for the offer, and I'll be in touch tomorrow.'

'Good. No obligation, just an idea. Cheers.' He left the shop with his new volume clutched in one hand and the other raised in a backward salute.

That evening over another frozen ready-made dinner Maurice mentally debated the prospect with Alice. 'An unusual youth but he seems sincere, and I could probably train him up. What do you think?' He imagined her response and concluded that she would have approved the appointment with her usual pertinent aphorisms—'Don't look a gift-horse in the mouth, dear. I believe in serendipity. Providence works in strange ways,' etc.. He poured himself another half glass of scotch and called Hemingway's mobile number.

The latter was evidently in a pub from the background noise. 'Yep?'

'Mr Hemingway? It's Maurice Aldridge here.'

Hemingway seemed momentarily confused. Then he responded with more deference. 'Oh, yes Mr Aldridge?'

'I've been considering your offer, and I'd like to give it a try. How about a month's trial employment, subject to you providing suitable references, and then see how we go?'

'Oh. . . . well that sounds good. Yes, thank you.'

'I'm going away to the country for the weekend, but I suggest you come in on Monday and we can discuss terms and routines and so forth. How does that seem?'

Hemingway thought it seemed fine, and so it was decided.

Having hopefully solved his staffing problem for the time being, Maurice emailed Donald Easterby about his meagre progress to date on the Darwin quest, and made his plans for the weekend trip to Shropshire with an optimism he had not felt for some time. He had decided to make a proper expedition of it. He would close the shop on Friday and drive up, calling en route on Felicity Trask, the old friend who had given him the tip, and possibly on other book dealing acquaintances at pleasant places like Stow-On-The-Wold and Woodstock. Then stay the night in Shrewsbury so as to be at the auction house in good time on Saturday morning.

His thoughts turned again to the decision concerning the other matter, the other significant place that lurked close to his itinerary. He took out his battered pocket address book, which had done worthy service for some twenty years. There was the address hidden inside the back cover and written in small letters in his meticulous handwriting: Delia Cornwell. 25, Cotswold Av, Cheltenham, followed by a telephone number. Would the woman still be there after all this time, he wondered? He hesitated, then reached for the phone and dialled directory enquiries. 'D. Cornwell, Cheltenham,' he said when the operator answered. As he waited he reflected that surely anyone would have moved away in the circumstances. The voice came back quickly. 'There's no D. Cornwell. Only a T. Cornwell.'

'Ah, yes. That's probably it,' he said. The operator gave him the number. Surprisingly it was unchanged. She just hadn't changed the directory entry since her husband's time.

He sat for a long moment staring at the address, then pushed it once more to the 'awaiting decision' section of his mind, took a swig of whiskey, and settled down to read another extract of the Fuchs chronicle. The Second World War and the Cold War were periods in world history so different to the modern era. Periods when the entire planet seemed on the brink of self destruction. Hard to imagine from this comparatively tranquil and affluent perspective. Perhaps due to the influence of the whiskey Maurice's attention wandered from the book and he became reflective. Was it a sign of humanity's progress that there had been over fifty years of relative peace since those times? Was it part of the Darwinian process that man was learning from past mistakes? Or was it merely the lull before the next storm? His mind returned inevitably to 9/11, and thence to the London bombs, and he concluded that on balance, no, man probably hadn't learnt a great deal.

CHAPTER THIRTEEN

June 15th, 1951. Wakefield

What is it about mathematics that is so wonderful?

It means nothing to the ordinary man in the street, as I have often been reminded. To him it is just 'sums', a means of knowing how many days there are left in the year, or how much money he has in the bank. What he forgets, or never knew in the first place, is that, coincidentally, 'sum' is the Latin for 'to be'. Not, 'I might be, I should be, I aspire to be', but what I demonstrably am. Mathematics is the pure, precise definition of that which—however hugely complex—is (as well as a great deal that is not, but that's another matter).

What the average person finds hard to grasp is that maths governs everything—from the orbits of the planets, to the design of a fir cone, to the composition of a Chopin nocturne. It enables a computer to think, it dictates the genetic makeup of a human being, it defines the interaction between the particles in a chemical formula, or in an atomic explosion.

One day we will be able to calculate in mathematical terms the precise activity between the neurons of the human brain. Which means we will be able to replicate it. We will be able to measure man's capacity for love, and decipher his propensity for evil.

Mathematics is the one invariable. Mathematics would exist even if nothing else did (yes, I realise that is a philosophically problematic statement, but as I interpret it, it is true).

People are often puzzled when a mathematician talks about a beautiful equation. How can a set of numbers and signs be beautiful? I always explain it by comparing it to the view through a child's kaleidoscope. When you look through the eye-hole you see what seems to be a miraculously symmetrical explosion of colour, a vision of perfectly contrived harmony. It is the same with a complex equation. When it is a true 'sum' all the elements come together in a suddenly complete arrangement of ciphers, with no flaws, no irregularities. The numbers synchronise in a perfect juxtaposition. A piece of magic is created and for a moment the universe is illuminated.

Mathematics is the language of the universe. And once we are completely fluent in that language we will be able to interpret the universe.

I am by no means completely fluent. No mathematician ever has been, or will be in this era. But we are getting close.

CHAPTER FOURTEEN

The competition will generally be most severe be-
tween the forms which are most like each other in
all respects. Hence the improved and modified de-
scendants of a species will generally cause the ex-
termination of the parent-species; and if many new
forms have been developed from any one species, the
nearest allies of that species will be the most liable
to extermination.

Origin of Species

One learns from the media about apocalyptic events, but they have little personal effect amongst the barrage of global activity, unless there is a direct connection. Only then do they achieve real significance for the individual. And only then do they have a serious effect on that individual's progress.

On the seventh of July nearly seven years previously Maurice had been sitting on a London bus heading for Bloomsbury. It wasn't his normal bus. It was around a quarter to ten in the morning and he was going to the British Museum for some reason that he afterwards couldn't quite recollect. As always he was watching the busy London scene from the upstairs window with detached interest. In the seat in front of him two school girls were chatting and laughing. Maurice wondered vaguely why they weren't yet in school. One of them received a call on her mobile, and he was mildly alerted by her excited tones as she relayed a message to her companion. He picked up the odd phrase—'King's Cross. . . .' 'bombs on the tube. . . .' 'terrorist attacks. . . .' He was trying to hear more as the bus stopped near Tavistock Square, and he barely noticed the number 30 bus passing by in the same direction. His own bus had taken on more passengers and was just starting off again, when there was a huge explosion. It blew in the front window and shook the whole vehicle as if by an earthquake. He was showered with glass, the girls in front screamed, everyone crouched instinctively in their seats. The vehicle came to an abrupt halt along with the rest of the traffic in the street, and for a few seconds there was an eerie silence broken only by the tinkling sound of falling glass and the occasional louder crash of falling metal. Maurice cautiously raised his head and looked around the upper deck for the source of the explosion but could see nothing. Gradually people recovered themselves and stared about them with bewildered expressions. A man in front of him was mopping blood from his face, and one of the school girls was sobbing hysterically.

Then Maurice peered out of the shattered front window. Sixty yards ahead, over the now motionless lines of traffic he could see the devastated shape of the other bus, scarcely recognisable. The top deck had all but vanished. A pall of smoke was rising from the twisted shell where it had once been. The street immediately around it was a chaotic jumble of halted vehicles and scattered debris. He could vaguely make out the forms of people lying on the pavement close by, and of others standing, kneeling, walking tentatively towards the bus. From other directions and from nearby buildings people came running.

He collected his wits and stumbled with the other occupants down the stairs and out onto the road. He made his way through the still immobile traffic to the stricken vehicle. By the time he reached it a number of passers-by were on the scene. The rear of the bus had been obliterated. The air was filled with the sound of moaning, sobbing, and a strange hissing which may have been from the bus's engine or some other source which he couldn't determine. People were heaving at the twisted metal blocking access. Passengers stumbled from the lower deck, shattered, bloody, wide eyed with shock. A woman collapsed into the arms of a helper. Two men staggered out carrying another human form drenched in blood. From the remains of the top deck came a series of moans, a desperate wailing, then an abrupt shriek. A middle aged woman was carried out, quite obviously dead. She had short dark brown hair and for an insane moment Maurice thought it might be Alice.

He wandered dazedly amongst the carnage. In his disorientation he almost fell over the form of a man lying on the pavement. He was barely conscious, lying awkwardly beside a lamp post where he had been dragged. What remained of his legs was a mass of blood and bone. Maurice stared for a helpless moment, then impotently took off his jacket and bent to place it over the lower half of the man's body. As he did so he was aware that the other was trying to say something. He bent lower, holding onto the lamp post, and tried to catch the whispered words. 'Tell Delia she must. . . . tell her she. . . .' He could hear nothing more. He let go of the lamp post, arranged the jacket over the carnage of the man's legs, then realised that the victim's head was resting uncomfortably on a twisted sheet of metal and he was moving it minutely from side to side as if to change its position. Maurice crouched further, brushed debris from the matted hair, lifted the head with one hand and pulled the offending object from under with the other. It looked like the jagged end of a vehicle panel and he slid it to one side. Then he realised that if he allowed the head to fall back onto the pavement it would be at an even more uncomfortable angle. He cast around for something to act as a pillow. His jacket was already covering the legs and there was nothing else to hand. The continuing aftermath of the explosion went on around them. Maurice was caught in an awkward position, half crouching, with one hand supporting the man, the other holding on to the lamp post. Small whispered words or moans were coming from the other's lips. For want of anything better to do Maurice sat clumsily on the pavement, his back against the lamp post, and using his thigh as a pillow let the head rest upon him.

The eyes had been closed, but now they flickered open and tried to focus on him. The face had a cultured look, and he judged the man must be in his late thirties. He heard the whisper again and bent to listen. 'Please. . . . tell Delia I'm sorry. Tell her to look after Clare. Tell her I'm so sorry. . . .'

'Delia?' repeated Maurice.

'Please. . . . Promise to tell her.'

'Yes,' he said. 'I'll tell her.

The victim's eyes closed again and he appeared to fall into a sleep.

Maurice didn't know how long he sat there, unable to move, unable to do anything but look at the unexceptional face, tranquil now in its unconsciousness. A thin line of blood was trickling from under his jacket to the gutter and he tried not to think about what lay underneath. He found himself imagining that it was not a stranger but Alice he sat beside. Alice, as he already knew, would probably be looking at some point in the future. He wondered whether he would feel the same helplessness whilst at her bedside waiting for the inevitable. He wondered whether he would feel so utterly separated from all that the world meant, all that he thought life was supposed to be about.

He sat in a kind of semi-trance until the he became aware of a hand on his shoulder and a voice saying, 'Sir? Excuse me, sir?'

He looked up to see a uniformed ambulance man leaning over him. 'Sorry,' he murmured and blinked to arouse himself.

'Is this a friend of yours, sir?' asked the man.

'Er. . . . no,' replied Maurice.

'Is he with you?'

'No. He just. . . . I don't know who he is.'

The man lifted Maurice's hand from the other's head and said, 'It's all right, sir. You can leave him with us now. He's dead.'

He beckoned to a colleague, and together they lifted the man's body from Maurice's side. He raised himself from the ground and looked around him. Sound came back into his awareness. The scene had changed little except that now there was the noise of sirens, ambulances were arriving, and uniformed figures were in evidence. The wreckage of the bus still stood with a haze of smoke around it. He saw that the medics were carrying the body towards one of the ambulances, so he turned and walked away.

Alice was at home when he got back. She was watching the news of the attacks on television as he walked in. She had always been able to interpret every nuance of his expressions at an instant—it was why he had never been able to keep any secrets from her. She took one look at him and knew immediately that he had been there. She sat him down and brought him water, and listened to his mumbled story through his tears. She held him and then laid him on the sofa. It was only then that he realised he had left his jacket containing his wallet and other possessions lying on the pavement beside the lamp post where the ambulance people had dropped it. No means of finding out what had happened to it. Also no way of finding out who the man was.

He did not tell his wife too much about it all. He could not bring himself to disclose the details of his part in the man's passing. It had happened just two months after Alice had received the cancer diagnosis, and death was not a matter he wished to dwell on. But the two events were forever linked in Maurice's mind.

A fortnight later the police rang. They had his jacket and its contents at Bow Street police station. They apologised for the delay—there had been so much to attend to—but would Maurice like to come round and collect it?

He did so the next day. The coat was intact and the contents of the wallet complete. There was a large stain of dried blood on the jacket's lining. He signed for everything, they asked him a few questions about his part in the incident, and said that he might be wanted to give evidence at any future inquest. He nodded and asked if the police knew the name of the man. They told him his next of kin had been informed, but when Maurice pressed for his details and told them the reason they broke the rules and gave him the name and address. It was a Thomas Cornwell, married to Delia Cornwell, and they lived in Cheltenham.

Maurice returned home and wrote a brief note. It said:-

Dear Mrs Cornwell,

I am the person who found your husband after the bomb. I am so sorry for your loss. He wanted me to tell you that he was sorry, and asked you to look after Clare.

Yours sincerely, Maurice Aldridge.

He could think of nothing else to say, so simply posted the letter. He did not get a reply, and he could not bring himself to make any further contact.

He gave his brief testimony to the inquest some time later. During it he learned that he had probably sat with the man for about twenty minutes. Most of the emergency services had been occupied up the road at Kings Cross, where the underground bombs had gone off forty minutes before the one on the bus. Some of the bus passengers had actually been refugees from the closed tube stations.

Four bombs had exploded altogether, and all four bombers had died in the attacks along with more than fifty other victims. The bombers were all British residents, most with families and young children, one with a pregnant wife. They left video messages which talked of the West's war against Islam, and which praised Allah and the prophets.

CHAPTER FIFTEEN

January 18th, 1847. Down House

My extraordinary husband is now obsessed with barnacles. Barnacles of all things! Having busied himself for years with such grand formations as coral reefs, volcanoes and icebergs, and having written papers on every single species and rock and leaf encountered on the Beagle voyage (even the dust from the decks has been analysed and 'phialled' away!) he is now left with just one tiny creature which he calls his ' Mr Arthrobalanus'.[13] He discovered it on some desolate shore of South America, and it is apparently the smallest barnacle known to man. It seems this unbeautiful midget has some particular significance in the evolutionary pattern of life, and this has led C to embark on a study of the whole clan of barnacle species, of which apparently there are legions, and of which there is, not surprisingly to my mind, no authoritative record. We are now inundated with specimens and collections from all points of the compass, and their odour permeates every corner of the house. As if we have not enough of the earth's detritus to cope with.

One consolation however is that dear Joseph Hooker[14] is with us a good deal these days to aid my husband in his work. Joseph, although eight years younger than C, has made a great impression on him since his return a few years ago from his own lengthy voyage to the Antarctic bearing almost as many specimens as C did from the Beagle, and

[13]*Meaning 'Jointed Common Barnacle', named by Darwin himself.*
[14]*Joseph Hooker, son of Sir William Hooker, Director of the Royal Botanical Gardens at Kew, b. 1817.*

they have talked and corresponded endlessly since that time. I welcome Joseph's presence in the household for various reasons. He is a most amiable presence to have about the place, he gives the children much entertainment, he makes a capable partner for me at the piano, he handles Charley and his ailments with great tolerance and tact, and, perhaps most important of all from my point of view, he has had a virtuous evangelical upbringing which I believe will act as a brake on some of my husband's wilder speculations against the will of the Almighty.

In particular I suspect that he is wary of Charles's theory about the arbitrary transmutation of species throughout the generations, this so-called 'natural selection'. My husband is in great need of an ally on this matter. He had not yet dared to reveal his thoughts about it to any other living person except myself, for it is far too radical a theory for even the most tolerant of his other associates to digest, let alone the authorities in the universities and the Church. I know he agonises constantly about the effect it might have were he to publish it. It is so contrary to all traditional teaching, so challenging of historic thought, that he fears he will either be dismissed as mad or reviled as some kind of Satanist! However he has now shown Joseph some of his writings on the subject. This is a gesture of immense trust, and I know he did it with much apprehension for he values Joseph's judgement greatly. He is awaiting the verdict with considerable trepidation, as indeed am I.

The other matter to record is that I am with child once again.

This will be my sixth delivery and, jubilant though I am with the Lord's bounteousness to us in this regard, I do not look forward to my confinement with eagerness. I am not built ideally for child bearing and it comes hard, even with the aid of C's chloroform administrations which provide some degree of anaesthetic. But the rewards are well worth the suffering, and we both delight in our thriving family, even though I do sometimes wonder how much further it will expand. The house already rings constantly with the running feet and shouting voices of the children and their frequently visiting cousins. How C manages to concentrate on his studies is a constant source of wonder to me. But he tolerates their noise and interruptions with great forbearance, and even claims to find the activity a source of stimulation.

Children are such a consolation in these difficult times, when there is so much tragedy all around. The potato blight is in its third year now, and tens of thousands have died of starvation in Ireland, and even in our own rural parts. The famine, aided of course by the infamous Corn Laws, raised the price of even basic bread and flour to heights which the poor could not begin to meet. On top of which the iniquitous Stamp Duty prevented them from owning their simple quarter acre from which to husband a living. Sir Robert Peel[15] has now been forced to repeal these unfair measures, against much opposition from the farmers and landowners it has to be said, but there is still real deprivation even within our own parish. We do our part and supply the village with all the surplus food and crops we have available, and I have organised a system of penny bread coupons which I give away to the most needy at the door and which can be exchanged at the baker's, but it is all too little in such times. They say it is the greatest humanitarian crisis of the century. Such events do make one wonder even more than usual as to the Lord's purpose for us on this earth, and whether we are being punished for our human misdeeds. Charles inevitably has it that such catastrophes are inescapable and haphazard and all part of nature's struggle to fashion method from the madness of the universe, but I naturally cannot go to that extreme either.

---

[15]*Tory statesman and Prime Minister, 1788–1850.*

Ah well—my task as I see it is straightforward enough. It is to ensure that this tranquil corner of England provides as safe a haven as possible for the benefit of our growing family, the progress of my brilliant husband's endeavours, and hospitality for our ever demanding circle of friends, relatives and associates. Thankfully I have been endowed with the energy of the Wedgewoods. I hope it is sufficient to the task.

CHAPTER SIXTEEN

If Mozart, instead of playing the pianoforte at three years old with wonderfully little practice, had played a tune with no practice at all, he might truly be said to have done so instinctively. But it would be the most serious error to suppose that the greater number of instincts have been acquired by habit in one genera- tion, and then transmitted by inheritance to succeed- ing generations. It can be clearly shown that the most wonderful instincts with which we are acquainted, namely, those of the hive-bee and of many ants, could not possibly have been thus acquired.

Origin of Species

'It's the way I work,' Donald Easterby had said. Maurice wasn't sure how much the man had uncovered when he ex- plored the book dealer's past and qualifications. He hadn't been more forthcoming on the matter, but his apparent famil- iarity seemed uncanny and was not a little disturbing. Mau- rice wondered how far back his researches had extended. Unlikely surely that they had reached to the book dealer's childhood. But given what had been disclosed so far it was conceivable. And as with most people his childhood was the key to understanding Maurice.

His journey, from his birth to lunch with the wealthy American at the Ritz, had been to all outward appearances unremarkable. However those appearances were decep- tive. His beginnings at any rate had been distinctly uncom- mon. His mother had been a seventeen year old prostitute in Leeds, who gave him away for adoption the moment he emerged. He never knew who she was, and untypically never had any desire to, not even in later life. It was enough for him that he was fortunate in his adoptive parents, who of course to a new born child were no different to real parents. He was fortunate, that is, until they were both killed in a car crash when he was eight years old. That was the first serious setback in the journey. They had been worthy alternative parents. Loving, caring, conscientious, and he had repaid them with his love. But then he lost them. Not through divine decision, nor through any astrological arrangement of the stars, but through sheer accident.

The only benign factor in this circumstance—if there could be anything benign about such a disaster—was that, although he did not become aware of it until much later, they had not been *inspiring* as parents, and that his new situation turned out, by chance again, far more propitious for his life's voyage that would have been the case if they had survived.

One reason for this was that the foster family with whom he now ended up was a completely different enterprise to his adoptive family. His first parents, despite their worthiness, had been a prosaic couple who lived in a prosaic semi in a prosaic suburb, and who passed the time in prosaic routines and paid affectionate but prosaic attention to Maurice's welfare. They did not even have the imagination to adopt another child to enliven his prosaic early years. His new family by contrast were a vibrant and intelligent collection of individuals, who were anything but prosaic.

A second reason was that, whereas his first family had lived in industrial Leeds, the city where he had been conceived, his second family lived some thirty miles north-east in York, a quite different place. York is an exceptional city. A truly extraordinary city, which had an influence on the rest of Maurice's journey in all sorts of direct and indirect ways. York's eventful history has been preserved perhaps better than any other major town in England, due greatly to the fact that the city centre is surrounded by a fortified wall that has miraculously remained almost intact since its Roman and medieval origins. This has ensured that most of the buildings within that encircling wall—from the stupendous York Minster, surely one of the greatest cathedrals in all Christendom, to the most dignified of institutional buildings and the humblest of crooked gabled shops—have also been preserved. And along with that preservation has come an ecclesiastical, a scholastic, and a commercial history that colours and informs the lives of many of York's inhabitants, including Maurice's new family.

The head of the household was Marcus Oldfield. A large, bearded, ebullient academic, who taught physics at York University, and had an unquenchable curiosity about the human condition and a complete inability to regularise his own. His wife, Audrey, was a tiny, long-suffering, but unfailingly optimistic woman who adored him and who kept their tumultuous household functioning by sheer good will and little else. Marcus and Audrey had two of their own children, and when the doctors advised Audrey not to get pregnant again they had promptly decided, out of their irrepressible largesse of spirit, to foster some more. When the social services arranged for Maurice to join the family in their lofty, rambling Victorian villa just outside the city walls, the pair had already adopted two other children whose circumstances had left them homeless. The ménage consisted of Marcus and Audrey; their natural daughter Gloria, a fifteen year old blond bombshell with a fierce temper and a sharp northern wit; their twelve year old son Sam, who had a passion for Elvis, animals and roller skates; the two foster children—Henry, a lanky ten year old black boy, rescued from the tribal wars in Nigeria, whose genial personality concealed an anguish at his experiences that was a permanent scar on his spirit; and Vicky, the same age as Maurice, who had been whipped away from an abusive step-father and step-brothers at the age of seven, and whose main functions seemed to be to hero worship Gloria, live on potato crisps, and intrude wherever possible on Maurice's privacy. There were also two dogs (a dalmatian and a York-shire terrier, mirroring their owners in size discrepancy), two cats, a vicious talking parrot, and possibly a fair number of cockroaches and other parasites.

Maurice, after the solitary years of his early childhood, when his own imagination had been his chief source of companionship, at first found this teeming household wholly intimidating. The presiding couple were both more flamboyant than his previous parents, and the other children in their various ways all individual and challenging. Evening mealtimes, when everyone came together, were argumentative feasts, erratically provided by Audrey and enthusiastically presided over by Marcus. Discussion ranged from sixties youth preoccupations with pop and cinema, to historic debate on science, politics and philosophy. Everyone was encouraged to have their say, and with Marcus prodding, questioning, commenting and criticising there was little room for reticence.

It took Maurice the best part of a year to come out of his reclusive shell and cautiously join the general exuberance, but it was a year of revelation and instruction.

He was instructed early on how to fight.

He was sent initially to a local Church of England school. It was housed in a Victorian brick building surrounded by concrete playgrounds where the law of the jungle ruled supreme. Like many such institutions, from prisons to army regiments to schools, the inmates instinctively divided into cliques governed by the rules of natural hierarchy and motivated by internecine rivalry. Maurice, being by circumstance a recluse and outsider, immediately found himself the object of scorn. Children can be primitive creatures, reacting fiercely to aliens in their midst. His chief oppressor was an evil Yorkshire thug called Winston Starkey, who was two years older and six inches taller than Maurice, and who took an instant delight in provoking him into fights which, in the first week, resulted in Maurice getting a number of painful bruises and two bleeding noses.

It was his new foster mother Audrey who first noticed his distress, and having gently prised the reason from him during his first weekend break from school, she then reported it to her husband. Marcus promptly led Maurice down to the huge basement of the house which served as hobbies store, games cellar, and general rumpus room, fished amongst the piles of debris and sporting equipment on the shelves for some boxing gloves, and said, 'Right my lad—we're going to have no more of this. We're going to show you how you look after yourself in this rough old world.' He tied the gloves, which were several sizes too big, onto Maurice's hands with the remark, 'I used to be an amateur boxing champion in my youth, and I'm going to give you some tips.' Then he arranged the boy's body in fighting stance and said, 'The secret of taking on fellows bigger than you is that firstly they're over confident, and secondly they're vulnerable low down on their bodies. So what you do is take them by surprise, and where you hit them is in the stomach and chest. Now you're wearing gloves at the moment so you won't hurt me or yourself, but believe me, when bare knuckles hit a solar plexus or the ribs over a heart they can inflict a lot more damage than merely hitting a nose. So let's see what sort of a punch you have.'

After a weekend's instruction in the art of prizefighting, Maurice was packed off to school on the Monday morning with trepidation in his heart and exhortations ringing in his ears. Sure enough the mid-morning break brought the expected playground confrontation with a leering Winston Starkey and his gaggle of sycophantic followers.

'Heyup, it's our little lad from the orphanage. Still here, are we? Not run off to Doctor Barnardo? Not found a new mummy yet to change our nappy?'

This witticism provoked a roar of laughter from his audience, which encouraged him to further provocation. He cuffed Maurice's head and danced in front of him like a grinning giraffe.

Maurice was a good pupil. He did exactly as he'd been taught. And though small, he was stocky and strong. His left fist came up low and hard into the other's solar plexus. His right followed immediately in a high curve straight to the heart. The tall youth went down as if struck by lightning. Then Maurice bent over him and punched him again, this time fair and square on the nose, from which blood spurted copiously.

The onlookers were shocked into silence. Only the sound of Winston Starkey's moans could be heard as he writhed on the ground. Maurice turned and went to the other end of the playground as the duty teacher came hurrying across to see what had happened. There were no repercussions. Presumably none of the witnesses had dared to speak up. And Maurice never had so much as another glance from Winston Starkey or any of the other playground despots throughout the next three years he was at the school.

The lesson learned was to prove a useful one in later life—certainly for Maurice, and probably for his opponent as well.

The next lesson was to prove even more beneficial. It was the lesson of history. Marcus Oldfield, although a scientist by profession, was a lover of all things historical, from books to buildings, from artifacts to actual facts, and he imparted his enthusiasm to the members of his extended family at every opportunity. Everyone had the run of the loaded bookshelves which ran the length of the large dining room, and he was for ever picking out volumes that he thought might interest one or other of his wards. The whole family was commanded to accompany him and Audrey on their various forays to the ancient sites and buildings dotting the city and the surrounding

Yorkshire countryside—which was never resented because he made the expeditions such occasions of fascination and drama. The stories ranged from heathen intrigues and medieval battles, to the demolition of great monasteries, to the Civil War and the Bonfire Plot. The cast of characters included Romans and Vikings, abbots and archbishops, Constantine the Great, William the Conqueror, Henry VIII and Guy Fawkes. The history as always comprised tales of strife, conspiracy, betrayal, bloodshed and heroic achievement.

On Sunday mornings everyone was similarly encouraged to accompany the pair to the anglican services, either at the Minster itself on the major religious festivals, or at local parish and country churches on normal days. Marcus was one of those imaginative scholars who quite happily combined an unwavering faith with his passionate commitment to science, and his church visits were inspired as much by spiritual devotion as by his love of sublime architecture and ecclesiastical music.

For Maurice in particular all this enthusiasm for matters hitherto outside his experience came as a constant source of wonderment. He acquired a love of books which never left him. He developed a fascination with the unfolding histories of people and nations. He discovered a respect for the beautiful rites and the remarkable buildings that had been fashioned through centuries of religious instinct. And he gained a curiosity about science that informed all the other topics.

This instruction had a great deal to do with his winning a place at the nearby grammar school, and eventually to his gaining a scholarship to Cambridge. He owed it all to Marcus and Audrey Oldfield. And to his own tenacity.

When, years later, the two surrogate parents eventually passed away, the five children, by then middle-aged and scattered around the world, and all in their various ways leading fulfilled lives, maintained irregular contact with one another.

The bonds forged in their youth remained among the strongest in their lives however little they saw of each other. It was one reason why Maurice's inner loneliness was never total.

However, whenever he thought about his childhood he was aware that his inability to rationalise his present existence was largely due to the conflict of early influences within him. He didn't need a psychoanalyst to tell him that. No need of counselling to come to terms with such an obvious conclusion. The books and the scotch bottle were a perfectly adequate means of doing that.

On reflection he decided that Easterby hadn't discovered too much about his past. It would have been more of a deterrent to hiring him than an incentive.

CHAPTER SEVENTEEN

September 15th, 1951. Wakefield

The revelation of Marxism is that the most important way to think of humanity is, not as divided vertically by nationalities or races, but as divided horizontally by classes. And that therefore the proletariat across the planet are bound by a common cause, as indeed are the ruling classes, the wealthy classes, the aristocratic classes—irrespective of their language, their religions, their nationalities. And that, by recognising this collectively, the members of each class need no longer stay passive in the face of historical forces, but can begin to challenge and direct them, just as man is beginning to direct the forces of nature.

The revelation of physics is that there is no limit to the energy available within those forces of nature. The quantum field is the source of <u>all</u> energy. All mass, all matter, all manifestations consist of quantum particles and thus of energy. During my four years at Bristol and subsequently at Edinburgh University where I progressed, I developed my knowledge of theoretical physics beyond all measure, and I began to comprehend the full truth of this fact. And when those two revelations are taken together, then it is surely evident that the potential of the second—the universe's resources—should be equally available to all who struggle to achieve the potential of the first—society's resources (I am not sure that all who read that sentence will readily understand it, but it makes sense to me).

It was this insight that motivated me to do what I did. It was this that obliged me to take the first momentous step to becoming a 'spy', a 'traitor', a 'Spanish fifth columnist' as I have been branded by the world's newspapers.

When war broke out in 1939 I was immediately interned as a former German citizen and sent to Canada with a large group including other foreign born scientists and academics, as a convenient way of getting us out of the way. Then after six months the authorities realised the folly of having such potential assets sitting around doing nothing in another country, and brought us back again! I went straight back to Edinburgh and my work on quantum properties and connections.

Then in the spring of 1941 I received a letter from a fellow scientist which changed my life.

Rudolf Peierls is a remarkable man who was then Professor of Mathematical Physics at Birmingham University and, although I did not know it at the time, he had been working for some years with other scientists around Europe and in America on the possibilities of harnessing the huge energy created by the splitting of nuclear particles or atoms. He was also a Jew, and another German refugee (how ironic it is that Hitler probably brought about his own defeat by his destruction or rejection of the most talented minds within his fiefdom!)

I had met Professor Peierls a few times at Bristol and at Edinburgh, and he had read some of my papers. In the letter he offered me a job as his research assistant at Birmingham for the princely salary of £275 a year. I accepted, and thence by chance found myself at the forefront of the British effort to split the atom. Little did I realise how this was to affect my entire existence and thinking. I will always remember the Professor's first words to me when I arrived at the research establishment. "You have an enormous responsibility, Mr Fuchs. You are joining one of the most vital enterprises ever embarked upon, which creates both practical and moral problems. We are attempting to create a weapon such as has never been seen in the history of warfare."

The words were commanding enough. It was some time before I understood their true significance.

CHAPTER EIGHTEEN

He must be a dull man who can examine the exqui-
site structure of a comb, so beautifully adapted to its
end, without enthusiastic admiration. We hear from
mathematicians that bees have practically solved a
recondite problem, and have made their cells of the
proper shape to hold the greatest possible amount of
honey, with the least possible consumption of wax in
their construction. It seems at first quite inconceiv-
able how they can make all the necessary angles and
planes. But all this beautiful work can be shown to
follow from a few very simple instincts.

Origin of Species

Maurice closed the shop at lunch time on the Friday, took a
rare tube journey home in the interests of speed, collected his
ready packed holdall, and set off for Shrewsbury in his eight
year old Rover which only ever left the garage at weekends
(buy British he and Alice had decided, even though the motor magazines didn't rate it the most reliable of cars). By now
he was again having misgivings about the whole business.
Why was he wasting time over such a nebulous commission?
What on earth was he doing spending an entire weekend tra-
versing the country on this vaguest of pretexts? But then her
inevitable voice whispered in his ear. 'Look on this as a voyage of adventure, old boy. A miniature Odyssey. You might
discover things other than just a tatty old manuscript.'

'Thanks, Alice,' he muttered, 'a tortuous Greek ordeal.
That's a big help.' His mood of ambivalence grew as he
joined the swathes of traffic leaving London. And increased
further by another decision he had made. The obvious route
to Shrewsbury was via the M1 and M6 motorways north,

but at the last moment he had decided to take the more devious M40 route out of London towards Oxford. Something at the back of his mind had been niggling for a day or two. He had been pondering as to why Easterby's revelation about the Darwin journal hadn't come as a complete surprise, and also why the only other response to his letter—the ambiguous email from his book dealer acquaintance in Oxford—was intruding on his thoughts. The man had mentioned a previous incident connected with Darwin, and during one of Maurice's sleepless nights a dim memory had surfaced. Only a hazy recollection, but it now had an extra relevance.

He conceded that if he was going to make one trip on a flimsy pretext he might as well extend it on another. He could of course have telephoned, but it seemed more pertinent to make the brief detour to the old university city. He reached the Oxford junction still not quite decided, hesitated, then nodded to himself and swerved off the motorway, provoking an angry horn blast from the vehicle behind him. 'All right, all right—keep your hair on,' he muttered at the rearview mirror.

As he drove into the heart of town, where the traffic was if anything worse than London's, he had a struggle remembering his way. He hadn't been there for some time. Eventually he found the right back street and got a parking space behind one of the colleges. Then walked the short distance through to Broad Street, past the grand college architecture which reminded him of his own student days amongst the similar gold-stoned piles of Cambridge. Significantly however it was this rival university town that a century and a half ago had hosted some of the most notorious debates over Darwin's great hypothesis.

Maurice was reflecting on this as he made his way down a narrow lane by the side of a college wall. The lane was virtually empty and his steps echoed on the paved sidewalk. Suddenly he had the impression that the echo was repeated by other footsteps behind him. He stopped and looked around. There were various openings and doorways onto the lane, and one or two other people distantly in sight, but he saw nothing suspicious. He frowned, inclined his ear, but could hear nothing further. Shook his head and continued on his way. The double echo had stopped and he dismissed it from his mind.

He gained the main thoroughfare, turned down another side road and entered a shop doorway. An antiquarian book shop like his own, but very different in character. Smart, immaculate, shining with polished mahogany counters and shelves, its name proudly announced in gold letters above the window, its leather bound wares precisely ranked for maximum effect. Maurice felt a twinge of envy, but then reminded himself that it took time, effort and money to keep a place in that state, and he would much rather use his resources on meeting the customer's needs rather than the proprietor's.

A dapperly suited man with gold spectacles and fastidiously brushed grey hair stood behind the counter leafing through a volume. In the background a groomed secretary tapped at a computer.

The man looked up as Maurice entered. His eyebrows rose. 'Maurice, dear boy! How are you? What brings you to these provincial parts?'

'Hello, James,' said Maurice. 'You look to be doing as well as ever.'

'Well if you can't sell books in this town you've no business being in the business, have you?' He grinned and closed the edition he was looking at. 'Haven't seen you in a long time. How are things in the big smoke?'

'Oh, ticking along. Can't complain.' Maurice glanced at the assistant and decided she was too far away and too occupied to worry about. 'James, this is just a flying visit. Thank you for your email. I was on my way north and I thought I'd drop in on the off chance.'

'Can't tell you any more than I mentioned in the email, I'm afraid.'

'No, but I did eventually remember what you were referring to. It was when we last met, about three years ago.'

'Yes. You'd just lost dear Alice. You were in a bit of a state, old boy.'

'That's right. I'm sorry, I probably didn't make much sense at the time.'

'Not at all. Dreadful thing for you. She was such a lovely lady. Hope you've recovered from all that.'

'More or less.'

'Anyone else in your life now?'

Maurice shook his head. How could he explain the impossibility of such a thing. He hesitated. Have to be a bit careful over this. 'James—the incident you mentioned. If I remember, we were trading some scientific stuff that time and you said something about a Darwin family book that you'd heard about.'

'That's right. Your note reminded me.' The other took of his specs and scratched his head. 'It was a couple of years before I saw you then. There was mention of a diary written by Darwin's wife.'

'Yes. Remind me, what was the mention?'

'Well. . . . someone came into the shop and asked me what such a thing would be worth.'

'Who was it?'

'Haven't the foggiest. Some old boy. Quite eccentric if I remember. Rather dirty, unshaven. Smelt too. What he was doing dabbling in such things I couldn't imagine. Didn't want to ask, to tell you the truth. There've always been rumours about the diary, but I couldn't imagine where he'd heard of it.'

'What did you say to him?'

'Well, naturally I said the value all depended what was in it, what state it was in, and a million other things.'

'That was all?'

James's brow furrowed again. 'Of course I asked him if he actually possessed such an object.'

'And?'

'He was quite secretive. Said he might know where it was. When I asked him how he'd come across it he said he was a Darwin family descendant. No—'sort of' descendant was how he described it. Refused point blank to divulge anything else or even to tell me why he'd actually come in, so I said goodbye to him as soon as was politely possible and forgot about it.'

'You didn't get his name?'

'No, sorry.'

'Did you gather that he lived locally?'

'It seemed he was from Oxford, but I'm not sure why I thought that.' He twinkled. 'I don't suppose he had direct connections with the university, although it does have its collection of oddballs amongst its population.'

'He never came back to you afterwards?'

'No. Oh—I saw him once in the street. Wandering along muttering to himself, looking like some old tramp.'

'So that was all?'

'Absolutely. As I said it was a while ago.' His eyebrows rose again. 'So you're on the trail of something?'

'Possibly. Wealthy client who's after the same thing.'

'Here in Oxford?'

'No, he's American. He has no real leads, but when you replied to my letter I. . . .'

'You thought it was worth coming all this way? Must be a serious customer.'

'Well, as I said, I was passing by, and. . . .'

'He has proof that the thing exists?' The man's eyes had that beady book-trader's glint. Maurice was wary.

'Nothing definite. But it seems it's possible. There are some clues.'

The other paused for a moment, then shrugged and pursed his lips cynically. 'Well, good hunting old son. We all need these fanatical collectors, don't we?'

'Yes.'

'Sorry I can't be of more help. One would imagine the Darwin compendium had been well and truly trawled by now. If something as important as that was around it would surely have surfaced.'

'Quite. That's what's strange about it.' He wasn't sure whether the dealer had really dismissed it from his mind, or was just playing cool.

'Have you got time for a cup of tea or something?'

'Thank you, James, but I must be on my way. Just thought I'd drop in.'

'Good to see you.' He raised a finger. 'Tell you what— have you read Darwin's own memoirs?'

Maurice's eyebrows went up. 'No.'

'I've got a rather tatty copy here. Would they interest you?'

'Yes, they would.'

The other vanished for a few moments and returned with the book. 'Rather cursory jottings really. Written for the benefit of his children rather than the public.' He held it out. 'Not a valuable edition. Have it on the house.'

Maurice took the battered volume. 'That's kind of you, James.'

'My pleasure.'

'Goodbye then. Glad to see you haven't changed much.'

'Oh, the grey hairs keep coming, but I'm probably the only one who notices. 'Bye, Maurice. Stay in touch.'

Maurice left the shop and headed back to the car with the book.

Now he had to make a decision. Should he stop off at that other place on his route which had loomed so large in his thoughts recently, or should he defer it until the return journey? Should he phone ahead and warn of his coming, or should he just roll up and play it by ear? He sat in the car and stared out of the front window for several moments. Memories of that distant event loomed again and he suffered a tremor of mixed emotions—guilt, remorse, grief. A group of noisy students passed by, laughing and joking. Ah, such carefree days. Make the most of them, people, he thought. The weight of responsibilities will come sooner than you think.

He came to a decision and started the engine. To break his journey now would be too distracting. It might affect the entire weekend. He would do it on the way back. He pulled out of the parking space, and just missed a passing van which had to swerve around him.

Maurice was never the quickest of drivers, but he made Shrewsbury in less than three hours including a motorway pit-stop en route, and settled into his adequate pre-booked room at the Coach House Hotel with a sigh of relief. It was one of those period hostelries that one only finds in the remote corners of provincial England, which still cling to their ancient past in both ambience and service, disdaining any attempt at modernisation bar the essentials of hot water, radiators and barely functioning TV sets. Maurice quite liked that. It suited his frayed mentality.

He dined in the musty smelling dining room on overdone roast beef and apple crumble, washed down with a passable Fleurie, which he knew should have been just a half bottle but wasn't. It was served alternately by a cheery girl barely entering puberty, and an elderly woman who could have been her grandmother. Then he went early to bed and, keeping aside the Darwin memoirs his Oxford colleague had given him, continued his reading of the John Bowlby biography which he had brought with him. The author was a psychiatrist and had approached Darwin's life from a psychological perspective, arguing that much of the naturalist's drive, and possibly his health problems, could have stemmed from the trauma of losing his mother at an early age. That gave Maurice pause for thought.

He tossed and turned a bit during the night—partly too much alcohol and partly the uneven bed—and for once he did not have his usual nightmares. Instead he dreamed he was forever hurrying down darkened city streets after a mysterious figure who was carrying the only known copy of some publication which Maurice knew was vital in some way but couldn't remember why.

CHAPTER NINETEEN

February 12th, 1848. Down House

My dear husband's thirty ninth birthday. Can it really be nine years since we wed? And more than five since we made the move to Down? Certainly those years have been eventful enough, but still it startles me that they can speed by so quickly. How ephemeral is human life! How little time we have to achieve anything of lasting importance in this world.

It was an auspicious day, for we had with us to celebrate several of C's closest colleagues, who all made the journey from London to join us for the weekend. As well as the ever loyal Joseph Hooker we had C's old friend and mentor Charles Lyell,[16] and the naturalists Richard Owen[17] and Edward Forbes[18] and Andrew Ramsay,[19] and the discussions around the dinner table were lively indeed. I never cease to wonder at the erudition of such men, for the subjects ranged from the origins of C's beloved barnacles to the formation of continents, from the creation of coal seams to the demise of the dinosaurs, from the development of apes to the global dispersal of plant seeds, and within the company there never appears to be any shortage of detailed knowledge or lack of opinion. One thing however I do notice is that, although these eminent men of science all seem to agree on the concept of evolutionary development generally, they are none of

---

[16]*Later Sir Charles L. author of the influential 'Principles of Geology', 1797–1875.*
[17]*Later founder of the British Museum of Natural History. 1804–92.*
[18]*Later President of the Geological Society of London. 1815–54.*
[19]*Later Sir A.Ramsay, geologist. 1814–91.*

them persuaded of my husband's view concerning the lack of planned design in the process, and the sheer accidental nature of its happening. Indeed Charles is so wary of provoking them on this topic that he refrains from raising it directly in their presence, and is content to argue only on specific principles and technical details, a pastime he anyway delights in.

The time will come however when he will have to make his beliefs known. The philosophical debate on such matters is growing louder with every passing month, for political issues around the world are emphasising its importance. The papers are full of the unrest of the underprivileged across Europe, with insurrection sweeping Italy, and France on the verge of revolution (the French king, they say, is preparing to exile himself to England—a historic irony indeed!). Even in London the authorities are dispensing arms to defend the chief institutions, for the Chartist movement is again threatening insurrection and planning to march on the capital with a hundred thousand souls. And behind it all the atheists and communists and anarchists are stoking the fires, for their aim is to destroy the established ruling order which they claim is there merely to preserve the supremacy of the rich and to keep the working masses subservient.

I can understand that they sometimes have just cause, but I cannot accept that all this is C's doctrine of haphazard development working within the heart of society itself. The doctrine that only the strongest (which in mankind's case means presumably the best armed and most aggressive) will prevail. To do Charles credit, when I challenged him on this, he agreed that the ideas of the extremists went too far. "Militancy rarely achieves its stated aims," he said. "It is only justified when countering other militancy or genuine oppression." I was relieved at his reply, although I could have wished that had said it was <u>never</u> justified. He then added, "The problem is how to define genuine oppression. Men feel oppressed in all sorts of circumstances. So the question is, how extreme does the oppression have to be to justify armed retaliation." Turn the other cheek then, does not feature in his interpretation.

Ah well, enough of such topical matters. They pale into insignificance when taken against the eternal issues of life and death. C's own infirmities seem to get worse with each passing year. He cannot endure either work or play for more than an hour or two at a stretch before he has to retire to his couch to rest, and his stomach and his skin are constantly in rebellion with every effort he makes. We have tried all remedies known to man, from orthodox medicines to home-made pills and potions, from sedatives to emetics, from compresses and poultices to his endless cold water immersions, and even to electric plate batteries which provide shocks to the stomach!—but nothing benefits him for long, and the slightest exertion produces vomiting and dizziness, accompanied by the most debilitating depressions. I wonder at how he manages the enormous volume of work he undertakes, but as he says, it is his inspiration and his motivation, and perhaps after all his salvation too. His fear is always that he will succumb to his condition before he has completed his researches and revealed the results to the world. My fear is of both occasions.

One of our greatest consolations is reading books together, for that is something he can do without taxing his constitution too far, and I succeeded some while ago in persuading him to read Coleridge's reflections on the spiritual life. He was somewhat critical, proclaiming that Coleridge's faith like many others is a purely instinctive longing rather than based on any rational evidence. I tried not to take offence at this indirect slur on my own belief, and instead asked him directly how much credibility he gave to the life of Jesus. He responded by asking, "Do you mean the human life, or the holy life?"

"Either or both," I replied.

He gazed at me for a moment or two, and said, "Well, as a historical character he obviously existed. And no doubt was an influential figure within the community he moved amongst. But as this supposed Son of God, with magical powers—no, Emma, I cannot accept that."

When I asked why, he countered with a question of his own. "How long do you think mankind has lived upon the earth?"

I gave the conventional reasoning that, judging from the generations recorded in the Old Testament, it was probably about six thousand years. He then replied at length. I cannot recollect his words exactly, but I need to record the thoughts and they were something to the effect, "Very well, we'll accept the possibility that it was six thousand years, and we'll include the possibility, evidenced by rock formations and fossil remains that it was several million years. In either case, it would seem extraordinary to postulate that God, after watching man fighting and philandering and sinning for centuries, suddenly decided he would start taking a hand in the proceedings. Presumably having abandoned all those previous generations to their fate in hell. And furthermore to do so, not by appealing directly as himself to the foremost minds at the centre of civilisation, such as the Roman senate or the Egyptian court, but by disguising himself as a human, approaching an isolated desert community, preaching a few vivid sermons and doing a bit of faith healing, and then, by getting himself martyred in the most horrible way possible, hoping to attract the attention of the earth's entire population and transform its habits. Which he patently failed to do. No, Emma, I cannot see the logic in such a concept."

"What about the virgin birth?" I asked. "What about the miracles? What about the resurrection?"

He smiled tolerantly and said, "Unnatural births are commonly proposed as origins for godlike beings; miracles are frequently reported but never proven; and as for the resurrection, I can think of a dozen more likely explanations for the disappearance of a body than that it was wafted up to heaven."

He left me wordless as always. I have not the means to counter him, nor to abandon my own secure convictions. We are doomed to remain opposites on this matter.

However I am pleased to say that, ironically, he has become quite friends with our new curate in the village, Revd John Innes. They now spend much time on devising enterprises for the benefit of the parish, and I have even heard them indulging in good-humoured arguments concerning the authenticity of the scriptures. I personally do not take to Mr Innes's method of conducting services—he is too much of a high church Anglican to my mind (I secretly wish there was a Unitarian church here at Down)—but I hope that perhaps he might have more success than I in dissuading my husband from trying to turn the whole world upside down.

CHAPTER TWENTY

There is no evidence that man was aboriginally en-
dowed with the ennobling belief in the existence of an
Omnipotent God. On the contrary there is ample evi-
dence, derived from men who have long resided with
savages, that numerous races exist who have no idea
of one or more gods, and who have no words in their
languages to express such an idea. The question is of
course wholly distinct from that higher one, whether
there <u>exists</u> a Creator and Ruler of the universe.

The Descent of Man

In the morning Maurice fought off his inevitable hangover
with a full English breakfast in the hotel dining room—
served by the same young girl, looking not quite so bright
at this hour—whilst temporarily depressing himself with the
Telegraph's usual litany of bad news from the Middle East,
worse news about the National Health, and truly appalling
news about the state of the nation's finances. He paid his
bill—a lengthy process involving complicated printouts and
old fashioned credit card signatures—received instructions
on how to find Alders auction rooms, and headed briskly in
that direction.

He was walking along one of the main city thoroughfares,
relishing the relative tranquillity compared to the crowded
streets of London, when once again he suddenly experienced
the odd sensation that he was being followed. There was no
particular reason for this, and as he looked about him at the
smatter of ambling people he could see no-one who looked
remotely suspicious. It was just a feeling. Maurice frowned,
clenched his fists in irritation, and told himself to stop being
paranoid. This business was infiltrating his brain.

He marched on to the auction house. He knew that the auction began at eleven, with a couple of hours viewing period beforehand, and he had left plenty of time to inspect the items he was interested in. At the building he found a typical scene with which he was well familiar. The business was located in a large converted warehouse near the river, where it had been for well over a hundred years, and was one of those slightly shambolic provincial establishments which, unlike the grand houses in London and the big cities, often provided a fruitful hunting ground for small-time dealers like himself.

He always warmed with anticipation when he entered such places. They smelled of musty belongings and ancient beeswax, and echoed with shuffling feet and lowered voices, rather as if one was in church. One never knew quite what one might come across in them, for they depended for the major part of their business on the estates of the recently deceased, and therefore often harboured items which had lain forgotten in family closets and attics for a generation or more. Maurice could never escape a sense of poignancy as the worn paraphernalia of recently ended lives were paraded before the coldly calculating eyes of persons mostly uninterested in their private history and sentimental significance, but only in their monetary worth. *'Memory is a man's real possession.'*

He picked up a catalogue at the desk and wandered along the aisles of furniture, paintings, volumes and memorabilia to be auctioned, his practised eye skimming the shelves for the hoped-for gleam of embossed leather or traditional binding that betokened something in the book line which might be of interest. Saw nothing immediately that attracted him, neither could he spot the numbers relating to the specific items he had come to view, so made his way back to the desk. A dour old boy in overalls, who'd probably been with the firm for half a century, was manning it. When Maurice asked about the effects of George Weldon, lot numbers 274 to 279, he was waved brusquely towards a set of double doors at the far end. 'They'm in the overflow store at the back.' The voice had a drawling Shropshire accent.

'Thank you,' said Maurice, and turned away.

'What sort o' stuff you looking for?' continued the voice.

Maurice turned back. 'I'm not sure really. Nature books, science. He was a keen naturalist, and that's rather my field.'

The other's gnarled features twisted sceptically. 'Well, I dunno if you'll find much there. The family took anything of value. It's mostly pretty ordinary stuff there.'

'Oh well, I'll have a scout around,' said Maurice. 'You never know.' He was about to turn away again, then on an afterthought asked, 'There aren't any of the family here for the auction by any chance, are there?'

The old fellow glanced around the room. 'There's a woman here somewhere who first brought in the stuff. I think she's one of them.' He pointed to a large alcove where there were a few tables and chairs and an apology for a tea counter. 'There she is in the snack bar. With the green coat.'

Maurice thanked him, and headed for the alcove. Then on second thoughts he changed direction and walked first to the outer display room to find the lot numbers.

As the man had said, there wasn't much of value. The first few lots consisted of ancient bits of furniture, the next of a large number of books—some of interest to students of botany and biology but not to Maurice—and the last lot was a jumble of household objects and naturalist's playthings, glass cases full of butterflies, stuffed birds, etc,—the sort of items that were frowned on nowadays by the conservation lobby.

Having scanned it all fairly thoroughly, Maurice abandoned his quest and headed once more for the main showroom and the snack bar. Only ten minutes or so now before the start of the auction, and the place was getting busier. A queue had formed at the tea counter, so he didn't bother to get himself anything but headed straight for the woman in the green coat, still sitting at a side table.

She looked up as he stood before her. 'Sorry to bother you,' said Maurice, 'but are you anything to do with George Weldon's family?'

She was a plain looking woman, in her fifties probably, with a blond-streaked hair perm and a strained but intelligent face. 'I'm his daughter.' Her accent was cultured.

'Oh. How d'you do? My name is Maurice Aldridge. I'm a book dealer from London. Um . . . may I sit here for a moment?'

Her expression wasn't particularly welcoming, but she gestured to the seat opposite and Maurice sat on the rickety wooden chair which was probably itself a leftover from some long ago auction. He suddenly wished he'd prepared his speech. 'I, er. . . . I was in the area and I thought I'd drop by to have a quick look at your father's effects. I'm sorry for his death.'

'Thank you,' she replied. 'He died some months ago. I'm afraid you'll have a long wait until his stuff comes up.'

'That's all right,' said Maurice, 'I've had a look and there's not much in my field. I probably won't stay. I'm doing some research, you see, for someone who is. . . . well, let's say doing a project on Charles Darwin and Darwinism. Am I right in thinking that you, er. . . . your family are connected to the Darwins?'

She appraised him over her coffee mug. 'Yes. My mother was a Darwin. Fairly remote. What project is this then, Mr. . . . Aldridge?'

He pulled a wry face. 'Oh, it's just another research program. As if there aren't enough already.' He glanced back at the auction room. 'I thought there might be something interesting among the items, but I couldn't see anything at first glance.'

'No,' she said, sipping her coffee. 'Anything in that line was kept back by the family. There wasn't much in any case.'

'Ah.'

'Tell me more about the project.' She didn't sound fiercely interested.

'Well I don't know very much,' he replied vaguely. 'It's a client of mine. Buys a lot of old books and manuscripts. Has an interest in biology and so forth. And he seems to think there's still undiscovered stuff about Darwin around somewhere.' He waved a dismissive hand. 'He's a bit imprecise, to tell you the truth, but he's very well off and he's paying me to do this.'

'I see.'

Maurice as usual wondered how much he should say. Well nothing venture, he thought, and leaned forwards a little. 'He did say that there's a rumour that Darwin's wife, Emma, kept a private diary which has never been discovered.'

Her expression did not change. 'Oh, yes,' she replied matter-of-factly. 'That rumour's always been around. It might be true.'

'Then why has it never come to light?' asked Maurice.

She shrugged. 'Emma was very emphatic that she didn't want it made public, so the family has obeyed her wishes. That's what they say. I wouldn't know. There were only a few copies made supposedly. I've never seen one.'

'Do you know which descendants might have copies?'

'No. Our branch certainly never have. It would have been the immediate surviving children who got them, and presumably they would then have been handed down.' She gave him a slight smile for the first time. 'I doubt if they'd be of much interest to your client anyway. The book would probably have been just a housewife's diary sort of thing. A lot of Victorian wives kept those.'

'Yes, probably,' agreed Maurice, casually. 'But you never know. And with so much interest in Darwin over the last century it's surprising that something like that has never surfaced.'

She shrugged again. She evidently didn't consider the matter of world shaking importance. But then she softened and a reflective shadow crossed her face. 'I'd quite like to have read it myself actually. She was a remarkable woman from all accounts.'

'Was she?'

'Had ten children, ran a big household, looked after a sick husband, and lived well into her eighties.' She pulled a wry face. 'And here's me—only two children and a bust-up marriage, and I feel half dead already.'

'Oh dear.' Maurice felt embarrassed. For want of something to say he mumbled, 'Do you live near here?'

'Yes. Not far. He . . . Charles was brought up in Shrewsbury, you know.'

'Ah, yes.'

She pointed vaguely. 'The house is still there. The Mount. It was turned into an old people's home at some stage.' She laughed, her face suddenly acquiring a hint of its youthful liveliness. 'Funny if I ended up there myself.'

'Not for a long time yet, I'm sure,' said Maurice, inadequately.

'Are you married, Mr Aldridge?'

'Widowed.'

'Oh, I'm sorry.' He shrugged. She contemplated her mug. 'I sometimes think I'd prefer to have been widowed rather than divorced. Easier to bear than the turmoil.' Maurice didn't attempt to disillusion her. She blinked as though suddenly realising what she had said. 'Sorry. That was insensitive.'

'No, no. . . .' He murmured, and tailed off. He had never been good with distressed women.

She was regarding him with a little more interest. 'Did your wife die recently?'

'No. Several years ago. Cancer.'

Her eyes showed concern. 'How awful for you.'

'Yes. But one moves on.'

'Does one? Have you moved on?'

This was becoming a little too personal for Maurice's taste. He tried to change the subject. 'Well, work is a great consolation. Hence my quest for things like this.'

The eyes did not leave him. 'It's all irrelevant, you know.'

He puzzled for a moment. 'What is?'

'All the Darwin business. Doesn't matter whether the earth was made in six days or six billion years of evolution. What matters is what we're doing here. Where's the sense in life unless it's for some greater purpose?'

The last thing Maurice wanted was a theological discussion, but he felt he ought to say something. 'Um, well. . . . yes, but it's interesting to find out about the scientific, er. . . .'

'Oh to hell with science!' Her tone was suddenly fierce. 'I'm sick of scientific arguments.' He nodded dumbly. 'If people paid more attention to what the Bible says instead of playing with their scientific toys, the world would be a better place.' She noticed his embarrassment and her voice softened. 'Sorry. Didn't mean to sound off like that. It's just one of my hobby horses.' She looked down and played with her tea spoon. 'I couldn't have gone on without my faith.'

He was saved from further awkwardness by a bell sounding loudly around the rooms. 'That'll be the start of the auction,' she said, and got up. People were gravitating towards the auction platform. 'I'm going to come back later. It'll be hours before Father's stuff comes up.' She hesitated and put her head on one side. 'Perhaps I'll see you then?'

Maurice felt a touch of panic. Further involvement with a lonely woman, and a fervent lonely woman too, did not feel like a good idea at the moment. 'I, er. . . . I doubt it. I have to be on my way.'

She looked only slightly crestfallen, and held out a hand. 'Nice to meet you then, Mr Aldridge.' Maurice too rose from his chair. 'Good luck with your quest.'

'Thank you.'

She was turning away, but then hesitated and turned back. 'There is one member of the family who might be of use to you. He's a distant cousin of mine—Cyril Catcheside—lives in Malvern.'

'Oh?'

'He's a strange man. Fixated with the Darwins—always rummaging round the family archives, and writing rather tedious pamphlets and such. You never know, he might tell you something.'

'Do you have his phone number?'

'Not with me. You'll find him in the phone book, I expect. Catcheside.' She smiled briefly and turned again.

'Thank you,' said Maurice, and watched her broad hipped figure weaving its way towards the exit doors.

'Good morning everyone, and welcome to today's auction.' The auctioneer, a florid man with a moustache and country tweeds who looked as if he'd stepped out of the pages of a P.G. Woodhouse novel, had mounted his rostrum.

Maurice too slipped quietly away.

CHAPTER TWENTY-ONE

September 30th, 1951. Wakefield

As I familiarised myself with the work being done in Professor Peierls' department at Birmingham, it became clear that he was not exaggerating about the importance of the work being done there. Here was the potential for an astonishingly powerful new device which could win the war outright. And it was a race as to whether the Allies or Germany would achieve it first.

So when in June of the following year Germany launched its unprovoked attack on Russia, the cradle of communism, it seemed to me a matter of the simplest logic that Russia too should have access to this knowledge. Indeed I could not understand why this was not already happening and why the allied authorities were so wary of cooperating with the Russians. I knew of course that there was an inbuilt antagonism between the capitalist and the communist regimes, but surely now was the moment of all moments to set aside such mistrust and combine against the common enemy.

One of the problems was that the people of Britain had still not appreciated quite how deranged the regime in Germany was. When I brought up the subject amongst my fellow physicists at Birmingham, they would say such things as: "Yes, of course we understand that Hitler has aspirations to world domination—but we have experienced such threats time and again throughout history, from the Romans to the Vikings, the Spanish, Napoleon. . . . and for the most part we have managed to repulse such threats." I would reply that they had not witnessed at first hand as I had, the barbarism, the sheer insanity that had overtaken my native people. They were going to have to recruit every available ally to counter this extremism—even such as Russia. Yet for all their alarm and for all Churchill's stirring rallying cries they still did not quite comprehend what extreme measures they had to take in order to defeat the menace. They would reply with such aphorisms as, "One does not have to sink to the level of one's enemies," or, "The problem of extremism is that it invariably causes more problems than it solves."

Radicalism just was not in their nature. That in peacetime is a virtue, but in war it is a hindrance.

After some soul searching I decided I had to take steps on my own initiative.

I had been assisted in my escape from Berlin by members of the German Communist Party, one of whom was a Polish emigré of fiercely committed beliefs. I knew that he, like myself, had also fled to Britain and was now heavily involved with organising German communists abroad in the fight against fascism. The British Communist Party was assisting in this effort, and through them I was able to make contact with him. I now approached him for advice as to what I should do.

When we met, I explained at some length my thoughts about my work and about Russia, and how I felt both could affect the outcome of the war. He was an extremely serious and intelligent man, and when I had finished he looked at me for a long moment in silence. Then he surprised me by saying, "As you know I am a committed communist. What you probably don't know is that I am also a member of Russia's foreign intelligence branch, the GRU."

It transpired that he had been recruited by the Russians some considerable time earlier, and had been operating as a passive surveillance agent in Britain ever since arriving there. Fate had led me to someone who could facilitate my approach to the cradle of communism in the most direct way possible. I took it as an omen that I was on the right path.

In a very short space of time he arranged a contact for me whom I only knew as 'Alexander', but whom I later learned was in fact attached to the Soviet Embassy in London. After some initial soul-searching, and with considerable apprehension, I typed out a technical report on my department's progress on the nuclear fission and uranium diffusion issues, and on one of my days off I took a trip to London as instructed, to meet with this Alexander.

I have to admit I was terrified. This was the moment, the irrevocable step. This was the point at which I had to act on my beliefs. To stop theorising and turn conviction into action. When I reached the capital I almost turned back. It was only my faith that this was something that <u>had</u> to be done, and that I was one of the very few who could do it, that urged me on. I walked across London from the train station to the secret address near Hyde Park that I had been given, all the while inwardly shaking and looking about me for imagined followers (I was not on those early occasions a very skillful agent!). As I approached the front door to the house I had a serious attack of dizziness, which I presume was psychosomatic, and I had to sit down on the steps for some moments to regain my composure. Then I rang the bell several times as instructed, the door opened and I was ushered inside. My career as a spy had begun.

I have to repeat here that I never thought of myself as a traitor. I simply considered it my duty to do anything within my power to aid the fight against Naziism. I have been called arrogant for taking it upon myself to make this decision. But my father always preached the message that it was not enough to search one's soul constantly as to one's true beliefs, but that one must also <u>act</u> on those beliefs.

Furthermore those beliefs extended to a greater dimension then merely aiding a political cause. How do I explain it? Ever since the defining moment of my discovering Darwinism during my early student days, I had viewed his theory of evolution as the explanation and motivation for all natural phenomena. I had believed utterly in the progress of nature and of humanity via its irresistible method. Yet suddenly the aberration of the Third Reich had exploded amongst my own countrymen, supposedly some of the most advanced and civilised on the planet, and thrown us back to the dark ages at a stroke. How could this have happened? How did this accord with the doctrine of natural selection? The only explanation I could find was that it was a hiccup in the march of progress, a reversion to the primordial forces that still lurked within us, and that the ultimate rejection of its perversity would leave humanity better and stronger. The greater the evil, the greater the reaction against it.

It was therefore up to every individual to react in the most effective way his talents allowed, to put right that which had gone wrong. Which, as I saw it, was what I was doing.

Even so I have to laugh at a joke Gordon Hawkins has told me: Capitalism is standing on the brink of the abyss. Communism is about to overtake it.

CHAPTER TWENTY-TWO

If a fair balance be struck between the good and evil caused by each part, each will be found on the whole advantageous. After the lapse of time, under changing conditions of life, if any part comes to be injurious, it will be modified; or if it be not so, the being will become extinct, as myriads have become extinct.
Origin of Species

A hundred and sixty miles North West of London, Maurice was in a phone booth in the Shrewsbury city centre. He did have a mobile phone, but invariably forgot to keep it with him as in this instance, so he was forced to use the public phone to get to directory enquiries. The voice gave him the number for the only C. Catcheside listed in Great Malvern. He irritably fumbled with his coins, tapped the number, and a female voice answered.

'Is this the home of Mr Cyril Catcheside?' asked Maurice.

'Yes, that's right. It's Mary Catcheside here. Do you want my husband?'

'If he's available, thank you.'

He heard the voice calling loudly, 'Cyriiil.' A lengthy pause and then an abrupt male voice. 'Yes?'

'Mr Catcheside? I'm sorry to trouble you. . . .'

'Speak up. Bad line.'

'Sorry, I'm in a phone booth. My name is Maurice Aldridge. I'm a book dealer from London. I was given your name by one of the Darwin family in Shrewsbury who told me you had done a lot of research on the family's history and so forth.'

'Yes.'

'I, er . . . I'm doing a bit of research myself for a client, and I wondered if . . . well, I thought it might be useful to talk to you, and, er. . . .'

'You're in London, you say?'

'No, I'm actually in Shrewsbury at the moment. I came up for the auction of George Weldon's effects, and. . . .'

'You won't find much there.'

'No, I rather gathered that. However I met his daughter at the auction, and. . . .'

'Celia. She tell you about me?'

'Yes. She mentioned you, and. . . .'

'Bet she said some funny things about me.'

'Er, not at all. She. . . .'

'Don't see eye to eye, her family and mine. Chalk and cheese.'

'Oh, really?'

'So what sort of stuff are you after?'

'Well, it's a bit difficult to say over the phone. I was wondering if, er. . . .'

'You going back to London this way?'

'I could do. I have to get back this weekend and I was thinking I could come down that way, and . . . well, if it wasn't too much imposition. . . .'

'Not trying to sell anything, are you?'

'Oh, heavens no. As I said, I'm doing some research, and. . . .'

'Call in. Malvern's only a couple of hours from Shrewsbury. You coming today?'

'I could do. It's very short notice, but. . . .'

'Come for tea. About four. The wife makes very good old fashioned fruit cake.'

'That's most kind.'

'Got a pen? Take down the address.'

The arrangement suited perfectly. Gave him time for other things. Other people.

An hour or so later he drove up outside the home of the person who had been the instigation for the whole trip. A rambling Georgian cottage overlooking the wooded hills on the outskirts of Ludlow, not too far off his route to Malvern.

As he climbed out, Felicity Trask, a buxom woman with unruly blonde hair wisping around a weathered but handsome face, came down the overgrown path wearing baggy linen slacks and an excruciatingly bright man's beach shirt. 'Maurice, darling! Good to see you, good to see you!'

'You too, Felicity,' replied Maurice with more modest exuberance. Indicating the shirt, 'Been holidaying in Miami?'

She looked down at herself and chuckled. 'Posh, isn't it? I wear it for painting—doesn't show the paint stains.' She enveloped him in a bear hug and kissed him on both cheeks. 'How are you, sweetie?'

'Surviving. How are you?'

'Oh, same as ever, same as ever. Bit older, bit fatter, bit poorer, but soldiering on.' She waved around the wildly out-of-control garden and the dilapidated cottage. 'Everything crumbling around me along with myself, but I like it that way. Come in, come in. Bit chilly for *dejeuner sur l'herbe*, so we'll eat inside, eh?'

The interior of the house mirrored the state of the outside. Chaotic and bizarre, books and paraphernalia piled everywhere, the smell of musty objects and oil paints and garlic infused cooking—an air of obscure and dedicated industry.

'Home-made soup and home-made bread and country pate for lunch. Will that do you?'

'Sounds wonderful.'

She waved to a huge and battered leather sofa as she went to the cluttered kitchen area. 'Sit down. Still drinking?'

'Too much.'

'Good, me too. Got some rather splendid vintage cider—try it.'

Maurice's good intentions about daytime drinking went out of the window, he felt the weight of concerns slipping from his shoulders, and sank back into the deep leather cushions with a relief he had not felt for a long while. He reflected gratefully on their past relationship as Felicity clattered things in the kitchen area and prattled on about the dire state of the business, direr state of the world, and even direr state of her waistline.

She was a semi-recluse, and since a stormy divorce many years ago, had led a bachelor life like Maurice. They had known each other since Maurice's early publishing days when the book world had brought them together. Alice came into the social equation about the same time as Felicity was disentangling herself from her alcoholic and violent journalist husband, and the newly bonded couple took the lone and distressed woman under their wing. She had remained a friend ever since. When, after various abortive romances and unsatisfactory jobs in London, she had moved to the country and opened her bookshop the trio maintained an irregular but affectionate contact. And over the whole ordeal of Alice's illness and passing Felicity had been a distant but solid support.

In the old days they used to meet regularly at events such as the Hay-on-Wye or Bath book festivals, but now Maurice saw her rarely. Her bookshop was in the once simply delightful, and now exceedingly trendy little town of Ludlow, renowned for its ancient winding lanes, its picturesque castle ruins, its Shakespeare festival, and its gastronomic restaurants. The shop survived thanks to all that and the regular trickle of tourists, but never seemed to make any money, due mostly, Maurice suspected, to the owner's lack of interest in all matters commercial.

A few minutes later the two were sipping home-made minestrone soup accompanied by pate and vintage cider, and the talk was of vintage books and book sellers, contemporary authors and publishers, and literature ancient and modern.

'So what's this Darwin business all about then,' asked Felicity eventually, her mouth full of wholemeal and pate.

Maurice told her the circumstances of his quest. He had no qualms about abandoning secrecy in this case.

'What a great commission!' exclaimed the other. 'Opportunity to scour the country, and be paid at the same time. Why can't I meet customers like that?'

'Something of a wild goose chase, I suspect,' said Maurice.

'Never mind. Chase the wild geese and enjoy the goose liver on the way.' Felicity waved her soup spoon in the air, reminding Maurice of Donald Easterby's love of conducting conversations with his cutlery. 'Always had a soft spot for Darwin. Read him in my twenties and thought, of course! That's what it's all about. Makes such common sense. Why didn't we all think of it before?'

Maurice nodded. 'How important do you think this work would be if it materialised?'

'D'you mean the diary or Darwin's postscript?'

'Either. Both.'

She pondered for a moment. 'Hard to say. A diary by Emma Darwin would have obvious historical interest and, if the content was revealing, historic interest also.' She sipped a spoonful of minestrone. 'A detailed conclusion by Darwin himself. . . . Wow.' She sat savouring her culinary creation. 'That could stir things up a bit. Get all the pundits at each other's throats again.' She wiped her mouth with a paper napkin, chuckling. 'I'd like to see that.'

'Yes,' said Maurice, sipping without guilt at his second half pint of cider. 'I'd like to read Darwin's opinion for my own sake. Not quite sure what I feel about the infinite.'

'Ah no, well me neither. Could never go with all the biblical stuff—tablets of stone and virgin births and miraculous resurrections. What nonsense—far too airy-fairy and apocryphal for me. Which is why Darwin came as such a revelation.' She brushed an unruly streak of blonde hair from her face and cut more slices of pate. 'However the overall cosmic picture, that's a whole other thing. I enjoy trying to keep up with the science. I don't deal much in science books like you, but I like to read them.' Maurice nodded. 'Such extraordinary strides made in the last century. You wonder where it will lead us in the next.' She shook her head. 'Mind boggling prospect.'

Maurice nodded again. 'The universe will look quite different to us in a hundred years. A different set of concerns.' He took another swig of cider. 'We'll probably laugh at the stuff we worry about now.'

'Mm,' said Felicity glumly. 'It's one reason I'm quite glad I don't have children. Well, grand children at any rate. Wouldn't like to have their generation's problems.'

'No,' replied Maurice. Although that was probably what grand parents had always thought. And the grand children usually managed to come off a bit better than their forebears. He glanced at his host. 'But you seem quite happy with your solitary life, Felicity.'

Her eyebrows went up as if she'd never considered the matter. 'I suppose I am,' she said. 'Living on one's own has its drawbacks, but it saves a lot of others. That whole bloody lottery of marriage for instance.' ('*Men marry because they are bored, women because they are curious. Both are disappointed.*') She was gazing out of the window. 'I get so much pleasure from the moment, you know. I love this tatty old cottage. I love the trees in the garden. I love the hills around here. I love my little shop and the odd people who come into it. I love my amateur painting. I love the wind and the frosts and the sun. I love seeing old friends like you. In fact I'm probably the most complaisant bugger you could ever meet.'

Maurice smiled. 'That's good,' he said, and stared at the table top. He was aware that she was studying him with concern.

'You all right?'

Maurice looked up. 'Yes, fine.'

'You look a bit frazzled, that's all.' She tipped her head enquiringly. Her green eyes were kindly. 'How are you managing yourself, Maurice? Life O.K. is it?'

Her visitor nodded. 'Can't complain.' He dipped his spoon in his cooling soup.

'It was a tough time with Alice.'

Maurice nodded again but didn't speak.

'Recovered now? Back on the rails?'

'It's taken a long time, but I'm doing all right.'

'Her going like that must have been so difficult.'

Maurice nodded slowly. 'Yes. It was complicated because. . . .' He stopped. He had never told anyone the true circumstances of her death, and he didn't wish to go into them now.

'Because?' prompted the other.

Maurice shook his head. 'No, nothing. I don't really want to talk about it. However I do. . . . I have been finding things difficult recently, Felicity. I don't know why. I should be getting over her loss by now, but for some reason I can't seem to shake free of it.'

His host pulled a face. 'Well they say it takes four years to get over a death, a divorce, or a bankruptcy. You've a bit to go yet.' She paused a moment. 'She was a touch special, Alice. Hard to replace. But it wasn't a unique relationship, you know. There are other people out there.'

Maurice frowned. 'Not unique?'

'Well, there's no such thing as the perfect couple. You two had some sparky old rows if I remember.'

Maurice blinked. 'I suppose we did. I'd forgotten.'

'Oh yes. Probably good for you. You need to find someone else to row with.' She put her head on one side as she regarded him. 'You wouldn't be disloyal if you went looking, you know.'

Maurice picked up his cider glass and again said nothing.

Felicity pointed a piece of bread. 'Yes, definitely time you did a bit of that.' She pursed her lips. 'Though I'm the last person to advise on such things. I gave up trying to find my ideal man years ago. Decided that either men are all hopeless or I'm just hopelessly intolerant.'

'Probably the former,' said Maurice.

She smiled. Then said pointedly, 'They tell me everyone meets up via the internet these days.'

Heaven forbid. How could he possibly get involved in something like that? A great intake of breath suddenly caught Maurice by surprise, and then for no reason he was sitting with the glass half way to his lips, the hand holding it shaking so violently that cider splashed onto the wooden table top. 'Damn!' he said. 'I'm so sorry.'

She got up, laid a hand on his shoulder and went to the sink for a cloth. 'Don't worry about it.' She came back with the cloth and a glass of water. 'Here. Probably best you stick to this now. That stuff's a bit powerful.'

Maurice took a sip as she mopped the table, and then sat holding the glass, occasional intakes of breath still shaking him. She waited, standing beside him. Finally he found his voice and looked up. 'I'm sorry. I'm so sorry. I don't know why. . . . .'

'That's all right, sweetie. It was a big thing for you.'

'She'd be so cross with me,' stammered Maurice. He took of his specs and dabbed at his eyes with his handkerchief. 'She'd give me such a ticking off for being so indulgent.'

'Not at all. If I knew Alice she'd have been in tears herself that you still cared.'

Maurice heard the latter's voice in his ear. 'Don't listen to him, you silly man. Snap out of it and stop making such an idiot of yourself!' He pulled blew his nose fiercely on the handkerchief. 'What a fool I am,' he said. 'Three years on and still. . . .' He broke off, not trusting himself to speak further.

Felicity took his head and pulled him towards her. He found himself nestling between her generous breasts. 'There now,' she murmured. 'It's all right. It's quite all right.'

It was comforting there. He stayed still, feeling relaxed and at peace like a small child consoled by a mother. Silence for several seconds, and then inevitably their position produced a stirring in his loins. The two were motionless, the erotic tension suddenly growing. Just as it was getting past the point of no return, Alice whispered in his ear again. 'Careful now, boyo. No harm in a fling, but do you really want to get involved to that degree? Do you really want the obligation?'

'No, no,' her murmured into Felicity's bosom.

He felt her stiffen. She let go of his head and pulled away abruptly. 'Sorry. Didn't mean to presume.'

He hadn't realized he had spoken aloud. He was urgently contrite. 'Oh, no!' he said. 'I wasn't talking to you.'

'You weren't?' She stepped away and contemplated him gravely. 'Oh dear, sweetie—you really *are* in a bad way, aren't you?'

He cleaned his specs and put them back on, feeling very foolish. 'Not really. It's just. . . . I just talk to her sometimes. Silly, I know, but. . . .'

'*Very* silly, dear. Especially when you're with somebody else.'

'Yes. Yes, I know. Please forgive me.'

She relaxed slightly, then chuckled, mopped the cider on the table and went back to the sink. 'Well, it's probably better that I don't try and fill the gap,' she said as she wrung out the cloth. 'But you definitely need to find someone who can. Seems to me you aren't nearly as good at being on your own as I am.'

'No. Probably not.' Maurice sat back a little. 'You see,' he said, 'her death was more complicated for me than it needed to be, and it left me with. . . .' He broke off and shook his head. 'I can't really explain.'

'No, well. . . . I'm here if you ever change your mind and want to talk about it.' She raised a wry eyebrow. 'And I promise I won't try and get your trousers off.'

There was no further reference as they finished lunch. They chatted on a bit more about books and politics and rural matters, and eventually Maurice got up, a touch unsteadily. 'I must be on my way.'

'Are you safe to drive?' asked his hostess. 'You've been knocking back the cider.'

'I'll be all right. Thank you, Felicity. It was good seeing you again. I'm sorry I got a bit. . . .'

She waved it away. 'Get in touch whenever. Don't leave it so long next time.' She saw her guest to the door. 'Good luck with the quest. Seems it might be quite important.'

Maurice nodded. 'Yes. Not sure why, but it does feel so.'

'Keep me posted if you find anything.' Felicity grinned. 'And if it makes you rich you can buy me dinner in Ludlow. I can't afford to eat there now, it's so posh.'

Maurice backed the Rover out of the weed infested driveway, waved to the brightly coloured figure filling the wisteria framed doorway, and drove off with the occasional intake still shaking his chest. A few hundred yards along the narrow country lane he was forced to pull out to get past a large black SUV parked on the verge and he vaguely wondered what it was doing there, but such was his mental state that he barely considered it. Time had passed, so he abandoned his planned meander through the Cotswolds and headed in a slightly befuddled state down the A49 towards Great Malvern. Fortunately there were few police cars in that area.

Three quarters of an hour later he turned off the main Worcester road and drove towards the high contour of the Malvern hills. As the car toiled around the side of the steep hill and into the town he wondered at the atmosphere of the place. He had never been there before, and its unique situation, bounded by the towering hillside behind, the great stretching Severn Vale in front, and the wide sky all around, instantly seized his imagination. '. . . *And I will have some peace there. For peace comes dropping slow . . .*' Alice would have loved this, he thought as he meandered through the town's leafy spaces and wide avenues, lined by a hotchpotch of period buildings dating back from late Victorian to early Georgian and probably beyond. He noted the quirky collection of antique and arty shops where a number of day tourists were wandering, but couldn't immediately spot any dealers of his own species amongst them. There must be some hidden away in such a place, but there wasn't time to go looking. He left the town centre and got lost amongst the outer lanes winding about the hillside as he searched for the road he wanted. He had to ask the way twice, but eventually found it and drove slowly along, an irritable driver hooting behind. Finally he saw the house, 'Heathfield', a picturesque but slightly dilapidated white-washed villa, standing in its own modest grounds next to similar tree-shaded dwellings. He edged cautiously in through the pillared gateway as instructed, and pulled up outside the green painted front door. It opened as he got out of the car. A small man with a greying reddish beard, rimless spectacles, and deeply lined, pinched features emerged. His short bandy legs were encased in green corduroys and his broad chest and shoulders in a multi-coloured woolen jacket zipped up the front. He made Maurice think of a leprechaun or an ageing monkey dressed for the circus ring.

'You found us. I'm Cyril Catcheside. Come in.' He shook hands and turned briskly around to lead the way indoors.

'What a lovely town,' said Maurice as he followed into the shaded hallway crammed with book shelves, racks of weather coats and walking sticks, and lined with so many assorted prints and paintings that one could barely see the colour of the walls.

'Eh?' said the other in front of him.

'Malvern. I've never been before. I didn't realise it was quite so beautiful.'

'Yes. One of Britain's best kept secrets. Long may it remain so.' Catcheside led the way into a spacious living room, similarly cluttered with books and paintings, but with a wide bow window looking out over the stretching hillside and the cloud scudding sky. 'This is my wife, Mary.'

A broad, hearty looking woman, slightly taller than her husband, straightened up from the tea tray. 'Welcome, Mr Aldridge.'

'Maurice, please. I was just saying what a charming spot.'

'Yes, we like it. We've been here a long time now. Do sit down.'

'Strong associations with Darwin, this town has,' said her husband, as Maurice sank into one of the deep, floral printed armchairs. 'Did you know that?'

'Really?' said Maurice surprised. 'No, I had no idea.'

'Oh yes. Came here regularly for treatment for his ailments. It had a great reputation in those days as a spa for health treatments and so on. Still has to some extent, but in those days the whole world beat a path here seeking miracle cures for its various ills.' Catcheside gave a sly sideways grin. 'Never found them of course, but it kept the doctors rich and the clients in hope.'

Maurice was struck by the fact that so many relatives of the family still seemed to maintain their ties to places linked with the great man. He glanced at the wife. 'Is that why you came to live here?' he asked. 'The Darwin connection?'

She simply raised an ironic eyebrow and deferred to her husband. Catcheside stuck out his jaw. 'Not consciously. But I suppose . . . Well, put it this way. I came here quite often in the early days when I was looking into his life, and we sort of fell in love with the place, so. . . . you might say it had an influence.'

She put a cup of tea in front of Maurice. 'We lived most of our lives in the Birmingham area. This was heaven compared to that. Would you like some fruit cake?'

'Yes, indeed. Thank you.' It was dark brown, heavy, and packed with fruit. He asked the husband politely, 'So you're retired now?'

'Ten years, thank God. Was a civil surveyor, but took early retirement. Thirty years of bureaucracy and incompetence—that was enough for me. Now I have my hobbies and walking and grand children. Busier than ever, aren't we, Mary?'

She nodded. There was an air of placid calm about her, in contrast to his fidgety energy.

'One of your hobbies being Darwinism?' said Maurice.

Catcheside didn't answer immediately. He sniffed and stared sideways out of the window. 'Intriguing topic. Ever more intriguing the more you look into it.'

'I can imagine.'

He looked back at Maurice. 'How much do you know about it?'

'Not a great deal, but I'm learning.'

'What's your specific interest?'

Maurice hesitated, a little put out by the aggressive questioning. 'Well, as I said, I have a client who's asked me to do some research . . .'

'What's *his* specific interest?'

'He's a . . . a collector of books, manuscripts, memorabilia. Particularly in scientific areas.'

'Not much left to find in that field. The museums and foundations have most of the Darwin stuff.'

'Yes, I realise that.'

'So he must be after something particular.'

Again Maurice was cautious about giving too much away. He sipped the tea, which was helping to clear his head after all the lunchtime cider. He countered with a question of his own. 'Are you closely related to the Darwins, Cyril?'

The other perused him with small sharp eyes. 'No. A distant line. We're a far flung bunch. But you'd be surprised how many of us maintain the links. Keep up the interest.'

'Yes, well . . .'

'Know why that is?' The beady eyes were still on him.

'Well, it's a fascinating subject, evolution. He was an extraordinary man.'

'More than fascinating. More than extraordinary.' Cyril pushed his spectacles back onto his nose. 'The idea of evolution had been around for a long time before he came on the scene. Even the ancient Greeks had theories about it. It was his interpretation of it that was so revolutionary.' He wrinkled his nose, looking more monkey-like than ever. 'Most important scientific theory ever arrived at, Maurice.'

Now where have I heard that before, thought Maurice. 'You think so?' he said.

'Without doubt. Explains everything. Explains the way the world works, explains the messes we get ourselves into, explains tragedy, aggression, struggle . . . Trouble is the world doesn't want to know. Won't take the message on board. And until it does . . .' He shrugged, and glanced at his wife.

Maurice looked at her. She was sitting with her tea. She raised her eyes to the ceiling with an expression of wry resignation. She had heard it all many times, he thought.

'Anyway, that's enough of that,' went on Cyril. He took a bite of fruit cake and said with a full mouth, 'So what is your client specifically looking for?'

'Well, anything connected really,' replied Maurice. 'Anything original, that is. Writings, manuscripts, notebooks . . .'

'Not a chance. I've got one or two minor things, but they came down through the family. Everything else, as I said, has been snapped up.'

Maurice took the bull by the horns. 'My client thinks that Emma Darwin may have kept some kind of journal. I'm not sure how authentic his information is, but it was one of the items he mentioned.'

'Oh, that.' The other said no more, just watched him.

'You know about it then?'

'Oh, yes. It's often talked about within the family circle.'

'But it's never come to light?'

'Not publicly.'

'But privately?'

Cyril shrugged, but said nothing.

'Why hasn't it come to light, do you think?'

Another shrug. 'It may not actually still exist. And if it does. . . . well it would probably only be in copy form. There were very few copies.'

The same repeated excuse. 'Why did Emma want it kept so secret?'

Cyril chewed purposefully on his fruit cake. Then he said, 'Maybe she just felt it was too personal. Or maybe . . . too contentious.'

'Contentious?'

'As I said, the whole theory's contentious.'

'Yes, but why should his wife's diary be any more so than everything he wrote himself? I mean it's all been debated over ad infinitum.'

'Quite so. Who knows?'

Maurice felt his irritation rising. 'But forgive me, Cyril, from what I've heard you've done as much research into their lives as anyone. You must have some ideas about it.'

The man took a sip of tea, and wiped his mouth carefully with a linen napkin. Then he said, 'Well, to tell you the truth, I've tried quite hard to find the thing myself. I've followed up most of the avenues, but I've never come up with anything. Anything concrete, that is.'

'But you do believe there are copies around?'

'Yes, I do.' He pursed his lips and again looked at his wife as if seeking confirmation. She gave only the slightest of shrugs. 'I wouldn't swear to it but I'd say there have to be. These things don't just disappear.'

'So have you found any clues at all?'

Cyril stared at Maurice over the top of his rimless glasses for a long moment.

'You may as well tell him,' prompted his wife, sipping at her tea.

She's the force behind the throne, thought Maurice. A bit like Alice and him. 'All right,' Cyril said. I'll tell you what I know on one condition. If you unearth anything . . . I don't think you will, but if you do . . . you tell me about it.' With a hint of ferocity. '*Everything* about it. Agreed?'

Maurice fought back the instinct to retaliate. 'Yes, absolutely.'

The other's chin jutted forward like one of his primeval ancestors sniffing the wind. 'I looked into this thing quite seriously some time ago. I was intrigued by the whole idea, and. . . .,' he threw another glance at his wife, 'Mary would say I became a bit fanatical about it.' She gave a slight smile but said nothing. 'I corresponded with a number of direct descendants of the family. They were all pretty non-committal about the journal, but the general opinion seemed to point to the theory that Darwin's third son, Francis, who was responsible for publishing the old man's letters and his autobiography after he died, also had a private printing of Emma's book done, and gave copies to all the children.' A beat. 'There were seven who survived the parents. Two others died in infancy and the second child, Annie, died tragically of tuberculosis at the age of ten. Here in Malvern in fact.' Cyril's face screwed into a yet more gnomic expression. 'These various copies—he only printed enough to give one to each of the children—were supposedly handed down through the generations. None ever came into the public domain. They were either kept hidden in deference to Emma's wishes or simply got lost amongst the family paraphernalia.' He paused for a moment to watch his visitor. His story corresponded with Donald Easterby's, and Maurice remained impassive.

'Well. . . . having failed to track down any of the copies, I then did some thinking. It seemed to me that, of all those which might exist, the most likely one to try and find was that which would have been given to the Darwin's eldest surviving daughter, Henrietta.'

'Why?' asked Maurice.

'Well, she had no offspring to hand the thing on to. But she was very close to her mother, and in fact was herself responsible for publishing Emma's own letters after her death.' Cyril raised a finger. 'The letters never mentioned the journal by the way.' The finger waved. 'So . . . she would surely have taken care over what happened to her copy, but the question was, what *did* happen to it? It's unlikely it would have gone to any of her siblings' families as they would all have had their own copies. It didn't surface amongst her own stuff after she died. So it seemed to me the most likely possibility was that she had passed it on to one of her numerous cousins amongst the other branches of the family.' He glinted at Maurice over the glasses. 'What do you know about the family tree?'

'It's pretty complicated,' replied Maurice.

'Quite so. Emma Darwin's mother came from the Allens. They were a prolific family of land owners at Tenby in South Wales. A tucked away spot, but a rather special place and a favourite resort amongst the well-to-do in those days. From there many of the family married well, and they all hobnobbed with politicians, diplomats, celebrities such as Sydney Smith, Florence Nightingale, Wordsworth, Byron, Coleridge, the list goes on. . . . It always amazes me how the Victorians managed to communicate and socialise as frequently as they did.'

'Yes,' said Maurice reflecting on the vast network of associations amongst the educated classes of the time—all before the advent of the telephone and the motor car.

'A grand child of one of the Allens ended up married to Lord Salisbury—Queen Victoria's Prime Minister. There's social climbing for you!'

Maurice smiled. He was warming more to the man.

'Anyway,' went on the other, 'Emma's mother, Bessie Allen, was one of eleven children. Emma's father of course was a Wedgewood. He was one of seven. Many of that gaggle of aunts and uncles in the two families went on to have large broods of their own, and through the generations there were several more unions between cousins within those two families and the Darwins. From that time to the present we are talking about at least six further generations. So you can see there must be several hundred people walking the planet today who have links with one or other of the three dynasties.'

'So you had a pretty impossible task,' said Maurice.

'Well, one would think so. However there were a few clues. Henrietta herself—or 'Etty' as the family called her—left a wealth of material and diaries, and she was a prolific letter writer. So I was able to shorten the likely list of first recipients to those cousins she corresponded with and stayed closest to after Emma's death. And by a process of elimination I ended up with what I considered to be the few most likely family lines worth following up.' Cyril sighed. 'However it was still a pretty laborious business, and to tell you the truth I was beginning to get disenchanted with the whole game. I had almost decided to give it up when I had what seemed like a breakthrough.'

Mary Catcheside came across with the tea-pot to top up Maurice's cup, and Cyril drummed his fingers waiting for the interruption to end. Then he went on. 'One of my most difficult lines of investigation was an offshoot of the Allen family which had a fairly direct line of descent from one of the cousins that Henrietta used to correspond with, and about which there was evidence of a collection of family memorabilia passed down through the generations. I had a hell of a time tracking them down, but I eventually discovered that there were at least five contemporary progeny. One of these died childless some years ago, one lives in Australia, two are fairly uncultured artisan types living in the North of England, but the eldest and most likely was a divorced school master with some indications of an interest in history and science, who now lives and works in London.'

He paused expectantly, the little eyes narrow. Maurice sensed revelations. He asked, 'Did you contact him?'

'Yes. He's called Robert Gresham. I wrote to him first, with a general innocuous enquiry about inheritance from Darwin's time. He wrote back, answering that, yes, he had inherited a few things but not much of importance he thought. I then followed up with a telephone call and asked a bit more. He was quite forthcoming. Said there was an old trunk full of family stuff which had lain around various attics and cellars for decades getting gradually fuller and fuller, and which nobody had the energy to investigate thoroughly. But he did believe there were a few oddments from the nineteenth century—books, photos, the usual musty clobber. He hadn't specifically noticed anything resembling a diary or journal, but admitted he hadn't looked closely and there were, he thought, one or two leather bound volumes amongst the stuff.'

'Did you ask him to take a closer look?' asked Maurice.

Cyril sat back in his armchair, glanced at his wife, and tapped his fingers together. 'Here's the interesting part. Gresham's flat was burgled last summer when he was away on holiday. The only thing that was taken was the trunk.'

Pregnant pause. Maurice's brain worked overtime. 'That's extraordinary. Why . . .? Who . . .?'

'Exactly. Why, and by whom?'

'Did he go to the police?'

'Of course. The police weren't very interested since nothing of any real value had apparently been taken. But they went through the motions, examined the method of entry—a forced flat door—took finger prints, etcetera. And went away again. The school teacher went back to his business and more or less forgot about the incident. But then a couple of months later he had a call from the police. They had arrested a small-time burglar after another job, and found various clues linking him to the trunk theft. The man had admitted it as part of his 'other crimes to be taken into consideration', but couldn't, or wouldn't say what had happened to the stuff.'

'Where is he now?'

'In Pentonville, serving nine months. He had used a young teenage accomplice—the trunk's quite big—but the boy got off with a caution.'

Maurice's mind ticked. 'Have you contacted him?'

'I wrote a letter making a general enquiry, but of course I didn't get any reply. How do you ask a criminal to explain the details of his crime to a stranger?'

'So you got no further?'

'Well, I followed up with a phone call but he refused to take it. Don't know why. And to be honest I'd sort of run out of steam by that time. The obvious explanation was that the man had been hired by someone to pinch the stuff. Someone who was well ahead of me in the game.' He shrugged. 'So I thought, well if there was something significant in the trunk, then by now it must be a well concealed item within a private collection somewhere—quite possibly abroad—and it probably wouldn't come to light for a decade or two. By which time any interest I might have would be well eclipsed by more powerful parties. The thought of traveling to Pentonville to interrogate petty criminals who had no desire to talk to me didn't fill me with much enthusiasm.'

Maurice nodded. 'No, quite.'

'You could do that of course, though I doubt he'd tell you any more than he told the police.'

There was silence in the room. What an odd business this was, thought Maurice. All these people interested in the hypothetical casual jottings of a Victorian housewife, who hadn't even done anything startling on her own accord. Still, at least it had given him a diversion and sent him on an interesting weekend's journey. He drained his tea. 'Well, thank you, it's been most interesting to talk to you,' he said. 'I won't take up any more of your time, but perhaps if you give me the man's name I might find a moment to contact him. One never knows . . .'

'Charles Derwent,' said Cyril, putting down his cup. 'Odd that, isn't it, so close to Darwin's own name? Charley D. the police call him. He's evidently an old customer.'

'Right.' Maurice got up. 'Thank you for tea, Mary. Delicious fruit cake. So nice to meet you both, and to see your lovely house.'

'Nice to meet you too, Maurice,' the wife replied, getting up.

Maurice hesitated. 'Do you know, I think I'd quite like to spend the night in Malvern now I'm here. Explore the town a bit. Is there a nice hotel here, not too expensive?'

'Several,' said Cyril. 'We always recommend The Mount. Bit old fashioned, but very comfortable, and not bad food.'

'The Mount?' said Maurice.

'Yes. Same name as the Darwin family home in Shrewsbury. Did you know that?'

'Yes. Your cousin up there, Celia, told me that. Another coincidence.'

'Life's full of them, as they say.' Cyril rose. 'The hotel gets quite full at the weekends.' He headed for the door. 'I'll phone them now and see if they can take you.'

'Oh, there's no need . . .' began Maurice, but too late. He smiled awkwardly at Mary and hovered as she collected the tea things.

'You've done him good coming to see us,' she said, picking up his plate. 'He always likes discussing Darwin.'

'Ah, good.'

'Are you married, Mr Aldridge? Children?'

Oh dear, thought Maurice, why did the topic always have to raise its head? 'No. I'm a widow. No children.'

'Ah.' She piled things onto the tray. 'We lost our only son some time ago. He was nineteen. A hit and run driver ran into him on his bike.'

'Oh. How awful. I'm sorry.'

'Cyril found his solace in Darwin. I found mine in church.' She smiled at Maurice. 'Men need to find reason, don't they?'

'I suppose so. Don't women?'

'Perhaps we're more philosophical,' she said. 'The driver was drunk. Got off scot-free because our son didn't have the legal lights on his bike. Which of course Cyril blames himself for. It was over ten years ago but it's hard to come to terms with something like that.'

'Yes.' He could not imagine their suffering.

Cyril came back into the room. He raised his eyebrows at the atmosphere.

'I was telling Mr Aldridge about Peter,' she said.

'Why?' he asked crotchily. 'He doesn't want to know things like that.'

'It must have been a dreadful tragedy for you,' murmured Maurice.

'Yes, well tragedy is part of life, isn't it?'

'Yes.'

'I've booked you a room at the Mount.'

'Thank you.'

'Do stay in touch,' his wife said, picking up the laden tray. 'Cyril would love to help with your search if there's anything else he can do.'

'I certainly will. You've both been most kind.' Maurice hesitated, looking at Cyril. 'One last thing. Have you ever heard rumour of a secret postscript to Origin Of Species?'

'Postscript?'

'Written by Darwin. Never published.'

'What sort of postscript?'

'An explanation of his philosophical deductions. An intellectual interpretation, if you like, of the implications of his theory.'

Cyril's eyes narrowed in curiosity. 'Why d'you ask that? Do you know of something?'

'Well, it's just that there are rumours about that also.'

There was a pause, then the other shook his head slowly. 'That's something I haven't heard about.'

'Ah. Well if *you* haven't heard of it, then it's probably apocryphal.'

The man made no movement. 'That would be extraordinary. That would be astonishing.'

'Yes, but. . . .'

'What do you know about it?'

'Very little. As I said, just anecdotal.'

Cyril blew out his cheeks. 'Whew! Never ends, this business, does it? Well, let me know if you find anything about that also. *Please* let me know.'

'I will.' And Maurice went down the steps to his car, aware of the other's eyes on his back all the way.

He stayed at The Mount, another quirky hotel, in an antiques littered room with an uneven wooden floor and a large Empire style bed from which he had a different view of the gorse-strewn hillside at the back. He ate rack of lamb and tarte tartin in the hotel dining room, and once again drank his way through a full bottle of wine whilst listening to two well-heeled couples dining together at the next table. The men talked exclusively together about cars, rugby, and the stock market; the women about shopping, children, and TV soap operas.

What a trivial species we are, thought Maurice, not for the first time, as he drained the last of the wine. How would such people react if he were to get chatting and told them of his quest? With interest? With indifference? With perplexity?

Well there was no danger of it happening. And he longed again through his semi-inebriated haze that he had Alice instead to discuss it with.

CHAPTER TWENTY-THREE

April 2nd 1849. The Lodge, Great Malvern

The whole family has travelled to this exquisite town for an extended stay in order that Charles might try the much vaunted cold-water cure for his ever worsening condition. The cure has supposedly been tested by many, including Royalty and the aristocracy, and has become particularly relied on by the literary set. Apparently such luminaries as Charles Dickens, Thomas Carlyle, Lord Tennyson and Macaulay all proclaim its benefits. It involves a strict diet and much cold water douching and dousing, hot sweating and cold compressing, spring water imbibing and ingesting, 'wet-sheeting' and 'skin-scrubbing', so that there is no corner of the body inside or out that is not thoroughly drowned in nature's fluid. This, together with the taking of vitamins and palliatives, and regular strenuous marching up and down the Malvern Hills in all weathers, is without doubt a revolution to anyone's normal practice. I suspect the phrase 'kill or cure' may have originated here!

C is under the personal supervision of the founder, Dr Gully, a most amiable man, and claims that the treatment is already having a beneficial effect on his constitution. Certainly he seems the better for it after only a month of the process. He came to me yesterday with a broad smile on his face, and said, "Oh, Emma, this place is good for me, no doubt! I feel so much better already."

I replied, "Are you sure that it is not because you are able to forget your work and indulge in such harmless occupations as playing with the children and discussing your maladies with the other patients?" But he waved such flippancies aside and hurried off for another douching. Well, far be it for me to question the worthy doctor's methods.

In any case we are all so pleasantly occupied here. We have rented this charming house, with gardens that open onto the mountainside where the children can roam freely in the bright Spring weather; there are picnics and donkey rides upon the hills; and the town has a constant programme of musical concerts and social gatherings, which altogether is providing the whole family with such a diverting holiday that I consider the expense of Charles's treatment to be money well spent on all our behalves.

It is such a joy to see the six children thriving so well. They are all in their various ways of delicate constitution and we have decided that their education shall be mostly by governess and tutor. But they have the liveliest and most willing of dispositions, and constantly surprise both Charles and myself with their progress in languages and literature, in music and painting, in pianoforte, singing and dancing—all of which instructions we are able to continue here. We are as ever criticised by some of their aunts and uncles for the casual nature of their routine, but we are both so confident that our indulgence is producing happy and fulfilled personalities that we ignore these imprecations.

I am hoping to persuade C to remain here for at least three months, so that his health might have a real chance of profiting. However I know that a part of him frets to return to his barnacles and his book writing. He has the abiding fear of all who have doubts about the afterlife that he will leave this one with no worldly achievement to mark his passing. He may secretly mock at the devout sentiment, which relies on the immortality of the soul and the hope of a life hereafter, but to me that is an infinitely more rewarding philosophy than that our feeble achievements here on earth are the only incentives for our lives.

When I behold the crowds of beggars and ragged urchins who hang about the streets of even such a genteel place as

175

Malvern, I cannot but ponder on the sheer inequality of existence that bedevils our species—to which the only logical redress is that we will all ultimately be equal in the eyes of God and in His eternal kingdom. But when I suggest this to Charles in another of my periodic attempts to challenge his philosophy, he simply shrugs in his disarming way and proclaims, "Oh, Emma, Emma—we are all simply struggling atoms in the gigantic march of progress. We are all at the mercy of the elements and capricious fate. These lofty principles such as the sanctity of the soul, equality and natural justice—desirable though they no doubt may be—are just wishful fantasies of the human imagination."

Can this dispute ever be settled, I wonder? It would truly seem to be a conflict between the innate desires of the sentimental heart and the harsh realism of the intellect. My one doubt is that the issue was supposed to have been resolved by Christ's coming on earth, and yet here we are almost two thousand years later and still it rages. Charles does have that conundrum on his side of the argument. I sometimes agree with him that, when the Lord decided to intervene by sending His son down to earth to save us, He could perhaps have made a more effective job of it. My husband has tried to console me by pointing out on our walks the inconceivable age of the planet's history as revealed by the composition of the rocks on these lovely hills. "Forget the stories of the Old Testament," he said. "Man's generations go back far beyond the tribes of Israel. And in comparison to the age of the earth, two thousand years is but an eye-blink. All prophetic theories and all religious doctrines are but transitory visions in the wider scope of time. They will be superseded just as belief in the ancient gods have been superseded."

At odds with the Bible once again! What am I to do with this infuriating man?

CHAPTER TWENTY-FOUR

*The mere sight of suffering would suffice to call up
in us vivid recollections and associations. With mankind selfishness, experience, and imitation probably
add to the power or sympathy. For we are led by the
hope of receiving good in return to perform acts of
sympathetic kindness to others.*

The Descent of Man

The town of Cheltenham is a mere twenty miles from Malvern across the Severn Vale. A tranquil, unostentatious place
distinguished by some rather splendid Regency architecture,
marred by eruptions of discordant modern corporate and
civic edifices. Its inhabitants represent a typical cross section
of affluent middle class England, who have the air of going
about their business in relative harmony and with little care
about the outside world. In fact, as Maurice knew well, they
suffered the same deviations and disruptions in their lives as
did everyone else.

After his Malvern sojourn he knew he could not delay the
decision to visit any further, and had driven here. He now
found himself in the meandering centre of town, lost his
sense of direction, and stopped at a petrol station to enquire
about the address he had in the back page of his notebook.
Naturally he had never got around to anything as modern as
a satnav. He eventually found the house in a quiet tree-lined
street on the North side of town. Parked the car opposite and
sat for a long time staring at the elegant white painted Regency semi. Now that he was actually there he realised the
folly of coming unannounced. What would the woman think
of this stranger rolling up on the doorstep on a Sunday afternoon? How would she react to meeting the last person

to see her husband alive? Would she not resent having the memories of that awful incident revived after so long? Several times Maurice almost lost courage and drove off again. After perhaps ten minutes he had seen no sign of life, and with the half-hope that no-one was in, he got out, crossed the road and rang the bell.

Thirty seconds passed, then the door opened and the woman he presumed was the wife stood there. He was thrown immediately. She was slim, dark and had the kind of vivacious attractiveness that always made Maurice tongue tied.

'Delia Cornwell?' he asked.

'Yes?' Her expression was curious but not unfriendly. There were strained lines around her eyes, the only blemish on her beauty.

'I. . . . I'm sorry to surprise you like this. My name is Maurice Aldridge. I'm the person who wrote to you some years ago when your husband died.'

The woman stared at him for a moment. 'Oh,' was all she said.

Maurice hesitated. He thought he had worked out what to say, but now couldn't remember what it was. 'I. . . . I was in the area and I thought I'd call in to see if. . . . to meet you and see if you'd recovered from. . . .' He realised what a ridiculous thing it was he was asking, and his nerve failed him. 'I'm sorry. This isn't. . . . I shouldn't have come. I. . . .'

'It's all right,' she said. 'Come in.' She held open the door. Maurice hesitated, then entered. He was in a wide hallway, decorated with William Morris paper and smelling vaguely of musty carpet and furnishings. A girl was coming down the stairs, perhaps fifteen years old.

Delia Cornwell closed the door behind them and said, 'This is my daughter, Clare.'

Maurice held out a hand. 'Hello, Clare. Nice to meet you.'

She shook hands, a limp teenager's shake. 'Hello.'

'Clare, this is Mr. . . .'

'Aldridge.'

'Mr Aldridge. He. . . . he's just called by to say hello.'

Maurice took his hand away for fear she would feel the sweat of his palm. He looked back at the mother, not sure what to do next.

'Come in. Have a cup of tea,' she said. 'Clare, set the table.'

They led the way into the back room, a large kitchen-cum-dining room with tall windows overlooking a leafy back garden. 'Do sit down,' said Delia indicating the oak dining table. She switched off the soap playing on the portable television on the sideboard, and went to the kitchen area. The girl fetched cups and saucers and sat herself at the table opposite Maurice, contemplating him with uncurious eyes.

Maurice was unsure what to do. He had not anticipated having a child—presumably the child—present. He said to her, 'Do you have brothers or sisters?' It was the first thing that came into his head.

'A brother.'

He looked round. 'Is he here?'

'He's at football practice.'

'Ah. How old is he?'

'Twelve.'

He nodded. He hadn't the remotest idea what one said to teenagers. The obvious questions—'Where do you go to school?', 'Have you lots of friends there?', 'Have you got a boy-friend?'—all seemed so banal.

It was she who saved him. 'Where do you live?' The question was direct, totally innocent.

'London.'

'Why are you in Cheltenham?'

'I, er. . . . I'm an antiquarian book dealer. Do you know what that is?' She nodded.   Well that was something. 'I'm here visiting some book-seller friends of mine who might have some old books that would interest me.'

'On a Sunday?' she asked. She had an appealing directness.

'Well, yes. It's only at weekends that I can get about the country, and we book people do business at any time of the week.' He turned the conversation from himself. 'Do you read books much? Your generation likes computer games and such, don't you?'

She pulled a face. 'My brother does. Not me. I read a lot actually.'

'Oh. Good.'

'I've got a Kindle.'

Another gadget to add to all the rest that were slowly killing off his kind. 'Those are brilliant,' he said. 'Make getting books very easy, don't they?'

'Yes.'

'Do you have a favourite book?'

'Middlemarch.'

'Goodness. That's an ambitious one.' He couldn't remember whether he read such things at her age. Was he completely out of touch with the maturity of modern youth? He glanced back at her mother, who was pouring water into a teapot with a slight smile on her lips.

'I like it that there are so many different stories. All connected.'

'Yes. Very difficult for writers to do that.'

'And I like reading about a different time.'

He relaxed a little. 'Shall I tell you something interesting?' he said. 'Many more women buy historical novels than men do. Why do you suppose that is?'

The girl tilted her head. 'I don't know. Perhaps they like the old world better than the new one.'

'Do you?'

She shrugged. 'I like them both.'

'That's good then.'

She asked, 'How old are the books you sell?'

'Well, they go from only a few years old, right back to the middle ages. But of course those are very rare and very valuable.'

'Like the Domesday Book?'

'Ah—well if I had an original copy of that I'd be very rich.'

'How many books have you got?'

Maurice pondered. 'Do you know, I haven't the faintest idea. Several thousand.'

'Have you read them all?'

He laughed. 'No, I haven't. But I'll tell you this. If I could live for ever I'd have a good try at doing so.'

She smiled brightly. 'Yes, that would be good. You could read all the books that had ever been written then, couldn't you?'

'Yes. The only trouble is, people would be writing new ones faster than one could read them.'

'Well, I suppose you'd just have to learn to speed read.'

Her mother came over with the tea tray. She poured tea for all three of them, passed around the biscuits, and sat down. 'Books,' she said. 'That's a noble profession.'

'Sometimes,' said Maurice. 'Sometimes quite ignoble.'

The girl dunked the rest her biscuit in her tea and took a bite. 'That's not very polite in front of guests,' admonished her mother mildly. The girl wrinkled her nose at her and rose, having evidently lost interest in the encounter. 'Can I watch telly in my room, Mum?' she said.

'As long as it's not gangsters or pornography,' she answered. Her daughter grinned back, said a cheerful 'Bye' to Maurice and went briskly upstairs.

'Bright girl,' said Maurice.

Delia nodded. 'She can be a monster like most teenagers. But on the whole not bad.'

Silence for a moment. Maurice could not look into the dark eyes for long. 'I'm sorry to surprise you like this,' he said, staring into his tea cup. 'I've been meaning to. . . . I mean, I should have come a long time ago. There must have been things. . . . you must have wanted to know more about what happened. . . . but I was in a bit of a state myself at the time, and I couldn't. . . . I wasn't able to. . . .'

'It's all right,' said Delia. 'I can understand. It must have been a horrific experience.' Her voice was low, with the slightest hint of a lilt. Welsh perhaps?

'My own wife was very ill at the time, you see, and so. . . .'

'I'm sorry. Is she better?'

'No. She died three years ago. Cancer.'

'I'm so sorry.'

'It's taken me a while to recover, but I've often thought about you and what a shock it must have been. I always felt I hadn't done enough, and so when I found myself in this part of the world I thought I ought to try and see you. I'm not sure what I can tell you. It's probably too late after all this time to be of any use, but I just. . . .' Maurice tailed off.

She nodded and stirred her tea. 'You were actually with Tom when he died?'

'Yes. I wasn't on the bus. I was on another one nearby, and. . . . Well there was chaos in the street after the explosion, and some of us tried to help, but there wasn't much we could do until the ambulances came.'

'But you found him?'

'I. . . .' How to describe it? 'He was lying on the pavement. I think he'd been pulled from the bus. He wasn't in pain, but he was. . . . he was in a pretty bad way. I just sat with him until the medics arrived.'

'They said his legs were badly injured.'

No need to give the details. 'It was hard to tell, but he lost a lot of blood. I think perhaps that and the shock. . . . It was quite a long time before help came, you see, and I didn't know what I could do to help, except. . . . except. . . .'

'It's all right. You did what you could. And he wasn't alone when he died, that's important.' Maurice nodded and was silent. 'And he talked to you.'

Maurice looked up. 'He didn't say much. He was barely conscious, he was peaceful. But he was very anxious that you got the message.'

The woman nodded and looked at him with sad eyes, forcing him to stare again into his cup. 'I expect you wondered what it meant.'

'Well, I. . . . I didn't think too much about it. I suppose we all have things we'd want to say if we. . . .'

'But he wanted to say he was sorry?'

'Yes. Just that. And to look after Clare.'

She nodded slowly, all the while gazing at Maurice. 'I wonder which is worse—to lose someone slowly over a long period as you did, or to lose them suddenly and not say goodbye.'

Maurice had no answer. 'It must have been hard for your children too,' he said.

She nodded. 'Especially for my son. He was only six at the time.' She turned her head and gazed out of the window. 'His sadness is sometimes unbearable to see.'

Maurice understood that all too well, but again said nothing.

Delia glanced towards the stairs and went on. 'We were happy together. I was blessed with a good man. However we had our crises as most people do.' Maurice nodded and waited. Her eyes came back to him. 'I ought to tell you what his words meant.'

He gestured in an embarrassed way. 'No, no—it's none of my business. I don't. . . .'

'Our crisis was that I got pregnant by another man. Quite early on in the marriage.' She spoke more softly. 'Clare isn't Tom's true daughter, you see.'

'Ah.' He didn't know how to react.

'Although he accepted her and loved her as if she was. But as you can imagine it made things very difficult for a while.'

'Yes,' said Maurice.

'The reason he wanted to say sorry was because he always felt that he hadn't accepted her, that he hadn't loved her enough. But it wasn't true. He was a wonderful father.' She bit her lip and her eyes were glistening. 'And he felt also that he was never able to forgive me properly. But that wasn't true either. He forgave me as much as it was humanly possible to do.'

Maurice took off his specs and cleaned them.

She took a deep breath and glanced back at the stairs. 'She doesn't know. I hope she never knows.' She turned her head again to Maurice with a wry expression. 'In fact now you are the only other person who does know.'

Maurice blinked awkwardly and put his specs back on.

She asked, 'Do you have children?'

'No.'

She didn't comment. 'I'm a family solicitor. I'm never sure whether it's harder dealing with other people's problems, or you own.' Maurice half smiled and nodded. 'The sad thing was that we seemed to have worked through most of ours when. . . . We seemed to have entered a really good period in our lives. Life isn't fair, is it?'

'No.'

She pursed her lips. 'Jihad. A strange concept. I will never understand the ways of religious fanaticism. Seems to be counter to everything life should be about.'

'Yes.' '*Oh senseless man, who cannot possibly make a worm, and yet will make Gods by dozens.*'

She threw him a brief smile. 'Well, at least with books you can stay detached. All those lives on the pages don't directly affect you.'

Maurice reflected for a moment. 'Not always true,' he replied. 'In fact I'm on the trail of a book at the moment which has. . . . might have a bearing on all that kind of thing.'

'What kind of book?'

'It's about Darwin. Darwinism.'

'Ah.' She frowned. 'How does that have a bearing?'

'Not directly. But it explains the irrationality of existence.'

'I see.' Pause. 'Have you found someone else?'

'No.'

'Me neither. I've been out with a few men. Old clients, divorcees. . . . the usual. But it's hard to start again after so many years.'

'Yes.'

She took another breath. 'Well anyway. . . . thank you for coming. I'm glad you did.' A hesitation. 'It must have been an ordeal for you.'

Maurice blinked. 'No, as I said, I've been meaning to come for a while, and . . .'

'No, not now. I meant then. Being with him all that time. Sitting with him until he. . . .'

Maurice thought back to that moment. And then to the other moment three years later, when he sat beside Alice. That put the first into perspective in a way that nothing else could have done. In whatever guise it came, death was always non-negotiable. The only thing that signified was how you dealt with it. '*I had seen birth and death, but had thought they were different.*' He said, 'I'm glad I was there. I wasn't glad at the time, but afterwards. I'm glad someone could be there.'

There was silence in the room. Alice murmured in his ear, 'Now's your chance, boyo. This one's a possibility. She's your style. Do something.'

'For Christ's sake, Alice!' he silently retorted. 'Stop interfering!' To the woman he said, 'I ought to be on my way. I'm sorry it took so long, but I'm glad I saw you.'

She smiled. 'So am I. Thank you.'

He rose from his chair and hesitated, wondering how to take his leave. As always he was waiting for someone else to take the initiative. Alice was thankfully mute. 'Well, thank you for tea,' he said. 'And say goodbye to your daughter for me.'

She had risen too and stood, still smiling. 'I will. Come and visit us if you're ever in these parts again.'

'Yes. Yes I will.'

But he knew he probably wouldn't.

He left her waving on the doorstep, and drove back to London at a sedate pace even for him.

CHAPTER TWENTY-FIVE

November 25th 1951. Wakefield.

One of the inmates accosted me in the exercise yard yesterday. He was a long term prisoner who was in for robbery with violence and murder, a detail which he had already informed me quite openly and without any indications of remorse. I was slightly apprehensive at his approach, but then he said, "Doc, I want you to explain Einstein's Theory of Relativity to me."

I was naturally taken aback, and when I asked him why he wanted to know, he replied, "I find it fascinating—know what I mean? All that stuff about time and space not being fixed. Varying according to the conditions of the observer."

Extraordinary! A man whom hitherto I had assumed could only speak in the primitive jargon of base society, here talking in sophisticated scientific terms. He had evidently grasped the fundamentals of the subject, so I regaled him with Einstein's own illustration, which in its way has never been bettered. It will fill the time to record it here:-

Take someone in a train travelling at fifty miles an hour. If he throws a tennis ball forwards down the carriage also at fifty miles an hour, the tennis ball, relative to himself, will only be travelling at fifty miles an hour. However, <u>relative to someone standing on the embankment</u>, the ball will be travelling at one hundred miles an hour—the speed of the train combined with the speed of the ball. If he throws it backwards, the person on the embankment will see the ball as staying in the same place. The speed of the train cancels out the speed of the ball.

But now comes the extraordinary thing—if the person on the train shines a torch forwards or backwards, the results are quite different. Why? Because light is in effect the essence of all energy, and so nothing can travel faster than light. Light always travels at its same fundamental speed (186,000 miles per second) whatever the speed of its source. It is not even affected by the speed the Earth is spinning. The projected torchlight therefore is not affected by the speed of the train— it still travels at its own precise velocity. And the crucial thing is that both the man in the train and the man on the bank, if they could measure it, would see the light going at that same speed. The speed of the train cannot be added or deducted because energy sets its own speed.

This affects the relationship between the two observers in extraordinary ways. As far as the tennis ball is concerned it takes the same <u>time</u> to travel down the carriage for the fellow on the embankment as for the fellow on the train, but goes a different distance at a different speed 'relative' to each of them. But speed is a ratio of distance and time: miles per hour, feet per second. If therefore you make the relative speed of the projected object the <u>same</u> for both of them, as with light—then plain arithmetic tells you that the <u>time</u> has to vary for each—relatively.

To us, so used to living by the apparently precise clock, this is an astonishing thing. Everyone and every thing in fact carries their own personal time around with them, even though superficially the times all appear the same. Even the clock itself does. A clock on top of a mountain will actually run minutely faster than one in the valley (which has indeed been proved). And, paradoxically, a twin who goes off on a long space journey will come back considerably younger than his twin who stayed on Earth. In his case the speed of his journey has slowed down his relative time. And the faster he goes, the slower goes his time. If his space-ship was able to travel at the speed of light itself, then his time would stop completely. He would have achieved eternal life.

Which a particle of energy has.

To my surprise my questioner appeared to understand and accept this explanation without hesitation. He had been nodding sagely throughout my explanation, and after it he said, 'Well, just goes to show doesn't it, Doc—nothing is really as it seems.' And he went cheerfully off to his cell, either to dwell further on the matter or to plan his next nefarious deed. I wondered whether, in different circumstances, this amateur scientist might have had the capacity to break another man's bones with an iron bar.

The incident left me to reflect that indeed nothing is as it seems. The more we discover, the more there is to discover. The greater the truths we unravel, the greater the truths which lie behind them. I suppose we will never arrive at the ultimate truth. We have only begun to sniff at the extraordinary conditions of the universe and the forces which govern it. And no doubt we will perish as a species long before we get anywhere near that ultimate answer, just as the prehistorics of the Jurassic and other ages perished.

As I said to Gordon Hawkins later that evening when I told him of the encounter, it put things into perspective. The present trials and struggles are insignificant in the grand scheme of things. The millions of Jews who died at Hitler's hands may represent one of the greatest atrocities of our time, but in the relative period of the earth's history they are but another small blip on the chart.

Gordon agreed and said, "Yes—their numbers must be added to the legions who perished before them, mere termites on the face of the earth. One can only look to one's own individual fate, make one's small contribution to the whole gigantic enterprise and hope that in some way it has an effect."

Precisely. Or perhaps it is simply as Shakespeare put it—'life is a tale told by an idiot, full of sound and fury, signifying nothing.'

CHAPTER TWENTY-SIX

Ignorance more frequently begets confidence than does knowledge: it is those who know little, and not those who know much, who so positively assert that this or that problem will never be solved by science.
The Descent of Man

As arranged, Roger Hemingway arrived to begin work at the bookshop at precisely nine o'clock on the Monday morning. He wore a white shirt and new business suit, his hair had been trimmed and brushed back, and he had quite an air of educated respectability. Maurice felt reassured. He was presented with two letters of recommendation, but his mind was already made up and onto other things, and he skimmed their positive endorsements briefly before photocopying them for the files.

Hemingway was taken through the routines and processes of the business, saying little except to seek clarification of the occasional detail, whilst making notes in a small notebook he had brought with him. Then, as he was shown the layout and system of the bookshelves themselves, he took more notes whilst emitting appreciative murmurs and occasionally picking out a volume for appraisal. By the end of the morning he was conversant with most of the necessary functions.

Come lunchtime Maurice was mightily relieved that he seemed to have found an assistant who at least showed signs of competence, although it would be some time yet before he could entrust him with sole care of the shop. He therefore sent him out for a lunch break, after getting him first to fetch in a lunch-bar sandwich for himself. Lunchtime was habitually quite a busy period, since the shop was often attended by a number of local workers browsing away their own lunch hours. Maurice knew from long experience that few of them were there to buy, and his main duty was simply to be present and keep a beady eye on the door, since regrettably this was the worst time of day for pilfering. Long gone were the days when one could confidently retreat to the back office, leaving the shop unattended until someone called for assistance.

He passed the time scanning Donald Easterby's lengthy compiled list of Darwin descendants for any of the names he had encountered so far. But without result. Then he sent a further email report to Easterby describing his visits to Shrewsbury and Malvern and his various meetings. He asked whether Easterby had come across either Cyril Catcheside or the teacher Robert Gresham in his previous enquiries, even though they weren't on the list. Added a question as to whether the American thought there might be anything to be gained from contacting the Pentonville prisoner. He did not however mention his earlier side visit to his Oxford dealer colleague and the obscure dead-ended clue there. Too nebulous at the moment.

When Hemingway returned from lunch, punctiliously on the hour, Maurice retired to his office and left his new assistant to man the desk. He kept his door open and listened to the other handling a couple of book sales with adequate competence, then relaxed enough to spend time updating the accounts. They did not reassure him. Whilst buried in the uninspiring figures the phone rang. It was Felicity.

'Hello, sweetheart,' said the unmistakable voice. 'Got home safely from your expedition, did you?'

'Yes, thanks, Felicity. And I apologise again for my emotional behavior.'

'Don't worry, darling. We all have our ups and downs. But I thought I ought to tell you—shortly after you left I had a visit.'

'Oh.'

'About twenty minutes later a man knocked on the door, and I rather unwisely let him in. Big ugly brute. Wanted to know why you'd come to see me.'

Maurice frowned. 'How did he know?'

'No idea. But he was rather adamant that I told him the reason. I was about to tell him to piss off and mind his own bloody business, but he started playing casually with one of my carving knives and I thought better of it.'

'Oh my God, Felicity!'

'Don't worry, he didn't actually do anything nasty. But I felt he was definitely capable of it, so I'm afraid I told him. I convinced him I knew very little about the details, but I did say you were after some original Darwin manuscript. I'm very sorry.'

'Did he leave then?'

'Yes. Just smiled nastily, told me not to mention his visit, stuck the knife in my kitchen table and walked out. All very melodramatic. I thought you ought to know.'

'Oh Felicity, I'm so sorry. It must have been terrifying.'

'Well, I wasn't too scared at the time, but I did need a strong cup of tea after he'd gone. And a stronger glass of something else after that. Where do you think he came from?'

'I haven't the faintest idea.'

'Well it seems you aren't the only one on the trail of valuable papers, so you ought to be a bit careful, sweetheart.'

'Yes. Yes, thank you for telling me.'

Maurice put the phone down with an unpleasant mixture of thoughts swirling about his brain. He sat for a while, then went through to the shop. 'Do you know anything about prisons, Roger?' he asked.

Hemingway looked taken aback for a moment and glanced behind him as though expecting a bevy of coppers to jump from behind the shelves.

'I mean, do you know the procedures for visiting people in prison? Have you ever visited anyone there?'

'Er . . . no. 'Fraid not,' replied the other. The smile shone like a beacon. 'Not my sort of place really.'

'No, of course not.'

'Why d'you ask?'

Maurice hesitated. 'Well. . . . it's just that I was thinking of going to visit someone there and I wasn't sure how one goes about it.'

Hemingway's smile broadened further. 'Oh, yes? Who's that? No-one in the family, I hope.'

Maurice smiled tolerantly. 'It's someone I've never met. But someone I need to talk to. I'm trying to track down a book.'

Hemingway's myopic gaze was curious. 'Oh? Something valuable?'

'Could be.'

'Something stolen, is it?'

Maurice felt awkward. He had said too much. 'Something like that.'

Hemingway grinned again. 'Have you got a dodgy customer then?'

Maurice bridled slightly. 'Well no, the customer isn't dodgy, but the item he's after might well have travelled a dodgy route. And a few other dodgy people seem to be after it.'

'Oh, right. Well no-one's likely to tell you much in prison, are they?'

Maurice nodded. 'No, you're probably right.'

Hemingway glanced towards the book shelves and scratched his ear. 'I could, er . . .' He hesitated, then said in a helpful tone, 'I could make some enquiries for you if you like.'

Maurice nodded gratefully. 'Oh, well . . . anything that might be of help would be welcome.'

'Yes, right. I'll see what I can find out.' And they both returned to their respective tasks.

Just before closing time that day Maurice checked his emails again, and found a reply from Donald Easterby:-

'Well done, Maurice, you're working fast. Yes, the guy in prison may well be worth a visit. But he must have been commissioned, so first of all you should talk to the Robert Gresham whose stuff was stolen. (I never came across him or the Cyril Catcheside guy in my researches by the way.) He may tell you who else knew he had the trunk. In which case you may then have some names to fire at the jail bird. See if any of them strike a response. Good hunting. Donald.'

Yes, of course, thought Maurice, should have thought of that. He began tidying up his desk prior to closing. As he did so he was vaguely aware that Hemingway was dealing with a late customer. Maurice glanced through the doorway and saw what looked like a youngish university graduate at the desk. He had a faintly arrogant manner and was enquiring as to whether they had an early edition of Stephen Hawking's *A Brief History Of Time*. Maurice listened to the exchange.

'A brief what?' replied Hemingway.

'History Of Time. It was first published back in the eighties.'

'Oh well, before my time,' said the new assistant jokingly.

'Well, you must have heard of it. It's probably the biggest ever scientific best-seller.'

Hemingway appeared to bridle slightly. 'Did you look in the science section?'

'Of course, but I can't see a copy there. I'd be surprised though if you didn't have it somewhere.'

'Well if it isn't there we can't have, can we?'

'I just thought it might be somewhere else. Under another heading perhaps.'

'Well, have you looked in the history section?'

The other cast a slightly supercilious look. 'Hardly likely, is it?'

'Why not? If it's called a brief history, that's where it should be, isn't it?'

'It's a science book, chum, not a history book.'

Hemingway had his back to Maurice but it was evident his manner had changed. His voice was suddenly lower. 'Listen, 'chum', don't patronise me. If I tell you we haven't got it, then we haven't got it, have we?'

The other looked taken aback, then bridled himself. 'But you haven't even looked to see if you've got it! All I'm asking is for a bit of assistance. That's what you're here for, isn't it?'

Hemingway was silent for three seconds. Then he moved around the counter. 'What I'm not here for is to take aggro from people who get in my face! You want to be very careful what you say, know what I mean?'

Maurice was out of his office in a trice as the customer backed away. 'Is something the matter here?'

Hemingway instantly recovered his composure and stopped advancing. 'Sorry, boss. This. . . . person here was getting a bit insulting and I'm afraid I lost my temper.'

'It wasn't *me* who was insulting,' said the young man, his face flushed. 'I was merely wanting to find a book, which I presumed was what your establishment was here for. Sorry if I've made a mistake.'

Maurice stepped in front of his assistant, his hands raised in placation. 'My apologies, we're a bit pressurised at the moment.' He took off his spectacles. 'I'm afraid we haven't got the book you're wanting. Probably best to go to Foyle's up the road.'

'You want to teach your staff some manners.' The man glowered at Hemingway, then turned and left the shop without another word. Maurice whirled on his employee with a surge of anger. 'You don't speak to customers like that! What do you think you're doing?'

Hemingway looked at the floor abashed. 'I'm sorry, Mr Aldridge. He just got my goat, that's all. Pulling his superior education.'

'It doesn't matter what his education was. Eton or Borstal, he's after a book and he must be treated like everyone else!'

The other's expression was full of contrition. 'Sorry. My fault. It won't happen again.'

His eyes blinked as if he was about to cry. He looked so repentant that Maurice softened and spoke more gently. 'It had better not, Roger. Otherwise this employment won't last very long.'

'No. Quite. Absolutely.'

They both returned to their respective posts. Maurice opened his desk drawer and took a good swig of scotch, well aware that solved nothing.

He closed the shop a short while later with some relief, and went home with his mind on other matters.

CHAPTER TWENTY-SEVEN

November 10th, 1849. Down House

This barnacle business is really getting out of hand! Charles is occupied with the wretched things night and day. Parcels of them arrive weekly from all corners of the world—from America, from Australia, from Europe, even from the Arctic! The entire house reeks of their malodorous presence, and C's trays and jars and slimy dissections are spreading out beyond his study to various parts of our living quarters. One would have thought that such primitive organs had little importance in the scheme of things, but Charles and his colleagues consider them to be greatly indicative of the methods nature uses to progress the species. Barnacles apparently have been around since the time of the dinosaurs, and are living examples of how the earliest mutations of organisms occurred. C has tried to show me through the microscope how one such mite actually divides into male and female with highly developed sex organs (he has no inhibitions about discussing such matters, although it makes me blush at times), and how their anatomy contains the elemental constituents which eventually evolved into crabs and lobsters and suchlike. All I can recognise is a very ordinary sea creature, which doubtless has its place in the natural order, but C is greatly enthused by his findings. He is constantly firing off letters and dissertations to his contributors, including of course Joseph Hooker, who is at this time on an exploratory expedition of his own in the Himalayas (though how he is supposed to help furthering the study of barnacles from there is beyond me).

At any rate Charles's preoccupation does seem to be keeping him energised, and thanks to his refusing to undertake any further journeys for meetings of the Royal Institution, the Royal Society, the Royal Geographical Society, and all the other Royal fraternities he belongs to, as well as to his continuation of the various water treatments learned at Malvern (he has gone so far as to construct a special 'douche house' in the garden, where he alternately sweats and freezes under the auspices of our patient Parslow), his health this winter is considerably improved.

Not so the rest of the family though. First Annie, followed by her sister Etty, and then the baby Lizzy have come down with scarlet fever, which affects them all distressingly. Annie in particular is not strong in her constitution, and though ever willing and thoughtful of others, struggles sometimes I know to keep up her spirits and maintain the pace of activity of her siblings. I do worry about her. In fact I fret about the family's health in general. There seems to be no pattern to the wellbeing of humanity. An ill-fed peasant, out in all weathers and living in a damp unhygienic hovel, can be fit as a flea, and yet a fortunate well provisioned family such as ours can be subject to all measure of afflictions.

I actually had the courage to ask C recently how that squared with his theories of survival of the fittest. He merely shrugged and said, "Chance, chance—all is chance." Then he added, "However it is a crucial fact that production of an apparent excess of offspring is one method by which the different species protect their future."

That makes sense. I myself am with child once again.

CHAPTER TWENTY-EIGHT

*Man scans with scrupulous care the character and
pedigree of his horses, cattle, and dogs before he
matches them; but when he comes to his own marriage he rarely, or never, takes any such care. He is
impelled by nearly the same motives as the lower
animals.*

The Descent of Man

Cyril Catcheside, on the phone from Malvern, was more
relaxed and forthcoming than previously. He and his wife
had evidently discussed Maurice's visit and decided that
the book dealer was a good egg. He was happy to provide
Maurice with the private telephone number of the Robert
Gresham whose trunk had been stolen. Catcheside added
that the man's teaching post was that of A Level History and
English at a comprehensive school in Chiswick. 'Good luck
with him,' said Catcheside over the phone. 'And remember
to let me know what happens. That's your payment for tea
and fruit cake.'

When Maurice rang the number on the Tuesday evening
he caught a rather worn sounding Gresham just finishing his
supper in front of the TV.

'I'm sorry,' said Maurice. 'Cyril Catcheside gave me your
number. Is this a bad time?'

'No,' replied Gresham. 'We're watching my girl friend's
favourite murder series. The body count must be in the dozens. If I miss another one or two it will hardly matter.'

'Ah, yes,' replied Maurice, trying to remember what Alice's favourite drama series was. Period no doubt, but she
did like the detective things too. 'Well, I'm an antiquarian
book dealer, and like Cyril I'm on the trail of mementos of
the Darwin family.'

'Ah yes, well—I can't be of any more help than I've given him, I'm afraid. Anything I might have had was stolen and there doesn't seem much likelihood of getting it back.'

Maurice this time had prepared what he was going to say. 'No, I understand that. But I was wondering if I might come to see you for a brief visit. I know it's a bit of an imposition, but this business is quite important, and it just might be that we can unearth some further clues over a chat.'

'Well, if you really think so. I'm pretty busy—it's coming up to mock exam time—but I could see you one lunch hour perhaps. Always glad of an excuse to get out of school.'

'That would be ideal. I'll come to you—tomorrow, or whenever suits.'

'The day after would be better. Say twelve thirty, outside my school gates? We can go to a pub on the river.'

'Perfect.' Maurice took down directions and replaced the receiver with relief that this step had so far been easy. Also with a small spark of anticipation. He had begun the hunt with some ambivalence, but now it was beginning to get into his bloodstream. He polished his specs reflectively. He was alternating his reading of the Fuchs record with explorations of Darwin's life through as many books as he could lay his hands on. He was intrigued by the latter's mentality. What a voracious curiosity! What an eclectic interest. What an infinite capacity for painstaking labour and investigation. *'What a piece of work is man. How noble in reason'*. Yes, if all humankind possessed the same attributes, how much better a place the world would be. He put his specs back on. Of course that was what evolution was about. Progress through individuality. Emergence of the superior being.

He noted the appointment with the school teacher in his desk diary.

It was with only minor trepidation that he decided to take a gamble and leave Hemingway in charge of the shop over the lunch period that Thursday. The young man had proved efficient since he started, and there were no further untoward incidents with customers. Maurice left him with various instructions and a list of what to say to a few potential clients whose calls might be expected, and with a strict admonition to keep his temper under control whatever the provocation. Hemingway was suitably humble, with the charm back at full throttle. Maurice locked the office where he kept his files and more valuable stock, and checked the till to see there was sufficient small change in it. Then left his new assistant to it.

He met Gresham as arranged at the gates of the school, which was the usual vast compilation of undistinguished architecture, surrounded by concrete and ringing with youthful shouts. Gresham himself was a tousled cynic in his late thirties whose intelligent demeanour and athletic physique spoke of youthful aspirations now somewhat diluted. They walked the few hundred yards to the river, and ordered lagers and ploughmans at the bar of the Bell and Crown.

It was warm enough to go out onto the pub's terrace overlooking the Thames, and for a moment they both sat silently with their beers, watching the smooth running waters, the rowers sweating up and down the river, the gently waving trees on the far bank. There are worse places than London, thought Maurice. Not quite the peace of Malvern (or Innisfree for that matter), but he'd settle for his final days contemplating a view like that. Trouble was one would need a king's ransom just to get a broom cupboard on the river now. His reverie was interrupted by a blast of sound from the bar, where the pub's television was switched to some sporting event. And an extra half million not to be near a pub, he thought.

'How do you enjoy teaching?' he asked by way of making conversation.

The other gave a dry snort. 'Enjoy is hardly the word.' He continued gazing out across the river. 'I don't know quite what's gone wrong with education. I used to think growing up was about challenge, and learning self discipline, and seeking ideals. Those are all concepts that seem to have vanished from the educational vocabulary.'

'Ah, yes, well . . .' said Maurice in sympathy. '*I have never let my schooling interfere with my education.*'

'Perhaps I'm just jaded, but I do seem to remember that lip service at least was paid to such matters when I was at school.'

Maurice thought back to his own school days at York. Pretty conventional curriculum but demanding in a rigid sort of way and, yes, disciplined and morally driven, despite what Mark Twain felt.

Gresham turned his head. 'So, what was it you people were hoping to find amongst this stuff?'

Maurice shrugged. 'I gather you're descended from the Allen family?'

'Yes. But a long way back. One of the Allens married a Gresham. Hence my name.'

'Didn't marry a Darwin or a Wedgewood then. Must be one of the few.'

The other laughed. 'Quite enough of that incestuous stuff without my lot joining in.'

Maurice got straight to the point. 'But it's true that one of your forebears may have inherited some Darwin memorabilia?'

Gresham waved a dismissive hand. 'There's no evidence of anything important. I told your friend in Shropshire that.'

'Yes, but. . . . there seems to be quite a lot of evidence that there *are* still some undiscovered Darwin relics. Papers, diaries, that sort of thing.'

'So. . . .?'

'Well nobody knows for sure, and there may not be anything at all amongst the things you lost, but we're following up every avenue.'

'Do you represent a museum or an institution of some sort?'

Maurice was glad his career hadn't taken that path. He was not an institutional man. 'No. Just an influential private collector. He has an interest in all matters to do with evolutionary science.'

'Hm, well . . . I wish he could find some way to speed up the process. We're in grave need of it on this little planet.'

Maurice made no comment and sipped his lager. 'Have you no idea what was in the trunk?'

Gresham shook his head. 'I'm sorry I never looked more closely. My wife . . . my then wife was always on at me to do so. But it was quite a big thing, and full of several generations of family flotsam. Photos, letters . . . mostly pretty uninteresting.' An expression of disdain crossed his face. 'The last time I had a look was when we moved house about two years ago. I rifled through it when it came up from the cellar.' He shook his head. 'It did cross my mind that someone ought to sort through it all properly but quite frankly it was too daunting a task, especially in the middle of a move.'

Maurice nodded. 'I know what moving house is like.' He and Alice had lived for over twenty years in their cottage in Surrey, and when they finally moved out the stress of the whole business took them by surprise. 'Didn't you notice any books or leather bound volumes amongst the contents though?' he asked.

Gresham shrugged. 'Well. . . . there were a number of things like that. Mostly just ancient photo albums, family accounts ledgers, children's workbooks, that sort of thing—but I simply didn't have the energy to go through it all, much to my wife's annoyance.' He pulled a rueful face. 'She had a tenuous connection with the Allens herself, and she used to say there could have been something of value there.' With irony, 'It seems she may have been right.'

'Your wife had an Allen connection?' said Maurice, surprised.

'Yes. Coincidental. One of her distant ancestors married an Allen. It was a talking point that gave us a connection. Helped a little in my pursuit of her, I suppose. She was a bit out of my league.'

Was the whole world connected to this family tree, thought Maurice? The pub waitress came out with their ploughmans lunches. As they broke bread and delved into the cheese there came another noise assault from the television inside, this time the strident tones of a commercial. Gresham frowned. 'Why do the commercials always seem to bump up the volume? Counter productive, I'd have thought.'

'Most commercials are counter productive,' said Maurice. 'Or at least mutually counteracting. All they do is double the cost of most that we buy.'

Gresham chuckled sourly. 'You're right.' His tone lightened. 'I was at a dinner party the other night. There was an advertising executive there with his wife. One of those smart-alec types who think they run the world. I made the mistake of asking him whether he really thought that periodic barrage of banal chunter and musak was really fruitful.'

'What did he say?'

'He tried to explain to me that it didn't matter what the conscious effect was, it only mattered that subconsciously the brand names were being impressed on the brain.' He snorted. 'That got my goat, and I said that to people of any brain at all they were being impressed as brand names to be avoided. At which he laughed condescendingly and shot his designer label cuffs!' Maurice laughed. 'So I then rattled off a list of products I'd sworn never to buy under any circumstances because of their fatuous, repetitive advertising campaigns, and before long the whole table was playing the game of which brand name was to be most avoided. He didn't talk to me for the rest of the evening.'

Ah, thought Maurice, a man after my own heart.

'So anyway, why did you want to talk to me personally?'

Maurice cleaned his specs on the end of his tie. 'Well,' he replied cautiously, 'your burglary was obviously commissioned. It was too specifically targeted to have been otherwise. And whoever commissioned it must have had some idea as to what was in the trunk. So we were thinking. . . . wondering if you could remember all the people—relatives, family friends—who might have known about its contents.'

'Are you suggesting our family circle consists of crooks and swindlers?' The man's tone was drily amused.

'Of course not,' said Maurice hastily. 'It's just that someone may have mentioned it inadvertently to some outsider who saw their chance.' He replaced his specs and gazed at the other over the top. 'Some collectors will go to extraordinary lengths, you know, to get hold of things that interest them.'

'Really? I suppose they will. I hadn't thought about it.'

Maurice ventured, 'If your wife was interested, she's the obvious suspect. She wouldn't have had anything to do with it?'

Gresham looked mildly irritated. 'Lord, no. She's a highly moral person.'

'I'm sorry, I didn't mean. . . .'

'We had our differences, but she's not the sort to do anything like that.' Gresham reflected a moment. 'I suppose she might have told someone. She could have. . . .' He broke off, and made a small startled move. 'Good lord. . . .'

'What?'

'It's just occurred to me.' He stared across the river, a hunk of bread in his hand and an expression of intense conjecture on his face. A rowing eight passed by, the splashes of the oars and the cox's exhortations clearly audible. Maurice waited. 'I wonder . . . Yes. D'you know, I think I've guessed what may have happened.'

'What's that?'

'I think it may have been. . . . not my wife. . . . but her bloody husband. Good God! Why didn't I think of it before?'

The rowing cox's voice dwindled as the boat glided on. Gresham sat in thought until it could be heard no longer, then he continued. 'We bust up a couple of years ago, you see. That's in fact why we were moving house. We sold it and took half each. I bought a flat, and she . . . well she moved in with another man, who is now her husband.' He pulled a bitter face. 'He's quite flash. Works in the City. Gave her a nice house, car of her own, dinners out two or three times a week. All the things I couldn't give her—not on a teacher's salary. It was just one of the things that broke us up.' He glanced at Maurice. 'She's the daughter of an earl, you see. Used to better things. It was why she kept on at me about the trunk.'

'She knew what might be in it?' asked Maurice.

'Not specifically. But she was more interested in the Darwin link than I was. In fact she was quite intrigued by the whole business.' He sniffed. 'I suppose the aristocracy concern themselves more with hereditary matters.'

'But you said she had a connection with the Allens?'

'Only by marriage. An Allen married into the powerful Cecil family in Victorian times. Became the wife of Lord Salisbury in fact, the Prime Minister. And my wife's family is related to the Cecils.' He raised an eyebrow. 'They're all interbred in one way or another—the so-called nobility. Anyway she was convinced there was something of value there. There were whole bundles of letters from that period which she delved into when she had time. But she couldn't understand me for not looking into the whole thing properly.' Gresham took a big bite of bread and cheese as if suddenly needing sustenance while he thought. Then, through a full mouth, 'Yes, I'm sure that's it! I remember her new husband showed quite a bit of interest too when he heard the story. I didn't think much about it then, but I heard recently that he'd got himself into a bit of financial bother.'

'So . . .?'

'So on thinking about it, I wouldn't be at all surprised if they're the ones who hired the thief. Or rather, *he's* the one. He'd have done it off his own bat. Probably didn't even tell my wife. She would never have had the gall. . . . no, let's be fair—she wouldn't have been so dishonest as to do something like that, but she would have told him all about the trunk, and . . .' He gestured emphatically. 'You see, I always wondered how the burglar could have had such detailed knowledge of where and what to look for. My flat isn't as spacious as our house was—no cellars or anything—but it's at the top of a big converted Victorian house, and I have access to quite a large attic area. That's where I stored the trunk, along with a load of other stuff. It's hardly the first place an ordinary burglar would search, is it?'

'No,' concurred Maurice.

'Not unless somebody told him specifically what to look for and where to go.' Gresham pointed an emphatic finger at the sky. 'It was him! I'll bet it was him! He'd have done it without her knowing. The shit!' His expression was part fury and part triumph, the look of a man who had nailed an adversary in the great battle of life. 'I should have thought of it before, but. . . . well to be honest I wasn't all that interested in the bloody thing. I was quite pleased to have it off my hands in fact.'

Maurice was thoughtful. 'I still don't . . .'

'What?'

'I don't quite understand why he would go to such lengths unless he had some specific knowledge. I mean, you said that your wife just had a vague idea there might be something in the trunk. That's hardly enough to commission a full-scale break in, is it?'

Gresham hesitated. 'No, but. . . . well, maybe she knew more than she let on. Or maybe she found out something after she left me, through her family connections.'

'Bit of a long shot.'

'I don't know, but the more I think about it the more I'm sure it was him. It all fits. She wouldn't have had anything to do with pinching it herself, I know, but she could have told him and. . . . yes, yes, it must have been him! The shit!'

'What is his name?'

'Nicholas Fanning. She's Frances Fanning now.' He pulled a face. 'Fanny Fanning—can you credit it? That alone is grounds for not marrying him, I'd have thought.'

'Where do they live?'

Gresham glanced at him. 'You're not going to go and accost them, are you?'

Maurice gave a diffident smile from behind his spectacles. 'No. I hardly think the evidence justifies that. But you never know, I might be able to find a way. Pin down the burglar for instance.'

'I doubt if he'll tell you anything.'

'Probably not. But it may be useful to know where they are.'

'They live in Highgate. 20 Fitzroy Grove. City salary territory—naturally.'

'But you think he's in financial trouble?'

'He started up his own investment business. Found it wasn't as plain sailing as he'd thought, that's what I heard.' His lips pursed. 'Not so easy to grant yourself six figure bonuses when you aren't employed by multi-national banks.'

Maurice risked a personal question. 'Are you still angry about losing her?'

Gresham's jaw jutted. 'I'm angry, but not really about that. We weren't really suitable. I'm angry about losing my two sons.' He looked suddenly forlorn. 'She has custody, even though it was she who left me. Fair enough. She's a good mother, and I. . . . well I had failings as a father.'

'Don't you see them?'

'Oh yes—every other weekend. I see them, but the occasional father thing is a bloody awful business.'

Yes, Maurice could imagine. The other went on, 'There's not much natural justice when it comes to marriage break-ups.'

'I'm sorry. Must be difficult.'

'Do you have children?'

'No. Sadly.'

'Children, no children, it's all sad, one way or another.' Gresham drew a breath. 'Anyway, I bet that's the link. If you nail the bastard let me know. I'll have a drink on you.' And as if to emphasise it he took a long draw on his beer.

They didn't talk much more on the subject. The sun continued to shine, the rowers sweated up and down the river, and they drank another half pint, or was it two? They talked about various unrelated matters including religion, although afterwards Maurice couldn't remember how they got onto it. All he remembered was Gresham saying that without it he could never have got through the parting with his wife. Another one, reflected Maurice. He wished he could have had similar help.

He returned to the shop slightly tipsy. As he approached the doorway to his premises a man was just leaving. A big man with heavy features, wearing a pale grey suit, who glanced at Maurice and strode quickly off in the other direction. He didn't look the type who might be interested in old books, but in his befuddled state Maurice didn't pay much attention. He entered to find his new assistant stationed formally behind the counter with the air of a diligent shop keeper.

'All well?' asked Maurice.

'Fine,' replied Roger cheerfully.

'Who was that just leaving? Man in a grey suit.'

Roger looked blank. 'No idea. Just browsed around and left. Had a few like that this morning.'

Maurice retired to the sanctuary of his office. This lunch-time drinking had to stop.

CHAPTER TWENTY-NINE

January 18th 1952. Wakefield.

Eureka! I have progressed from reading 'Origin of Species' to 'The Descent of Man'—which Gordon Hawkins lent me since it is not in the library—and this remarkable book, even more than the previous one, has answered so many questions for me. Darwin's genius was that, not only did he observe the minutiae of the development of species, but he also <u>interpreted</u> them with a logic that is clear to follow. This is the mark of all great scientists—interpretation. What he makes so evident, to me at any rate, is that the apparently incomprehensible behaviour of 'civilised' men towards their fellows throughout history has its roots in their primeval origins, which are never far from the surface. Thus he wrote: "The evidence that all civilised nations are the descendants of barbarians consists of clear traces of their former low condition in still-existing customs, beliefs, language, etc.". And then: "With mankind some of the worst dispositions, which occasionally without any assignable cause make their appearance in families, may perhaps be reversions to a savage state, from which we are not removed by very many generations."

With reference to my own countrymen, some of his observations seem especially pertinent:- "All animals living in a body, which defend themselves or attack their enemies in concert, must indeed be in some degree faithful to one another; and those that follow a leader must be in some degree obedient. When the baboons in Abyssinia plunder a garden they silently follow their leader, and if an imprudent young animal makes a noise he receives a slap from the others to teach him silence and obedience." And: "The half-wild cattle in S. Africa cannot endure even a momentary separation from the herd. They are essentially slavish and accept the common determination, seeking no better lot than to be led by any one ox who has enough self-reliance to accept the position." Do these not describe the unquestioning acceptance of Hitler's leadership by the all those who subscribed to his Third Reich?

Then further: "With all animals, sympathy is directed solely towards the members of the same community, and therefore towards known and more or less beloved members, but not to all the individuals of the same species. This fact is not more surprising than that the fears of many animals should be directed against special enemies." Thus, when a despot proclaims that specific types are enemies of the state—Jews, gypsies, communists or whoever—his declarations are accepted as true for all the above reasons.

And resoundingly: "The rudest savages feel the sentiment of glory, as they clearly shew by preserving the trophies of their prowess, by their habit of excessive boasting, and even by the extreme care which they take of their personal appearance and decorations." What better description of the typical Nazi military character could there be?

When it comes to the frequent puzzling examples of neighbour turning on neighbour during times of oppression, we get this illuminating passage:- "So it has almost certainly been with the unusual and opposite feeling of hatred between the nearest relations, as with the worker-bees which kill their brother drones, and with the queen-bees which kill their daughter-queens; the desire to destroy their nearest relations having been in this case of service to the community." Again a course directed by Adolf's own psychopathic leanings.

However Darwin then offers us this reassurance:- "To believe that man was aboriginally civilised and then suffered utter degradation in so many regions, is to take a pitiably low view of human nature. It is apparently a truer and more cheerful view that progress has been much more general than retrogression; that man has risen, though by slow and interrupted steps, from a lowly condition to the highest standard as yet attained by him in knowledge, morals and religion."

One has to hope that he is right!

However at lunch time today I had an experience that made me wonder. I found myself in the canteen sitting next to my murdering Einstein enthusiast. He greeted me with the usual 'Wotcher Doc', and seemed in an affable mood so, with reference to my readings, I took the risk of gently questioning him about his crimes. He was unashamedly open about them, and when I asked who was the victim involved in his murder conviction he said, 'Oh, just some bloke.'

I probed further, asking if he was an acquaintance or a relative or some such.

'Oh, no, nuffink like that,' he replied. 'I'd never met him before.'

'Then why did you kill him?' I asked.

'He pinched my wife's parking place,' came the answer.

Of course I was bemused. I dared to ask, 'Did you not think of the effect on those close to him? His own wife, his mother, his children?'

He stared at me with complete incomprehension, and then said simply, 'No', and reached across me for the boiled potatoes.

I thought it safest not to press the matter further. However it confirmed my appreciation of Darwin's observation that many men quite simply feel no affinity with any of their fellows who aren't immediate members of their own small circle of family and friends. It is the frequent case with criminals, gangsters, torturers. In their case evolution has a long way to go.

CHAPTER THIRTY

*We must, however, acknowledge that man with all
his noble qualities, with sympathy which feels for the
most debased, with benevolence which extends to the
humblest living creature, with his god-like intellect
which has penetrated into the movements and constitution of the solar system—with all these exalted
powers Man still bears in his bodily frame the indel-
ible stamp of his lowly origin.*

The Descent of Man

Maurice was sitting at his desk, pretending to study the sales
figures whilst fighting off the after effects of his lunch with
the school teacher, when Hemingway tapped on the door
and put his head in. 'Sold a couple of books while you were
gone,' he said. 'Nothing special. Here are the receipts.'

Maurice scarcely looked up from the figures. 'Good,
Roger. Well done.'

The young man was about to leave again, but then on an
afterthought turned and asked, 'Good meeting?'

Maurice pulled himself from his reverie and replied non-
committally, 'Interesting'. Then, as much to himself as to the
other, he added, 'I never cease to be amazed at the power of
the written word. Much greater than the spoken—except I
suppose for the odd historic speech, but then they're usually
written beforehand anyway.'

'Sorry?' said Hemingway with a frown.

Maurice raised his head properly for the first time. 'The
written word. Its importance, its worth. Once it's in print it's
assumed to have value.'

'Oh, yes,' said Hemingway. 'Extraordinary.'

'I suppose it's because everyone assumes that, if it's written down, it must be the truth—or at least the result of careful thought. Not haphazard, unconsidered conversation.'

'Mm. Yes, that's probably it.'

Maurice threw his assistant a dry smile as if to an academic confidant. 'Perhaps we should ban the spoken word. Make everyone communicate through the pen. It could improve personal relations enormously.'

They were a lot of words for Maurice. Hemingway contemplated the wall opposite as if they were written there, but could think of no further response so said nothing.

'So how much did you take over lunch?' Maurice asked, glancing at the receipts.

'Nothing much. About fifty quid.'

'Better than nothing,' said Maurice.

'Oh, and, er. . . . I forgot. There was a phone call for you.'

Maurice's eyebrows went up. 'Who?'

'Some American.' He fished in his jacket pocket and took out a scrap of paper. 'Tommy Houseman. Said to call him in Michigan.'

Maurice frowned. 'Did you talk to him at all?'

'Um. . . . no. Just took the message. He seemed quite insistent, if you know what I mean.'

'Right,' said Maurice. 'I'll call him later.' He had no intention of doing so.

Hemingway shifted position and half smiled his beguiling smile. 'So . . . was this the same thing today?'

'The same thing?'

'That you went to lunch for? The thing you were talking about connected with your jail bird.'

'Oh. Yes.'

Hemingway put his head on one side. 'It's really valuable then, is it?'

Maurice shrugged. 'Could be. No-one's very sure, that's the trouble.'

'What is it—a science book?'

Maurice was weary of being secretive. 'Sort of. Something to do with the Darwin family.'

'Oh.' The youth frowned thoughtfully. 'Charles Darwin? The evolution guy.'

'Yes.'

'Interesting.'

'Well it would be if it turned up. It was only produced as a very limited edition, so if there are any copies about they could be—yes—pretty valuable.'

'And you're on the trail of one?'

Maurice waved a hand. 'A fairly faint trail.'

Hemingway persisted. 'So if you were the one to discover it you'd be famous.'

Maurice shrugged. 'Well, not famous probably, but a source of some recognition amongst my peers.'

'Amongst your what?'

'My fellow dealers. Yes, I'd enjoy that. I'd have left my small mark on history.'

'Yes. Nice one.' They smiled at each other, the smile of fellow associates in a business enterprise. Maurice felt an innocent gratitude towards the younger man that he had not felt for anyone in a long time. However he pushed it aside before it might embarrass him, and turned back to the sales figures.

Hemingway too turned away, but then on another afterthought stopped. 'By the way, if you want to visit someone in prison you just have to write to them and then they send you a Visitor's Order.'

'A Visitor's Order?'

'Yes. That allows you to make an appointment.' He added with a self-deprecatory smile. 'I found it on Google.'

'Oh, thank you, Roger. Very kind of you.'

At that moment the shop bell pinged behind Hemingway. He was quickly off the mark and back at his post, closing Maurice's door.

Maurice shook his head as if to clear it, took a scrap of paper from his own pocket, opened his desk diary, and beside his entry for that day's lunch appointment with Robert Gresham he wrote, 'Nicholas & Frances Fanning. 20 Fitzroy Grove. Highgate.'

He was to wish later that he had not done so.

CHAPTER THIRTY-ONE

<u>April 16th, 1850. Down House</u>

Oh Lord, if ever you had mercy show it now. I can scarcely write in my battered journal, my hand is trembling so with trepidation. Our beloved Annie is at death's door. The message came from Malvern, where we had sent her as a last resort to treat her desperate condition. She had a serious relapse there yesterday, high fever and vomiting, and we were urged to come at once. She is just ten years old. I am eight months gone with child and cannot make the arduous journey. I was so distressed that I tried to board the carriage this morning, but Charles and the servants held me back. Charles set off himself with all haste, his face grey with anxiety. Nurse Brodie and sister Etty are at Annie's bedside, thank heavens, so she is not alone in her crisis, but it pains me beyond measure that I cannot be there to cradle and comfort her. There is such a physical ache in my heart that I fear it might impart itself to the unborn child within me and I know not where to turn for comfort.

As with Charles himself, no one seems able to make a precise diagnosis of our darling's condition. For the better part of a year now she has been dispirited, complaining of headaches and nausea, and unable to participate in the family activities which she used to lead with such enthusiasm. None of the well tried remedies in my own father's Book of Medicines have had an effect, and the doctors in London have managed nothing beyond administering the usual pills and potions and advising quiet rest, and so taking her to Malvern and the attentive Dr Gully has been the only resort left to us. C had high hopes of the good doctor's treatment since it has proved so efficacious for himself. He is convinced that

Annie has inherited her condition from him. Certainly the early signs were that she was rallying under the care. But now comes this dreadful news of her decline. Surely, surely it cannot mean the worst.

Being our eldest daughter Annie has always held a special place in C's affections, and as she has grown she has taken such pleasure in attending to his wants, participating in his experiments, and assisting him in all ways with his work. A great bond has grown between them. Her sweet nature is so amiable and willing to please that neither C nor I can recollect any instance of our having had to scold her, and her siblings have always looked to her for succour and advice in their own pursuits. There cannot be a more loving and blameless disposition alive on earth, and if God sees fit to take her from us then I will not know what to think. Certainly for Charles, who has been wrestling with his doubts about the Creation and the Kingdom for so long, it will seem the final confirmation of all his misgivings.

I struggle over and over again in my mind with the one fundamental question. Why, oh why is it that we have to suffer such great torments and injustices here on earth in order to earn our place in heaven? What is the purpose of such universal pain? Were it that all men had to endure an equal test of their good will and fitness for eternal life, then I could understand—but it is quite evidently not so. The truly deserving suffer appalling tragedy, the guilty so often sail through life without trial or challenge. There has to be method behind this, I know, but it is hard to fathom. When I discuss it with men of the church or other devout minds I receive no enlightenment there either, other than the catch-all, 'God moves in a mysterious way'. He does indeed.

I will pray now with all the faith that is in me.

April 24th, 1850. Down.

Annie has left us. Thy will be done.

CHAPTER THIRTY-TWO

More individuals are born than can possibly survive.
A grain in the balance will determine which indi-
vidual shall live and which shall die, which species
shall increase in number and which shall decrease or
finally become extinct. . . . The slightest advantage in
one being over those with which it comes into com-
petition will turn the balance.

Origin of Species

Four days after his Chiswick lunch meeting Maurice received
a letter from Charley Derwent in Pentonville Prison containing a scruffy note and visitor's pass. As Hemingway had
advised, Maurice had written to the petty thief requesting a
meeting on the grounds that it might result in some financial
benefit to them both. On receiving the prompt reply, which
simply read: 'All right—come any afternoon. Charley D.', he
immediately rang the prison and requested an appointment
the next day.

A grey, drizzling afternoon fitting the ambience of the
building, as he arrived and stared up at its inhospitable Victorian walls, painted white presumably to relieve the stark-
ness. Hard to believe that when first erected the place was
hailed as a breakthrough in innovative prison design. 'Just
the place to revive the human spirit,' he muttered to himself
as he approached the entrance. '*Vile deeds like poison weeds*
bloom well in prison air.'

Admittance was straightforward, accompanied by a brisk
body search, photo, and fingerprint recording, all of which
made him feel a bit like a criminal himself. By contrast
with the exterior, the visiting room was surprisingly light
and airy, if starkly impersonal. He sat at the appointed place

and whilst waiting for Derwent to appear curiously studied the few other visitors and inmates already conversing there. There was little to distinguish them. One might have been at a social services office, or perhaps a job applications center, rather than an establishment for the condemned of society. Should he have expected anything else? Popular portrayal invariably had criminals' outward features as betraying their dispositions, but he saw no immediate evidence of that here. Just everyday people having everyday chats.

Then the exception. A short, thick chested, balding prisoner was admitted and pointed in his direction. Ah, thought Maurice as the man rolled on bandy legs towards him—there is type casting after all. He watched with some apprehension as the other seated himself opposite. He must have been in his fifties and had a coarse, expressionless face—the face of someone for whom life held no more challenges or surprises. He sat upright with his knotted hands together on the table and stared at his visitor blankly.

'Thank you for seeing me, Mr Derwent,' said Maurice.

'What's this all about then?' He had a flat London accent.

'I'm a . . . let's say, a dealer. . . .'

'A wot?'

'A dealer in old books and manuscripts. I'm on the trail of a particular item which might be worth quite a lot of money. It's possible you might be able to help me find it.'

'Ow's that then?'

Maurice felt even less confident. How do you talk to a convicted criminal about his crimes? Just discuss them openly as one would a job carried out by any other professional—a plumber for instance, or a garage mechanic? Once again, as so often with this quest, he was forced to plunge straight in. 'I believe you have admitted stealing a trunk from the attic of a Mr Robert Gresham in Chiswick about a year ago?' He made the statement on a rising wave of embarrassment.

He needn't have worried. Derwent was totally unfazed. 'Yeh. What about it?'

'I also gather you wouldn't tell the police who it was who hired you to do the job.'

'Well, naturally. I'm not going to grass on them, am I? They paid me good money for that job. *I* didn't know what was in the bleedin' thing.'

'No, of course, I understand that,' said Maurice. Well, nothing venture, nothing gain. 'But would I be right in thinking it was a Mr Nicholas Fanning who hired you?'

The man's hesitation and tiniest twitch of an eyelid told him all he needed to know.

'Why would you think that?'

'Ah, so you do know him?'

'I never said that.'

'Think carefully, Mr Derwent.' Maurice did his specs polishing thing. 'It might be worth, let's say, five hundred pounds if we were able to recover certain items from that theft through your information.'

There was a pause. He could almost see the wheels turning. 'Well, let's put it this way . . .' The man sniffed. 'You're puttin' a case to me which you obviously know something about. So if I was to say nothing, but at the same time didn't deny anything, then you could draw your own conclusions, couldn't you?'

'Conclusions?'

'That maybe you was right.'

'I see, yes.' Maurice put his specs back on. 'And if I drew the conclusion that I was right about Mr Fanning, could I also draw the conclusion that you never discovered anything about the contents of that trunk?'

Derwent stared and sniffed again. 'When I do a job for someone, I do the job that's asked—no more, no less. I don't ask questions or try to find out more than I need to know.'

Maurice nodded. 'Thank you. That's really all I need to know myself.' It seemed to have been ridiculously simple, but he could think of nothing more to ask. However he didn't feel he could just leave abruptly. He glanced round the room. 'Do they treat you quite well in here?'

Derwent stared at him blankly for a second. 'Oh yeh—bleedin' Savoy innit?'

'Right. . . . well I won't trouble you any further.' Maurice rose.

'Wot about the money you mentioned?'

'You can trust me that, if I get the hoped for result from my investigations, then I will pay you your money.' Maurice turned and left the room, as briskly as was seemly.

CHAPTER THIRTY-THREE

February 25th, 1952. Wakefield

It is now more than one year since I was interned here. I feel that I have known nothing else but these grey walls, this monotonous regime. The stress and the excitement of those far off days when I was at the heart of the nuclear experiment and the core of the espionage operation seem a distant dream. Another world entirely to this dull, unfulfilling existence. I fret that I am not utilising my talents to any good effect. It is such a waste of an individual's potential.

However I console myself with the thought that I <u>did</u> contribute to the cause of scientific advancement. And I fulfilled my vow to do everything I could to help bring the war to an end. It lasted longer than any of us at the start thought possible. By the end of 1941 it had expanded across Europe, the Japanese had lost their heads and bombed Pearl Harbor, and America was in the fray. It seemed that the monsters who had hijacked my country had committed the entire planet to endless conflict. The urgency to create the atomic bomb intensified with every day that passed. The complications were immense, but we knew we were getting closer and the work was all absorbing, the pressure intense.

The whole key to the creation of a bomb was finding the way to split atoms with the right properties and release the huge energy contained within their neutrons in a chain reaction. No-one has ever seen an atom, let alone a neutron, but for decades we had known they were there through the mathematical calculations based on the behaviour of the elements that we <u>could</u> see. I well remember the extraordinary moment back in 1941 when I was working at Birmingham with Professor Pieirls, and he showed me the calculations he had done on this theory with Otto Frisch (another brilliant Jewish scientist who had fled Hitler's regime). The atom considered most suitable for splitting, or 'fission' as it came to be known, was that of the heaviest element, uranium, but for years no-one had believed the practical process was possible, or at any rate that it was possible to split enough atoms simultaneously to create a big enough chain reaction for an explosion. Pieirls and Frisch had however calculated that such a reaction <u>could</u> in fact be produced from only a few pounds of the particular isotope 235 of uranium. Which meant that the nuclear bomb was theoretically possible. The problem was to turn theory into practice.

By now of course others were also urgently working on the same thing, the Germans and the Russians predominantly amongst them. And since I was passing to the Russians much of the information on our researches, they were almost as far advanced with their program as were we. It is not true to say that I had no qualms about this process for I searched my heart before every secret meeting, but I was clear in my mind that I was doing the right thing in the circumstances.

Furthermore I was confirmed in my cause by another extraordinary personal event. I have explained in this record that throughout my youth, as I watched the rise of Hitler and the descent into depravity of so many of my countrymen, I constantly struggled to come to terms with the enormity of man's capacity for barbarity. I could find no sense in the explanation that this was the eternal battle between God and the Devil, for if God was all powerful and had created the universe in the first place then how could he possibly have allowed such perversity to stem from it? Despite my father's lifelong convictions it seemed to me that the Bible itself was such a welter of fact and fiction, such a tangle of mysticism and contradiction, that no reliability could be placed on it as any sort of realistic blueprint. Furthermore the researches within my own profession were revealing ever more clearly how the universe had formed and was evolving, and this excluded still further the probability that there was any guiding force behind such a gigantic and haphazard transformation. The only explanation for the aberrations that have occurred throughout man's brief and turbulent history had to be that he was still in thrall to the prehistoric instincts that had governed his battle for survival in the past. As I have read in 'Descent of Man', his aggression, his sadism, his antagonism towards those of a different race or mindset, his urge to seek power, wealth and territory, all these must stem from those ingrained primeval urges which were once essential for the protection and proliferation of his tribe. So, while man grows ever more sophisticated in his scientific and technological prowess, he is yet at base a primal and instinctual animal.

One of my associates at Birmingham was a highly intelligent researcher who, for reasons which will become obvious, I cannot name here. He and I became quite friendly, and on occasions in our lunch breaks or after work at the pub we would indulge in speculative discussions about our experiments, about the state of the world, and about man's condition. One day, when I was elaborating on my fascination with evolution and the findings of Charles Darwin, this man said to me, 'You know that I am a direct descendant of the Allen family?' When he saw the look of puzzlement on my face, he added, 'Emma Darwin's mother was Elizabeth Allen.' He explained that the prosperous Allens were based in South Wales and were closely integrated with the Darwins during the nineteenth century, along with the Wedgewoods. They were all large families and many of the offspring of all three intermarried (I should add that his own surname was not Allen).

This was fascinating to me, and I encouraged him to talk at some length on the connections and the history of those three dynasties, about which I was extremely ignorant at the time. He then became quite conspiratorial and, glancing about the pub we were in, leant forward and muttered in my ear (I'm confident I can recall him almost word for word), 'My own family has an extraordinary piece of memorabilia from the Darwin era. It has been handed down through various family lines and ended up in our possession. It's a copy of a secret diary which Charles Darwin's wife Emma wrote during their years together. Totally enthralling!'

Naturally I was intrigued and questioned him at some length about its contents. In the end he agreed to let me have a look at the work, although he was distinctly nervous about it as there was a strong tradition within the family that the writings were private and not to be circulated abroad. Under a good deal of pressure he smuggled the volume to me a week or so later, with the condition that I must never let anyone know he had done so, and that I could only keep it for a day or two.

I read it as soon as I could from cover to cover. It was an intimate account of the family's day-to-day activities during the middle part of the nineteenth century, and of Emma Darwin's phenomenal husband's working methods. All told from a woman's point of view—a far more personal chronicle than any of Darwin's own writings.

What made it doubly interesting was that Emma mentioned towards the end of the diary that Charles himself had written an addendum to 'The Descent of Man', in which he finally described his own spiritual attitude. He had until then kept even more silent about this than about his evolutionary conclusions. However, for whatever reason this addition was never added to the book. Probably because of his habitual fear of provoking controversy.

When I asked my friend if he knew anything about the addendum he just shrugged and said that so far as he could glean it had never come to light. All he knew was that towards the end of his life Darwin had written a short autobiography for the benefit of his children in which he did expound to some extent on his thoughts about God, religion and so forth, but only in brief unscientific terms. Presumably the addendum had considerably more to say on the subject.

After we parted the thought of that document remained in my mind. It must have been contentious if Darwin had excluded it, and it would presumably have been written with more deliberation than any musings in an autobiography. I felt it would be intriguing to read. I had no idea what Darwin's political affiliations were—knowing a bit about his character by now, I guessed that he probably remained fairly conservative in those as in all things—but his philosophic deductions, based on his scientific studies, now those were surely of supreme relevance.

Still, Emma Darwin's own testimony was intriguing enough, and the force of its contents have stayed with me ever since. Her writings revealed that her generation had their own great struggle with oppression and tragedy, their own wrestlings with the eternal questions of morality. Whilst having no direct bearing on my specific work, her personal reflections persuaded me still further that my convictions were the right ones.

I also found it deeply moving to read her descriptions of the kind of rich and bustling family life that it seems I will never experience. Such existence is the traditional and natural way of things. Without it the evolutionary process cannot continue. I have been remiss in allowing all the other considerations of my life to distract me from such experience.

I was enthralled by her writings, but they left me with immense feelings of sadness.

CHAPTER THIRTY-FOUR

*We have now seen that actions are regarded by sav-
ages, and were probably so regarded by primeval
man, as good or bad solely as they affect in an obvious manner the welfare of the tribe—not that of the
species, nor that of man as an individual member of
the tribe. This conclusion agrees well with the belief
that the so-called moral sense is aboriginally derived
from the social instincts, for both relate at first exclusively to the community.*

The Descent of Man

Maurice sat in his back office fighting the urge to open his
whiskey flask as he leafed through the edition of Charles
Darwin's own memoirs that his Oxford colleague had given
him. Roger Hemingway was handling things adequately in
the shop and, apart from leaving his office door open so that
he could hear if anything untoward was happening, Maurice
felt relaxed enough to leave him at it and concentrate on his
own concerns. His growing preoccupation with the Darwin
business was starting to unsettle him. It was dominating his
life. He had now come across the entry in the Fuchs journal
which connected it to the Darwin one, and there was little
doubt it confirmed the existence of the latter in an emphatic
manner. It also confirmed the Allen connection to at least
one of the copies. And now, the slim volume he was reading
was not so much a memoir as a series of reflections on various aspects of life, and apparently written more for the benefit of Darwin's own offspring than for the general public.
Nevertheless it provided further insights into the mind of the
scientist. The more Maurice read about the man the more,
in a strange way, he identified with his preoccupations. And

consequently with his dilemma. How to reconcile prevailing currents of thought with the real world as he observed it. How to accommodate the speculations and superstitions of the human species as it searched for some meaning behind its tortuous progress, whilst at the same time promoting his own theory of the total randomness of that progress. A paradox that might unsettle anyone. It was not surprising that Darwin had hesitated for so long before publishing his major commentaries.

However the Victorian had himself conjectured from time to time that it might be healthier to just get on with life rather than spend so much of it trying to analyse its workings. A part of Maurice felt perhaps he was right.

He gave in to temptation and took a good swig at the whiskey before turning his attention to his other dilemma. A more mundane one by comparison. How to physically progress things further. He had traced the vaguely possible path of one copy of Emma Darwin's journal to a specific address. But how was he to continue the investigation? He could hardly knock on the Fannings' door and enquire as to whether the stolen trunk had produced anything. He could scarcely write to them and say, 'I believe you have acquired certain Darwinian memorabilia through illegal means. If it's still available I have a client who would be interested in purchasing such for a considerable sum.' Apart from anything else that would make him an accessory. And Maurice had never done anything illegal in his life. Except of course for murder.

He frowned, resisted the temptation to take another shot of whiskey, irritably tossed the flask into his drawer and sipped at a lukewarm mug of instant coffee instead. Not much use consulting Alice over this one. She would be as non-plussed as he was.

As he pondered the phone rang. It was Donald Easterby.

'Maurice, I'm back in London. How are you doing?'

'You're in London already?' The casual globe trotting of the rich was something way beyond Maurice's experience or ambition.

'Yes, I had to come back for business reasons. And also it was a good excuse to catch up with our little enterprise. Can I pop over and see you?'

Maurice blinked. 'Well, yes by all means. You know where I am.'

'I'm on my way.' The phone went dead.

The man's eagerness over what must surely have been a relatively minor item within his overall activities seemed odd. However Maurice was glad to know he now at least had someone to consult with over the situation. A bare half hour passed before the towering figure walked into the shop. Easterby took in the presence of Roger Hemingway behind the serving counter as he headed for Maurice's office.

'Who's that?' he asked sotto voce as he entered and hovered in the middle of the floor.

'My new assistant,' replied Maurice, getting up and closing the door. 'I lost my old one under rather awkward circumstances and this chap happened to be available.

'Doesn't look quite the type for antique books,' said Easterby.

'No, but it was an emergency. And actually he's not doing too badly.'

Easterby frowned suspiciously. 'What does he know about our little project?'

Maurice as usual felt daunted in the proximity of the much taller figure and headed back to the safety of his desk. 'Oh, don't worry—very little.'

'Good. Don't tell him if you can help it.'

Definitely a touch of paranoia here, thought Maurice. The American sat in the leather chair and leaned forward intently. 'So, where have you got to? What's happening?'

Maurice wasn't sure where to begin. 'Well, I've read the entry in the Fuchs record which relates to him seeing a copy of the journal.'

'Yes. Crucial that, isn't it? Lucky I remembered it.'

'It would seem to put beyond doubt the fact that she wrote such a thing.'

Impatiently, 'Yes, yes, I never had much doubt about that. But have you got any closer to finding it?'

Maurice described his meetings with the school teacher and the prison inmate.

'Great,' commented Easterby. 'That's productive.' He seemed more on edge than previously. As if the outcome of the quest now had an added significance.

Maurice went on, 'I'm in a bit of a quandary as to what to do next.'

'Why?'

'Well I can hardly go and confront this Fanning man and accuse him of having stolen the trunk, can I?' He reined back his impatience. 'And in any case—it was nearly a year ago, and well. . . . in the unlikely event that it did contain a copy of the diary, wouldn't he have sold it by now?'

The American pondered for a moment. 'It's possible, but I don't think so.'

'Why not? Surely that would have been his first consideration?'

The other shook his head. 'It would have been too risky for him to approach any of the orthodox customers with such a thing—museums and so forth. This is stolen property. The news of its appearance would have spread like wildfire.'

'Yes, but. . . .'

'His only other hope would have been private collectors such as myself.'

Maurice frowned. 'Well, he's a city banker—he must know all sorts of wealthy people.'

Easterby shook his head. 'There aren't many in the market for something like this, who would buy and ask no questions.' He thought some more. 'No—if it was on offer on the black market I would have heard about it.'

This seemed a touch optimistic for Maurice's pedantic nature. 'All right, but surely, if he stole it for financial reasons then he must have had some idea how to dispose of it?'

'Yes.' Easterby grimaced with frustration. 'Yes, it's a mystery.' He scratched his head impatiently. 'Look, Maurice, why don't you go and at least take a look at their place—where was it—Highgate, you said? You never know, it might tell you something.'

'You don't expect me to break in and search the house, do you?'

'No, no—nothing like that. But you may get some idea of their setup. How well off they seem. Whether there might be an excuse to approach them on some seemingly innocent matter—you know what I mean?'

Maurice hadn't the faintest idea what he meant. This sort of detective work wasn't his line at all. 'Well, I. . . . I don't know. . . . I mean, I can't quite see how I could. . . .'

The impatience increased in Easterby's voice. 'Just take a look at the address—that's all, Maurice. You can tell a lot about people from the places they live in. You never know what you might spot.'

'Very well, if you say so.' Maurice adjusted his spectacles. 'But just to have a look, nothing more.'

'Sure, don't do anything too daring. I'd hate for you to get in trouble.' The sarcasm was clear. He rose and paced the room. 'Meanwhile I'll have a think about how else we might approach this thing.'

Maurice sat for a moment watching as the man walked up and down, covering the length of the office in about four huge strides. 'If I may say so, Donald. . . .' he began.

Easterby stopped. 'What? What?'

'You seem extremely obsessed by this search.'

A pause. 'Well, yes. Yes, I'm enthusiastic about it.'

'It seems a bit more than mere enthusiasm.' Maurice peered over the top of the specs. 'Does it have some significance I'm not aware of?'

The American hesitated, then sat again in his chair. He closed his eyes and passed both hands over his face. 'Yes. Yes, I'm sorry. I'm far too impatient. It's only a book for Christ's sake!'

Maurice sensed an unspoken turmoil. 'Is there some reason? Does it have a special importance beyond. . . . beyond the obvious?'

Easterby took a deep breath and relaxed a little. 'No, not really. That is. . . . it has acquired an importance in my mind, yes. Especially now you seem to have found a lead. I feel it might be the final piece in a. . . . a jigsaw that I've been trying to put together for long time now.'

'Would you like to tell me?'

The other paused again, was silent, then said, 'You were involved in one of history's big disasters, weren't you, Maurice?'

Maurice stared at him in surprise. 'Sorry, I. . . .'

'I wasn't meaning to pry. But when I looked into your record I came across a news item that mentioned you'd been a witness in the inquest on the London bombings.'

A beat. Was there nothing this man didn't know about him? 'Yes, I was. I was quite close when it happened.'

'The article didn't say much. Did it affect you?'

'Affect?'

'Were you involved? Did it have a personal impact?'

How could he possibly explain? 'Yes, I was involved. And yes, it did.'

Easterby nodded slowly. 'Then you'll know how the fact of its being a national. . . . or should I say global news story, adds somehow to the significance. Everyone knows about it, but you were *there*.' Maurice waited to know the point of the diversion. Easterby stared down at his knees. 'I was involved in something like that also. But it was a natural, not a man made disaster. The extraordinary thing is that it happened less than two months after your experience—which is why the article struck me so forcibly.' He looked back and inhaled deeply. 'It all goes back a long way, you see, Maurice. It goes back all the way to my childhood.'

Maurice waited. 'I've got time if you want to tell me.'

'Well it's not a distinguished story.' He took another breath. 'I was brought up in a wealthy environment. I won't bore you with the details, but you can imagine. . . . big houses, retainers, nurses and tutors, lots of comings and goings but none of them for my particular benefit. Older brother and sister, parents who were well meaning but whom I hardly ever saw. Mother whom I adored, but was like some distant angel who every time I got to touch vanished again like a mirage.' He pulled a wry face. 'The only time the family was together was church on Sunday. Traditional Catholics, which always seemed ironic to me given their lifestyle. So as a kid I was indoctrinated with all that high church stuff. All that shenanigans about original sin and confession and preparing for the afterlife and so on.' His voice hardened. 'We didn't live near any primary schools, so my early education was put in the hands of a private tutor. A Catholic priest who lived with us. He was a bastard. A sadist. If I didn't recite the catechism correctly he would beat me with a knotted cane. If I made a sound he would double the strokes.' He took a deep breath. 'That so-called man of God made my childhood a living hell. He made me so confused about religion it took me decades to recover. In fact I never recovered. My main childhood recollection is of loneliness and fear and bewilderment. My only escape was into my head, with my dreams and my fantasies. In later life, when I knew a bit more about the world, I learned that that priest wasn't alone. Religion was responsible for much of the world's pain—from the Crusades to the Inquisition to the modern jihadists. Which only served to confuse me even more.' He gestured. 'At college I was to outward appearances a privileged confidant guy just like all the other privileged confident guys. I kept up the pretence of faith. I went to church and prayed to something I hoped was there. But inside the loneliness and confusion was always present. I was dead. Same with romance. The girls I met, some of them gorgeous, bright, eligible—and often, let's face it, because of my wealth available—they none of them meant anything to me. None of them could replace the one woman I wanted, who was my mother.' A dry smile. 'Text book Freudian case, eh?' He went on. 'And none of it was helped by the fact that I had no real career, no vocation, no purpose to my life. Only my collection of literature and scientific stuff, which I was gradually building up. Through which I suppose I was seeking more meaning to existence than the Bible provided.' His expression was frank. 'This went on until I hit thirty. A rich, clever, lost soul amongst a million others.'

He paused, stared down and brushed an imaginary speck of dust from his trousers. 'Then something happened that changed my life. I met a man, four years younger than me, and we fell in love. I realised I was gay, and everything fell into place.' His pale gaze came back to Maurice. 'You wouldn't think it possible, would you—that it could take a person until his thirties to realise something like that? But my whole upbringing, my whole family's history and ethic argued against such a possibility, and it wasn't until I actually found someone I could love that I was able to suddenly adopt the right state of mind and be myself.'

He rose again from the chair. Paced the room, slowly this time. 'His name was Richard and he was a musician with the Boston Symphony Orchestra. Played the clarinet. Had aspirations to being a soloist, but there aren't a lot of slots for solo clarinetists, however good. We began a relationship which lasted for fourteen years. He was all I wanted in a person, as I was to him. I went with him on his concert tours, he became the chief curator and partner in my collection. We travelled the world, attending all the top concert halls, visiting all the top libraries and museums, holidaying in all the top places. We barely had a difference of opinion. We faced a future that was for each of us meaningful at last.' He stopped pacing for a moment and gazed out of the rear window. 'Then in August 2005 we were in New Orleans where Richard was playing at some concert or other. Great city, great music, great time. We just lapped it all up. Until the warnings of Hurricane Katrina came through. We didn't worry too much the first couple of days. Then the warnings got more serious and the mayor ordered the evacuation of the city. We were staying at a hotel to the east, on a rise some way back from the sea. We debated as to whether to leave, but by then there were reports of huge traffic jams and petrol shortages, and we figured we were probably better off where we were. That night the wind was pretty fierce and the rain was lashing down, but it seemed the worst might pass us by. It was quite a scary night, but the hotel was well built and it didn't seem too cataclysmic—rather exciting actually. In the morning we put on rain jackets and ventured out to the front of the hotel to watch the drama. Quite a few other people were there. There was a terrifying sky, fierce gusts of wind and lashing rain. For the first time we both simultaneously felt things were getting a bit out of hand. Then we became aware of shouting and screaming coming from down by the shore. A strange crashing which we couldn't really interpret over the noise of the wind and rain. And by the time we saw the water coming it was too late. We tried to run back to the building but it hit us like a. . . . an avalanche. No, not so much an avalanche as a surge of black water that came from nowhere and was suddenly up around our waists, then over our heads, over everything in sight and sweeping us away, god knows where. I lost sight of Richard immediately. I was thrown around, sucked under, smashed against debris, palm trees, walls. . . . I was convinced this was it. I wasn't scared. Just thought, oh well, I've had my time. I've found happiness and it's O.K. to go now. But I didn't go. I was somehow washed up on a roof and managed to hang on. I was bloodied and half drowned and I was there for something like six hours until the water partially receded again, but I survived. Richard didn't. I never saw him again. Not until two weeks later when I finally identified his body at one of the makeshift morgues.' He turned back to Maurice. 'You've seen the pictures. You saw what happened to New Orleans.' Maurice nodded. 'Well that finally did it for me as far as religion was concerned. I had lost the only person who had ever really mattered to me. If there was a God then he certainly had nothing to do with love and mercy and forgiveness and all that other stuff.'

Maurice inevitably thought of Alice, but banished the comparison from his mind.

Easterby went on. 'All I could feel was anger. Especially when I saw the mass of survivors pouring into the few churches that were still standing, and praying for salvation to the being who had supposedly allowed it to happen in the first place! I mean, how ridiculous was that?' He opened his hands in a gesture of resignation. 'So the last vestiges of my Catholic upbringing were banished. I began to understand that morality has nothing to do with catechisms or tablets of stone. It's just basic common sense—what is best for society. However I had to find something to replace God. I needed some other philosophy, some other explanation for the apparent mad state of the universe. And of course it was Darwin and his evolution that seemed the most likely candidate. I already had a fair bit of material on that subject in my collection and I set about gathering more. I started learning what Darwinism was actually about. And the more I learned, the more I realised that for me this was the answer. So, as I collected more and more stuff, I eventually came to the discovery of the journal and the postscript. The postscript which might be Darwin's own final comment on the whole business.' He looked up at Maurice, and for the first time there was the glimmer of a smile in his eyes. 'Which is why I'm so keen on finding the damned thing.'

'You think it will provide some sort of revelation?'

The other shook his head. 'No. No, I don't expect that. After all, the revelation was his theory of evolution itself. The route to it is well explained in his writings. No, I just want to read his personal take on the philosophical implications.' Easterby's lips tightened. 'They've been delved into ad nauseam since his time, yet they're still rejected by a large part of the human race. Basic superstition still takes precedence over logic. It took me a long time to understand that what most people want above all is not genuine knowledge, but security. They find a religion, or a political creed, or some mad world theory, and they cling to it against all argument because it's their safety. They won't entertain doubt because they haven't the mental courage or the open mindedness to question their mind-set. Do you know, in the States almost half the population vote for a political candidate, not because of his policies, but according to what his faith is. And we're supposed to be a sophisticated race!'

Maurice gave an imperceptible shrug. '*God is a comedian playing to an audience too afraid to laugh.*'

Easterby waved a hand. 'Well, whatever. There will always be those who reject Darwin. And sure, he may not shake the heavens, but he must surely have some relevance here on earth.'

Silence. 'Yes,' Maurice said. 'I understand. Thank you for telling me all that.'

Easterby gazed at Maurice with a softness in his expression that was not often there. 'You have sadness in your own life, Maurice, I know that. I suspect it has led you to make some very hard decisions?'

Maurice frowned and blinked behind his spectacles. 'You seem to know a lot about me, Donald.'

The other waved a dismissive hand. 'It's no mystery, Maurice. Details are easy to find these days. I knew about your involvement with the London bus bomb. I also saw an obituary article on your wife. It seemed to indicate that desperate measures might have been needed to end her suffering.' A beat. 'Just a guess of course. Would I be wrong?'

A long silence in the room. Maurice found himself in urgent need of distraction and cleaned his specs furiously.

'That's all right,' said Easterby. 'You don't have to say anything. But few of us can escape tragedy in one form or another. It's a condition of human life.' His tone lightened. 'Anyway, all I'm saying is that if we can be partners in this business then perhaps it will be good for both of us.' To give Maurice time to recover he rose and wandered along the book shelves once more, peering at the titles.

After Easterby had left Maurice considered his options. No harm surely in simply driving over to Highgate and taking a look at the house. It wouldn't achieve much, but might assuage their curiosity a little. He had already planned a weekend trip to Down House—the Darwins' home in Kent—to view the setting where it had all taken place. This meant a pretty tortuous journey across London, so he might as well extend it further and take in Highgate en route.

Yes, he'd wait until Sunday and do that. Another lonely Sabbath taken care of.

He glanced out of the office at Hemingway, who had been counting the change in the desk till. The youth caught his eye through the doorway, smiled and went to deal with a new customer by the bookshelves. Maurice had another sip of cold coffee, weakened, reached for his drawer and took a slug from the whiskey flask. Then he went through and Googled Hurricane Katrina on the computer.

CHAPTER THIRTY-FIVE

August 5th, 1851. Down House

Oh, what an astonishing week we have had! The whole family has been in London to see the Great Exhibition. We stayed at Erasmus's[20] Mayfair house, and went daily to visit the exhibition in Hyde Park. The Crystal Palace[21] in which it is housed is surely one of the finest creations ever built. I could never find the words for my humble journal to describe its lofty, soaring, glistening splendour. It is like a fairy-tale glass palace, more magnificent than any cathedral, grander than any nobleman's castle. And inside! Oh, the astonishing display of man's enterprise and ingenuity—huge roaring engines and clattering machines, the wondrous products of his scientific invention, the beauteous plants and trees of his cultivation, the glorious creations of his artistic soul. If ever there was proof of his divine nature then here it is.

And the greater part of it stemming from the effort and creativity of the British peoples and their Empire. We are surely leaders of the world, and the joy of it is that we have done it, not by war and aggression and conquest like other empires (well not wholly, Charles might say!), but for the most part by trade and pioneering instruction and missionary example.

The entire country is thronging to see the marvellous show. The Queen and Prince Albert (who instigated the whole venture) have been several times, all of London appears to be

---

[20]*Erasmus Darwin, 1804–81. Charles's elder brother.*
[21]*Crystal Palace—huge and famous glass and iron exhibition hall designed by Joseph Paxton.*

there daily, and there are great lines of carriages encroaching on Hyde Park from every direction. Never have I seen so many people all together in one spot before, and of every class and culture which is a great encouragement. The children too were quite overwhelmed at it all, and we had to keep careful watch on them for fear of losing them in the melee.

As for Charley, who has had a small input into the designs of some of the exhibits, he was of course enthralled by the entire spectacle. He insisted on rushing there each morning as soon as was practical, striding ahead to every new section and burying himself deep in all the information and literature on display. He would spend all day immersed in the exhibits, then stagger home exhausted and ill, throw himself on the bed for a tormented night, only to rise next day equally eager to begin again. I cannot decide which weighs heaviest in the balance—the stimulation it provides to his spirit, or the strain it imposes on his body.

Inevitably the Exhibition is causing controversy amongst the leading thinkers of the land (why is it one cannot create a purely innocent spectacle without the pundits having to pronounce some moral judgement upon it?) The members of the new intellectual movements, who call themselves 'positivists' and 'secularists' and 'materialists' and I know not what, are claiming that it is living proof of man's development and supremacy on earth, and that all this extraordinary creation is happening without any Divine influence. They say it proves that society itself is in process of evolution, with the elite nations such as Britain leading the way, and they espouse the theories of the heretical Revd Malthus,[22] that backward nations and communities who cannot control

[22]*Economist working for the East India Company, who through his radical 'Essay on the Principle of Population' proposed that birth control and the cessation of charity to the underprivileged were essential to the development of society.*

their economies and their population growth, automatically contrive their own demise through famine and plague as exemplified by the tragic experience of the Irish. This may have a cold logic in the vast overall scheme of things, but it seems to me a highly uncharitable reasoning, and anyway has little to do with the exhibition.

I'm glad to say that C is careful not to associate himself directly with any of these particular factions, but I know from his conversations that his opinion follows similar paths and it pains me that such a generous heart can accommodate such a bleak philosophy. I wish I could get him and the Revd Malthus in the same room together. I suspect they would soon disagree on their theories and might even come to blows!

The more orthodox clerics however are claiming similar substantiation in the celestial grandeur of the great show. The Anglicans in particular are trumpeting that it proves the Kingdom of God is finding its rightful (i.e. British) place on earth. I'm not sure where that leaves all the other nations, but in any case it is a strange paradox that both sides of the religious debate can find equal justification in this fabulous testimony to human progress.

At any rate our London expedition has served as a welcome diversion, and lifted our spirits for the first time in the year since our darling Annie's passing (how she would have loved the exhibition). This in fact is the first entry I have felt able to make in my journal since that awful day. It is a loss from which neither C nor I will ever properly recover—she was truly the light of our lives—but this experience has at least shown us that life <u>can</u> continue after death, and gives us the strength to move onwards once again. Even though I suspect that for Charles her death extinguished any last remaining spark of belief in a divine guidance. I see a shadow cross his face whenever anyone mentions such matters, and I take care not to do so myself in his presence.

For myself, I could not have continued without my prayers to sustain me.

CHAPTER THIRTY-SIX

We need not marvel at extinction. If we must marvel, let it be at our presumption in imagining for a moment that we understand the many complex contingencies on which the existence of each species depends. If we forget for an instant that each species tends to increase inordinately, and that some check is always in action, the whole economy of nature will be utterly obscured.

Origin of Species

It was the last Sunday in March, a distinctly damp and chilly one, when Maurice found himself sitting in his car contemplating the exterior of the Fanning's home. One of those spacious ranked brick villas that the Victorians threw up in such immense numbers around London's outer suburbs to meet the ever growing demands of the affluent middle classes. Its rooms were spacious to accommodate large families and frequent entertaining, its attics generous to house the servants, and its garden vast by most modern city standards. It had probably been built at the time for a few hundreds of pounds, and the constructors would have gasped at the sums such places fetched now. They would have been even more astounded at the size of the loans outstanding on the vast majority of them. Especially this one, if the owner was in as much financial trouble as Robert Gresham had suggested.

That owner was managing to keep up appearances though. Two newish looking Mercedes, his and hers, were parked on the forecourt, and elegant pot plants guarded the approach to the front door. 'All right for some,' muttered Maurice. Apart from the cars there was little sign of life. As he watched from across the street he thought he saw shadows cross the ground floor windows once or twice, and a blind had risen at one point upstairs, but that was all. However he was in no hurry, and sat listening to some Mozart on Classic Radio for a good twenty minutes as he waited, for what he wasn't sure.

He was just pouring himself a second cup of coffee, laced with a second shot of scotch from the thermos he had prepared before coming out ('Shut up, Alice, I've earned it'), when there was a tap on his passenger side window and he looked up to see a faintly indignant male face peering in at him. He lowered the window and the man, a middle-aged fellow with the sallow features of an accountant or an IT consultant, leaned lower and said, 'Excuse me but did you know that you were partially blocking our driveway?'

'Oh, er. . . . I'm so sorry,' Maurice apologised. 'It was hard to find a spot and I thought I'd left enough room.'

The other mollified his tone. 'Well it doesn't matter too much as long as you aren't going to be there all day. It was just that we weren't sure what you were doing sitting there for so long.'

'Oh, I was just um. . . . killing some time. I was a little. . . . early for a meeting,' stuttered Maurice. 'It's all right, I'll move on now.' Flustered over where to put his coffee, eventually started the engine, and pulled out. In his haste he almost collided with a black SUV with tinted windows which was approaching from down the street. An angry blast from its horn and Maurice stopped abruptly, just in time. This was becoming a habit. Waved his apologies at the black anonymous windows as it passed, then drove on, his heart rate doubled. He looked back in his mirror and saw the local resident standing on the pavement staring after him, whilst the SUV was backing into a parking space beyond. He was to remember the significance of that image all too well before long.

He drove on towards the South East suburbs.

The village of Downe, as it is now spelt, is a strange place. Something of an anomaly. A mere fifteen miles from the centre of London and yet it still has the air of a remote country hamlet. For some reason the relentless growth of the capital's suburban tentacles has bypassed this little corner of Kent and left it a rural oasis, considerably more affluent than in Darwin's day and doubtless inhabited mostly by well heeled commuters, yet in aspect little changed for all that.

Down House itself, having survived for almost a century in a slowly deteriorating state, was now a museum, restored to probably a much sprucer and better groomed state than ever it was as a bustling family home. As Maurice drove into the public car park to one side of the property he noted with pleasant surprise the respectable number of cars and a couple of tourist buses parked there. Still quite a lot of interest in the old boy, he thought.

He walked the short distance to the house, masked from the road by a thick stone wall and a barrier of foliage, and looked up at its rather stark, white-painted exterior. Not especially distinguished architecturally to be sure, but it had an air of space and grace, a feel of solid and reflective respectability, whilst preserving the privacy of its interior with an aloof anonymity. Very appropriate, thought Maurice.

He pushed open the tall front door and went in. The ticket desk was manned by one of those ubiquitous middle-aged ladies without whose volunteer services the stately homes and small museums of England would be unable to function. Just the sort of thing Alice would have enjoyed doing. Bought his ticket and received a cheery smile and a brief tour instruction in return, and mingled with the assortment of visitors treading the corridors with hushed deference.

It was one of the more fascinating experiences of Maurice's life. He wandered about the unostentatious rooms, where the atmosphere of genteel Victorian family life was so lovingly preserved, with something akin to reverence. It was not hard to picture the long ago coming and going of servants, tradesmen, family visitors, the scampering of children, the clattering of kitchen cooks, the tip-toeing past the study where the head of the family was engaged in his precise and arcane experiments. And within that study itself, where all his books and files and instruments were so astonishingly intact, it was easier still to imagine the atmosphere of intense investigation, of murmured consultation, of painstaking notation that filled the hours, weeks and years during those exploratory times.

The revelations continued when he went out into the grounds and meandered amongst the well tended lawns, the large seed beds and original glass houses, where all manner of plants had been propagated and biological experiments conducted. And of course the famous sand walk where Darwin himself had regularly strolled, his cane clicking amongst the stones like a metronome to his meditations.

Not surprisingly however, there were no clues anywhere as to hidden manuscripts or undiscovered archives. He could hardly have expected such after more than a century, but a small part of him had hoped that perhaps a Sherlockian clue which no-one else had spotted in all that time might have leapt to his notice. Even so, thank heavens he had made the trip, thought Maurice. This brought the whole enterprise to life. It took the quest from the realms of intellectual supposition, and made it human. He wanted to find this journal. He wanted to know more about this extraordinary family which one hundred and fifty years previously had nurtured within its bosom the seeds of a philosophical revolution.

'Oh, Alice,' he muttered as he headed back to the car park some three hours after arriving, 'Oh, Alice, what a place, eh? Wasn't that fascinating? Wouldn't you have loved to have run a household like that?'

'No thank you, dear,' she would have replied. 'Ten painful births, constant squealing children, a plethora of servants to manage, and a husband with his nose permanently in rotting plants and decaying corpses. Not for me, my dear, but very interesting all the same.'

Yes, all right, concurred Maurice mentally, but if we can discover her book we'll find out how she felt about it all herself. That, you and I would both surely love to know.

As he climbed into his car and began the journey home he went over the topography of the house in his mind, trying to imagine where Emma might have written the record of her life. Did she sit daily at an appointed hour at the same desk where she composed her numerous letters? Did she retire to the privacy of her separate bedroom? In summer did she have a favourite secluded corner of the garden to which she retreated? And where did she keep her musings safe from the prying eyes of servants, family and friends? In a secret drawer in her desk? Hidden behind a skirting or under some creaking floor-board? Tucked behind the volumes in the library? Who knows, perhaps a few original pages might still be there—having survived the comings and goings of subsequent generations—rotting and yellowing in some dust filled crevice of the house.

He wondered whether the house had affected Easterby in the same way when he visited, or whether he had merely looked upon it as another object of dry historical interest. Knowing more of the man now, he thought that unlikely.

'All right, Donald,' he murmured at the road ahead, 'let's find this bloody thing.'

CHAPTER THIRTY-SEVEN

May 16th, 1952. Wakefield.

I am still managing to keep myself quite well occupied here despite the tedium. I have my journal, my books, my chess games, my duties in the library. And of course my mathematics. The fortunate thing about being a theoretical physicist as opposed to a practical one is that I don't require equipment. All I need is a pencil and paper, and with those I can let my imagination run riot. I can test the most fantastical hypotheses about the quantum world, I can explore the wildest theories about the cosmos.

It was during my years in that extraordinary country America that I started to truly appreciate the infinite possibilities of scientific discovery. By the end of 1943 everyone was convinced the creation of an atomic bomb was no longer just a theoretical concept but a real possibility, and I was sent with a group of other scientists to New York to collaborate directly with the Americans on the joint effort to achieve it. I had by this time attained my British citizenship and I was granted an American visa in my capacity as an 'official' of the British government. This might seem ironic as I was still passing on all technical data I could lay my hands on to the Russians, but they were after all our allies and had already done more than any other nation to wear down the resources of the Third Reich.

It was arranged with them that I should have a new go-between in New York, and I was given the most complex of instructions as to how to make contact. Thus it was that I found myself, at a specific date and time, walking along a specific street between the astounding skyscrapers of

Manhattan, wearing specific clothes and carrying, of all things, a tennis ball, whilst looking out for another man, also wearing specific clothes and carrying a specific book, to whom I was to introduce myself with a specific phrase and whom I was only ever to know by a specific codename. I felt like someone who had stepped out of the pages of a Joseph Conrad novel!

Looking back on that time from the perspective of my cell, I often wonder how history would have turned out if my actions had enabled Russia to achieve the bomb before the allies did. I know now that they did not have an immediate effect on the outcome of the Second World War, since it anyway ended abruptly when America dropped the bomb, but they had considerable effect on what came after. What they are calling the Cold War. It is a fact that Russia is now virtually equal to the West in its nuclear capability, due largely to my efforts, and I worry occasionally that this is the right consequence given the enmity that prevails between the two sides. But it is a major factor in maintaining the status quo. A balance of power must surely be right. As is a balance in all things.

This is a short entry. I am tired of writing. I am tired of looking for answers to questions I am no longer sure are relevant. Actually I'm tired of wondering even what the questions are.

I look up at my small patch of sky and count the days until I am released from this dreary place. Even though I won't know what to do when that happens.

I suspect I will still be in a prison. The prison of my mind.

CHAPTER THIRTY-EIGHT

He who believes in separate and innumerable acts of creation will say that in these cases it has pleased the Creator to cause a being of one type to take the place of one of another type. . . . He who believes in the principle of natural selection, will acknowledge that every organic being is constantly endeavouring to increase in numbers; and that if any one being vary ever so little, either in habits or structure, and thus gain an advantage over some other inhabitant of the country, it will seize on the place of that inhabitant, however different it may be from its own place.

Origin of Species

Looking back, it seemed to Maurice that the Monday after his visit to the Darwin home was the most traumatic day of his life. Even including the day Alice died, for that was after all expected. And even the day of the London bombs, for that was pure chance.

The first hint he got that all was not as it should be was when Roger Hemingway failed to turn up for work. There was no indication, no message, and when Maurice tried his mobile number there was no answer. Once again he was unaccountably without assistance in the shop. He managed all right by himself during the morning, made do with a coffee and his mints for lunch, and was rearranging the military and warfare section (one of his least favourite, but needs must) when a youngish man in a raincoat came into the shop accompanied by a uniformed policeman.

'Mr Aldridge?' said the first man.

Maurice was gazing at his colleague's uniform. He looked back. 'Yes?'

The man showed an identity card. 'Detective Sergeant Macintyre.' His nondescript face was impassive. He glanced round the shop. 'Are you the proprietor here?'

'Yes.'

'Are you on your own?'

It sounded like some sort of accusation. 'Yes.' A brief silence followed. Maurice felt obliged to fill it. 'My, er. . . . my assistant isn't here at the moment.'

'Your assistant?'

'Yes. He . . . failed to show up this morning.' He glanced at the uniformed man, who looked as if he should still be in the fifth form. 'What's this about?'

The plain clothes man was fishing in his inside pocket. 'What is your assistant's name, sir?'

'Um. . . . Hemingway. Roger Hemingway.'

A postcard sized photo came from the pocket and the man held it out. 'Is this him?'

The Hemingway in the photo looked gaunter and grimmer than the one Maurice knew. 'Yes, that's him. Has something happened to him?'

'Why did you call him Hemingway?'

Maurice frowned. 'Because that's his name.'

The man's face was inscrutable. 'It's not actually.'

'I don't. . . . I. . . .' Maurice waited for enlightenment. Neither of the policemen showed any expression, or gave any clue as to their mission. 'Can you tell me what this is about?'

Again the detective looked round the shop, then back at Maurice. 'We need you to come with us to Hampstead Police Station, Mr Aldridge. Are you able to lock the shop up?'

Maurice put a hand to his tie. 'Lock up? I don't understand. What . . .?'

'We have to ask you some questions. It would be best if you came of your own accord.'

'My own accord. . . .? What sort of questions? Can't I answer them here?'

'My superiors are wanting to talk to you. I'm afraid we need you to come to the station.'

A police car was waiting around the corner from the shop. The ride to Hampstead seemed interminable. Not one of the policemen said a word throughout the journey, and neither did Maurice. He desperately wanted a drink, and his collar seemed to have shrunk. He barely took in the police building in Hampstead where the car arrived, and the corridors and stairways whence he was led passed in a blur. He eventually found himself seated behind a table in a bland, bare room, with just the same uniformed bobby for company. The detective sergeant had vanished somewhere along the way. They waited for perhaps five minutes, Maurice motionless, his eyes fixed on the table in front of him.

The door finally opened and the detective sergeant entered accompanied by an older man, also in plain clothes. Mid forties perhaps, tall, and remarkably handsome in a slightly worn sort of way. He could have been a semi-alcoholic and much married film star whose career was beginning to slide. He placed a file on the table, took the seat opposite Maurice and gazed at him. Maurice blinked behind his spectacles and waited.

'I'm Detective Chief Inspector William Ramsay, Mr Aldridge. From Scotland Yard.'

Maurice was never sure how high up a Chief Inspector was. They always seemed to be Chief Inspectors on TV. But whether he was the army equivalent of, say, a Brigadier, or just a mere Colonel he had no idea.

The man opened his file. 'We have a few questions.'

'What about?' Maurice's voice was one degree louder than a whisper.

'We're investigating an incident involving a Mr Nicholas Fanning. Do you know him?'

Maurice stopped blinking. 'Incident?'

The film star eyes were unflinching. 'Do you know him?'

'No. At least. . . . I know of him. I've never met him. What . . .?'

'Where were you yesterday?'

Through all the exploding lava in Maurice's brain something told him to be extremely cautious.

'Yesterday? I, er. . . . I went to Downe in Kent. I went to visit the Charles Darwin home there.'

'What time was that?'

'Um . . . late in the morning.'

'Was that the only place you visited?'

'Yes.' Well, it was true it was the only place he had actually entered.

The man looked down at the file in front of him. 'Weren't you at Highgate before that?'

Oh God. How often in the past had Alice said, never lie to the authorities—it rarely pays. 'Highgate?'

'We have a witness who says that you were at Fitzroy Grove in Highgate at around eleven o'clock yesterday morning.'

'Yes. Yes, I was.'

'So why did you say you didn't go anywhere else?'

'I didn't. . . . didn't actually visit anywhere. I just stopped there for a while.'

'Why would you wish to stop in Highgate?'

No more lies, whispered her voice. 'I went to . . . I went to look at Fanning's house.'

'You went to look at it?'

'Yes.'

'Why?'

'I . . . It. . . .' How could he possibly explain the complex series of events that had brought him to that place the previous day?

'We gather that you sat in your car outside his house for at least twenty minutes, Mr Aldridge. We do have a witness.'

Maurice remembered the neighbour who had accosted him as he watched the Fanning home. The policeman was continuing. 'The witness was concerned enough about your behaviour to take down your registration number. Which is how we found you.'

Maurice found his voice. 'Yes. The man who lived opposite.'

'Why would you want to look at that house for twenty minutes?'

'I. . . . It's complicated.'

'Try and explain.'

'I. . . . I'm trying to find something for a client. I'm a rare book dealer, you see. I believed that this. . . . this item might be at the Fanning's house. . . . or they might know something about it.'

'Item?'

'A manuscript of sorts.'

'Why didn't you go in?'

'Well I. . . . I don't actually know them, and I. . . .' He gave up the impossible task of explaining himself and lapsed into silence.

The policeman looked at the file again. 'This man you call Roger Hemingway. . . . He's your assistant, you say?'

'Yes.'

'Since when?'

'Oh, only a week or so. He's quite new.'

'Why?'

Strange question. Maurice frowned. 'I don't understand. What do you mean, why?'

'Why would you take on someone like this to be an assistant in a book shop?'

'Someone like what?'

'Did he have experience? Did he know about books?'

'Well, not much but. . . . It was an emergency. My previous assistant had left me and I needed someone urgently. He happened to be there, and. . . .'

'He happened to be there?'

'Yes.'

'Convenient.'

'Well, he did have references, and. . . .'

'Ah, references.' The tone was cynical.

At last Maurice found his mind again. 'Look, will you please tell me what's happened? What is this all about?'

'A murder.'

The ground shook.

'Murder? Who's been murdered?'

'Mr Nicholas Fanning.'

Time had stopped. 'Fanning? Murdered?'

'Murder or manslaughter—we're not sure which yet.'

'How? Who. . . .?'

The man was watching Maurice intently as he spoke. 'He was tortured, Mr Aldridge. Tortured we think to reveal the whereabouts of the manuscript you were interested in. He died either because of the torture, or because of a heart attack suffered during the torture.'

Maurice wasn't sure whether the volcano was in his stomach or his head. He could not connect any of this with reality. 'Tortured?'

'Badly.' The policeman left a long pause. Then he leaned forward slightly, the first time he had changed his position. 'We think he was killed by your assistant in the shop and an accomplice. A man known as George Cummins. Would you know him?'

Maurice shook his head. The other took a photograph from the file and pushed it across the table. It was of a middle aged man with broad shoulders and a heavy square face. He was wearing a pale grey suit and a rather gaudy tie. He seemed vaguely familiar, but Maurice had no idea why. He whispered, 'I don't know him.'

'Are you quite sure?'

'Well, I. . . . Yes, quite sure.'

'Yet he and your Roger Hemingway entered the house at about the very time you were there yourself.'

'The same time?'

'As near as we can tell.'

'I didn't. . . . I never saw. . . .'

'They drove there in a black BMW four-by-four and parked quite close to where you parked.' Oh God, thought Maurice—the car he had nearly driven into. Ramsay was tapping the photo. 'This man works closely with your man.'

'Works with?'

'He runs what might loosely be described as a detective agency. But you know that.'

'No. I told you I've never seen him.'

'You haven't employed his agency to help you find your manuscript?'

'No. Certainly not.'

'Yet he—George Cummins—employs your. . . . assistant as an assistant himself. They're both known to us, Mr Aldridge. They tread a fine line with the law. Cummins already has various convictions.'

Maurice closed his eyes and his breaths were swift and shallow.

'The man you call Hemingway is actually Roger Farringdon. I think you knew that.'

Maurice could only shake his head wordlessly.

'Well, we'll soon know. We have him and George Cummins in custody here in the building.'

Maurice's spectacles had misted over, or perhaps it was just that his sight had stopped functioning properly. 'Here?'

'By strange coincidence our associates at Marylebone Police Station had been investigating a complaint against them.'

Maurice waited.

'Your previous assistant. . . .' he consulted his file again. '. . . . Mr Rupert Johns?' Maurice nodded minutely. '. . . . had filed a complaint that he was assaulted, threatened and forced to leave your employment by the man he identified as George Cummins.'

258

'Assaulted?'

'Yes. He was accosted near his home, knocked about quite painfully, and warned not to come in to work again. He was also warned not to tell anyone, but he thought about it for a day and then very bravely went to the police at Marylebone.' Oh, god—poor Rupert, thought Maurice. The policeman was watching him intently. 'Would you know anything about that?'

'No. No, I don't. He said. . . . he told me there was a family emergency. . . . He just left without any notice.'

'Just left?'

'Yes.'

'Of course, had you in fact *wanted* him to leave it would have been a little difficult—employment conditions, redundancy payments, all that.'

'Why would I want him to leave?"

'You were immediately able to hire this new assistant. Rather conveniently, as I said.'

Maurice's brain refused to function. 'Well I don't. . . . I didn't. . . .'

'You see, Mr Aldridge, we were fortunate. These two were pretty clumsy operators from the start. We got onto you very quickly thanks to the neighbour who took down your registration number. We tracked the car to you and your shop, and that of course connected up with the Marylebone enquiry into Cummins and his associate Farringdon. That was just a minor investigation at the time, but it turned into a major one.' For the first time there was a hint of expression on the man's face—ironic humour perhaps? 'Police methods of communication and cross reference are quite sophisticated these days.' The expression vanished. 'They were identified as the people who assaulted Mr Fanning by his wife—who incidentally was also treated pretty badly and traumatised. We arrested both men this morning, which is why Farringdon didn't turn up for work at your shop today. Although it's highly unlikely you would have wanted him there anyway after what happened. Wouldn't you say?'

This time the silence went on for even longer. The eyes of all three policemen were on Maurice but he could find no word in response. Finally the matinee idol drew a breath and asked, 'Have you anything to add to what you've told us, Mr Aldridge?'

Maurice shook his head. His neck muscles seemed to have barely enough strength to hold it upright.

'Then I must tell you that I'm arresting you on suspicion of conspiracy to cause grievous bodily harm to Mr Nicholas Fanning and his wife for the purpose of procuring information which might lead to financial gain. You do not need say anything which. . . . .' The voice went on for some time, but Maurice heard nothing through the volcano's roar.

Eventually he regained his senses enough to understand that he was being asked a question. '. . . . there must be someone. Do you have a lawyer? Is there anyone you'd like to contact?'

He looked about him vaguely, then took out his wallet. Donald Easterby's card with his email and various phone numbers was in it. It was the only thing he could think of.

CHAPTER THIRTY-NINE

November 31st, 1853. Down House.

(We are now supposed to write the village as 'Downe' to prevent confusion with County Down in Ireland, but I cannot bring myself to use such an ugly spelling, and anyway the house stays as Down House whatever the bureaucrats think.)

Charles has been to London to receive the Royal Medal from the Royal Society! It is awarded annually, with great ceremony in front of the whole membership, to the naturalist who has made the most distinguished contribution to science. It is the highest honour that illustrious body can bestow. I am so proud of him.

The award was initially intended as a tribute to his great book on the Beagle voyage and his other studies from that journey, but dear Joseph Hooker, who of course sits on the council, reported that when C's new volume on barnacles was mentioned at the latest meeting the whole room burst into spontaneous applause, and so his award was confirmed on the back of the simplest of living creatures.

Well, thank heavens all his efforts and all our tribulations over barnacles have come to an end and been suitably rewarded. It began with a short little treatise on his 'Mr Arthrobalanus' and ended eight years later with a detailed study, almost sixteen hundred pages long, of every wretched barnacle species on the planet. Most of which have passed through our house at one stage or another! I do believe that C is as relieved to be rid of the creatures as are the rest of the family. I am still not certain quite what their relevance is to the whole concept of transmutation and evolution, but evidently the Royal Society considers them crucial so who am I to question it?

Joseph Hooker is now as eminent in his own field of biology as C is in his. He is still the only person apart from myself who knows C's ultimate vision of the true nature of evolution. Joseph has always of course supported the theory of the gradual development of species through the generations, but never admitted to accepting C's concept of it as an accidental treelike structure whence all species have branched off haphazardly from the same primordial microcosms. However I suspect from the conversations at the dinner table when he visits, that he is gradually coming round to C's opinion. Indeed when there was a gap in the conversation yesterday evening, I taxed him on the matter. He was reluctant to answer, but then glanced at C and said, "I know this is an issue between you and Charles, Emma, but I have to say I cannot now accept the biblical version of the Creation. Thanks especially to your husband's researches I can no longer believe in an organised nature with man and the beasts all preconceived by God. In fact I would go so far as to say that the whole notion is no more credible than that of the Trinity and the life hereafter—nothing more nor less than mythology."

My heart sank at such an emphatic loss of someone I counted as an ally. "Where then did such ideas originate?" I demanded.

"It seems to me," he replied, "that they are imaginary concepts which have filled the gap of what the human mind cannot grasp, because science up till now has not been able to produce a better logical explanation."

Charles said little, but sat back with what I recognise as a replete look on his face. His revered disciple was expressing his own long held secret thoughts.

However I cannot abandon the beliefs and instructions of a lifetime for such a philosophy. Later that night, when we were alone together, I dared to query it more directly to

Charles. For the first time that I recollect I made a serious attempt to challenge him on the premise. I asked whence came his confidence in his own belief? Why should he think that his conception was right when it contravened that of the vast majority of thinking persons? How he could presume that all those centuries of spiritual teaching, the writings of all the most learned minds through the generations, the entire vast edifice of church and biblical tradition are all built on superstition?

To do him credit he has never tried to dissuade me of my faith. Nor did he now. He merely said, "Mankind has always relied on divine traditions and supernatural hypotheses to explain the mysteries of life. It is in fact a tribute to man's evolving intelligence that he can invent such towering concepts by which to make sense of a mystifying universe. And it is up to each individual to choose their own creed from all those on offer." But then he put the sting in the tail by adding, with that twinkle in the eye that I know so well, "They cannot however <u>all</u> be right. Therefore it is incumbent upon individuals to make a proper study of each proposition in order to fully understand it. And you, Emma, are a highly intelligent person who could readily understand our propositions if you chose."

Well I do try to understand his propositions. But my mind is ever in conflict with my heart over them. Which of course is part of his thesis. Intellectual interpretation versus emotional instinct.

Ah well, I take consolation however from the fact that neither C nor any of his fellow thinkers have yet come up with an alternative answer to the question, whence did the initial spark of Life originate in the first place? That is a conundrum that pure science will surely never solve. One to which only the Almighty knows the answer.

C is now sucking the juice of two whole lemons a day to add to the therapy of his regular cold water douches. He does seem somewhat the better for it, and is going up to London rather more frequently to enjoy the company of his fellow scholars. He is sleeping better too. For purely personal reasons I am glad of that. To put it as delicately as possible, the less wakeful and restless his nights, the less likely I am to get with child again!

CHAPTER FORTY

It is the most closely-allied forms, species of the same genus or of related genera, which, from having nearly the same structure, constitution, and habits, generally come into the severest competition with each other. Consequently each new variety or species, during the progress of its formation, will generally press hardest on its nearest kindred and tend to exterminate them.

Origin of Species

'Oh, Maurice—dear man, I am so sorry. How can I apologise enough?' Donald Easterby had risen from his seat as Maurice was conducted into the room. Another man in a Savile Row suit rose at his side. He was stern faced and distinguished looking. In his bewilderment Maurice misinterpreted his presence—was this another official sent to torment him with demonic facts? Donald introduced him. 'This is Justin Laurenson, a criminal lawyer. We'll have you out of here soon, don't worry.' The man smiled then and shook Maurice's hand. Maurice's only thought was how sweaty his own palm must feel. He was pale and unshaven. The volcano had rumbled on and off all night, and he had slept little in his cell. When he did sleep the nightmares had almost immediately woken him again. He glanced at the copper standing by the door. 'I don't understand what's happened,' he mumbled.

'Sit down, Maurice, before you fall down.' Donald had taken his arm and was guiding him into a chair by the central table. He stood at his side and put a hand on his shoulder. 'What's happened is that you've fallen foul of a move to beat us at our own game. One which went catastrophically wrong.' He moved round the table to stand opposite again. There was genuine concern in his eyes. 'I'll explain shortly, but the first thing is to get you out of this place and back home.'

'How. . . . how can you do that? They think I'm to blame.'

The lawyer spoke for the first time. 'They were a little premature in their assessment, Mr Aldridge.' His voice was deep, cultured, like an actor's. 'They may come to regret it. At any rate we'll do our best to make them do so.'

The door opened and Chief Inspector Ramsay entered with the detective sergeant who had first accosted Maurice. Donald stepped back a pace. 'Can we get this over as quickly as possible, please? This is my lawyer—Justin Laurenson. You spoke on the phone this morning.'

Ramsay nodded. 'Ah, Mr Laurenson. Yes, we've checked some of the facts you gave us and they appear to be correct.'

'Of course they're correct, Chief Inspector.' The lawyer's tone was abrupt. 'It's a pity they weren't checked before you made the arrest.'

Ramsay stared back at him impassively. 'This is a serious case, Mr Laurenson. We did what needed to be done on all the available evidence, and we had to move fast.' He turned to Maurice. 'We're letting you go, Mr Aldridge, for the time being. It would seem that you might have been the victim. . . . I should say another victim—of an involved fraud aimed at getting hold of this mysterious Darwin document. I gather it could be valuable.' The film star gaze remained fixed on Maurice for a second. 'However we must ask you to remain available for further questioning. An extremely serious crime has been committed and until we get to the bottom of it you remain a key witness.'

Maurice blinked through his spectacles and nodded. As always in this place he could think of nothing to say. His need for a drink was desperate. Donald and the lawyer talked for several minutes with the police but he paid little attention. All he could think was, how on earth could such a seemingly innocent business as the search for an old book have brought him to such a situation? How could such an innocuous quest play such havoc with his life? Anger began to take over from fear, which perhaps was no bad thing.

Eventually he was asked to sign various forms, the content of which he was again incapable of digesting, and the two men conducted him from the building. Outside on the pavement, with the London traffic growling impassively past, Laurenson spoke briefly to Maurice about his legal rights and the procedures that would now follow—none of which Maurice remotely remembered afterwards. Then the lawyer departed to whatever lofty sanctum he dwelt in and Donald ushered Maurice into a taxi, awkwardly contorting his long body to climb in after him.

He gave the driver instructions to Maurice's home at Primrose Hill, then settled back beside the other and put a hand on his arm. 'It's all right, dear man. I know how awful that must have been for you. You're in shock, but you needn't fear. You won't be going back there again.'

The anger furrowed Maurice's brow. 'How. . . . what happened exactly?' he asked. Then wished he hadn't. He wasn't sure he wished to know.

Donald was staring ahead out of the taxi. 'Maurice, you're not going to believe this. Soon as I got your call in France, the first thing I did was get onto my London lawyers and told them to raise hell. Then I did some serious thinking. I wasn't sure quite what had happened of course, but whatever it was it obviously had to do with the thing we're chasing. And whoever was behind it obviously knew where we'd got to.' Maurice listened with more concentration. His brain was beginning to function. 'Now there are very few people who knew about our arrangement, least of all what it's purpose was. Top of the roll call of course was Tommy Houseman who gave me the introduction to you in the first place.' Flashes went off in Maurice's head. 'Now Tommy's a ruthless son-of-a-bitch when it comes to his collection, but he's not a gangster.' Donald turned his gaze to Maurice. 'I phoned him yesterday, soon after your call.' Satisfaction glinted in his eyes. 'It was early hours of the morning in Michigan so I woke the bastard out of a deep sleep and caught him off guard. Told him what had happened, with embellishments, and threatened him with every reprisal in the book unless he came clean.'

Maurice was still, expressionless. 'What did he say?'

'He blustered a bit, but eventually opened up. He admitted to having been curious about what I was after.'

'Yes,' said Maurice in a cold voice. 'I didn't mention it, but he called a couple of times, trying to find out about it.'

Donald's eyebrows went up. 'Why didn't you tell me?'

'I didn't think it mattered.' Maurice suddenly felt foolish. 'I was naive. I never imagined. . . .' He took off his specs and got to work with his tie.

Donald grunted. 'I wish you'd said, Maurice. I would have realised it might get serious.' He rubbed his brow. 'You see, he made some more enquiries after I'd talked to him that first time. I don't know how, but he got some inkling of what I was about. Being Houseman he couldn't resist trying to discover more details.' He waved his hand in a gesture of disbelief. 'Arsehole! It seems he approached some one-horse detective agency here in London on the flimsiest of recommendations, and in his haste commissioned them to keep an eye on you and find out what they could about our search.' He raised a cynical eyebrow. 'He didn't realise—at least I'm pretty sure he didn't realise—that they were just a bunch of punks operating under the guise of an agency, who used it as a front for every type of scam that's going. Turns out they're probably into drugs, prostitution, pornography— all the usual crappy operations. Well, rare manuscripts are a new departure for them, but Tommy evidently gave them a lurid account of how much the things he was after might be worth, and they pulled out all the stops.' Donald's expression was dry as he looked at Maurice. 'They were quite ingenious actually. Certainly took you for a ride.' Maurice replaced his specs, feeling even more foolish. 'They got rid of your old assistant with strong arm tactics, and cleverly installed this Hemingway character in his place. He was able to find out about your business and trace all your moves. I gather he even got from you that it was a Darwin manuscript we were after.' Maurice wilted with embarrassment. Donald gazed reflectively into space. 'It's an ironic thing. Natural science and evolution is not one of Tommy's main interests—you probably know that. But philosophy is. Why a banker should have such a leaning I don't know, but he's got a huge collection of philosophic papers and first editions by big names in the business—Wittgenstein, Russell, Hoyle, Stuart Mill—an impressive list. When he learned this could be some important new Darwinian item, he told me he just had to have it.' Donald shook his head. 'I asked him, why the hell?—and he confirmed what I've always said to you. Darwin was the daddy of them all. Darwin puts all the rest into context.' He gestured again. 'So he lost his head and told his guys to go after it, no expense spared. He didn't realise he was giving criminals carte blanche to turn the search into a major crime job.' He looked back at Maurice with a rueful expression. 'It's the trouble with compulsions like ours, Maurice. Once you get wind of something really interesting you just can't relax until you get hold of it. Art collectors are the same. There's only the one Van Gogh, only the one Rodin—and no amount of copies or reproductions will fill the bill. It's why the international market for stolen works is so flourishing.' He shook his head and tapped the taxi's arm rest with his fingers. 'It's a weird contradiction in values. God knows how many rare pieces, pictures, manuscripts are locked away in hidden vaults, never to be seen by the common eye.'

Maurice nodded silently. He was too angry to care about the compulsions of billionaire collectors.

'Anyway—soon as I guessed what the scene was, soon as I tumbled that you'd probably fallen foul of these motherfuckers, I caught the first plane from Nice. And here we are.'

'Thank you,' murmured Maurice. 'I couldn't have. . . . I didn't. . . .'

'No, thank *you*, Maurice. You've been through a horrendous experience on my behalf, and I feel very bad about it.' He patted Maurice on the knee as if he was some faithful hound. 'The one good thing about it all is that we don't think they got anything from the Fannings.'

Maurice was fearful of asking his next question, but he needed to know. 'What. . . .? What actually happened there?'

Silence for a moment. Donald stared out at the passing traffic. 'You've got to admire their ingenuity. Seems they'd been following your every move, Maurice. The younger of them, the guy you knew as Hemingway, first wheedled his way into your trust by coming in to talk books—quite a new angle for him I imagine—got talking to your assistant, and found out where he lived. Then the other one visited the poor boy and bullied him into leaving. So, in the emergency they'd created for you Hemingway was able to take his place.' Donald cast an ironic look at his co-passenger. 'Got to hand it to him—he pulled the wool over your eyes pretty smartly, Maurice. He's obviously a bit of a charmer but I think you may have been a little naive there.'

Maurice stared into space.

'He was able to listen to your phone calls, read all your notes and diary entries or whatever. . . . Do you keep your office locked when you go out?'

Maurice nodded. 'Always.'

'Well, I don't suppose old door locks are much of a challenge to guys like that. Anyway, the upshot was that when they found out about the Fanning connection, they simply followed the trail and turned up there themselves—it would seem shortly after your visit.' His lips twisted. 'However they didn't content themselves with merely observing the Fanning house. They had to go barging in there. They had to go the whole hog and use mafia methods to find out whether the Fannings had anything.'

'What. . . .? What did they do?'

'It wasn't good, Maurice.' Donald clasped his hands together and stared at the floor of the cab. 'They slapped the wife around, then beat up the husband. Then when they couldn't get any joy from him—either because he couldn't tell them anything or because he was pig-headed—they stripped him and started splashing boiling water on him from a kettle.' A beat. 'Hard to credit, isn't it?'

Impossible for Maurice to credit—that any human being could do that to another.

'The wife was forced to watch, but couldn't do anything tied and gagged. After some while of this the husband apparently had a heart attack. The thugs realised they'd gone too far, panicked and fled the scene. The wife eventually managed to free herself and get to a phone, but it was too late. By the time the medics and the police arrived he was dead.'

Silence in the cab. The familiar streets sailed by as so often before, impassive, unknowing, uncaring. Maurice tried to prevent images of the scene from looming too vividly in his mind, and wondered at this latest example of man's inhumanity to man. For once he wasn't moved to look to Alice for consolation. He had no wish to imagine her pain at such circumstances.

They arrived at his address and Donald opened the cab door. 'Can I come up?' he asked. Maurice nodded, and Donald leaned forward to speak to the cabbie. 'Can you wait here? I'll be down in a few minutes.'

Maurice led the way up to the flat. It was the first time Donald had been there but he gave it little attention as they entered. He paced around in his usual manner, then stood in the middle of the wide living room and said, 'I'll quite understand if you want to drop this whole business, Maurice. Seems we were up a dead end with the Fanning thing anyway.'

Maurice, who was finally pouring the drink he had been desperate for during the last twenty four hours, looked up. 'Oh?'

'Mrs Fanning has admitted to the police that they did have access to the stolen trunk, but there was nothing of much interest in it—certainly no Darwin journals or papers. She claims it was her husband who instigated the robbery without her knowledge. Don't know if that's true, but it's too late to bother about now. The police aren't going to press charges over it.'

He waved away the proffered scotch bottle, and Maurice slumped wearily into his chair with his glass. He was home, and for the first time since leaving the police station he experienced relief—a wave which flooded over him and left him calmer but totally exhausted. He felt he had aged ten years in twenty four hours.

Donald contemplated him for a moment, then awkwardly levered himself down into Alice's neat boudoir chair opposite. He was far too big for it. 'Hell of an ordeal, Maurice. I can only apologise for getting you into it. I just hope they put those morons away for the rest of their lives.'

'I can't. . . . I don't know how I can have been so stupid,' mumbled Maurice. 'He had references, but to take him on with so little thought, without. . . .' He lapsed into silence.

Donald shrugged. 'Yes, well—they're cunning these operators. Not intelligent, but cunning. I guess it's the law of the jungle. The more primitive the species, the cleverer their hunting techniques.' He crossed the great legs. 'Now look—I have to take the plane back to France in the morning. I suggest you take a day or two to get back on an even keel. The lawyers will stay in touch. I don't think you'll have much more trouble with the police, but if you do we'll be there to help.' He spread his hands. 'Meanwhile let's just step back and look at all this from a distance. You probably don't want much more to do with it for a while, and I have to decide whether I'm still interested in pursuing such a nebulous thing.'

Maurice nodded. He couldn't begin to think about such matters now. His social graces clicked into action. 'Sorry— if you don't want a drink, would you like a cup of tea or something?' He looked at his watch. 'I don't even know what time it is.'

'No, no, nothing for me. Unless you'd like me to stay, perhaps I should leave you now to recover and gather your thoughts about everything.'

'Yes, that might be best.'

The other rose again. 'I'm at the hotel tonight. Call me if there's anything you need. Anything at all.'

Maurice nodded. Donald looked around the room for the first time. The chintz furnishings, the crowded book shelves, the assorted prints and nicknacks. He went to the books and scanned them for a long moment. Turned and smiled at Maurice, shaking his head. 'You clever old fox.' Maurice acknowledged the compliment with a wry shrug. Donald's gaze swept the room again. 'Nice place. So English. So you. Just what I would have expected really.'

'Thank you.' Maurice heaved himself out of his chair, then stopped on the way to the door. 'The wife. . . . Mrs Fanning. What happened to her?'

'She was badly shaken up. They handled her roughly, hit her a couple of times, but they didn't torture her. But I gather she's pretty shocked by the whole thing. Not surprising.'

'No.' He saw Donald to the stairs.

'Don't come down,' said the American. 'I'll call later to see if you're O.K.' Gestured at the whiskey bottle. 'And don't drink too much of that stuff.' He took the stairs down to the waiting taxi.

CHAPTER FORTY-ONE

June 2nd, 1952. Wakefield

I have never quite understood why I have always felt such an instinctive affinity with Charles Darwin. Not so much the man himself, but his researches. After all his interests lay in a completely different field to mine—although doubtless if quantum mechanics had been discovered in his time he would have shown the same investigative curiosity in that sphere as in all his others. It is something to do with the universality of his investigations, the all embracing scope of his findings, which have such a relevance to everything that mankind dabbles in. That same universality pertains to my own work, although to the vast majority of the species it is far too impenetrable to capture their interest.

Actually the more one thinks about it the more one realises that Darwin's discovery (I use the singular because in effect all his researches led to the one gigantic overriding concept) lies at the heart of even my particular domain. There is little doubt, in my own mind at least, that in the teeming maelstrom of chemical reactions all those billions of years ago the creation of elementary life came about through a providential conjunction of nuclear particles at some chance moment in time and space, in exactly the same way that Darwin's chance genetic combinations produced variations and thence modifications to that elementary life, which eventually advanced it to the relatively sophisticated state we now inhabit. It is all part of the same process.

When I was ultimately recruited to go from New York to Los Alamos in the summer of 1944, it was to join the top secret mission established there for the sole purpose of finalising creation of the atomic bomb. I had very little idea at the time as to what I would discover there or what my role would be. When I arrived I was astounded to find myself amongst the greatest collection of scientific minds ever assembled in one place. That place was to all extents a purpose-built and self contained army base in the heart of the New Mexican desert, but with basic housing, shops, schools, meeting halls, everything for the maintenance of a community of several hundred people, where the families of the scientific team could reside in as near normal conditions as possible, yet still within the barbed wire confines of a clandestine military establishment. I encountered there, not only many of the brilliant people I had worked with over the years in England, but also most of the legendary names I knew by reputation from all over Europe and America. Geniuses such as Robert Oppenheimer, Niels Bohr, James Chadwick, Victor Weisskopf, Richard Feynman, Enrico Fermi, Martin Deutsch, George Kistiakowsky, Edward Teller—the list went on and on. I can honestly say that, although as always I was fairly reticent socially, it was professionally the most exciting two years of my life.

Atomic research had now progressed far beyond the merely theoretical, to the purely practical task of creating a functional bomb as urgently as possible. It was known that the Germans were working on the same project, so speed was of the essence. There was a great deal of debate amongst all the scientists as to the ethics of producing such a monstrous weapon, and what the future effects might be for the human race, but all were agreed that the immediate consideration was to end this terrible war as quickly as possible. For that reason I still could not understand why our side was not combining forces with the Russians in this business. They were after all our allies in the war, and they had expert minds on their side which could have contributed to the enterprise. I discovered that many of the scientists at Los Alamos thought as I did. It was openly discussed during moments of relaxation, and it was even felt among some that it was an act of betrayal that America and Britain should keep their main ally in ignorance of their progress. Deputations were actually made to President Roosevelt and to Churchill to this effect, but it appeared that the long established antagonisms between the two great opposing philosophies could not be surmounted. I mention this here, not just as a statement of self justification, but also to show that the rights and wrongs of the issue were not as straightforward and universally accepted as was made out at my trial.

I continued to act on my own beliefs as I had done previously. During my months in New York I had met quite frequently with the go-between provided by the Russians, and I had passed them enough information to enable them to build a uranium diffusion plant very similar to the first one built by the Americans in Tennessee. I maintained contact with this man after going to Los Alamos and was able to arrange occasional meetings with him now on trips away from the camp. I gave him as much detailed information as I could about the headway of the work there, which, since we all at the base freely exchanged notes about progress within our various units, was quite comprehensive.

One should understand. It was not only that I saw Russia as an ally in the fight against fascism. It was as I have stated before, that I was convinced—and still am—in the deepest core of my being, that the principles of communism, when adhered to in their true substance (which I concur has rarely been the case so far) are the only way forward for the human race, and indeed the only way for it to survive the primitive and perverse instincts which bedevil it. The fact that human ingenuity had so far outstripped human morality that it was now on the point of devising a weapon which could be used to obliterate itself, made the adoption of a viable modus vivendi all the more imperative. I saw it as my absolute duty to do whatever was in my power to help bring this about. That is the simple case of the matter.

I explained this the other night to Gordon Hawkins on a rare occasion when we discussed my situation. After I had finished speaking he was silent for a long moment. Then he asked simply, 'Was it then up to every individual to break the accepted laws whenever he felt they were standing in the way of progress? And if that were so, how would we deal with the anarchy that resulted?'

I could not answer. I felt he would think me arrogant if I said what I thought. That there are some who see further than the common herd, for whom such laws are created.

He was watching me carefully as I sat there. Then he said to me, 'You have given me the intellectual reasons as to why you did what you did. I sense there were emotional reasons too. Do you want to talk about it?'

I wanted to answer him, but I couldn't. Then—why I have no idea—I found that I could not breathe. I suddenly felt I was suffocating. Tears welled up and I found myself sobbing. I hadn't cried since I was a child, but I could not control it. I wept for what seemed an eternity, and then I sat there shaking for another eternity. Neither of us spoke, and eventually I left the room. I lay in my cell for two hours until the shaking had subsided.

When I saw Gordon next, neither of us referred to the incident. I am still mystified by it.

CHAPTER FORTY-TWO

Both sexes ought to refrain from marriage if they are in any marked degree inferior in body or mind. But such hopes are Utopian and will never be even partially realised until the laws of inheritance are thoroughly known.

The Descent of Man

The evening after his release from police custody Maurice was sitting staring at an unappetising looking concoction from the local pizza parlour when the phone rang. He was still in a state of semi-trauma and he answered with apprehension. He didn't immediately recognise the male voice at the other end.

'Was it you? Were you involved in the murder?'

'Sorry, I. . . . Who is this?'

'Robert Gresham. Was it you?'

It took a moment for Maurice to register the school teacher. He couldn't answer immediately. The panic had risen again, the pain in his chest returned. 'I. . . . no. . . . well, in a way. . . . I. . . .'

Gresham's tone was vitriolic. 'You put those bastards onto my wife, didn't you? You shit! Why the hell did I tell you about her and the bloody trunk?'

'No. . . . it wasn't like that. . . . it was a mistake. . . .'

'A mistake? You don't torture someone to death by mistake!'

'No, no, it was a mistake they found out about. . . . It was my fault. I didn't realise who they were.'

'You didn't realise?'

'I was taken in by them. I didn't. . . .'

'Taken in? What the hell were you doing telling anyone about it in the first place?'

'I didn't tell them. I. . . . they found out. They read my diary, and. . . . Look, it's too complicated to explain. I'm still in shock myself and. . . .'

'You're in shock?'

'Well I realise. . . . I'm just so sorry that. . . . Look, can we meet, and I'll tell you how. . . .?'

'No, thank you. I haven't the faintest desire to meet. The last meeting caused quite enough damage. I just hope the police handle this properly and you get what you deserve!'

He rang off. Maurice was trembling so violently he had to sit again immediately.

The next three weeks passed in a fog. Maurice received another visit from Detective Sergeant Macintyre, who asked more questions, warned him that he had to be available to give witness at the trial in a month or so's time, and then went away again. He received a number of reassuring phone calls and emails from Donald back in France, who showed a gratifyingly conscientious concern about the whole thing. There was a brief flurry of interest in the press over the case, but surprisingly the police managed to keep both Darwin's name and Maurice's name out of things, so the hacks had to be content with making the most they could out of Frances's aristocratic connections. "Earl's daughter in mystery death case" was the most lurid headline they could come up with, and then dropped the story until the trial for want of further detail.

But the storm in Maurice's brain and the pain in his heart would not recede . Nothing he could find to excuse himself, and nothing that Alice's voice could say to absolve him, lessened the awful thought that he had been responsible for the loss of another man's life. And therefore the possible ruin of the wife's life. For the sake of some wretched manuscript which, if the truth were told, was probably of little importance in the grand scheme of things.

He did pluck up the courage to phone his old assistant at the shop, Rupert, and proffer his apologies for what had happened. Rupert was fairly terse and non-committal, and when Maurice tentatively offered him his job back politely turned him down. So Maurice was forced to resort to the services of an agency and obtain a new assistant by orthodox methods. They found him a woman with suitable experience and qualifications, and he installed her in the shop, wishing he had chosen that route in the first place. He still went in to work himself, merely as a routine and a less depressing alternative to sitting around the flat. But his heart was not in the business and his customers got untypically short shrift.

The passing of the days did little to assuage the feelings—if anything they increased as the incident faded into the past and the trial date loomed in the future. He could not sleep at night, and he could not think properly during the day. His sole salvation was the scotch bottle, and he was well aware that this was the downhill road to perdition but there was nothing he could do about it. It was the only method he had of finding oblivion during the dark hours, and tranquillity in the light.

Finally, after three weeks of this existence, Maurice woke one morning to find himself lying on the top of his bed, still fully dressed, with a shattering headache, a vile taste in his mouth, and a smattering of vomit on the bed quilt. He knew he had reached the nadir and he had to make some sort of decision. He shook the sludge from his brain and the mist from his eyes and half climbed, half fell off the bed. Staggered to the bathroom, washed out his mouth, took three tablets of paracetamol, flung his dirty clothes into the linen basket, and stood for a long period under the shower—first warm, then icy cold—until he felt semi-human again. Then forced himself to do a minimal amount of his morning exercises to get some clean air into his lungs, and made a pot of strong coffee instead of his usual tea. He sat with his cup beside the telephone, looked up the Fanning's number in the phone book and dialled.

He wasn't even sure that she would still be there, but he knew immediately that it was she who answered. The voice was dull, lifeless, but had that unmistakable upper class nuance to it.

'Hello?'

'Is that Mrs Fanning? Frances Fanning?'

'Yes.'

He hesitated only a fraction. 'This is Maurice Aldridge. I'm the book dealer who was the cause. . . . well partly the cause of your husband's murder.'

The silence seemed interminable. He did not break it, merely waited. Eventually: 'You mean, my husband's manslaughter. That's what they are calling it.'

'Yes. Whatever it was.'

'What do you want, Mr Aldridge?'

'I want to see you.'

'Why?'

'To try and explain.'

'I don't want any explanations.'

'Then to say how sorry I am.'

'I don't want any apologies.'

'It's for my sake as much as yours.'

'I'm not concerned for your sake.'

'No, I. . . . I can quite understand that. But you see. . . .'

'What?'

'I know what it is to lose someone dear. . . . to lose one's spouse. . . . and I can't forgive myself until I apologise to you in person.'

Another pause. 'I can't see how that might help either of us. What's done is done.'

'Yes. But the pain of it won't go away. And it's the only thing I can think of.' His voice wavered. 'At least it can't make it any worse.'

Silence again. 'I know nothing about the book.'

'I know that. That's not my concern. I wish I'd never heard about the wretched book.'

'What can you possibly hope to say that will make things better?'

'I don't know. I just know I want to meet. I don't. . . . I don't know what else to do.'

A small sigh, barely audible over the phone. 'When do you wish to come?'

'Whenever would suit you. Tomorrow perhaps?'

A slight pause. 'Come around four o'clock.'

'I'll be there.'

Her end of the line went dead.

He was punctilious the next day, arriving at four on the dot. He had not touched a drop since the two nights before. He took care to park the car well away from the neighbour opposite who had shopped him to the police. Walked the few yards to the house, past the two Mercedes still parked on the forecourt, one now looking dusty and unused, and climbed the front steps. Hesitated, wondering whether to ring the bell or use the door knocker. He rang the bell. It seemed a long wait but he did not ring again, and eventually there were footsteps inside and the door opened.

She was not what he expected. He had formed an image of a tall dark-haired person, handsome, but perhaps with those slightly aquiline features that the aristocracy often possess (the Plantagenet, or possibly the Roman influence?). But she was fair-haired and slight, with the sort of figure that might once have graced a ballet dancer but was now showing just a hint of approaching middle-age plumpness. Her eyes were the kind men would fight over—a paler blue-grey than Alice's—but now they looked exhausted and defeated.

'I'm not sure this is legal, is it?' she said in a matter-of-fact voice.

'Legal?'

'We are both principal witnesses in the trial. Should we be communicating?'

'Ah. I don't know—it didn't occur to me. The police didn't say anything.'

'Well, come in.' She stood aside to let him enter, and closed the door behind him. The hallway was wide and light, the walls haphazardly covered with a multitude of prints, lithographs and family portraits—nothing very valuable, Maurice judged, but quality none the less. She took his coat, and whilst she was hanging it up he glimpsed a large kitchen through the doorway at the far end of the hall—modern country style with the obligatory Aga. Was that where it had all happened, he wondered? She led the way through to a spacious lounge, similarly adorned with pictures and graciously if arbitrarily furnished, including a number of continental antique pieces. She gestured for Maurice to sit.

'We have an hour before my sons come back from school. I would like you to be gone by then.' Her voice was expressionless but not rude.

'Of course.' She had probably calculated the timing so that she could get rid of him in reasonable time, thought Maurice.

'Tea?'

'That would be very kind.'

She left the room. He looked around more intently. There were family photographs scattered around the tables and shelves—ancient ones of what were obviously her own family, the earl and countess presumably, posed in front of a fine Georgian portico, various siblings and family groups—and then more modern pictures of her two sons and a large, slightly florid man who must have been her second husband.

Now deceased. Maurice could not bring himself to look closer.

She eventually returned with a tray, and poured tea without a word. She came to him with a bone china cup and saucer in one hand and a silver sugar bowl in the other. He helped himself to sugar. 'Thank you.'

She sat opposite and took up her own tea cup. He noticed her fine ankles and delicate wrists. There was the trace of a bruise remaining beside her right eye. 'Well, Mr Aldridge, what did you want to say?'

He had tried to prepare the answer to that question but, not knowing what her attitude might be, could not, and had left it to his instincts. 'I don't know what I want to say. I just felt. . . . I have been in a fairly terrible state since. . . . since it happened—as I'm sure you have—and I. . . . well I just felt I had to apologise in some way. Well, apologise is not the right word, but. . . .'

'I must say you don't look the sort of person who would be mixed up with gangsters. If that's what one calls them.'

'I'm not. I've never been involved in anything like this. I'm just a book dealer who got caught in something I. . . . I still don't really understand.'

'But it was you who led them here?'

'It seems so. Unwittingly.'

'And you were led here via my first husband. Is that right?'

Maurice hesitated. This was the embarrassing part. 'Yes.'

'It's all right. I have talked to him. He's extremely angry with you. . . .'

'Yes, I know.'

'. . . . and of course with me—or at least with my husband over the theft. But that's his problem. I'm not angry. Not about that anyway. That's all old stuff. And as it happens, he was right.'

'Right?'

'About my husband and the trunk.' She pursed her fine lips. 'He did commission its theft.'

'I see.'

'I've sent it back now. But when it was delivered, some time ago now, I didn't know what to do. I was caught in a cleft stick. I couldn't report it without getting Nicholas. . . . my husband into trouble. So I just left it. But I wasn't pleased.' She turned her head slightly to gaze past him at the family photographs on the table. The bruise was clearer at that angle. 'I suppose we all make mistakes in life, Mr Aldridge. Most of mine relate to my choice of men.'

He didn't know what to say to that, so said nothing. She looked back at him. 'We had an almighty row when I discovered what he'd done. I didn't know at the time how much financial trouble he'd got himself into—he was very secretive about all that. Male pride I suppose. But there was still no excuse to go to such insane lengths chasing what was a long shot at the best of times. I. . . .' Her mouth tightened. '. . . . well it almost split us up.'

'I'm sorry.' It was inadequate, but he didn't know what else to say.

She looked at him. 'You said you'd lost your wife.'

'Yes. Three years ago. Cancer. Nothing as bad as this, but. . . .'

'Were you happy together?'

'Yes.'

'Well, at least you have that.'

'Yes.'

She was silent for a moment. Then she said in a different voice, 'This Darwin diary or whatever it is. . . .'

'Journal.'

'What is your interest in it?'

'It's not personal. I was approached by a rich American who collects such things. These collectors can be rather fanatical.'

'I know.' She glanced again at the photos. 'My father is.'

'He collects?'

'Just family records and letters. Stuff for the archives. He's titled, you see.'

'Yes, I know.'

She turned the pale eyes on him. 'The family goes back a long way, and like many aristocrats he's obsessed with its history.'

'And you?'

'Me?'

'I gather this trunk came down through your first husband's family. He said you were interested in what might be in it. Well, initially at any rate.'

The eyes flashed momentarily. Maurice wilted slightly. He wouldn't want to get on the wrong side of this one, he thought. 'It wasn't of much specific interest to me,' she said. 'But I did think Robert should have investigated it more thoroughly than he did. There *might* have been something truly interesting in there.'

'But there wasn't?'

'No, as it happens. Those. . . . thugs wouldn't believe it, but there was nothing of value. And even if there had been it would presumably have been disposed of long before they arrived.' She took a sip of tea. 'It was all so stupid. . . .'

'I'm so sorry. It must have been. . . .' He could not think of the right adjective.

She gazed into space. 'I used to chivvy Robert about the trunk from time to time, but neither of us got around to seriously exploring its contents. There was an awful lot of stuff there, and we had other things to worry about at the time.' Her nose wrinkled slightly. 'But then after the break-up and the divorce. . . . well a lot of things happened. I got married again. My new husband got into financial difficulties. I had mentioned to him the possibilities of the trunk, but it never occurred to me that he would go to such ridiculous lengths as to have it stolen. . . .' She looked back. 'It's funny—you can live with someone, but you often don't discover what they are really like until you find yourselves under threat. Then all the deepest instincts come to the surface. The primeval responses.'

'Survival of the fittest,' said Maurice.

She smiled for the first time, and her face lost ten years. 'Very good. Well he certainly didn't turn out to be the fittest.'

Maurice hesitated. 'I still don't understand. . . .' he stopped.

'What?'

'I don't quite understand why he *did* go to such lengths. I mean. . . . well, in order to commission the theft of something like that he must have had reason to believe it had real value.'

She stared down at the carpet. There was silence. He sensed she was struggling with something, and didn't break it. Finally she looked up again. 'I'm afraid. . . .' she said, and hesitated. 'I'm afraid that may have been my fault. I'm afraid I may have been partly responsible. I gave him the impression that there could be really valuable stuff in the trunk, you see. I didn't say so directly, but—partly because of my own enthusiasm, and partly because of my anger with Robert and his lackadaisical ways—I. . . . I may have exaggerated the chances.' She turned her head and stared out of the window. There was a suspicion of moistness in her eyes. 'I have a rather romantic nature, you see, and I had been fantasising that there were astonishing documents from Darwin's time in it—records or revelations of some kind. . . . although I hadn't imagined anything as dramatic as an entire journal. But I think. . . . I suspect I conveyed that impression to him. I'm terribly afraid I may have contributed to the whole awful business.'

Maurice was silent. She took a ridiculously small embroidered handkerchief from her sleeve and held it to her eyes. Then she took a deep breath. 'You have to be so careful, don't you? So careful in life. The slightest, most innocuous thing can turn it upside down. . . .'

'That doesn't make it your fault. You weren't the one who broke the law.'

'No, but there are other ways of being guilty.' She took a deep breath and glanced about. 'I wasn't sure that I could stay in this house after it all, but. . . . well the ordeal of moving elsewhere seemed too much.' She looked at him with for the first time just the hint of kindliness. 'And it's given you a hard time also?'

He shrugged. 'I deserve it. For being so careless.'

'Well, we can't cater for all life's eventualities, can we? It's too complicated.'

'Life?'

'Yes.'

'Yes.' A beat. 'Yes it is.' '*Life is the farce which everyone has to perform.*'

'I'm sorry for you.'

'I'm sorry for both of us.'

She took a sip of tea. 'So you think this journal thing does really exist?'

'It would seem so. Maybe just a few copies. Amongst the family's descendants.'

'Strange it's never come to light.'

'Emma Darwin was apparently adamant it shouldn't. It was probably a very personal record.'

Her voice was ironic. 'Not like today. Everyone seems to want everyone to know everything about everyone.'

'Yes, quite.'

'So if it had been in the trunk. . . .'

'Oh we didn't really expect that. Those criminals obviously had an exaggerated idea of the chances. But there might have been some further clues about it.'

'So what did you intend to do? Were you going to steal it yourself?'

He wasn't sure whether she was being serious or flippant. 'Good heavens, no. I didn't know what I was going to do, to be honest. It's just that my American client was rather insistent on my following up all avenues.'

An odd inflection to her voice which he couldn't interpret. 'Would it be important if it was ever discovered? I don't know much about the science world.'

'It could be. Not that it would add much to our knowledge of Darwin's own work. Just that it would cast further light on his life. And also there might be. . . .' He stopped. He wasn't sure how much he should reveal.

'Might be what?'

'Well, information in it about things he wrote himself. Things that haven't yet been discovered.'

'More about how evolution works?'

'Not so much that. More about what he thought the philosophical implications of evolution were. . . . are.'

She nodded, and sipped tea again reflectively. 'Do you believe in God, Mr Aldridge?'

He shifted uncomfortably. Very direct, this daughter of the nobility. 'I used to. . . . I think. Now I'm not so sure.'

She nodded. 'People do get more sceptical as they get older.'

'Do they? Some seem to get more convinced.'

'Probably just more hopeful—as their time approaches. It depends, I think, whether you choose to continue being questioning in old age, or simply accepting.'

'Yes. I wish I was more accepting.'

'Oh, no. Never stop questioning, Mr Aldridge.'

'Well, it can get you into trouble—can't it?'

'Yes. But what was it Bernard Shaw said? "The reasonable man adapts himself to the world. The unreasonable man tries to adapt the world to himself. Therefore all progress depends on the unreasonable man."'

He couldn't remember which play that came from. 'That's good. I like that.'

She smiled again, but without humour. 'I just wish I didn't meet so many unreasonable men.'

Maurice sensed an adulthood of disappointed expectations. 'How old are your sons?' he asked.

'Twelve and fourteen.'

He looked across at the photos. 'They look. . . . fine boys.'

'They are.'

'Were they. . . . were they very upset about . . .?'

'It's hard to tell. Shocked certainly. But they weren't specially close to their step-father. They greatly resented the break-up with their father. It's something I have to live with.'

He nodded. 'I don't have children. But I can imagine. . . .'

She raised her eyebrows. 'Why don't you?'

'My wife couldn't. It's something I. . . . we both regretted.'

She nodded. 'It must be hard if you wanted them.' She glanced at the photos again. 'Mine are the most important thing in my life.'

'They must bring you great joy.'

'No. Not always. But importance, yes.' She took a breath and drained her tea cup. 'Well—thank you for coming, Mr Aldridge. . . .'

'Maurice, please.'

'Was there anything else you wanted to say?'

'Not really. I don't know what I wanted to say. Except I'm sorry. I can't imagine. . . . It must have been. . . .'

She nodded. 'Not the way anyone deserves to go.' She took a breath. 'Well . . . I wasn't looking forward to your visit, but now I'm quite glad you came.' She smoothed her hair in the way that carefully turned out women do. 'I presume we'll meet again at the trial. I'm certainly not looking forward to that.'

'No. Me neither.' He put down his cup and got up. 'Thank you for tea.' Suddenly he felt dizzy, staggered and had to put his hand on the chair back. 'Oh dear. . . .'

She rose urgently. 'Are you all right?'

He recovered quickly and nodded. 'Yes. Sorry, I must have got up too quickly.'

'You're not going to have a heart attack on me too, are you?'

'No, no. Really. I'm quite fit. It's probably just the strain of the last weeks.'

He became aware that she was holding something out— the same small handkerchief she had used. 'What's that for?' he said.

'You're crying.'

'Am I?' Groped hastily for his own handkerchief but couldn't find it.

She pushed hers into his hand. Red with embarrassment he wiped his cheeks. For heavens sake—this was becoming a habit! The thing smelt of perfume and powder as Alice's used to do. 'I'm sorry,' he said. 'How foolish. I'm so sorry.'

'Don't worry. Keep the handkerchief.' She showed him into the hall. There he put on his coat, fumbled with the handkerchief, wondering whether to give the tiny damp thing back, then finally stuffed it into his coat pocket.

'Good luck with your quest,' she said.

'Oh. . . . thank you but I think that's probably over. I've no desire to go on looking now, after. . . . Nothing is that important.'

Her lips parted. 'Oh, well that's a pity in a way. It would be consoling to know whether there was anything in the whole business.' She opened the front door for him.

He hesitated, then on an impulse took out his wallet and proffered an address card. 'I don't. . . . this may not. . . . well, it's just my business card in case you should ever want . . .'

She smiled briefly and took the card. 'Thank you.'

He turned when he reached the pavement. She was still standing in the doorway—a slight, blond figure in a neat blue dress. She raised the briefest of hand gestures and went back inside.

CHAPTER FORTY-THREE

March 29th, 1854. Down House

Heaven forbid, we have declared war on Russia! I tremble to think what dreadful effects will come from this. The Tsar has been attacking Turkish ships and ports for months now, and threatening the whole of the Mediterranean and the trade routes to India and the Far East. Something had to be done. We have joined forces with France (for once we are on the same side!), the fleet has set sail through the Bosporus and is laying siege to Sebastopol. They say the slaughter is already appalling, and all the young men of England are drilling and parading and learning how to use the fearful new weapons (even our own Georgy and Franky are bitten with the bug and constantly playing war games in the garden). Aunt Fanny[23] has written from Tenby to say that their young friend Florence 'Flo' Nightingale, who is a dedicated nurse, has gone to the Crimea to work with the doctors there. She sends back moving letters describing the fearful conditions, and the tragic suffering of the young mutilated soldiers. We are all sending parcels of clothing and small comforts out to the front, but they will be of modest help.

Why is it that man has always to revert to warfare and butchery to gain his ends? I say 'man'—I ought say 'men', for I am sure that if women were ordering great affairs there would be none of such bellicosity.

Charles of course, as is his way, looks at the whole business from his own perspective and seeks to find parallels in Nature. He has been struggling for some time with an obstacle

---

[23]*Frances 'Fanny' Allen, 1781–1875. Emma's maiden aunt.*

to his grand theory. He has not been able to fully explain how similar species, if all descended from common origins, can occur in different continents on opposite sides of the globe. His opponents proclaim this is proof that such similar development must have been designed universally from the beginning. The modernists reply, why is it then that there are also species which are <u>unique</u> to the continents, such as the extraordinary beasts of Africa and Australasia? They contend that the common species must have travelled by means of shifting land masses, volcanic disturbances, wind patterns, and all manner of natural methods. Whereas the unique ones have developed in isolation within their original habitats. None of them can agree and so the dispute continues to rage.

C himself sees in the Crimea a metaphor for his own theories. That it is mainly by sea born invasion that the species have spread—seeds and plants, small floating creatures long ago, birds and frogs and snails—all swept by tide and wind to invade the alien shores, battle for survival with the native residents, and there evolve in similar ways to their ancestors back home. Just as men do in their constant urge for new conquests.

The one puzzle which he cannot yet solve, and which obsesses him day and night (I know for he is constantly repeating it to me and to Hooker as the only confidants he can trust), is <u>why</u> the species should constantly divide and subdivide and so develop new strains. <u>How</u> do offspring use the differences in physiognomy from their parents to take a new fork along the tree of evolution. He is convinced that they do, but he cannot comprehend the biological force. He believes that future science will have the answers as it finds the means to explore the structure of living bone and tissue, but it frustrates him greatly that he is not able to do so himself. He will not rest until he has mastered every aspect of creation. I fear there is a hint of arrogance there!

For my part the answer to his puzzle seemed obvious, and I could not resist letting slip the remark recently that man may not have the ability to master all aspects of creation, but the Almighty has. I should have known better than to think I might have scored a point over my husband. He promptly replied, "Well if the Almighty has, what is His motive? What is His purpose for such diversity? Why has he made such an imperfect job of it? Why invent such a myriad of species which are inferior and so become extinct? Why did he not create a perfect world while he was about the business?"

I should learn never to take issue with Charles. He has an answer for everything. Thank heavens I have my journal to confide in.

CHAPTER FORTY-FOUR

A struggle for existence inevitably follows from the high rate at which all organic beings tend to increase. As more individuals are produced than can possibly survive, there must in every case be a struggle for existence, either one individual with another of the same species, or with the individuals of distinct species, or with the physical conditions of life.

Origin of Species

A month or so after his eighteenth birthday and towards the end of his last term at the grammar school in York, Maurice was summoned by his agog foster sibling, Vicky, to the head of the household's study. His foster father, Marcus Oldfield, was behind his vast cluttered desk studying an envelope with a college crest on the back. He looked up as Maurice entered and motioned him to close the door against the inquisitive eyes outside. Then he held out the letter and scratched his beard.

'It's from Christ's College Cambridge. You'd better open it.'

Maurice took the letter and did so. It was a letter of advice that he had been awarded a scholarship to the university.

'Congratulations,' said Marcus with a wide grin. 'I knew you had it in you.'

Maurice stuttered his thanks and tried to convey his appreciation of Marcus's own involvement in the achievement. His foster father waved the acknowledgement away, then folded his big arms behind the desk. 'We'll have a family celebration later,' he said. 'But first of all, let me give you a bit of worldly advice, Maurice. Just this once, then I won't preach to you again.' His eyes were candid beneath his large bushy eyebrows. 'You may feel, having won this recognition, that the onus is now upon you to achieve great things in life. Do not be seduced by this imperative. I'm not sure in any case that you are cut out for the burden of greatness. As Shakespeare so famously said, some are born great, some achieve greatness, and others have greatness thrust upon them—but in any case the search for greatness is an illusion. If you become a politician you are expected to change the world, which few politicians manage to do; if you become an artist, you are forever seeking a perfection which you can never attain; if you become a scientist, the more you discover the more you discover there is to discover; if you become a tycoon, your success is measured by how much money you make, which you then end up wondering what the hell to do with.' He paused and studied the young Maurice's face. Maurice nodded and waited. 'In the final analysis there is only one rule for happiness, and it's a difficult one to adhere to. *Now* is the only time that matters. The present moment is the only one there is. The past is gone and you can do nothing about it. The future is to come and you cannot foretell what it will bring. This moment, good or bad, and what you create from it is what life offers you. This second's experience, and whatever joy, or knowledge, or riches you can wring from it is the only second you have. If you miss it, it is gone for ever.' He sat back in his chair. 'So when you get to that great place Cambridge, don't get diverted by the huge array of experiences on offer. Don't feel pressurised to go down roads that don't appeal. Take everything *you* want from the adventure and ignore the rest. And who knows, greatness may be thrust upon you.' He relaxed and grinned his great bearded grin. 'Here endeth the lesson.'

It was one Maurice often remembered, even though there were indeed many times when he failed to adhere to it.

Two days after his visit to the Highgate house he had received a phone call at the shop. He recognised her voice immediately. 'Mr Aldridge? This is Frances Fanning.'

'Oh. Hello.'

'Are you free to talk for a moment?'

'Yes. What is it?'

'There is something I didn't mention when we met. I've been thinking about it since, and I don't know if I should tell you, but. . . . I might as well.'

'What's that?'

'I wasn't quite telling the truth when I said there was nothing of interest in the trunk.' The slightest pause. Maurice waited. 'I didn't realise the significance of it until I learned what it was everybody was after. Then I remembered. I'm not sure it's relevant, but it could be.'

He prompted her. 'Go on.'

'Robert. . . . my first husband—was related to the Allen family, whence the trunk originated. You know who they were?'

'Yes. Emma Darwin's mother was an Allen.'

'That's right. She was one of a large family. They were nearly all large families then. Well, the Allens were quite well connected, and one of her many sisters had a grand daughter who ended up married to the Marquis of Salisbury.'

'Yes.'

Her voice showed a small surprise. 'You knew?'

'Robert told me.'

'Ah. Yes. Well, the Salisburys—or Cecils as their family name was—were an extraordinary family. They rose to power with the Tudors and were as influential in politics and the social world as the Wedgewoods were in the industrial, and the Darwins in the scientific worlds. Only grander.'

'Yes.'

'My father's family also has distant blood connections to them, which was one reason I was intrigued by the trunk.' She paused a moment. 'Well, when I heard about this book of Emma Darwin's I remembered something.' Her voice became contrite. 'As I told you I had a huge row with my husband when I discovered what he'd done. However, once I'd decided it was too late to do anything about it, I'm afraid my curiosity got the better of me and I helped him to go through the trunk. It took quite a while.' She took a deep breath. 'Anyway, amongst all the stuff were several bundles of old letters—you know, family letters from way back.'

'Yes?'

'They were mostly ordinary gossipy sort of things. People wrote letters in those days the way we make phone calls and send emails.'

'Yes.'

'There were a number written by someone who signed herself as Gwendolen. This, I'm almost certain, was Lady Gwendolen Cecil, the youngest daughter of the Allen descendant and the third Marquis of Salisbury.'

'Why do you think that?'

'There was no address on the letters, but they were dated around the turn of the nineteenth century. They were written on expensive parchment paper and had the Cecil family crest at the top.'

'Ah.'

'Lady Gwendolen never married, although there was some scandal which reached the newspapers about a possible illegitimate child. Instead she stayed at home and became her father's secretary—he was three times Prime Minister under Queen Victoria. Then ultimately she became his biographer. She in fact wrote what is generally accepted to be the most authoritative biography of him—his life was an unorthodox journey to say the least.'

'And the letters?'

'They appeared to be to one of her Allen cousins. They contained a lot of inconsequential chit-chat and I rather skimmed through them. But one sentence caught my attention. I remembered it when I heard about the Darwin journal. It went something like, 'I've finished Great Aunt's book. What a delight to read. Rest assured it will remain in safe keeping here at Hatfield.'

'Hatfield?'

'Hatfield House in Hertford was—is—the Salisbury family seat.'

'Ah, yes of course.'

'I wondered at the time what was meant by 'Great Aunt's book'. Well, Emma Darwin was a Great Aunt. So you can see why it struck home when I learned about her journal.'

'Yes, I can.'

'I just thought. . . . it seemed to me you ought to know about it.'

'Well, thank you. It's very. . . . very kind of you to tell me.'

'I didn't mention it when we met because I. . . . I wasn't sure whether your involvement should be prolonged, if you know what I mean. But anyway. . . . well, it's up to you as to whether you wish to follow it up or not. Maybe it's the clue you were looking for.'

Maurice pondered for a moment. 'I'm not. . . . I'm not quite sure how one *would* follow it up.'

'Well, I'd have thought the obvious place to look would be the library at Hatfield House. It's still owned by the family, but it's open to the public. Of course the book itself may have long since departed the shelves, but there's no harm in taking a surreptitious peek.'

'No.'

A slight hesitation. 'I'll come with you if you like.'

Maurice was taken by surprise. It was the last thing he might have imagined. 'Oh. . . . Well, that's very kind. I. . . .'

'I'd be quite curious myself. And I'd love to see the house again. I went years ago. It's quite magnificent.'

'I imagine so. I haven't been.'

'Why don't we both go then? Next weekend perhaps?'

It felt like a royal command. He had no reason to say no. 'Yes. Very well.'

'Good. How about Sunday? The boys will be with their father. We could go in the afternoon.'

'Splendid.'

'Would you like to pick me up?'

He didn't like to say that a Mercedes would be a much smarter form of transport than an ancient Rover. He agreed and put the phone down with uncertain feelings.

He pondered for a moment, then went back to what he was doing before the phone rang. He had spread in front of him on his desk several pages of charted information. They were Donald Easterby's records of the researches he or his minions had made previously into the Darwin family connections over the generations. He had as promised emailed them to Maurice shortly after their first meeting. They included several carefully drawn family trees depicting the main branches of descent over the past hundred and fifty years, and then page after page in chronological sequence of descendants' names, dates, affiliations—all carefully typed in columns. When the modern generations were reached two extra columns had been added. The first showed the contact address, telephone number, or in some cases even email address of the descendant, where these had been obtained. The second column contained a note of the action taken in each case to make contact. It was these contemporary entries that Maurice was studying.

Following up on his visit to his antiquarian colleague at the Oxford book shop, he had marked with a pencil three or four entries, all with addresses in Oxfordshire. Only one address however was actually within the Oxford city confines. The entry read simply: Samuel Matheson. 21 Arnos Avenue. And in the final column was the note: 'LETTER June 2009. No reply.'

Maurice sat for a moment staring at the entry, then rang Directory Enquiries. He gave the name and address and asked for the phone number. 'We have no record of a number under that name,' said the operator. Maurice replaced the phone. Sat for a long moment, then shook his head irritably and sighed. Did he really want to go on with this business now? Hadn't he endured enough effort and wasted time and appalling effects because of it? Did he have to dedicate his whole life to the cause of another man's compulsion?

His wife's voice murmured in his ear. 'Come on, dear, you can't give up now. Isn't this what your life's work is all about? Discovering the past? Seeking out the fundamental truths?' In his mind he saw her wagging a school-mistressy finger. 'You've come this far—I shall be very disappointed in you if you abandon it now.'

He muttered 'Yes, dear, if you say so', got up and went through to the shop, where his new assistant, a thin, brisk woman in spectacles, was officiating.

'Would it be all right if I went off early and left you in charge, Joan?' said Maurice. 'I have a lead I rather want to follow up.'

'Of course, Mr Aldridge. I can manage quite well here.'

He had no doubt she could—she had proved highly capable from the moment she arrived. And in any case he was beyond caring much about the shop. Let the fates decide where his business was going—he no longer had control of such matters. He got his hat and coat and left.

He caught the tube home, and there picked up his car and a city map of Oxford. It was by now around four in the afternoon. He would beat the worst of the rush hour. He took the M40 motorway towards Oxford for the second time in two months and made it in an hour and a half. Consulted the road map and eventually found Arnos Avenue. It was in one of the poorer suburbs, a street of largely terraced Victorian cottages, almost directly fronting the pavements, their inmates probably a mixture of artisans and poverty stricken university students. Number 21 was one of the most dilapidated. The dingy green paint on the woodwork was worn and peeling, the roof badly needed retiling, the windows were dark and mostly curtained. The tiny strip of earth in front was a mass of weeds and straggling bushes. Maurice watched the house from across the road for some time, but there was no sign of life. Eventually he plucked up courage, crossed the virtually traffic free street, took three paces to the front door and pushed the rusted bell button beside it. He heard no ring within, so concluded it wasn't working and knocked instead. Waited several moments and knocked again, loudly. Still no sign. His shoulders dropped and he turned away. A wasted trip.

He was crossing the road back to where his car was parked when he heard a noise behind him. He turned in the middle of the street. The house door had opened about six inches, and a beaked nose showed through the gap. Still no word. Maurice retraced his steps. Through the narrow space he could just make out the nose, a fraction of unshaven skin and a rheumy eye.

'Mr Matheson?' said Maurice.

'Eh?'

'Are you Mr Matheson?'

'What d'you want?' The voice was hoarse, with an uncultured accent.

'I'm sorry to trouble you out of the blue, but I wondered if I could have a word?'

The gap in the door remained inhospitably narrow. 'What about?'

'Er, well. . . . Might I come in?'

'Can't open the door. Cats.'

'Oh. I see, er. . . . well it's difficult to talk like this. Um. . . . is there any way we can. . . .?'

'What d'you want to talk about?'

'I'm a dealer in antique books and so forth.' No response. 'I'm told you might be a descendant of the Darwin family. Is that right?'

'No.'

Maurice felt defeated. 'Oh.' He grimaced resignedly. 'Sorry, I must have been misinformed. . . .'

'Who told you that?'

'Someone who was doing some research. I'm sorry, they obviously got it wrong.' He turned to go.

'I'm the Allen family. Different branch.'

Maurice paused and turned back. 'Ah. I see. That's interesting.'

'Why?' The nose was still the main organ of visual contact.

'Well, I'm aware of the connections between the two families. . . .'

'Yes. Bloody nuisance.'

'What?'

'Always causing bother. People interfering. People sticking their noses in.'

'I do apologise, Mr Matheson. I'm not meaning to interfere. I just. . . .' Irritation rose in Maurice's chest. 'Look, I've come a long way to see you. Could I at least come in and have a brief word?'

'I've nothing to tell you. I've nothing to tell anyone.'

'Well maybe not, but at least let me tell *you* why I'm here.'

A pause and an audible sigh. The door almost closed and there was the sound of shuffling and muttered commands from within. It opened again about two feet this time, and a gnarled hand beckoned. 'Quick! The little bastards'll run out given a chance.'

Maurice entered. The first thing that assailed him was the smell. The cloying odour of animals. Then the scuffling of paws, and the movement of blurred shapes through the dark confines of the narrow hall and stairway. The front door closed behind him, increasing further the darkness and the sense of claustrophobia.

'This way.' The figure pushed past him and shuffled down the passage towards the only source of light filtering from the rear. The feline shapes ran around and in front of him, small mewlings sounding through the dank air. 'Watch out for them. They'll trip you up if you're not careful.'

Maurice followed cautiously, the awful smell invading his nose and airways. He reached into his coat pocket for some form of defence and found the tiny handkerchief Frances Fanning had given him, which he had completely forgotten about. He put it over his nose. It still smelt of her perfume, a miraculous antidote to the stench. He followed the other into the back room, using the flimsy article like a medical face mask.

The rear was an open kitchen of sorts, cluttered with ancient stoves and kitchen furniture, bounded by worn sofas, tables sagging under unwashed dishes, tins of pet food, old newspapers, god knows what else. The walls were an expanse of stained and yellowing paint, the floor a minefield of tattered rugs and cat dishes. The cats, of all ages, colours and sizes, ran amok around and over everything.

'Goodness,' exclaimed Maurice, the hanky still over his nose. 'Are the cats all yours?'

The man turned and Maurice saw him clearly for the first time. He was like a run down version of Cyril Catcheside in Malvern. Short, wizened, unshaven—his thinning hair straggled over the filthy collar of his shirt, his woollen cardigan sagging and stained. 'Yer,' he said. 'All mine. Sorry, they probably smell a bit. I'm used to it.' He opened the door to the back yard and shooed some of the cats out. 'Go on, get out there!' They ran for the yard, and a welcome breath of air passed back in the other direction.

'How many have you got?' asked Maurice in wonderment.

'Dozen or so. Never quite sure.' The man picked up a spilled saucer of rancid looking milk from the floor and tipped it into the cluttered sink. 'Started with just a couple. For company, you know. And then one or two strays wandered in. 'Fore long I seemed to have acquired a bunch of them.' He sniffed. 'They come and go though. Never quite sure how many.'

Maurice was at a loss how to proceed. The smell was either receding a little or he was getting used to it himself. He looked around for somewhere to sit, then decided to remain standing. 'Look Mr Matheson, I'll come straight to the point. I was under the impression you were a Darwin, but since you are an Allen this may not be of any relevance. I'm searching for Darwin memorabilia—old records, writings, you know. I thought it might be possible you had inherited some stuff like that. I couldn't find you in the phone book, so I thought I'd drop by on the off chance.'

The man contemplated Maurice beadily. Impossible to tell how old he was. Seventies at least, thought Maurice. His suspicious watery eyes and his stooped figure betokened either unrobust health or premature ageing.

'How d'you find me?' he asked.

'Er. . . . well a client of mine has been doing some research into Darwin genealogy and. . . .'

'That book shop feller put you onto me?'

'Book shop?'

'Here in Oxford. Posh place off Broad Street.'

Ah, thought Maurice, so it is indeed the same man. His heart quickened. Better play this carefully. 'Oh, you mean James Goodwright? He did mention that someone had told him something. He wasn't sure who it was though.'

Matheson was silent. His stare made Maurice distinctly uncomfortable. Then he shook his head. 'Nah. I haven't got anything.'

'Ah. Pity.' Maurice hesitated. 'Since you went to the book shop I thought perhaps. . . .'

'Used to have a few bits. Family hand-downs and stuff. Not now though.'

'From the Allen family?'

'Yeh. You're not the first to come here.'

'Really? Have other collectors been in touch?'

'Time to time. Given them short shrift though. They all want somethin' for nothin'.'

'I never want something for nothing, Mr Matheson.'

'Good. 'Cos I ain't got nothing.'

'How closely are you connected to the Allen family?'

'Way, way back. Don't know any of them now. Never did really.'

'I see. So did you in fact sell the things you inherited?'

The beady eyes flashed. 'Why? Valuable is it, that sort of stuff?'

'It depends what it is.'

'Well, you know—family letters, papers, that sort of thing.'

'It totally depends what they are, Mr Matheson. Who wrote them, who they belonged to, what was in them. Of course there's a lot of interest in the Darwins. . . . and possibly the Allen connection. But any new discoveries would have to have some historical relevance to be of any true worth.'

The other nodded slowly. 'Well I've not got anything.' He waved around the room. 'You can see—I'm not much one for books and papers. Racing pages is about the nearest I get to reading stuff.'

Maurice wondered whether there was anything to be gained by staying. Then on an impulse he said, 'I'm a bit weary after my journey. Would you mind if I sat down for a second.'

The other nodded suspiciously, and Maurice pulled out a rickety kitchen chair and sat at the table. 'Thank you.'

Reluctantly: 'I don't have any booze. D'you want a cup of tea?'

The thought of tea out of an unwashed, cat smelling mug didn't entice and Maurice shook his head. 'I'm fine thanks.

I'll be on my way soon.' For want of anything else to say he asked, 'Have you lived here long?'

The man nodded, and went to the sink where he made a pretence of clearing up. 'Years. Years and years.'

'Ah.'

'Won't be here much longer though.'

'Oh?'

'They're chucking me out.'

'Who?'

'Landlords.'

'You don't own the house then?'

'No. College owns it. The colleges own most of this town.'

'Yes. So why are they throwing you out?'

Matheson gave up his rattling at the sink, wiped his hands on a filthy tea towel and sat in a chair across the table from Maurice. He puffed out his cheeks and ran a hand through his grimy locks. 'Needs repairs. Needs updating they say. I'm not keeping it up to the standards of the lease.'

'Oh dear.'

'That and the cats. The neighbours complain.'

'Ah well, I suppose. . . .' Maurice tailed off.

'I can't afford to spend on the place, y'see. Needs ten thousand spending on it to bring it back to how it was, before they'll even come and mend the roof. They say I'm responsible for not maintaining it to standard. Where am I going to get ten thousand, eh? Lost my job a long time ago and I never had a pension or anything. Spend most of my state pension on bloody cat food!'

Maurice glanced around at the half dozen moggies remaining in the kitchen, who were mostly draped contentedly over the sofa and the various tattered rugs. 'Do you need to be quite so philanthropic to the neighbourhood's cat population?'

The other squinted moist-eyed at him. 'They're company, aren't they? I don't have anyone, see. I don't have any family or anyone.'

'None at all?'

Pause. 'Well. . . . I've got a son. But I never see him.'

'Ah.'

'Don't know where he is—Canada or somewhere, last I heard.' He blinked, staring down at the table. 'He's a civil engineer. Works on big projects. Done a lot better than me.'

'You never hear from him?'

He shook his head, then glanced up at Maurice, a vulnerability showing through the cynicism, a wealth of regret in the narrow, tired eyes. 'My fault. I was no good as a father. Drunk too much, you see. Drunk my marriage away, drunk my job away, drunk everything away.' He rubbed his lank hair again. 'I was a right bastard, I suppose.'

Maurice could think of nothing to say, so just grimaced sympathetically.

'I'm off the booze now. Nearly killed myself so I finally came off it. Never touch it now. Strongest thing I ever did in my life.'

'Well done. That's good.'

A grunt. 'Too late though. Lost the lot by then. Family, job, everything.' His voice was little more than a hoarse mutter. 'I miss him now. He's all I. . . . Well there isn't anybody else. It's all my fault. . . .'

Maurice felt too embarrassed to say anything. The old boy glanced around the room. 'I don't want to leave here. It's not much I know, but I've always lived here you see. Ever since. . . . I like it here. It suits me.'

'Where will you go?'

He shrugged. 'Dunno. Social services say they'll find me a place, but. . . . well I can't have the cats there, can I? Can't have my son visiting there.'

'He's coming to visit you?'

'Well. . . . he might one day. I mean, despite everything I am his dad. He was close to his mother, you see. He blames me for. . . .' He waved away an imaginary spectre in the air. 'I've written to him. He doesn't answer but he's got to some day, hasn't he?'

'Probably.'

'And I don't want him visiting me in some bloody hostel or somewhere.' One of the cats jumped onto the table with a miaow. He irritably brushed it off again—'Gerroff!' He gestured at the room. 'You see, if I knew he was coming I could clean up this place. I've got a spare bedroom upstairs. Nicest room in the house. We'd be fine here. I'd even get rid of the cats.'

'Is your son married?'

He nodded. 'Yeh. Never met her but I've seen her photo. They've got a couple of kids, maybe more now. That's another thing. . . .' He rubbed his eyes with the back of his hand. 'Grand kids. I've got grand kids and I never. . . .' He tailed off, staring at the table top.

Far too much sadness here, thought Maurice, and rose from his seat. 'Well I'm sorry you can't be of any help to me. I'd better be on my way.'

'Sure you won't have a cuppa tea?'

From hostility to hospitality in such a short space of time. Maurice shook his head, then paused. As always the only way was to take the bull by the horns. 'Just one last thing though. James Goodwright at the book shop said he thought you'd said something about a diary written by Emma Darwin. She was the wife of Charles Darwin. Do you remember anything about that?'

The man looked up quickly, his eyes sharp once again. 'Diary?'

'Yes.'

'Did he say that?'

'Yes. He said you'd asked how much such a thing might be worth.'

Matheson shook his head. 'Don't remember that. Dunno what he's talking about.'

'You've never heard anything about such a diary?'

'Nah. Why? Would it be valuable?'

'Something like that could be, yes. Very valuable.'

'Ah.' He shook his head again. 'No. Don't have anything like that.'

'Pity.' Maurice instinctively felt that something wasn't right, there were things unsaid, but he didn't know how to get to them. Out of habit he put a business card down on the table. 'My card. If you ever think of anything. . . .' He tailed off, went to the door. 'Nice to meet you. Don't bother to get up, I can show myself out.'

He was careful not to let the cats out as he edged through the front door. The last thing he saw as he closed it behind him was the silhouette of the old man framed in the kitchen doorway, staring after him.

CHAPTER FORTY-FIVE

September 16th, 1952. Wakefield.

So now I will record the final stages in the journey that brought me to this place. The last accelerating events. Early in 1945 it was decided at the Los Alamos research base that it was urgent we should conduct a first test of a plutonium explosion. The war in Europe appeared to be coming to an end, but the war against Japan was at its height and it seemed, from an American point of view at least, that it might be just as prolonged and bloody. The pressure to produce the bomb was intense. I myself was working on the precise calculations involved in plutonium fission, and I had intricate knowledge of the whole design of that first test bomb. And of course I passed all this on to my Russia contacts, including a detailed drawing of the device itself.

When the test happened, out in the remote desert towards Las Vegas, the result came as an extraordinary shock to everyone who witnessed it. We all knew the theory of course. We all knew the hypothetical power of the weapon we were trying to create. But none of us were prepared for the gigantic effect of the explosion we witnessed from twenty miles distance through dark glasses. The astounding way that both heaven and earth lit up as if by some cataclysmic supernatural force; the speed and power with which the immense dust cloud unfurled far above the plains and mountains; the roar and shake as the very planet beneath our feet seemed to rock on its foundations; we were none of us quite prepared for all this. And it brought home to me as never before the vast potential for both good and evil that man has at his disposal. The immense discrepancy between his intellectual accomplishment and his aggressive instincts.

What has followed is of course the stuff of history. The destruction of Hiroshima and Negasaki, the swift capitulation of Japan, the worldwide celebrations of the end of the war, followed by the huge task of rebuilding the peace—all this is the continuing saga of man's struggle for survival and progress. In which I continued to play my part.

On my return to England in 1946 I was given the prestigious post of head of the theoretical physics department at the new Atomic Energy Research Establishment at Harwell. One might think that, with the war ended, I could now relinquish my espionage activities. However, so ingrained was the habit, so involved was I with the development of communism—still as I saw it the main hope for the salvation of mankind and the end to all wars—that I continued the process. My techniques were by now well practised, and for the next five years, right up to the moment of my arrest, I passed all my relevant information on to Russia.

Was I naive in thinking I would never be caught? Should I have known that destiny would eventually catch up with me? Perhaps I did. Perhaps deep in my subconscious I knew it had to end. But not in the way it has. Of course I now realise that, thanks to the new methods of deciphering Soviet codes and information, the authorities had suspected me and had me under surveillance for a considerable time. But because I never thought of myself as having genuine guilt I never really took the idea of discovery too seriously. Even when their suspicions became clear and they sent an officer from MI5 to interview me, I suppose I saw him as a sympathetic confidant rather than an enemy. I allowed myself over time to admit everything to him, more with the intention of unburdening myself of the enormous responsibility I was carrying than in the belief that I was confessing to serious crimes. With hindsight that might appear extremely ingenuous, but at the time, such was my faith in my cause and in the sincerity of my actions, that it did not seriously occur to me I was in real trouble. A dressing down and possible demotion from my position at Harwell was the worst scenario I anticipated. When I was ultimately formally arrested by a senior police officer for 'communicating information useful to an enemy'—which was another way of saying treason—it took a long time for the implications to sink in. Right up to the moment of my trial some four weeks later—during which period I cooperated totally with the authorities, giving them a full statement of my activities during all those years, omitting nothing—I still believed that I would eventually be exonerated. Or at least pardoned. It came as a profound shock to realise that the world saw me in a completely different light.

Yes, to the extent that I must have been astonishingly naïve, that I betrayed my so-called intelligence, that I did not see the world as it really is—to that extent I am guilty as charged.

I am running out of paper. It is in short supply still amongst so many other things, even years after the war. I am having to use old laundry lists and even toilet paper for my jottings. How are the mighty fallen.

CHAPTER FORTY-SIX

*With animals having separated sexes there will in
most cases be a struggle between the males for possession of the females. The most vigorous individuals, or those which have most successfully struggled
with their conditions of life, will generally leave
most progeny. But success will often depend on having special weapons or means of defence, or on the
charms of the males, and the slightest advantage will
lead to victory.*

Origin of Species

For the third time in a month Maurice parked his car near the
Fanning house. He felt his usual awkwardness as he walked
up the steps and rang the bell. A fine spring day in early May.
The well-tended front gardens were bursting with spring
flowers and along the streets the cherry trees were in late
bloom. Her was wearing (after considerable thought) a pale
pink shirt, a red striped tie and a rather dashing gold but-
toned blazer, rarely worn, that Alice had once bought him in
an attempt to jazz up his dress style.

She opened the door wearing a turquoise summer dress
with a cardigan round her shoulders. She was looking
brighter and more alive than the last time. The bruise by her
eye had almost gone. 'You look smart,' she said with a brief
smile.

'So do you,' he answered. Then daringly, 'I felt I ought to
dress up a bit for all this aristocracy visiting. I'm not used
to it.'

'Ah well, if it's any consolation, neither am I. I'm the
youngest in my family and I've never felt the least aristocratic.' She wrinkled her small nose. 'I could certainly never
bring myself to use my own prefix.'

Maurice wondered what earls' daughters called themselves—'Lady'? 'Honourable'? He held the door for her as
she climbed into the Rover. He had carefully swept it out that
morning, and even gone over the bodywork with a cloth. The
old girl looked quite springlike herself.

They didn't talk a great deal during the hour or so it took
to drive to Hatfield. Just enjoyed the relative Sunday peace
of the roads as the London suburbs fell away. He wondered
whether to bring up the subject of her ordeal, but decided
it best to wait until she felt like talking herself. Typically
for Maurice some things were too large or too sensitive to
approach. He preferred to wait until they resurrected themselves of their own accord.

When they finally reached their destination and drove
through the lofty entrance gates to the already crowded car
park, he parked to the attendant's directions and hurried
round to open the passenger door for her, feeling foolishly
old-fashioned. But she smiled gratefully and took his hand to
pull herself out onto her flimsy high-heeled sandals.

The house stood vast and imposing in its Jacobean splendour, its gardens clustered about it like bedecked courtiers
around their monarch. Maurice had done a bit of reading
before he set out, and he knew that it was in these surroundings that the young Elizabeth I had grown up, and indeed in
these very grounds that she had learnt of her accession to
the throne. He warmed as always to the aura of history that
pervades such places. The powers-that-be may not always
have got their jurisdictions or their moral conduct right, he
thought, but they could certainly build houses.

They bought their tickets at one of the oddly old fashioned
booths scattered about the approaches. Maurice insisted on
paying for hers, saying it was all down to the expenses of his
commission. Then they climbed the steps to the mansion's
huge front entrance and joined the throng of sight-seers in the
state rooms. Maurice almost forgot the purpose of their visit

as they wandered through the place, murmuring occasionally to each other at this painting, that superb piece of furniture. It was Frances who reminded him as he stood transfixed before Nicholas Hilliard's 'Ermine' portrait of the first Queen Elizabeth. 'Come on,' she whispered, 'the library's this way.'

'Oh, yes.' And he followed her lead, glancing about him like a guilty schoolboy fearing detection.

The library was less crowded and quieter than the other great rooms. The task of finding what they were after looked impossible as they gazed upon the towering ranks of book filled shelves, separated by high windows which stared impassively over the magnificent West gardens.

'Have you any idea what it might look like?' murmured Frances at his side.

'Not the faintest,' he replied.

'Well, if it was only a private publication, I can't think it would be very grand,' she said. 'Look for something not too big and probably without any wording on the spine. You start that end, and I'll start this.'

He nodded and they parted company. There was no public access to the gallery running around the upper shelves, and they were forced to focus on the lower levels. It soon became apparent that the collection was made up almost entirely of early editions of well known collected works. Maurice pause for a while beside a shelf containing what appeared to be all the John Murray publications of Darwin's writings. Was this significant, he wondered? Or was it merely that no self respecting library of the times would be without such an item?

He moved on and after several moments of working his way along the rows, during which he found it hard to concentrate on his objective so absorbing were the contents to his antiquarian's eye, he met her coming the other way.

'Nothing that I can see,' she whispered, glancing towards a portly bearded attendant nearby. 'They're all professionally published titles on the main shelves.'

'Yes,' he agreed. 'If it was here it would most likely be tucked away up there'—he nodded at the upper gallery. 'Or do you think it might be in a drawer somewhere?'

She shook her head. 'It would surely have come to light then. The family would have discovered it at some stage, and I can't believe they wouldn't have made its presence known. They're not after all bound by Emma's wishes as her own family were.'

He peered up at the gallery, which was reached by steep metal steps at each end of the room, and fenced by a flimsy iron rail. 'That's the most likely place. Stuck in some corner.'

She too gazed upwards. 'Well, short of sneaking up there in full view of the staff, I can't think how we can look.' She chuckled suddenly, an uncharacteristic schoolgirl giggle. 'And anyway I'm not letting Mr Charles Dickens over there get a view up *my* skirt!'

He was taken aback for a second, then added, 'Well he wouldn't let us go up there anyway.'

'Just a moment,' she said, and walked across to the attendant in question. Like most such he welcomed approaches from visitors to enliven his tedious hours of duty. He beamed as she flashed her eyes at him. 'Excuse me,' she said in her most gracious upper class manner. 'I wonder if you can tell me whether there's an inventory of all the books in here?'

The beam changed to a puzzled frown. 'Inventory, madam?'

'Yes. You know—of all the titles. I would have thought there must be, for such a distinguished collection.'

'Well, yes I'm sure there is,' he ventured. 'There's inventories of everything in the house, I think. But I'm not sure where. In the archives probably. Or in his Lordship's private quarters.'

'It's just that my friend here. . . .' she indicated Maurice, '. . . . is a distinguished academic, and he's trying to seek out a particular title. We think it may be in the Cecil collection, but it's hard to find amongst so many.'

The man scratched his beard in an exaggerated gesture of contemplation. 'Hm—well. . . . I dunno what to suggest. Probably the best way is to write to the librarian. He's in charge of all this. Or perhaps to his Lordship directly.'

'Yes, that's a good idea. I'll write to Lord Salisbury personally.' She said it as if she was on intimate terms with the said nobleman. 'Thank you so much.' Then as if on an afterthought she added, 'I don't suppose there's any way you could let us up onto the top gallery?'

He shook his head with an expression of deep regret. 'Sorry, Madam, strictly off limits there. They can't have the risk of public liability, you see.'

'Of course. I understand.' She smiled again and returned to Maurice, leaving a well smitten custodian behind her. 'No luck,' she murmured. 'But it might be worth a letter to the Marquis—you never know.'

'Yes,' said Maurice. He wondered if that would be better coming from her, from him, or from Donald Easterby.

'Let's get a cup of tea,' she said, and taking him by the arm, led him off out of the house towards the noisier public facilities in the old stable yard. They found a restaurant situated in what had once presumably been a coach house, and sat with tea and scones in a relatively quiet corner of the big room.

Maurice said, 'Well, I'm glad I've seen the house anyway. So close to London and yet the sort of place one never gets to.'

She poured tea. 'Sorry it was abortive.'

'I don't really mind,' he said. 'I'd more or less given up on the whole thing anyway.'

She raised her eyebrows. 'Well, you shouldn't. Not after all the effort you've put into it.'

'It wasn't wasted. It's been fascinating. I've learned so much about. . . .' He cleaned his glasses on his napkin.

'About what?'

He felt unaccountably embarrassed. 'About myself, I suppose.' He put the specs back on. 'It's made me think about. . . .'

'Yes?'

'Oh. . . . things. Life. Fundamentals.'

She sipped thoughtfully at her tea. 'How did you find out about our connection with the Darwins anyway?'

He told her about his book friend up in Shropshire, and his visit to Shrewsbury and thence to Malvern.

'Ah. Quite a trail,' she said.

'I enjoyed it. Got me out of London and showed me parts I've never seen.' He gazed out towards the gardens. 'England is still lovely.'

'I was brought up in the country. At heart I've always thought I'd move back.' She too looked towards the grounds. 'Perhaps now I will.'

He glanced at her. 'Did you grow up in a place like this?'

She laughed. 'Not quite.' Her gaze was distant. 'But still rather special. Once you've had that you always hanker for it.'

'I can imagine.'

'Ridiculously privileged of course. And I didn't have the worry of all the upkeep and so on.'

'I've ceased to believe in privilege,' he said.

She frowned. 'What do you mean?'

'There's always someone better and worse off. And always pros and cons. Who is more privileged—the oil Sheik with six palaces and a harem to worry about, or the tribesman with his own well and a flock of goats? It's all relative.'

She gazed at him thoughtfully. He felt vaguely embarrassed. It was again a lot of words for him.

'Are you happy, Maurice?'

He blinked and hesitated. 'I was. With my wife. Then she died and. . . . Well, there you are. One moment you're up, the next you're down. All relative, as I say.'

'How did she die?'

'Cancer. Usual thing.'

'Bad?'

The image of himself at the bedside that final day—so long engraved on his brain—appeared before him like a projected film. He didn't answer immediately, fearing an embarrassing return to the tears. 'Yes. Rather bad. I can't really. . . .'

'It's all right. You don't have to.'

He fished in his pocket and brought out the hanky which he'd washed and ironed. 'Thank you. You can have this back now.'

She took it with an acknowledging smile. 'You *seem* happy,' she said as she put it away in her bag.

He raised his eyebrows in surprise. 'Do I? Well, I suppose. . . . I suppose deep down. . . . I certainly used to be. Now I get by with my books and the shop. And with too much to drink.'

'Ah,' she said. 'That's a dangerous road.'

He nodded. 'I keep trying to stop, but haven't quite managed it yet.' She smiled but said nothing. He dared to return the question. 'Were you happy? I mean. . . . with him?'

She was frank. 'No.' She pursed her lips. 'Though he didn't deserve. . . . I wouldn't have wished that on anyone.'

Since she had brought it up, he said, 'I can't imagine how people could. . . . how anyone could. . . .'

'No. But then I've realised, there is no limit to man's perversity. Just as there's no limit to his heroism.'

'Is that what it was—perversity?'

'I don't know what it was. I am beyond analysing such actions.'

Silence as she spread jam and cream on a small piece of scone. She said, 'Poor man. He was exciting and sexy at first. In contrast to my first husband, who is one of the world's pessimists. I think I saw Nicholas as an escape route from all Robert's half empty glasses. But then I discovered that, with exciting and sexy can come rashness and irresponsibility.' She gave a small rueful smile. 'Hard to get the balance right, isn't it?'

'Yes,' he said. 'Balance—that's the word. Probably the most important word.'

'After love.'

He paused. 'After beauty. Which love and balance are just parts of.'

Another pause. 'Wow,' she said, and was quiet.

They talked further on the way home. He told her more about his acquired interest in the Darwin story. And the Klaus Fuchs story—both men struggling with the same questions, but in such different ways. She told him about her manor house upbringing, and related stories about her boys. When they got back to her house, she asked him in for a drink. He politely declined, citing stuff to do before opening the shop tomorrow. He didn't tell her the real reason was that he was feeling illogically disloyal to Alice. Or perhaps just that he didn't feel like getting too involved. With anyone.

'Well, thank you for the day,' she said.

'No, thank *you*,' he replied.

'See you at the trial,' she said.

'Yes, see you then.' And he drove away in the Rover, which preserved the faintest whiff of the perfume amongst its leathery smells.

CHAPTER FORTY-SEVEN

June 4th, 1857. Moor Park

Looking back over the years I have kept my private diary it seems to me that I have been constantly preoccupied with the same concerns. The trials and tribulations of my ever grow-ing family, which in some way are always inextricably linked to the work my husband is involved with, and the supposi-tions about life in general that this work has pointed to. I am writing this entry at the clinic of Doctor Lane at Moor Park in Surrey—yet another medical establishment where I have come to try and conquer my own and my family's ills. This time it is my continuing exhaustion after the birth of little Charles (my tenth confinement, not counting miscarriages), added to by my worry at the constant frailty of Etty,[24] now fourteen, who has accompanied me here. Nor do the rest of the family leave me free of concern. C's health as ever goes up and down as if on a pendulum, the constitutions of Lenny, Bessy and Horace are all susceptible to every ailment that blows by on the wind, and already we can tell that Baby Charles, though not yet six months old and of the sweetest disposition, is backward in his development and afflicted by the oddest little mannerisms and convulsions. I worry about him constantly, but as always am aware that we are in the hands of a greater power than we can contend with and must simply accept its purposes.

   Charles of course is much concerned with the effects of breeding between the differing strains of a species and be-tween different generations. He worries always that the death

---

[24]*Henrietta b.1843—now the oldest daughter.*

of Annie, which even now has him weeping, and the fragility which affects the rest of the family might be due to the fact that he and I are immediate cousins. I cannot say, although such a liaison is common enough and does not appear to affect all others in the same way.

I have left C at home this time, in the good care of Parslow and the servants, for he is now in the throes of his most intense period of work yet (is it any wonder that his constitution wilts under the strain?). There are signs that others working in his field are approaching similar conclusions to his own about the nature of existence, and his friends are all exhorting him to publish his findings before some upstart comes out with a superficial pamphlet or paper and steals his thunder. That would be a catastrophe, negating all his decades of painstaking research. It is now more than four years since we ejected the last of the odious barnacle creatures from the house, and since then C has been concentrating on what he sees as his grandest work—the book which will summarise all his thoughts about nature and explain his conclusions on the evolutionary process. So exhausted is he by the magnitude of the task that I have heard my mild mannered Charley refer to it as his 'abominable volume' and his 'everlasting species opus' and various other epithets too extreme to mention here. He worries as do I about the furore the book will provoke, and yet he still feels it is his duty to write it, else all his years of work and contemplation will have been for nothing.

As always I struggle with my doubts that in some obscure way the afflictions that affect our family are perhaps the Lord's way of warning him against the nature of his conclusions. These are so against all that the human race has ever held sacrosanct, all that the Bible and the Prophets have taught us, that it must come as no surprise that God should react in some way against such an assault on his sovereignty. Yet when I hint at this to C he simply says mildly, "Why would He visit His displeasure upon our children, who are surely not responsible for their parent's misdeeds?"

Of course he is right. It is 'the sins of the father' on the one hand, and 'suffer little children' on the other. The more I wrestle with the whole question of my dear husband's doctrine the more confused I become!

And yet there is a part of me that cannot help but take pleasure in his researches. Without them our lives would have been immeasurably the poorer. Despite all the years of vile smells and sights throughout the house, the jars bubbling with fermenting vegetation and the pots with boiling corpses, the sinks and buckets filled with rotting carcasses, the shelves and surfaces piled with skeletons and specimens, the daily arrivals of foreign parcels containing ever stranger and more macabre samples, the greenhouses and beds sprouting with strange flora—despite all this there is an everlasting fascination at the gigantic enterprise, which affects not only me but all the children, and even the servants (who have to attempt to maintain some sort of order in the midst of the mayhem). I can reflect back over the years at such a wealth of incidents, which are like a kaleidoscope of images in my memory: my husband and Revd Innes huddled together over a honeycomb crawling with bees with no thought for their own protection from stings; our beloved Annie patiently taking down endless pages of notations in the study as her father measures and weighs; the younger children rushing around the fields and woodlands with nets and buckets in the quest for some obscure plant or insect; the cluster of young heads around the table as their father delicately cuts open the gruesome corpse of a dead beast; the thunder down the stairs in the mornings to see if the tadpoles have appeared or the pigeon's eggs hatched; dear long-suffering Joseph Parslow patiently standing for hours at a time holding the ladder as C forages amongst branches and hedgerows for buds, blossoms, bird's eggs, ant's nests, and I know not what; Nurse Brodie screaming in fright at finding a family of toads housed temporarily in a bread bin in the pantry; the entire household searching fearfully throughout the premises for an escaped poisonous reptile from some tropical region; myself playing the piano whilst C observes the reactions to the music of a jar of earthworms placed on the lid; his own exclamations of delight at receiving a parcel of animal dung from the Far East which he then proceeds to dissect in search for undigested seeds and insect eggs; the animated arguments around the dinner table of all our learned academic friends whilst C sits at the head silently listening with that benign smile upon his face that I know so well. The memories are so many and so dear that I would not be without them for all the sermons from the pulpit that I ever heard. Thine be the glory.

CHAPTER FORTY-EIGHT

As all men desire their own happiness, praise or blame is bestowed on actions and motives according as they lead to this end. And as happiness is an essential part of the general good the greatest happiness principle indirectly serves as a nearly safe standard of right and wrong. But with the less civilised nations reason often errs, and many bad customs and base superstitions come within the same scope.

The Descent of Man

'Hatfield House! That's extraordinary!' said Donald Easterby on the telephone from France. 'Who could have guessed the trail might lead there?'

'It's only a tenuous link,' cautioned Maurice. 'There's no real proof a copy ended there, and even if it did, no evidence that it's there still.'

'No, no, but I like the story. It feels good.' Donald was in his earnest mode again. 'It's just the sort of place a thing like that might be found. What's more, Maurice, I have connections there.'

'Oh?'

'I've corresponded in the past with the librarian at Hatfield over the odd manuscript and so forth. I can write to him about this. He has access to all the Cecil archives. I'll do it immediately!'

'Well, no harm in trying,' replied Maurice.

'If I get anything I'll let you know straight away, and we could visit together.'

'Right.'

'Oh, and incidentally, I've been called as a witness in the trial of those two thugs. Strictly speaking I don't have to attend as I'm not in the country, but I feel I should so I'll see you then in any case.'

Maurice hung up with mixed feelings. He was a great deal more pessimistic about the chances of finding the journal than was the American, and he was getting weary of the responsibility. Deep down all he really wanted now was to get the wretched trial over and done with, and then forget about the whole business. The project had brought a temporary distraction in his life, but now his humble being hankered to get back to his books and his calm solitary existence again.

The trial loomed ahead in Maurice's mind like the nuclear cloud Klaus Fuchs had described in his diary—huge, threatening, unprecedented. It concerned primal behaviour that was quite incomprehensible to him, a capability that was unimaginable. Life in general, he knew, harboured endless examples of such, yet he could find no connection between them and the personal life he himself lead, the aspirations he held.

A week before the trial was due to start he received a call from Frances.

'Not long now,' she said. 'I was wondering how you felt about it.'

'Dreadful,' he said. 'I'm having nightmares.'

'I'm sorry.'

'I'm just a bit part player,' he replied. 'I can't imagine how you must be feeling.'

'My family has a few centuries of blood and treachery behind it. I suppose I should be unfazed. Actually I've just tried to blot it from my mind.'

'I wish I could do that. I need to practise mind control.'

'As you say, Maurice, you're only a minor witness in all this. Don't take it too much to heart.'

'I can't help it. I feel responsible.'

'You aren't. My husband was the main culprit, and he paid a dreadful price for it.' Slight pause. 'I was to blame too. More than you.'

'How are your boys?'

'Oh, they're fine. I count the hours until they get back from school. It's funny. I'm quite lonely without him. I never thought I would be.' He said nothing. 'Perhaps. . . . perhaps we could do another trip after the trial is over. See more stately homes.'

Mixed feelings. 'Yes.'

'I could even show you ours. Not quite a stately home, but it's rather beautiful. Eighteenth century.'

Feelings even more mixed. 'Ah. . . . that would be nice. '

'You'd have to run the gamut of my parents. My mother's quite eccentric—some might say dotty. But you could talk books with my father. He has an impressive collection.'

'No Darwin pieces, I presume?'

She laughed. 'That would be ironic. Sitting at home all the time. Not much chance, I'm afraid.'

At the Old Bailey a plea of manslaughter was accepted by the court, but the judge had insisted on hearing evidence before sentencing. Maurice was called as a witness on the second day of the hearing, along with Donald. The latter picked him up in a taxi and they went together to the famous law courts. They talked little en route, and as they entered the daunting halls of marble and stone Maurice felt the same sensation of being involved in some weird fantasy that had no basis in real life. He knew that Francis had been called on the previous afternoon and he was surprised to find her there again in the witnesses' waiting area. He gave her a nod and a wan smile, but did not say anything as he and the American sat. Then he noticed his ex-assistant Rupert sitting across from her. For some reason it had not occurred to him that he might see the young man there, but of course it was obvious. Maurice rose again and went over to him.

'I'm so sorry about all this, Rupert,' he murmured. 'Sorry about what happened.'

Rupert nodded, his tangle of black hair half hiding his eyes. 'S'all right. I'm sorry for you.'

'Did they. . . . did they give you a bad time?'

'Wasn't funny. But nothing serious.'

'You were brave to go to the police.'

'Nah. They just made me f. . . . bloody angry. I wasn't going to let the sods get away with that.'

Maurice nodded. 'Well, if ever you want your job back. . . .'

'Thanks, Mr Aldridge, but I think I've done the book trade. I'm working at an accountant's now. And trying to finish my course at the LSE at the same time.'

'Well, good for you. You'll have a much better career that way, I'm sure.'

He went back to his seat. Frances was called to continue giving evidence soon after. She waggled her fingers as she left, and made telephone gestures. He nodded. It was a couple of tedious hours before Rupert was called, and a further half hour before Maurice himself was summoned. As he rose from his seat Donald said, 'I'll probably be next. Wait for me, and if it doesn't take too long let's have lunch together.'

Maurice nodded and followed the usher to the court room. As he entered the large hushed chamber he was immediately aware of the two men in the raised dock, but couldn't bring himself to look directly at them. He was shaking a little as he entered the witness box and took the oath.

The ordeal was surprisingly brief, and he remembered little about it afterwards. He was somewhat briskly questioned about his role in the story. When he was asked to indicate the fraudster who had temporarily been in his employment he glanced at the dock for the first time. He barely recognised the impassive figure he knew as Roger Hemingway, and he still could not recall the large man in the grey suit next to him. Hemingway himself was staring straight at him, the offset eyes expressionless, no trace of the beguiling smile. When Maurice pointed at him and said, 'That's him,' he barely reacted, just the flicker of menace crossing his features. What thoughts were going through his head, what his feelings were about the whole surreal episode, Maurice could not remotely conjecture. Conceivably he had none.

It soon become apparent that the judge—a dry character with a public school voice and a slight speech impediment—was personally more interested in the nature of the sought-after journal than in the precise circumstances of the crime itself. Maurice told the court what little he knew about it.

'Extraordinary,' said the judge. 'And you think this book really exists?'

'It would seem so, Your Honour,' said Maurice quietly. 'There is quite a lot of evidence.'

'You say you've read Klaus Fuchs's account of seeing it?'

'Yes, Your Honour.'

'What does he say about it?'

'Nothing specific. Only that he thought it an interesting read.'

'And it mentioned the existence of a postscript to 'Origin of Species'?

'Yes.'

'Extraordinary! Do you think you might find it?'

Maurice hesitated. 'I don't know, Your Honour. It's doubtful. No-one has been able to find it so far.'

'Extraordinary!' The judge snorted. 'That would set the cat among the pigeons, eh?'

'Yes, Your Honour.'

'Well, I look forward to hearing more about it.' He consulted his file. 'Now then, you say the first time you ever saw this character was when he came into your shop looking for books. . . .?'

Hemingway's face remained immobile, hostile through Maurice's entire testimony.

Maurice left the court some half an hour later, with the firm desire that he would never have to see the place again. Donald passed him on the way to give evidence himself, and murmured as he went by, 'I shouldn't be too long. We'll have lunch together and talk.'

Maurice wasn't sure that lunch with the instigator of the whole affair was what he wanted, but he nodded and sat down to wait.

An hour or so later the two were once more seated at Donald's favoured table in the corner of the Ritz dining room, their sole meunière in front of them and the New Zealand Sauvignon idling in their glasses.

'You're very quiet, Maurice,' said the American as he dissected his filet.

'I'm not sure I can go any further with this quest,' said Maurice.

Donald looked at him intently. 'Oh. I'm sorry to hear that.'

'We seem to have reached a dead end. You say you got no joy from the librarian at Hatfield House?'

The other shook his head. 'Disappointing. He was very cooperative. Replied immediately to my letter. But said there was definitely nothing original in the library or the archives. And he thought he would have known if anything like that had ever surfaced within the last half century.'

'Then I can't think where else to look. And it seems to me. . . .' Maurice hesitated.

'What? Say what you're thinking.'

Maurice was diffident. 'Well, it just seems that. . . . if things don't want to be found then perhaps they *shouldn't* be found.'

'Shouldn't?'

'Well, Emma's journal was evidently a very personal reflection, which she wished to be kept private. And the Darwin postscript. . . . I don't know. That too was his own personal conclusion. They both plainly had concerns about making it public.'

'You don't think the world ought to know about such a thing?'

'Possibly. I don't know. I find myself in a dilemma about it. Particularly considering the effects that have happened so far.'

'That was an aberration, Maurice. A one-off freaky sideshow. I'm sorry it ever came about, but it doesn't alter the main purpose of the exercise. To discover what might be one of the most important documents ever written.'

Maurice toyed with his fish. 'Do you think so? Will it change anything? The debate will go on. People will still believe what they wish to believe, whatever Darwin thought about it all. The beliefs and the superstitions and the myths will survive whatever the evidence.'

'I don't agree. The myths are gradually dying out as science discovers the true facts. Look how far we've come since the middle ages. Since even the last century.'

Maurice nodded. 'Yes, perhaps. But even so. . . . well, let's just say that, much as I'd love to read either of these things. . . . I feel I've come to the end of the road on a personal level.'

Donald accepted defeat graciously. 'O.K., Maurice. I understand. You've been through enough. I'm very grateful for all that you've done so far, and I must say that in any case you've added to my knowledge of the whole shebang.' His eyes flashed momentarily. 'I won't say that I've completely given up on the chase myself, but maybe it's time to take a break and reassess the options. Maybe we were barking up the wrong tree. Maybe there are other routes to finding this thing.'

'Well, I wish you luck,' Maurice replied. 'If I can help in any. . . . less direct way, let me know.'

'Sure.' Donald waved the long finger. 'It will come to light one day. These things always do.' Maurice nodded. 'And if I'm the one to find it, you'll be the first to know.'

'I'd appreciate that.'

'And I'd suggest you don't do any more business with Tommy Houseman from Michigan.'

Maurice smiled and nodded again.

The American took a sip of the Sauvignon, savouring it pleasurably. 'Now, how do you fancy a little vacation in the South of France?'

Maurice's smile broadened. He felt remarkably relaxed all of a sudden. 'That's so very kind of you, Donald. And one day I might like to take you up on it. But do you know, just at the moment, all I want is to settle back into my routine and find my own world again. I've rather lost touch with it recently, and I. . . . I miss it.'

Donald nodded. 'I understand. You're a lucky man to know what your own world is. Not many do.'

Maurice considered. 'I think perhaps you do. Despite your setbacks.'

The American hesitated. 'To some degree. But it's incomplete. There are a few pieces missing.' He grinned, the beautifully modelled teeth flashing. 'That's why I need to keep up searches such as this one.'

'Well, good hunting.'

Donald sat back, wiped his mouth with his napkin, and gazed up at the superb chandelier-hung ceiling. 'Speaking of which. . . .

'Yes?'

'Well. . . . I don't think I can let you go quite so easily, Maurice. I have another little project which might interest you'

'Oh?'

'I think you'll like this.' He paused for effect as was his wont, then leaned forward. 'I've got wind of the possibility that Shakespeare's wife, Anne Hathaway, may have written a series of letters to one of her family describing her life with the playwright at Stratford. Now my informant has told me. . . . .' He broke off. He could only sit and stare for the next minute as Maurice almost laughed himself into a heart attack.

CHAPTER FORTY-NINE

<u>August 8th 1858. Sandown, Isle of Wight</u>

At last I feel able to write in my journal once more. We have come to this delightful place for a holiday, and the sunshine and the sea air have revived my health and spirits at a time when I felt that they would never recover again. The last few months have been amongst the most distressful of our lives. Tragedy and anxiety have tormented us from so many directions that at times I have not known where to turn. Since May our darling Etty has been battling diptheria, whilst the dreaded scarlet fever has been sweeping the village again and knocking at our door, threatening both Lenny and Horace and several of the servants. Then baby Charles caught high fever, and it transpired that it was indeed that awful disease. Poor backward deprived little creature that he was, he had not the physical resources to resist, and he mercifully died in my arms after days of torment. I myself had not long recovered from the ordeal of his birth and I scarcely had the strength of will to go on caring for my household of stricken invalids. Fortunately Charles himself was enjoying a period of relative good health in the fine weather of those weeks, and close friends and relatives brought help from all quarters, but even so it was a grievous time.

Then in the midst of our distress came explosive news on my husband's front. A paper arrived from Alfred Russell Wallace, a fellow biologist currently foraging in the Far East, which outlined a theory of 'Natural Selection' that C proclaimed was almost identical to his own. In fact he said that he could scarcely have worded it better himself. This threw him into an agony of despair for it confirmed all his worst fears that someone might pre-empt his long years of work and research. Mr Wallace, in his innocence, was asking my husband's authoritative opinion of the paper, little realising the impact it would have.

Charles, being wholly honourable, immediately sent the treatise on to his colleagues Lyell and Hooker for their judgment. They agreed that it mirrored his own deductions, which he had described in his paper all those years previously but never dared publish. Staunch friends that they are they immediately took charge and decided that the solution was to present both papers simultaneously to the influential Linnean Society, whose members represent the cream of scientific authority.

Charles was not there for the reading, little more than a month ago now. It coincided with the funeral of Baby Charles, and nothing could deflect C from being present for that occasion. Joseph Hooker reported on the reading. The extraordinary thing was that, when the two presentations were read to the assembled Wise Men, they apparently provoked barely a stirring of interest! Not one amongst the gathering appeared to recognise the significance of what they were hearing. This seems strange to me, for if an ignoramus such a myself can comprehend the immensity of the proposition then how is it that the greatest experts in the land can fail to appreciate it? Is it that my dear C's grand theory is not so consequential after all, or is it that it is so momentous those learned minds simply dared not contemplate its implications?

Whatever it is, the expected cataclysm failed to materialise—much to C's relief it has to be said. He knew however that he could now no longer delay completion of the full exposition, and as I write he is already immersed again in his 'abominable book'. I trust it will not cause him further affliction from his 'abominable constitution'.

As I gaze from my Isle of Wight window at the serene seascape beyond, the undulating grass covered cliffs, the peaceful ocean, the immense sky over all, it seem to me that ultimately none of these things matter anyway. All that matters is to try to live as the Lord meant us to live, and to enjoy the small moments. The rest will become clear when time decides.

CHAPTER FIFTY

The instinct of self-preservation is not felt except in the presence of danger; and many a coward has thought himself brave until he has met his enemy face to face. The wish for another man's property is perhaps as persistent a desire as any that can be named, but even in this case the satisfaction of actual possession is generally a weaker feeling than the desire. Many a thief, after success, has wondered why he stole some article.

The Descent of Man

At home, the evening after the court hearing, Maurice got a call from Frances. Her voice was contrite. 'Maurice, you won't believe this, but I think your conman friend from the shop may get off without a prison sentence.'

'What? Why?'

'His counsel are pushing the story that he was just duped by the other man.'

'That's ridiculous.'

I know, but it's why I was called again as a witness. I must have been in the box for more than two hours altogether.'

'I don't understand. How can they say he was innocent?'

'Well, not innocent exactly, but they're saying he was under the other creature's influence and didn't really know what was going on. They're saying he was intimidated by the man and had been bullied into playing his part. His only role was to trick his way into your employment in order to get information, and he didn't realise it would get so serious.'

'That's ludicrous. I explained his whole deceit to the court.'

'Yes, but his barrister is very clever. He has no previous record, and my counsel thinks they're going for a caution or a suspended sentence or something if he cooperates. What they really want, you see, is that he gives evidence against his boss.'

Maurice sat down, the phone still to his ear. 'That's. . . . that's a travesty! The other one may have been the brains, but he's just as bad. He's just as much to blame.' He thought back to all those hours and days of the youth's involvement at the shop. The calculated queries, the seductive smiles, the apparent fascination with books and with Maurice's world, the whole insidious strategy. 'I couldn't imagine a more premeditated deception.'

'I know, but. . . .'

'Didn't you tell them what happened at your house?'

'Of course, but you see. . . . .'

'What?'

'It's difficult. They're so clever. They twisted my words, and. . . .'

'What do you mean, twisted your words?'

'Well for instance, when they. . . . when the big man was. . . . was torturing Nicholas the other one kept mocking him. He was imitating Nicholas's words, saying, 'No, no, no. . . .' in a high pitched voice, like that.' Maurice tried not to imagine the scene. 'Well when I described this, the lawyer made out that what he was really doing was saying 'no, no, no' to the other man—trying to get him to stop, do you see? And I couldn't. . . . I wasn't able to explain well enough that that wasn't it at all. When they asked what his expression was I had to say that he wasn't actually laughing, but that he had this wild, wide-eyed look. I knew he was enjoying the whole thing, but they made out that he could have been just appalled at what was happening. I said no that wasn't it, but they kept on and on at me and I couldn't explain. I just. . . .' Her voice broke and she lapsed into silence.

Maurice was silent too. 'Are you sure he's going to get off lightly?' he asked eventually.

'No, I'm not sure. But my lawyer didn't look too hopeful. It's the other thug the police are really after, and they may take a plea bargain from your man in order to get his testimony. The judge is pronouncing sentence next week.' Pause. 'I'm so sorry, Maurice.'

'Don't be sorry. It's not your fault. Let's see what happens.'

'Yes. Right. Let's see.'

Maurice put down the phone and sat for several minutes. Why was it, he thought, that the law so often appeared to be acting against, rather than for, the interests of the victim?

It wasn't the first time he had encountered the paradox. He thought back to the last six months of Alice's ordeal. It had been his insurmountable problem then. The law, or the prevailing morality, or both, had been the chief obstacle to ending her suffering. He was himself so conditioned to obeying both that the act of defying them seemed beyond him. She asked him again and again to bring it all to a close, but it was something he was incapable of doing. He could only weep as she wept, feel pain as she felt pain. He could only hope to die at the same time that she was dying.

Finally her distress was so awful that he could endure it no longer and forced himself to pay a particular visit to their doctor. This was an old friend who had been their physician for many years—one of a decreasing species—which at least made it easier for Maurice to bring up the subject. He could remember clearly the conversation which took place in the local surgery one bright summer morning. The doctor, a world weary but conscientious practitioner who had attended Alice through all the stages of her illness, was sitting at his desk playing with a pen as he listened to Maurice's hesitant words.

'It can't go on any longer, Peter. She can't bear it any longer. And neither can I. It can't go on.'

The other watched him for a long moment, his head nodding slightly with each turn of the pen in his fingers. Then he

340

sighed and said, 'No. No, it must seem that way. I'm so sorry for you both. It's a terrible dilemma.'

'I need. . . . I need your help to end it. I don't know how one. . . . how I would go about such a thing.'

'Would you consider the option of going to Switzerland?'

Maurice shook his head. 'She's too sick to make the journey. And it's expensive, isn't it?'

'It's not cheap.' The doctor paused. His voice was low. 'Well, it's not the first time I've come across this situation. But I don't know how to help, Maurice.'

'Can't you. . . .?' Maurice waved a helpless hand. 'I wouldn't want you to do anything yourself. But couldn't you just give me some pills or something which would. . . .?'

The other shook his head. 'Some doctors might help you. But I can't. However hard it may seem I have to hold to the principle that the sanctity of life is inviolable. The law may change in this matter one day, but even then I could not approve. All my moral and religious beliefs would dictate against it.'

Maurice sat for a moment, then nodded and got up slowly from his chair.

'I'm so sorry,' the doctor said as he went to the door.

Maurice opened the door, and turned. 'You know what, Peter?' he said. 'Fuck your religious beliefs.' Then he left.

Back home that evening he gave Alice the maximum dose of pain killers, than sat beside her bed holding her hand until she fell into a coma-like sleep. Then he took a pillow, and with the tears steadily soaking it, he held it firmly over her face until she stopped breathing. He sat for several hours by her side before calling the emergency services.

He was perhaps fortunate that it was Peter himself who was called to make out the death certificate. The doctor's face was impassive and he said nothing to him at the hospital. Merely wrote a rather ambiguous report which included the words 'death by natural causes.'

CHAPTER FIFTY-ONE

December 6th, 1952. Wakefield.

Gordon Hawkins is a quite extraordinary man. He has never again mentioned the embarrassing incident in his room when my emotions had got the better of me, but during our talks he always has an authoritative opinion or some revealing piece of information which casts light on my own concerns. Yesterday we were discussing how scientific developments had radically changed philosophical theories throughout the centuries, and more specifically how they had influenced my own opinions throughout the much briefer period of my career. I happened in passing to mention the incident several years previously in which a colleague of mine at Birmingham had shown me his family's copy of Emma Darwin's private diary.

Gordon then leaned forward and said, "Did you know that, whilst awaiting publication of *Origin of Species*, the Darwins were actually staying just a few miles from where we are sitting?"

I sat up in my chair in surprise, and asked him to elaborate. "Well it was almost a hundred years ago of course," he said, "but there was—and I believe still is—a well known hydropathic spa establishment known as Wells House on the Yorkshire moors at Ilkley. It's a small town north of the prison on the far side of Leeds."

I had heard of the place but knew little about it.

"Well," he continued, "Charles D, on one of his perpetual quests for a cure for his bad health, went there at the time of publication. Partly to try and alleviate another severe period of sickness and partly, from all accounts, to hide whilst his magnum opus exploded on the world. The recurrence of his sickness was more than likely brought on by the exhausting task of finishing the book and proofs in time for the publication date."

I asked how he knew all this. He told me that Ilkley itself is a well known tourist spot, and there are a number of records of its connections with Darwin and others of the rich and famous. Gordon in his spare time likes to delve into the region's history, and it seems that on one of his foraging expeditions he came across in some archive or other the notebooks of Dr Edmund Smith, the founder of Wells House. "These were not by any means comprehensive," said Gordon, "but they contained all sorts of jottings, reports of conversations, diary entries—anything that Dr Edmund considered of interest—and of course he had recorded the visits to his establishment of any patients of note, including Darwin. He had held several discussions with the great man during his six weeks stay there, and wrote about him at some length."

"That's extraordinary!" I said. "What else do you know?"

"Well, only that Darwin was extremely on edge when he arrived—concerned about the reaction of the establishment to his new book. And when he found that Dr Edmund was a sympathetic soul with some understanding of the issues, he spoke quite freely about its contents and its controversial aspects. The intriguing thing is that in the course of this he admitted to the doctor that he had in fact written an addendum to the book which explained much further his own thoughts about the relevance of evolutionary theory to the question of religion and the existence of God."

This of course coincided with what I had read in Emma's journal and I questioned Gordon further, but he could tell me little more. It seems that—partly due to his own qualms and partly to the exhortations of his wife—Darwin had at the last moment omitted the addendum from the publication, intending to keep such opinions for a later date. Dr Edmund apparently mentions in his notes that he was fascinated to know Darwin's conclusions and questioned him about them, but was unable to elicit much on the subject. Darwin was as ever modest and reserved about such things.

I was of course intrigued by Gordon's story, and told him how this report confirmed all that Emma Darwin mentioned in her own diary, although there she said that Charles's post-script was meant for his next book, 'The Descent of Man'. Perhaps he intended to include it there but once again 'chick-ened out' as the Americans say. It only makes it all the more enthralling to know what was in it!

One might ask why I am so involved with the thoughts of a fellow scientist working more than a century ago. Hav-ing now read the prison copy of 'Origin of Species' several times, and each time found something new in its pages to marvel at, the overall impression is not just that his revela-tion was so all encompassing—it was also that his methodol-ogy was so complete. All scientists know, even if they do not always adhere to it, that nothing is proven until all possible variations are covered. I can only wonder at the painstaking industry of a man whose field was the whole of nature, and yet who, when he encountered such a variation never failed to explore it, when he met an inconsistency never rested un-til he had solved it, when he was challenged with a possible anomaly never left it until he had proved or disproved it. Of course there had to be gaps in his research, but he always ad-mitted such and recognised the unsolved problems, usually before his critics did. And of course he knew there would be many who would question his findings—as there are still—but it is inevitably because they haven't his perseverance or his objectivity to investigate such questions to their ultimate conclusion. As one studies his writings one cannot help but come to the opinion that, whatever the examples in nature of mysterious or still unexplained deviations amongst the species, his overall concept has to be right, and it is not the theory that is at fault but our research that is yet incomplete. Much as in my own field.

Gordon and I talked last night until well past the time I should have returned to my cell. I told him how I instinctively felt that Darwin held the key to all those things that have so tormented me down the years, ever since that terrible time in Berlin when man's true propensity for evil became so clear to me. I said words to the effect that, "We struggle to find answers to the irrational torments and tragedies which so bedevil our existence, and in our innocence we seek these in the stars, the heavens, the mystical motives of the gods. But to anyone of an analytical or logical nature these explanations are not enough. Certainly not for me. Which is why, if Darwin's postscript has anything to say on the matter, I would dearly love to know what it is."

Gordon replied, "But you are an advanced scientist. Do you really think it would contain anything new after all this time? Haven't we discussed most of the implications over the last hundred years?"

I agreed, but responded that much of the world refuses to accept those implications. I am still unsure of their ultimate consequence myself, which is why I would be fascinated to read Darwin's own interpretation.

He nodded. "I would too, I suppose," he said. "If only to have confirmation from the horse's mouth. How about a game of chess?"

We played until the early hours and I allowed him to beat me, which gave us both pleasure.

CHAPTER FIFTY-TWO

A moral being is one who is capable of reflecting on his past actions and their motives—of approving of some and disapproving of others—and the fact that man is the one being who certainly deserves this designation is the greatest of all distinctions between him and the lower animals.

The Descent of Man

Frances Fanning was right. George Cummins, the brains behind the criminals, got twenty years. Roger Hemingway/ Farringdon got off with a six months suspended sentence. Maurice heard the news via a phone call from the lawyer Justin Laurenson at the shop late one afternoon. At the end of the conversation, during which he hardly spoke, Maurice put the phone down and sat immobile in his office chair for a long while. His feeling of impotence was overwhelming. He was back in the playground with a superior mocking opponent against whom he had no defence. And this time he had no mentor to tutor him in the ways of retaliation. He understood why so many victims of ineffective justice feel a bitterness they are incapable of handling.

He sat until he had lost track of time. Then he suddenly straightened and looked at his watch. Twenty past five in the evening, almost time to shut up the shop. He looked out to where Joan was tidying up preparatory to closing. He opened his desk drawer and rummaged amongst the contents. Found what he was looking for—the copy of the employment contract he had given 'Hemingway' after the man had served his first month's apprenticeship. It had an address in the relevant box.

86 Templeton House.
Camberwell, London SE5

Whether it was genuine Maurice had no way of knowing, and it seemed an odd area of London for the character he had imagined he had been acquainted with. However, as he now knew, the acquaintance had been illusory. With the contract were the two letters of recommendation that the youth had presented when first employed. They had lain there unconsidered since that unfortunate day. Maurice now read them properly for the first time. The first was headed *Markham and Partners Ltd,* with an address in South London, and read:-

> *To whom it may concern:-*
> *Mr Roger Hemingway has been an extremely efficient and dependable employee of this firm who is wholly honest and trustworthy. We would reccommend him for any responsible post requiring competence and initiative.*

> *Signed Jonathan Markham.*

Maurice noted the misspelling of 'reccommend' and pursed his lips. He looked up Markham and Partners in Yellow Pages and of course found no company of that name. He then turned to the other letter, which was too similarly worded to be coincidental and which boasted another fictitious enterprise on its heading.

It had all been too easy.

Maurice sat for a further moment, expressionless. Then jerked into movement, put the papers back in the drawer, took out his whiskey flask, and rose from his chair. Donned his hat and coat, saw a startled Joan brusquely off home, and locked up the shop. He hailed a taxi in St Martins Lane and gave the address in Camberwell.

On the twenty minute journey there he barely glanced out of the windows. He did however consume half his flask of scotch. When he arrived at the address it was approaching six o'clock and the sun had sunk behind the looming bulk of what turned out to be a council built estate. Templeton House was one of those vast, characterless apartment blocks that had been thrown up in the fifties and sixties as the simplest and cheapest way to house London's army of disadvantaged families, immigrants and low paid menial workers. From its appearance it had since been largely sold off to its tenants during the Thatcher years and some modest attempts made to smarten it up and give it an aura of greater affluence. Maurice paid the taxi driver and walked the few yards across the concrete forecourt dotted with bland potted shrubs. Number 86 was on the fourth floor. He rejected the inhospitable looking lift and took the stone stairs two at a time. At the top he paused briefly for breath, then rang the bell of number 86, at the same time knocking loudly on the door.

It was opened by Roger Farringdon himself. He looked much as he had done in court, dour, expressionless—although now casually dressed in scruffy shirt and jeans. The fair hair was swept greasily back, the myopic eyes were bleak, the trademark smile nowhere evident.

'What. . . .? What the. . . .?'

Maurice pushed him aside, and as he fell back against the wall entered the flat. The place smelt of stale dust and cigarette smoke. He went briskly down the narrow hall, glancing into the single bedroom to one side, and found the living room at the rear. Sparsely furnished, unadorned, characterless, but with an array of expensive looking electronic gear. A towering sound system and speakers ranged along a wall, a desk top computer occupied a table, a huge flat-screen TV blared in one corner. Maurice glanced round, saw there was no-one else in the place, and turned as Farringdon followed him into the room.

'What the fuck d'you think you're doin' 'ere?' There was no pretence at the grammar school accent—the tones were now pure Essex man. Maurice noticed behind him by the doorway the half dozen books purchased from his shop, piled haphazardly on a shelf.

'So,' said Maurice, indicating them, 'interested in books, are you?'

The faintest smile played on the other's lips. 'When it suits me.'

'Have you ever read anything other than the football results?'

'Yes, actually.' Nodding behind him, 'Not that old rubbish though.' His tone became ominous. 'What's it to you?'

Maurice took off his spectacles and put them in his breast pocket. 'And you got off with a suspended sentence?'

'Yer. So wot?'

'Just an innocent victim who didn't know what was going on?'

Farringdon moved closer, dangerously. He was a good four inches taller than Maurice, and probably the best part of twenty years younger. 'That's what the court said, yeh. You wanna say anyfing different?'

'No.'

Maurice did exactly the same as he had done all those years ago in the playground. Left to the stomach, right to the heart. And it had exactly the same effect. Farringdon hit the floor like a fallen tree and lay gasping. Maurice did not follow up with the punch on the nose. He stooped, grabbed the other by the scruff of his shirt, and heaved him onto an upright chair by the formica topped dining table, the shirt buttons popping in the process. The man's chest was white and hairless. He sat there doubled up, fighting for breath as Maurice switched off the TV, glanced around, found an ancient vacuum cleaner in one corner and ripped the flex from it. Grabbed the still gasping Farringdon by the hair, pulled back his head, and wound the flex several times around his torso and the back of the chair, roughly tying the end at the back. Not very secure but it would do. He went to the adjoining kitchen area, grimaced with distaste at the chaos there, half filled the electric kettle and set it to boil. Farringdon, by now semi-recovered, stared at him in horror.

Maurice stared back impassively as the seconds ticked. He glanced at where the books lay, their traditional colours and gilt letters looking ridiculously incongruous in such surroundings. The kettle boiled. He lifted it from its base, grabbed a dirty tea towel from the sink, and walked over to the helpless man.

'Have you any idea?' he said in a low voice. 'Have you the slightest idea how hard it is for ordinary people to get through life? By doing the rights things? By trying to stick to the straight and narrow? Have you any idea?'

The other stared at him, his misaligned eyes panic stricken, his body shaking. Maurice placed the kettle on the table beside him, grabbed his open shirt and ripped it further aside under the electric flex, almost pulling both man and chair over in the process. Farringdon gave an animal shriek. 'No, no, no!' he gasped.

'No, no, no,' repeated Maurice. 'No, you haven't, have you? No idea.' He twisted the tea towel into a rope, and tied it round his victim's head, cutting across his mouth between his teeth. Then he picked up the kettle. Some of the water slopped from the spout onto the table top, and a few small splashes hit Farringdon's arms and chest. He shrieked through the towel.

Maurice lifted the kettle and held it above the other's exposed torso. His mind was blank. He had no idea whether he was going to go through with it or not. Farringdon's eyes stared at him over the tea-towel with a terror such as he had never seen before in any man's gaze.

He couldn't have said how long he stayed there motionless, the half naked body trembling a foot beneath his arm. Then he gave a little grunt and his shoulders relaxed. He put the kettle down and walked from the flat, leaving a blubbering, shaking wreck behind him.

CHAPTER FIFTY-THREE

November 26th, 1859. Down House

I have just returned home with the children from what I can only describe as one of the most inhospitable places on earth. Dear Charley was so exhausted at the completion of his book, so utterly afflicted in all parts of his body, partly with the sheer weight of the task and partly, I suspect, with the worry about its reception, that he travelled for another attempt at recuperation to a new hydropathic establishment we had heard about in the far North, built by Dr Edmund Smith, a man with a respected medical reputation. It is at Ilkley on the Yorkshire moors and its additional attraction was that it was as distant as C could reasonably get from London and the hullabaloo he anticipated when the book came out. However his letters from there told us that he was even so in such an agony of suspense over the birth of his 'wretched tome', and so oppressed by the bleakness of the surroundings and the weather in that place, that I feared for his very life. I and the children made the endless expedition North by coach and train to a rented house nearby where C could join us and seek respite in the family's bosom for a while. However the journey had exhausted everyone, and though the house was pleasant enough, the frozen elements at this time of year and the gloomy landscape were a drain on all our spirits. It was only the anticipation of news from London about the book's appearance that kept us lively (and myself in as fearful apprehension as C, although I could not say so to him since it was for different reasons.)

The volume finally went on sale to the book-sellers in a very elegant green covered edition of 1200, priced at 15 shillings each. Its publisher, John Murray, is a man of the most remarkable patience. He knew of the impending work many months in advance, and never having read a word of it, agreed to publish merely on my husband's reputation and on the recommendation of Sir Charles Lyell and all his scientific friends. He then had to endure an endless progression of editings and revisions—partly on my own advice it has to be said, partly at my husband's constant rethinking, and partly at his own suggestion. He also suffered much debate over the title. C originally wished to call it 'An Abstract of an Essay on the Origin of Species and Varieties through Natural Selection.' Both Mr Murray and myself feared that this was far too much of an indigestible mouthful for any reader to swallow, and we persuaded him little by little and letter by letter to reduce it to 'The Origin of Species', which title I feel has an imposing ring to it. It appears that all this work was worthwhile because, as we heard from London, the whole printing sold out the first day, causing Mr Murray immediately to order a second printing of 3000 copies. What a splendid indication of my husband's reputation, which did more for his health than all the spa treatments in the land! All that feeds his apprehension now is the suspense of waiting for the opinions of his many peers and adversaries amongst the scientific establishment.

My own apprehension however is of a different nature. As this journal testifies, for many years I have struggled with my concern for Charles's salvation as he interferes in matters which, deep in my heart, I feel are really only for God to know. Up until this moment I have been able to contain my fears since he has confined his publishing to general treatises on specific subjects within the natural and biological worlds. He has said very little about the relevance of his propositions to the greater question of God's kingdom and authority. Although I have been well aware of how C's own thinking on this matter has developed over time, he has refrained from making such thoughts public, and for that I have been grateful and somewhat reassured as to his future place in heaven. This book however, it seems to me alters everything. It brings together all his researches and findings into one great manifesto whose conclusions are clear for anyone to see. And as I have so frequently stated, such conclusions are contrary to everything the Bible and the Church has taught us throughout the centuries. I fear that it will be taken as a direct challenge to every ecclesiastical and canonical decree since the dawn of time, and in the depths of night when I lie awake thinking I suffer the most terrible doubts, not only for Charles's own soul, but for those of myself and our children also since we have been collaborators in his efforts. The worst of it is that I have no-one to turn to for advice or assurance on this matter for, of all who are aware of C's premise, those learned enough to fully understand it are now mostly converted to his way of thinking, and the rest are orthodox believers and churchmen who will simply confirm my worst fears with no offer of salvation. I am literally twixt the damned and the devil!

It is this terror in my mind that has led directly to my influence, or should I say my interference in two particular matters concerning the book, and these are now exercising my conscience. One is that I have had considerable sway in dissuading C from commenting in it as to how he specifically sees man's place in the evolutionary process. I am all too aware, having heard the endless debates around the dinner table and about his study desk, that he and his fellow 'homo sapiens' are mostly agreed on their descent from the early primate species. This of course is one of the major contradictions of all that we read in the Bible about the sanctity of the human soul, and I argued strongly that the proposition might create such a furore and such a distraction from the main thrust of the book that it could not be to C's benefit to include it. He did agree with me, and fearing such controversy as much as I did he confined his remarks on the subject to a few brief phrases.

The second matter is perhaps more serious, and in truth arises from the first. It embodies the crux of my whole dilemma. The early drafts of the book ended with a summation or postscript in which C explained the implications he believed his evolutionary theory held for <u>all</u> fundamental spiritual beliefs. This was the thing I most feared. This was the issue that had cast its huge shadow over his work for all these years, and which had been perhaps the only serious bone of contention between us throughout our marriage. I could not allow him to include this final piece without arguing against its inclusion with all the force I could muster. I feared so greatly for both his own reputation and the distress it might cause for all the family should it become the ultimate debating point of the book within the public forum. After a great deal of contemplation and soul searching C agreed to at any rate to postpone revealing it until a later date, or perhaps a later publication.

I must confess that, although concerned at influencing him to such a degree, I am greatly relieved at his concession. He has entrusted me with the safe keeping of this final peroration, which responsibility I do not entirely welcome. I am even apprehensive at mentioning it in my journal. My problem now is where to keep it safe and secure from future curious eyes until C feels the time is appropriate to reveal it. My hiding place beneath the boards of my bedroom will have to suffice for the moment, but that will never do as a permanent resting place and I must put my brain to work to discover such. It <u>must</u> not be discovered.

However I know that wherever I hide such a proclamation, its contents will always be known to the Lord. Why, oh why, Charley, did you have to give expression to such thoughts? Why do you put me through such torments?

CHAPTER FIFTY-FOUR

In all civilised countries man accumulates property and bequeaths it to his children. So that the children in the same country do not by any means start fair in the race for success. But this is far from an unmixed evil. For without the accumulation of capital the arts could not progress, and it is chiefly through their power that the civilised races have extended their range, so as to take the place of the lower races.
The Descent of Man

A month after the trial Maurice was almost back to his old routine. He had heard nothing from Roger Farringdon or anyone else connected with the court case, and he didn't expect to. His mind was now on classical books and traditional customers, his evenings occupied with reading and television and ready made suppers. Even his dreams had reverted to their old form, distressing as ever, but at least he knew what they were and where they came from. About his last violent intrusion into Farringdon's life he felt nothing but a vague grim satisfaction.

It was Tuesday morning and he was standing behind the reception desk in the shop whilst Joan busied herself amongst the book shelves. He himself was going through a bundle of books bought via telephone bid at a Birmingham auction of some deceased academic's effects. He had been tipped off that there might be some items of worth amongst them, but so far nothing had materialised. It was the gamble one had to take on these occasions. He was examining a worn copy of Forbes's *History of Astronomy* when the shop door bell pinged and he looked up. A figure stood there silhouetted against the bright June sunshine and at first he did not recognise it. Then it moved, and to his surprise he realised it was that of Samuel Matheson. The old man was stooped and frowning through the relative darkness of the shop, his form encased in a shapeless overcoat despite the warmth of the season.

Maurice came quickly forward. 'Mr Matheson!'

'Ah. It's the right place then.'

The old boy's voice was even huskier than before, but he seemed to have made some attempt to clean himself up. His lank hair was vaguely brushed, and he wore a wrinkled collar and tie beneath the overcoat's folds.

'What are you doing in London?' said Maurice.

'Bit of business,' was the reply.

'Did you come from Oxford by train?'

'Nah, bus. Cheaper.'

'Ah, yes.' Maurice waited, but there was no further offering. 'Well what can I do for you?'

Matheson peered around the premises. Joan was up a set of steps arranging things on an upper shelf. 'I need to talk to you. Private. Is there somewhere we can go?'

'Yes, of course. Come into my office.' Maurice signalled discreetly to Joan and led the visitor into the back office. He closed the door behind them. 'Shall I take your coat?'

Matheson pulled it closer around himself. 'Nah. It's all right.'

Maurice gestured to the chair opposite the desk and the other sat gingerly, glancing about him still.

'Lotta stuff you've got here. Lotta books.'

'Yes, well it is my business.'

'Pretty valuable I expect, some of these.'

'Yes, but the really valuable items I only trade as commissions. I don't have them here for long.'

'Commissions?'

'Specific deals for specific customers.'

'Ah yes, right.'

A beat. 'So, how are the cats?'

'Fine. Got to go though.'

'Oh dear.'

'Me too. I've had notice.'

'Notice?'

'Two months notice to quit.' Matheson tugged at his shirt collar.

'Ah. Where will you go?'

He shrugged. 'Dunno. I'll find somewhere.'

Pause. Maurice waited in vain. 'So. . . . why have you come to London, Mr Matheson?'

'To see you really.'

'Just to see me?'

'Yeh.'

'Why?'

The other screwed up his face and looked about him again. 'You seemed to me a decent sort. You seemed someone I could trust.'

'Well thank you. I hope you can.'

'I didn't know who to go to, y'see. I don't trust most of 'em.'

'Most of who?'

He waved a vague hand. 'Them. All them out there. You can't trust people these days.'

Maurice tried to be patient. 'What is it you want to trust them with?'

Silence. The old man sucked his lips as if they were perpetually dry. 'You promise you'll keep quiet about this? It's confidential, you see. You promise you won't tell anyone. You can't trust them. I need to know I can. . . . I can trust you.'

'I promise you, Mr Matheson, you will have my absolute confidentiality. In my business one has to earn trust or one will never survive.'

'Yeh, right. I can imagine that. It's why I came to you.' He pulled the coat closer and leaned forward. 'I need to tell you a bit about myself. About my family.'

'The Allen family?'

'Well, yes. . . . not exactly. . . . it's a bit complicated.'

'Go on.'

'I need to go way back. I need to tell you a story.' He glanced at the door and lowered his voice. 'You see, way back in the last century. . . . . no, the one before that. . . .'

'The nineteenth century?'

'Yeh. In Victoria's time. One of the old Allen family—four or five generations ago—married the aristocracy.'

'Which aristocracy?'

'The Cecils they were called. The Marquis of Salisbury and all that lot.'

Maurice's heart skipped a beat. Were the coincidences in motion again? Matheson went on. 'She married the feller who was head of the family and became Prime Minister.'

'Lord Salisbury?'

'Yeh. You know about him?'

'A little.'

'He was a real toff. Huge houses, and estates all over the place, and god knows what. You couldn't have someone like that Prime Minister nowadays, could you?'

'No, it's highly unlikely.'

'Mind you, he couldn't do much worse than this bunch of wankers.' He sniffed disdainfully. 'Anyway they had various children, who you could say were all descendants—well half descendants—of the Allens.'

'Yes.'

'And one of the children was called Lady Gwendolen. I think she was the youngest daughter.' His rasp became yet more conspiratorial. 'Now she never married. Dunno why. You'd think a toff's daughter like that would be a catch for anyone, wouldn't you?' His eyebrows were furled over his small rheumy eyes. 'But anyway she apparently lived at home with her parents, and when her dad was Prime Minister she acted as sort of secretary for him. Wrote all his letters and sorted his papers and stuff. They must have run things very different then. Whoever heard of a Prime Minister working from home?'

'I expect he spent a lot of time in London. He didn't live far away.'

'No, that's right. Hatfield.'

'Yes.'

'Even so, nowadays they have to have a million secretaries and stuff, don't they? So they can look busy.'

Maurice smiled. He was resigned to this taking a while.

'So anyway, here's this Lady Gwendolen sitting in this bloody great palace, working away at her dad's papers and such, and not getting much social life by the sound of it.' His watery eyes narrowed. 'Then there's this big scandal.'

'Scandal?'

'They kept it hushed up. Secret. You could do it in those days, not like now. Until that is. . . . until there was a case in court.' He raised an arthritic finger. 'A woman who worked in the. . . . on the estate went to the magistrates and complained she'd been given the sack. She said it was because she'd had an illegitimate baby.' He hesitated. 'Or because she. . . . well, it was some story like that. I'm not sure exactly how she described it.'

'How do you know all this?' asked Maurice.

'My mother told me. Years ago. She had letters about it and so on.'

'But your mother's no longer with you?'

'No. She died a long time ago. When I was just a teenager.'

'So?'

'So—the thing is, it was reckoned the kid. . . . the baby was really Lady Gwendolen's, you see. After an affair with one of the social circle. You know, some randy toff or other.'

Maurice remembered that Frances had mentioned an incident.

Matheson was continuing. 'But the family had paid the servant to say it was hers. So there wouldn't be a scandal and that.'

'I see. Was there proof of this?'

'No, no, nothing like that. But the woman obviously felt hard done by for some reason. Maybe they didn't pay her enough, or they sacked her because she started telling people, or. . . . Anyway there was this hell of a scene when she went to the magistrates and claimed it was Lady Gwendolen's baby. They threw it out of course. I mean naturally they were going to be on the side of the toffs, weren't they? But it all caused a bloody great row at the time, and the case got in the papers and everything, even though they tried to hush it up.'

'So then what happened?'

The old man sniffed and his eyes shifted back and forth. 'The thing is, you see. . . . that baby was actually my grandmother.'

There was silence in the room. A score of thoughts went through Maurice's brain in as many seconds. 'You know this for certain?' he asked eventually.

A nod. 'My mother told me. It was always known in the family. And what's more. . . .' He hesitated as if afraid to say it aloud. 'What's more, if it was Lady Cecil's. . . . Lady Gwendolen's baby, then I'm actually descended from her. She's my great grandmother.' His face cracked and he chuckled, a high pitched wheeze. 'Never think I had toff's blood in me, would you?'

Again silence. Maurice considered the implications. 'But there is no evidence of this link to the Cecils?'

'Well, no. . . . none they'd accept. They weren't going to admit it, were they? They weren't going to admit having little bastards running around the estate. That's why they had to get rid of the woman. That's why they paid her off or whatever.' He sniffed again. 'Mind you they can't have paid her much. There's never been any money in my family.' He rubbed his nose with the back of his hand. 'But you see the kid—my grandmother—wasn't christened with the woman's own name. After the magistrates chucked her case out, she decided to say. . . . or p'raps she was told to say she'd adopted it. And it was given the name Allen. That's how we know.'

'Ah. Right.'

'My name's changed since of course, through her marriage later and that.'

Maurice nodded. So that was how the old man had come to be on Donald Easterby's list of descendants. One had to admire the collector's research thoroughness. But Maurice was still unsure as to where this was going.

His visitor had become very still, and was staring at him with an untypical directness. 'But you see, there's other proof.'

'What's that?'

Matheson fumbled with rheumaticky fingers at the buttons of his coat, opened it, and with difficulty pulled from his trouser waistband a heavy object wrapped in a tattered plastic bag. 'This.'

Maurice had virtually stopped breathing, but he showed no sign. Just waited for the man to reveal it, which he eventually did with more fumbling and muttering. He laid it on the desk—a thick, untitled, dark leather volume. The edges were worn, the spine faded and frayed, the pages rough edged. He sat back and watched Maurice.

'What is it?' said the latter.

'The book you were asking about. The diary of that. . . . of Darwin's wife.'

Maurice made no move. 'How did you come by it?'

'Well that's the thing. My mother gave it to me. It was she who told me the story about. . . . all that. She told me that it belonged to Lady Gwendolen, who'd had it from her ancestors in the Allen family. Or the Darwin family. I don't really know—they were all connected by marriage and such.'

'How did your mother get it?'

'Well it was handed down from *her* mother. That's the whole thing, you see. They reckoned that Lady Gwendolen was so guilty about the baby. . . . so sad about losing it and everything, that she wanted it to have something. Something special to show where it came from. Something to keep to show it wasn't just some servant's bastard, but descended from an important family, see what I mean? So she gave it to the woman servant and told her to keep it in the family. Said it was really precious and a record of the baby's ancestors and so on. But it had to be kept secret until the right time, know what I'm saying? It had to be kept locked away until she and all the family and the Darwin lot were long gone, so there couldn't be any more scandal.' He sat back in his chair, hunched in his overcoat. 'So that's how I got it. It's the only thing my mother ever gave me. But she told me to keep it hidden until. . . .' He shrugged. 'Until I could hand it on to *my* kids.'

Maurice reached out a hand. 'May I?'

'Yeh. Take a look.'

Maurice didn't lift it. Just opened the front cover where it lay. The slightest odour of dusty grass wafted from it. The thin foolscap pages inside were yellow with age. He could make out the title on the frontispiece, in traditional Baskerville typeface. It said simply:-

THE JOURNAL OF EMMA DARWIN

1808-1896

He gazed at the words for a long moment, then closed the book again, and sat motionless. Eventually he spoke. 'What do you want me to do with this, Mr Matheson? Do you wish to sell it?'

'No, no. Oh no. I never want to sell it.'

'Then what. . . .?'

'It's for my son, you see. I'm keeping it for my son. It's the only thing. . . . I mean, I've got nothing to leave him. I've got no family stuff, or anything about my life. He wouldn't want that anyway. But this is different. This is his heritage—know what I mean. This will show him he really is somebody. I want him to have it.'

'So why have you brought it to me?'

'I didn't. . . . I didn't know who else to go to. I went to that posh book bloke in Oxford a few years ago, but he was a smoothie, I didn't trust him. I've kept it hidden in the house for years, but now they're throwing me out. Ten thousand quid they're telling me I need to put it all right, and I haven't got that. And I can't take this with me. Not to one of those hostels or wherever. Someone'd pinch it for sure. I didn't know what to do with it. But you seemed to know all about it so. . . . . Well I just thought you could keep it safe for me. You'd know how to prove its. . . . its. . . . .'

'Provenance?'

'Yeh. You'd know how to prove it was genuine and how much it was worth and all that. Then when the time came he'd really have something valuable from me.' His head was nodding, minute little nods as he sat forward again in his chair. A dank strand of hair had fallen across his face and his finger quivered as he pointed at the book. 'Do you think you could do that?'

'It could be worth a lot more than ten thousand pounds, you know.'

The old man's eyes narrowed. 'Yeh, but I'm not selling it. It's for him. I owe it to him.'

Maurice had to ask. 'Was there. . . . was there ever anything else with the book? Another document or a separate paper or anything?'

'No, just that.'

Maurice nodded. 'Well, certainly I could keep it some-where.' He indicated the safe at the back of the office. 'I have a safe here where I keep anything of real value. But how long do you think it might be for?'

'I dunno. Not too long p'raps. I got a card from him a couple of weeks ago.'

'A card?'

'Yeh. It was my birthday. He'd never sent me a birthday card—not for years. Then suddenly I got this card.'

'What did it say?'

'Just 'Happy Birthday dad.' That was all. But at least he hasn't forgotten me, eh?'

'I'm sure he hasn't.'

'So there we are. That's why I've come.'

'Right.' Maurice pondered. 'Do you have an address for your son?'

'Address? Yes, there was one on the envelope. It's at home. He's not in Canada any more—he's in Australia.'

'Well if I'm to keep this then I ought to have the address. So that if anything. . . . if anything happened to you I'd know how to get in touch with him.'

'Oh yeh. That's right. I'll send it. But you won't tell him, will you? Not unless. . . .'

'No, no, of course not. I won't tell anyone.'

'It's got to be our secret, you see. I don't want anyone else knowing. There's all sorts out there who'd get hold of this if they could. I mean I owe a bit of money here and there. . . . and then there's all these bloody crooks about. . . .'

'I promise.'

His face cracked into the semblance of a smile, showing his yellow teeth, and he sighed as if a burden had lifted from his shoulders. 'That's good. That's settled then. You look after it. You can read it if you like. I don't mind you having a look.'

'Have you read it?'

'Some of it. A while ago. It's quite interesting. Hell of a family those Darwins.'

'Yes. Quite a family.'

He looked about him. 'Well that's that. I'd better. . . .'

'Do you want a cup of tea or something?'

'No thanks. I thought. . . . Now I'm in London I thought I'd look around a bit. Haven't been for years. Thought I'd go to a caff or something. Might as well blow what little I've got left before they cart me off, eh?'

'Are you going back to Oxford today?'

'Oh yeh. Got to feed the cats.'

Maurice rose from his chair. 'Well. . . . I'll tell you what, Mr Matheson. I'll write an official note to say that I have your book in safe keeping, and I'll post it to you. Then you'll have a record of it, and if ever you need to prove it's yours, or you want to tell anyone how to get hold of it, you only have to show them the note.'

'That's good. That's a good idea.'

The old fellow got up with an effort, sniffed, wiped his nose on the back of his hand and looked around again. 'You must have tons of stuff like that here.'

'Not much as interesting as yours though.'

'I used to read books once. Quite liked books.'

'You should go back to them. They can give a lot of pleasure.'

'Yeh. I should do that. Well. . . .' He headed for the door. There he turned. 'Well, thanks, I'll. . . . I'll leave it with you then.'

'It will be quite safe, I promise you.'

Maurice watched through the shop window as the hunched figure in his shabby overcoat shuffled off towards Covent Garden and merged with the crowds on the pavement.

'Not your usual sort of customer, Mr Aldridge,' said his assistant beside him.

366

'No, Joan, he's not. And not many come bringing the sort of wares that he's brought.'

'Oh?'

'It's a long story. I might be able to tell you one day.

CHAPTER FIFTY-FIVE

May 24th, 1959. Wakefield.

I have learned that I am to be released. Almost five years before my allotted fourteen are up. It came as a shock. I presume it is for good behaviour, but I am not quite certain. They have told me little so far. However it is welcome news. Over nine years I have spent in this place. And although I have been treated quite well and have found compensations here, it will be a wonderful thing to be free again. Not without its challenges I'm sure, for I have no idea how the world will look upon me after what has happened. Indeed I have no idea what the world itself will look like. I have tried to keep up with developments through the newspapers and the wireless, but they only report events. Events such as the so-called Cold War, the Korean conflict, the hydrogen bomb and Russians' astonishing feat of launching their space satellite—both of which I am eager to know more about. But in matters of culture, of attitudes, the world must have altered fundamentally during that time. I am not a little nervous as to what to expect.

I would like to remain here in England. I like the English. Even the English criminal is a breed with a certain amount of character and resilience. I admire the English lifestyle and the English work ethic. However I suspect I would not be welcome here now, especially since my British citizenship was revoked after my trial. I will probably have to return to Germany, where I am even more in ignorance as to what kind of country I will find. How have my countrymen responded in the years since their defeat? How has the collapse of their guiding political philosophy affected them? How is their collective conscience after the revelations of the death camps and the tyranny of the Third Reich? These are matters about which I have so little knowledge. It is probably best not to dwell too much on what I may find outside. I must take it as it comes. But I can see why some habitual criminals come to prefer their life in prison to being out in the wide world.

What I do know is that I desire above all to return to scientific research. If my years of reflection and contemplation in this place have taught me anything, it is that science and factual discovery is the only way forward for the human race. Man's ancient dogmas have not served him well. Somehow he has to learn to put aside his prejudices and his primitive instincts. He has to harness his skills and act according to his reason, or he is on the road to self destruction.

Gordon Hawkins has kindly procured for me a large notebook, and I am spending my last days copying all my various jottings from my years here into it. But then I will not write any more. My writings have been a comfort to me. They have been my companion in times of loneliness. They bear witness to my ambitions and to my moral intentions. It's true that I do not seem to have fulfilled the concept of survival of the fittest, for I have no family of my own and it's unlikely now that I ever will have. I will not pass on my gifts to any progeny. But I will try to resurrect my reputation as a scientist, although that too is unlikely.

I don't know what I shall do with this book. It is I suppose a humble thing, of little interest to anyone now, despite my original ambitions. The world has passed on. I am no longer of much interest to it. Perhaps I will keep the book on some dusty shelf somewhere, and look at it occasionally to remind myself of what I had become. To remind myself of what the struggle was about. Is about.

I shall continue the struggle. It is all there is.

K.F.

Note written by Margarete Kielson Fuchs attached to Klaus Fuchs's journal (translated from the German).

January 1989.

My husband was too modest in his assumptions. On arrival in East Germany he was elected to the Academy of Sciences and appointed deputy director of the Institute for Nuclear Research at Rossendorf, where he served with distinction for twenty years. He also married me soon after his return. I was widowed and had known and admired him since we were students and young communists together at Kiel. He remained a committed communist, was elected to the Communist Party Central Committee, and received the Fatherland's Order of Merit and the Order of Karl Marx. In later life he campaigned constantly for a ban on nuclear tests and for nuclear disarmament. On his seventieth birthday the leader of the East German Communist Party, Erich Honneker, sent him a message which read, 'You can look back on a distinguished career as a communist, scientist, and teacher.' It made Klaus very proud.

My husband died in 1988.

CHAPTER FIFTY-SIX

*Each organic being is striving to increase at a geo-
metrical ratio, each at some period of its life, during
some season of the year, has to struggle for life and to
suffer great destruction. When we reflect on this struggle we may console ourselves with the full belief that
the war of nature is not incessant, that death is generally prompt, and that the vigorous, the healthy, and the
happy survive and multiply.*

Origin of Species

Maurice sat in his office staring at the closed volume. It was
noon on the day after the old man had visited. Maurice was
red eyed and physically exhausted. His mind was anything
but. He had stayed at the shop until late last night reading,
left the book in the safe, and then continued reading all that
morning. He now sat motionless, his third cup of coffee
growing cold in his hands.

Joan knocked on the door and stuck her head in. 'Are you
all right, Mr Aldridge?' she asked.

He came out of his reverie. 'All right?'

'You've been in here an awful long time.' She frowned.
'And you look very tired.'

He gave a small rueful smile. 'Yes, I am rather.' He indicated the book. 'I've been reading this.'

'Is that what the old man brought yesterday?'

'Yes. It's something that has played quite a large part in
my life recently. But I never thought I would actually get to
read it.'

She opened the door further and came a step into the room.
'Well, it must be important.'

He pondered. 'I don't know how important it is. The problem is that I've come across it under conditions of trust and I can't reveal its whereabouts.'

'So you can't trade it?'

'No, I can't trade it, but it's not just that. I can't disclose its contents to the world, and that's a small tragedy.'

'The world would be better off knowing?'

'The world is always better off knowing more, I think.'

She smiled. For some reason, despite his previous experience, he felt relaxed and confident in this woman's trust. He roused himself. 'I'll tell you what, Joan, I need your help. We have some photocopying to do.'

They laboured at the shop's small photocopier for almost an hour. When they had finished Maurice had a thick pile of A4 sheets which he put into a cardboard file and placed in his desk drawer. The journal he put back in the safe.

'Well, I hope that was worth the effort,' said Joan as she watched him lock the safe.

'Yes, Joan. As I said, I've been at unsure as to what to do with it, but I think I know now.'

'Good.'

He smiled at her in a paternal way. 'Do you like working here?'

She smiled back through her thin silvered spectacles. She was not pretty but had a pleasant face. 'Yes, Mr Aldridge, I do very much.'

'That's good. I can tell you it's a relief to have you here. I hope you'll stay for a while at least.'

She went back to the reception desk. He looked at his watch and picked up the phone. He dialled Easterby's number in France. A male voice replied in English with a strong French accent. Presumably a minion. Donald came on the line.

'Maurice—good to hear from you. What can I do for you?'

'I've got something for you.'

'Oh?'

'How soon are you coming back to London?'

'I had no immediate plans, but if it's something worthwhile I'll always come back.'

'I think you'll find this worthwhile.'

A beat. 'I'm all agog. Tell me.'

'Not on the phone. It's a bit complicated. But I think you'll be pleased you came.'

Another brief pause. 'I'm tied up here for the next thirty six hours, but I can get a plane day after tomorrow.'

'Good. I'll expect you at the shop. Bring your cheque book.'

Two days later Donald walked into the shop at around four in the afternoon. He was wearing the same bright red jacket that he had worn the very first time Maurice had met him at the Ritz.

'Hey, Maurice! I've hardly slept for two nights. I hope this is good.'

Maurice led the way into his office. They both sat, and Maurice took the file from his desk drawer.

'This is for you.' He placed it on the desk between them.

Donald's eyebrows went up. 'Is it what I think it is?'

'It's a copy. A photocopy of one of the original editions. You will know it's authentic the moment you start reading.' Maurice's voice was calm. 'However this is all you can have. You can't have the original. You won't be able to publish it or sell it. There is no proof of it's provenance or authorship. There is no clue as to where it came from. And if you want it, just to read for your own satisfaction, it will cost you ten thousand pounds. Cash.'

Donald sat for a long moment. He shook his head from side to side. 'You bastard, Maurice. Can't you tell me anything?'

'No. Sorry.' Maurice pushed the file across the desk. 'I can tell you this though. I don't imagine you'll regret a single pound of the expense.'

'Did it cost you that much to get it?'

'No. The money isn't for me.'

Donald opened the flap of the file and glanced at the sheets within. 'Is it just the journal? Nothing else?'

'Nothing else. I'm sorry. The other's a whole different business. I have no clue as to where it may be.'

Donald nodded. 'Have you read this?'

'Yes.'

'So it's as interesting as we hoped?'

'I thought so. I imagine you will too.'

Donald closed the file and took a cheque book from his inside coat pocket. 'Ten thousand?'

'Cash.'

He wrote out the cheque. 'You'll have to be careful with this cheque.'

'You'll have to be careful with that file.'

Donald laughed out loud. 'How about dinner at somewhere other than the Ritz?'

'Thank you. That would be very nice.'

Frances telephoned the next day. Maurice had not contacted her since the trial, although he had thought of her from time to time and wondered how she was. She of course knew nothing of his encounter with Farringdon. Against all instincts he found himself pleased to hear her voice.

'How are you, Maurice?'

'Fine.'

'I thought you might have called me.'

'Yes. I have been meaning to. I've been a bit. . . . well it's taken me a while to get my life back on track.'

'Yes. Me too.' Brief pause. 'I'm going down to Dorset with the boys this weekend for Sunday lunch. Would you like to join us?'

'Dorset?'

'My parents. They summon us for a visit once a month or so. Rather a long drive just for lunch, but. . . .'

Maurice was thrown off balance and hesitated. 'Won't they. . . .?'

'Won't they what?'

'They don't know me. Won't they wonder what. . . .?'

'Oh, don't worry about that. I'll just say I'm bringing a friend. They're used to that. It'll help break the monotony of the usual family chat. The boys get very annoyed at being interrogated as to how they're doing at school.'

'Oh, well. . . . it's very kind of you. But I. . . .'

'But what?'

He was at a loss as to how to respond. 'Why would you want to ask me?'

A slight hesitation. 'I like your company. I like being with you.'

'Oh.'

'Of course, if you don't wish to be with *me. . . . .*'

'Oh no, no. It's not that at all. I'm just not used to. . . .'

She laughed then, an amused happy laugh. 'You dear man. Stop being so self-effacing. How often do you get invited out by earl's daughters?'

'Not often, it's true.'

'And I'd like you to meet my sons. Do them good to talk to a man with some knowledge of the world.'

'Well I haven't much of that.'

'Oh, I think you have.'

He was silent again. She went on. 'And you'll find my parents an entertainment in themselves. Come on, it'll do you good.'

'Very well. Thank you.'

'I'll pick you up en route. Say nine o'clock, Sunday. It's a bit of a way, I'm afraid. Don't dress up. Summer casual.'

'Right. I'll . . . look forward to it.'

She rang off. He stood for a moment, disconcerted. 'Should I have said yes, Alice, do you think?' he asked.

'Don't be such a wimp, dear. Of course you should,' came the answer. 'Or don't you think you can look after yourself?'

'Of course I can.'

'Well then. Go and enjoy yourself. It's high time, if you ask me.'

CHAPTER FIFTY-SEVEN

<u>August 8th, 1861. Torquay</u>

I am sitting here in my room overlooking another sea at this pleasant town where we have come for our summer stay. I can see gardens and palm trees and blue sky and bluer water, and I have an hour or so's peace whilst the family go scavenging along the shore, so I may commune with my journal again.

I think this may be almost the last occasion. I think it is time to have done with these reflections. It will be like saying goodbye to an old friend who has been my companion and confidante through good times and bad, through traumas and triumphs, but who is now too tired and jaded to serve me for much longer. I am fifty three years old, and although still as vigorous as maybe, I have found it a growing burden of late to regularly record my thoughts in this book. The desire for simple leisure and contemplation is now more seductive, and the entries have become increasingly sporadic over time, and dare I say a little less fulsome and considered.

We have passed too what might be described as the high point of our lives at Downe. After all the years of toil and turbulence, all the debate and the doubt, C's great work at last presented itself to the outside world, and the anticipated furore over its content has raged ever since. As expected, commentators on all sides have taken their stance and proclaimed their opinions and vented their anger or their approbation. The newspapers and the scholastic periodicals have had a field day, and every expert, every scholar, every priest and every boot-boy has had his say on the topic. All of which has added hugely to the publicity and gratifyingly to the sales, Mr Murray having to do ever more numerous reprints, and foreign editions already let loose or planned in half the countries in Europe it seems.

The argument reached its zenith last summer, when a major debate on C's theory was mounted at Oxford by the British Association for the Advancement of Science. Charles himself was so ill and so worn out by the controversy that he declined to attend, and retreated as is his habit to the protection of Dr Lane's hydropathic establishment. However our ever reliable Joseph Hooker reported in great detail on the event, which made highly entertaining reading. It seemed that the hall chosen for the meeting was crammed to overflowing with almost one thousand persons, and the organisers were forced to move to a larger premises. Thomas Huxley stood in for Charles as the leading champion of his hypothesis, whilst Bishop Samuel Wilberforce[25] no less, led the assault. The latter, a bombast at the best of times, apparently thundered for the best part of half an hour against such unorthodoxy and such blasphemy, and ended with the sarcastic query to Huxley as to whether he was descended from an ape on his grandmother's or his grandfather's side. This produced much laughter, but Huxley bravely turned the tables by proclaiming that, if he had to chose between an ape for an ancestor and a supposedly intelligent and learned bishop who yet could only make ill-informed mockery of a serious scientific matter, then he would unhesitatingly choose the ape. C roared with laughter and clapped his hands when he read this. But better was to come. When it was Joseph Hooker's own turn to speak it seems that he took the bishop's argument and demolished it word by word, proving that he had not understood a single premise of the theory, that he was ignorant of all the basic rudiments of botany and biology, and furthermore that he could not even have read most of C's book! 'Soapy Sam' Wilberforce was left speechless

---

[25] Samuel Wilberforce, Bishop of Oxford 1805–73—known as 'Soapy Sam' for his unctuous manner.

and defeated, his weapons were all smashed, and the field was clear for the victors to celebrate.

However I suspect that the celebration will not be an enduring one, and I myself, whilst delighting in Charles's vindication, have my own constant fear to endure on the question. It is another reason to relinquish my journal. The struggle to reconcile my support for my husband's work with my own faith is one that has almost destroyed my wholeness of mind. It would seem to be an insoluble issue between C and myself and not something I wish to persevere with over the coming years. I prefer now to keep it as a private matter at the back of my mind, knowing that at the end the answer will be forthcoming whatever the earthly debates and dissensions.

Meanwhile I anticipate that our lives will continue much as before. The Powers-That-Be have not yet seen fit to bestow on C the knighthoods and honours that other less celebrated savants have received, but such things matter little to him. He will continue his researches and his writings, for he knows nothing else (he has already embarked on a book about orchids—which at any rate are preferable to barnacles, and less demanding than the origins of all species!). The children will continue to worry us with their health problems, whilst at the same time delighting us with their activities and their industry (all the boys show serious indications of following in their father's footsteps, and with distinction). My own time will be occupied with the running of our dear old Down House, with the affairs of the village, and with the endless visits and correspondence between the numerous members of our far-flung families. The seasons will come and go, the church bells will ring, the politicians and the philosophers will argue, the thrushes will sing, the sweet peas will bloom, and mankind will celebrate and suffer and depart. I have had a truly fulfilled life. I have been blessed with a privileged upbringing, I have produced a loving and creative family, I have seen remarkable times, I have been married to a brilliant and wholly good man. I am not regretful of anything but one or two misfortunes. And even these have taught me the ways of the Lord, and have made me what I am.

I give thanks.

CHAPTER FIFTY-EIGHT

The men who are rich through primogeniture are able to select generation after generation the more beautiful and charming women; and these must generally be healthy in body and active in mind. The evil consequences, such as they may be, of the continued preservation of the same line of descent without any selection, are checked by men of rank always wishing to increase their wealth and power. And this they effect by marrying heiresses.

The Descent of Man

Frances's sons were sitting in the back of the Mercedes. They were silent and expressionless as Maurice said hello and climbed into the passenger seat beside their mother. Daniel, the elder was already taller than her, fair haired with the same pale bluish eyes. Andrew, aged twelve, was smaller and darker both in looks and temperament. They were mute as she wound her way expertly through the London traffic towards the M3 motorway and the open countryside, chattering casually as she drove.

Maurice's head was full, as it had been for days, with thoughts of a different family, a different era, and he said little. But during a pause he felt obliged to contribute something and he turned awkwardly in his seat towards the older boy. 'When I was you age I was reading lots of books. Walter Scott, Conan Doyle, all that sort of thing. What do you read?'

The boy regarded him with a blank stare. Maurice continued. 'Harry Potter, I suppose? Philip Pullman?'

'Yes—that stuff.' A beat. Then, 'But I like Walter Scott too. And Dennis Wheatley.'

Maurice's eyebrows lifted. 'Wheatley? That's interesting. I didn't know anyone read him nowadays.'

'Oh yes. I like all that occult stuff.'

Frances laughed. 'What price Darwin now?'

Maurice said, 'I think I've got a couple of Wheatleys on my shelves. I sell books, you know.'

'Yes, I know.'

'But I don't think I've sold one of his in years.'

'Which ones have you got?' There was interest in the boy's voice now. As the conversation went on the younger boy remained silent and disinterested, until Maurice happened to mention that he had a military section at the shop. Then the boy pricked up his ears and asked, 'Do you have any books about the Battle Of Waterloo?'

'I certainly do. On all the Napoleonic wars.'

'We're doing that in history. I'd like to see those.'

'We'll have to arrange that,' said Maurice. 'What other wars are you interested in?'

'The Second World War. Especially the planes.'

'Ah. Well I have a few books on that as well. . . . .'

The talk didn't stop until they were deep in the rolling Dorset countryside, bathed in the early summer sunshine and voluptuous in England's deepest green. The Mercedes crawled slowly along a lane almost too narrow for its width, bounded by hedgerows twice the height of a man, until it emerged in the main street of a small hamlet, thatched and timbered, that could hardly have changed in three centuries.

'Here we are,' said Frances, and turned in at tall stone gate posts with a wrought iron sign which said simply 'The Manor'.

The drive was several hundred yards long between open sheep-strewn pastures lined with oak and ash. 'There used to be some magnificent elms,' she said, 'but the Dutch elm disease got most of them. And the ash are under threat now.'

They rounded a lake bounded on one side by rhododendrons and dotted with mallards and moorhens. Then the manor house unfolded before them, whitewashed, pillared and porticoed and Georgian paned, serene with the unique serenity that historic houses have.

'Beautiful,' said Maurice.

'I told you it was,' she said.

The earl and countess appeared at the front door and came down the steps as the car pulled up. Both skirting their three-score years and ten; he tall, angular, tweedily dressed despite the season—not unlike an older British version of Donald Easterby really—she slight like her daughter, fluttering with floral chiffon, eager as a yellow bird.

'Oh, here you are, here you are!' she sang, flapping her hands. 'My boys, my boys—come and give gran a hug.'

The boys dutifully did so, whilst the earl enveloped Frances in a bear clasp and took her offering of lilies and irises from the boot. He waved at the sky. 'Brought the weather with you—well done! Bet you're glad to be out of the smoke. Got lots to show you in the garden. Who's this then?'

'This is Maurice, Daddy—I told you about him.'

'Yes, yes. Deal in old books, I gather?'

'That's right,' said Maurice.

'Good, good. Man after my own heart. Got plenty to show you in the house. Like your opinion on some of them.'

'I'd be delighted.'

'Come in, come in. Game pie for lunch. Bit early in the season, so it's probably mostly rabbit and duck—but there you go. Hello there boys! How's the cricket? You in the team yet?'

And in they went, chattering and chuckling like a bevy of chickens.

Lunch was in the long bow-fronted dining room at a polished mahogany dining table that could have sat twenty or more. The meal was a kaleidoscope of pies and hams, salads and sauces, fruits and cheeses, all served up by Frances's mother aided by a stout housekeeper who, from the familiar way she ordered everyone around had obviously been part of the family for most of her life. The talk was of relatives and family gossip, village affairs, politics and politicians, sport and sportsmen—the usual kindred talk in fact, in which the boys were fully included, and coloured by that indefinable English upper class patina of irreverent and critical involvement.

Maurice was a back seat participant in the conversation, offering his contribution when addressed, but otherwise content to sit and observe the further interactions of family life of which he had so little experience. Frances occasionally threw him a quick glance to see if he was at ease, and then went back to her role within the circle as mover, advisor, disciplinarian and supportive giggler to her mother, whose evident delight at the occasion manifested itself in a continuous flow of exclamations, imprecations and chirrups of amusement.

After lunch the earl, whom by now Maurice had become accustomed under orders to address as James, suggested a quick visit to the library to see the 'ancestral tomes', followed by a 'post-prandial amble round the park'.

The library, which evidently doubled as a TV room, such gross modern appliances being banned from the elegant lounge, held a relatively modest but distinguished collection of books from Chaucer to Cervantes, Bunyan to Lawrence, as well as a number of leather bound family records and histories.

'Splendid,' murmured Maurice as he browsed the carved mahogany shelves. 'Fascinating stuff.'

'Yes,' said the earl, towering beside him. 'Hope we can keep it all intact. Bit of a struggle though.'

'Oh?' said Maurice.

'Takes a lot to keep up a place like this, you know. Death duties are a killer, despite the best efforts of the lawyers. My father managed to keep most of the land together, but we've had to sacrifice a few works of art—one or two Holbeins, even a Rembrandt would you believe.'

'That's a shame.'

'Made approaches to the National Trust, but they've got their hands full.' He gazed out of the window, head forward like an eagle's. 'So much history fading away in this crowded little island. So much of our past, our heritage.'

'Yes.'

The other sighed. 'Still, we've kept the land, that's the main thing. Not a vast amount but significant. Buildings and paintings will always come and go, I suppose, but land can never be replaced.' '*The land was ours before we were the land's.*'

They all, except for the countess who stayed 'to help Bessie with the crocks', donned wellington boots from a vast collection in the old stable block behind the house, and ventured out into the alternately manicured and muddy, formal and wild, open and secretive spaces of the estate.

The boys ran off whooping and whirling to their familiar stomping grounds, whilst Maurice, Frances, her father, and two boisterous dalmatians marched around the gardens, across the fields and through the woods on what was obviously a well-trodden route. The dogs appeared and disappeared on wild charges, and the earl waved his stick as he went at various landmarks and points of interest, giving a running commentary on their significance to the history of the place and the family. Maurice made the necessary appreciative comments, and Frances walked a step or two behind, saying little, having no doubt heard it all many times.

Then as they climbed an open hill, the perfect Dorset shape of a woman's breast, with a vast view of the rolling wield about them, James asked, 'Is it important then, this Darwin thing which has caused so much trouble?'

'Well. . . .' replied Maurice, carefully. 'It depends what one means by important.'

'Important enough to cause a man's death.'

'No, of course not. Nothing's that important.'

'So what do *you* mean by important?'

'Well, as a dealer in old books and manuscripts, a private reflection by Darwin's wife would be of great interest. From a scientific point of view, not so much. From a Darwinian academic's perspective it could be intriguing. From a general historian's less so. And so on.'

James nodded, and shouted to the dogs distantly galloping. They paid no heed. 'Have you any idea what's in it?' he asked.

'I have an inkling.'

'Frances thought there may have been something at Hatfield, but I gather that drew a blank.'

'Yes.' Maurice threw her a glance. 'Though she may have been closer than she realised.'

Frances's eyebrows went up curiously, but she said nothing.

'And there's something about a secret treatise by Darwin himself?'

'Yes, that's right.'

'What on?'

'Possibly a final comment on what he sees is the significance of his theory.'

'For whom?'

'For everyone. The philosophical significance.'

'Ah.' The earl marched on for a moment, sprightly for his age, approaching the summit of the hill. 'We're Roman Catholics, you know—the family.'

'Oh. I didn't know.'

'Well, my generation are probably the last. The modern lot aren't interested in all that.'

Maurice threw another quick glance at Frances, who smiled and wrinkled her nose at him. They gained the top, panting, and gazed out over the wide earth and wider sky. There was a distant glimpse of grey-green sea. 'But it's a shame,' continued the earl. 'It's a lot to do with what's wrong with the modern world.'

'Perhaps, yes.'

The other turned his watery but sharp eyes on Maurice. 'Of course he was a great man, Darwin. Explained so much. I have no problem with evolutionary theory. But it isn't the whole story, you know.'

'You don't think so?'

'Oh no.' The dogs raced up, panting. 'Sit!' he commanded, which they did for fully five seconds. 'No. Evolution reveals a lot. But it's a description, not an explanation. Describes the how, not the why. Can never explain the motivating force behind it all.'

'Isn't that its point? That there is no motivating force?'

James shook his head, his thick eyebrows bristling. 'I could never accept that. There has to be a supreme force to bring it all into being. To direct it, however mysteriously.' He waved a finger. 'For instance 'Origin of Species' may tell us how birds developed from pterodactyls or how we descended from apes, but it can't explain the miracles of sight, or sound, or creative thought.'

'It does actually,' said Maurice diffidently.

'Eh?'

'If you read it carefully you'll find that it suggests an evolutionary explanation for all those things.'

'Really?' The earl stared at Maurice, his eyebrows raised. Maurice nodded. Frances was pointedly peering off in another direction. 'Goodness. Well perhaps I'd better go back to it. Have to admit I never read the whole thing word for word.'

'Not many have. It's a bit of a challenge. But it's worth the effort if one can do so.'

The earl gave a throaty chuckle. 'Some of my cronies would love to debate with you on it.' He sniffed the air. 'I still go up to Westminster from time to time, you know. Put in my ha'porth in the chamber. But the time is up for us hereditary lot.'

'Yes, it would seem so.'

'Pity really. May not be exactly democratic, but they'll be losing all that wealth of public service and experience, all that historic wisdom. And the objectivity too. None of the jockeying for position you get in the other place—people forget that aspect.' He grimaced. 'No, it'll become just a carbon copy of the other chamber. Then they'll all wonder what they've lost.'

Maurice gazed across the rolling acres where the two dogs were once again mere racing dots in the distance, and wondered too what would be lost. Just another species, he supposed, or would it be called a sub-species?

'So d'you think you'll find this thing?' went on the earl.

'Well,' said Maurice cautiously, 'I'm more or less giving up on it. It's caused enough tragedy.'

'Hm.' Pause. 'Pity in a way. The sort of thing that *should* be found.'

'Perhaps. In which case no doubt one day it will.'

'Yes, right.' The old boy gazed at the far horizon. 'Won't change anything though.'

'Maybe not.'

'Just explain a bit more of how God works his mysterious way. No one will ever disprove the existence of God, y'see. There's no point to it all without God.' He threw a quick smile at Maurice, then looked back at the horizon and waved his stick. 'Never tire of that view. Sometimes think they should have built the house here.' He grunted. 'But then I suppose one would take the view for granted. You need something to aspire to.'

On the way back to London the boys were asleep in the back for the most part. As they left Dorset and hit the motorway, Frances said, 'Well now you know a bit about my family.'

'Yes,' replied Maurice. He minutely shook his head and smiled. 'Remarkable.'

'I know hardly anything about yours. Do you have siblings?'

'Yes. Four. Through adoption.'

'Goodness. I wouldn't have guessed. Where are they?'

'One is in Yorkshire, one in New Zealand, one in Nigeria, one in the States.'

'Goodness again. Do you see them at all?'

'Not enough. It's time I did.' He watched the passing landscape. 'I was thinking about closing the shop for a while and taking a trip actually.'

'Yes, you should. Go round the world and see what's happening out there.'

'Yes.'

By the time she dropped him back at his flat it was late in the evening. The boys had slept most of the way back and Maurice too was tired. She must have been exhausted after another three hour drive, but she didn't seem so.

'Thank you for a wonderful day,' he said as he climbed out.

'I hope you meant that,' she said.

'Oh yes. Really. I love your parents.'

'A dying breed.' As he closed the car door and stood on the pavement she lowered the window and leaned across. 'By the way, what did you mean when you said we might have got close at Hatfield?'

He hesitated. 'I shouldn't really have said that. I'll tell you one day.'

'Right.'

The boys had stirred with the stopping of the car. He tapped on the rear window. 'Bye boys. Nice to meet you.'

'Bye', they said in unison.

He hesitated on the pavement. 'Perhaps. . . .'

'Yes?' she said.

'Perhaps we could have lunch next week?'

'I'd like that.'

He had a sudden impulse. 'I'll take you to the Ritz.'

Her eyebrows went up. 'The Ritz?'

He risked a little exaggeration. 'I go there from time to time.'

'Well, well, Maurice. You are a man of surprises.'

'Shall we say Tuesday?'

She smiled. 'That would be wonderful.'

He watched them drive off, then took a deep breath of the mild summer air and turned towards his front door. 'Is that all right, Alice?' he murmured.

'Of course it is, you silly boy,' she answered. 'Quite a nice girl under all the posh veneer.'

'Yes.'

'Bit over the top though, the Ritz, isn't it?'

'Probably.'

'You'll be taking a room there next, to seduce her after lunch.'

His neck reddened at the thought. 'Don't be ridiculous, Alice!'

He could hear her laughing as he put his key in the door.

CHAPTER FIFTY-NINE

<u>April 28th, 1882. Down House</u>

I have taken my ancient journal from the dusty hiding place where it has rested for more than twenty years. I have to make one more entry in it before I return it there for what may be eternity, or at least the remainder of my lifetime.

They buried my Charley in Westminster Abbey two days ago. I recorded the details in my small diary, but this is my private reflection, my own benediction, for I could not bring myself to attend so large and grandiose a ceremonial. It was for the sake of others and for the nation, it was not the private farewell that C and I would have wished, and in truth that I planned. The family and the village had prepared for a simple burial in the churchyard, and John Lewis the village carpenter had already made the rough coffin that C had requested. Nevertheless, I was prevailed upon by the great and the good from all quarters—his colleagues in the sciences, politicians of every persuasion, the newspapers, the Dean of Westminster himself—to allow the larger occasion, and indeed it seemed to me only just that, whatever our personal instincts, such a tribute to my husband's achievements should be honoured in this way. I could not deny him his final recognition after so long passed over in the honours lists, and in his secret way I know that 'the Devil's Chaplain' as he was branded, would have been proud to be granted a final resting place within the chief sanctum of the creed whose doctrines he had been challenging for much of his life. It is the reconciliation between faith and science that in his heart I like to think he secretly desired.

The entreaty which finally convinced me came from the Standard newspaper, whose words I feel I should record here lest they be forgotten: ". . . One who had brought such honour to the English name, and whose death is lamented throughout the civilized world, should not be laid in a comparatively obscure grave. His proper place is amongst those other worthies whose reputations are landmarks in the people's history. . . . We owe it to posterity to place his remains in Westminster Abbey, among the illustrious dead who make that noble fane unrivalled in the world."

Although I was absent from the service, resting alone at home with my prayers, the children and the main household went, and of course all the extended family—thirty three Darwins and Wedgwoods and Allens altogether I am told. The children (I still call them that despite that they are all mature people with distinguished careers of their own) returned to Downe and gave me a full description of the occasion. I have also seen the newspaper reports, and letters from other witnesses are already beginning to flood in from all quarters. It seems to have been the most impressive and moving of events. The abbey was full to overflowing with all C's associates from the science and academic worlds, half the nobility of the land, many parliamentarians, the Lord Mayor of London, representatives from all the embassies of the empire, and countless other worthies in attendance. The service was solemn and majestic, and the tributes by the prelates adulatory, and by all accounts almost eulogistic. There was a specially commissioned hymn sung after the lesson, and the choristers sang 'I am the Resurrection' with those glorious words, 'His body is buried in peace but his name liveth evermore.' I could not have asked for more.

I am old myself now—seventy four next month—and though relatively robust for my age my bones are weary and my mind perhaps a little overfull with memories. I do not fear death and will not be sad to be at my husband's side once more. I am glad to have kept this humble record of my life, poor and incomplete though it may be. I shall return it now to its own resting place, known only to my nearest and dearest.

God be merciful.

E.D.

CHAPTER SIXTY

Thus, from the war of nature, from famine and death, the most exalted object which we are capable of conceiving, namely, the production of the higher animals, directly follows. There is grandeur in this view of life. . . . that, whilst this planet has gone cycling on according to the fixed law of gravity, from so simple a beginning endless forms most beautiful and most wonderful have been, and are being, evolved.

Origin of Species

He was sitting on the stone bench in front of the house. From there one could look down the narrow tree framed valley to where the grey sea lapped at the Dorset cliffs and the famous outline of the Cobb at Lyme Regis could just be seen in the far left distance. The view was the main reason they had bought the house, although he was not seeing it at the moment—his mind was on other things. The massive stone wall behind him reflected sunlight onto his back with a comforting warmth. It was not the most convenient of homes, but the building had that indefinable historic aura which carefully converted old places retain, and which colour the lives of their occupants in subtle ways. It was the other reason they had chosen it.

Frances came out of the oak framed doorway and rested a hand on his shoulder. 'What are you thinking about?'

'I'm working out what to say to them.'

She gazed down the valley at the distant water as she usually did. 'It's good of them to come all this way.'

'I practically insisted they did. There are quite a lot of issues involved. I want to be sure they understand them.'

She nodded towards the stone patio at the other end of the house outside the kitchen. 'Is it warm enough to have lunch on the terrace, do you think?'

'Why not? Bit chilly for Australian dwellers, but we can come in if it clouds over.'

She looked up at the sky, then cocked her head. 'I think I hear a car.'

He looked at his watch. 'It's probably them. I'll go down and see they don't miss the gate.'

She went back indoors as he walked briskly down the short graveled drive between the shrubs and her well tended flower beds, and stood in the roadway looking up the hill. A silver saloon appeared round the top bend. Presumably hired, he thought, and by no means the cheapest category. He waved as the car approached. It slowed and turned in before the gate. The driver's window slid down.

'Maurice Aldridge?' asked the man.

'Come in, come in,' said Maurice, and indicated the parking space at the top of the driveway. He followed on foot and arrived as they were climbing out of the car. The man was in his forties, smart suited, athletic, confidant looking—with only a slight facial resemblance to his father. The woman was fair haired and attractive in that outdoor, sun-burnt way that well travelled people often are. Maurice shook hands. 'Good of you to come all this way,' he said. 'I know you're not in the country for long.'

'We were glad of the chance to get out of London,' said the wife with a smile. 'And this is such a lovely part of the world.'

'We like it. My wife's family have always lived in these parts, so we sort of drifted down here.' He pushed open the front door. 'Come in and meet her.'

They all chatted for a few moments in the stone flagged kitchen whilst Frances laid out gazpacho and quiche and salad on a tray, and Maurice fixed long drinks and got out a bottle of wine just in case. Then they sat round the garden table on the terrace.

'I'm sorry about your father's death,' said Maurice.

The man shrugged. 'He lasted quite well considering. Seventy eight years after all the alcohol he got through—not a bad stretch really.'

'No.'

'We weren't actually that close. I had a. . . .' He hesitated. 'A difficult childhood.'

'I gathered as much.' Maurice threw him a quick glance as he offered the wine bottle.

'How much did he tell you?' asked the other.

'Not a great deal. But I know he felt deeply remorseful about the past. You meant a great deal to him during his latter years.'

'Really.' His expression was sardonic. 'A bit late.'

'Yes, well. . . . You've obviously done well in life. He was proud of that.'

The man nodded briefly with pursed lips. 'When did you last see him?'

'Six years ago. I only met him twice. Once when I tracked him down in Oxford whilst on the trail of the journal. The second time when he brought it to me at my book shop in London.'

'With instructions that it was for me?'

'Yes.' Maurice threw a glance at Frances. 'It was an odd step for him to take, putting it in my keeping, but he was in a rather parlous state and he didn't know where else to go with it. I told him he could get a lot of money for it, but he was adamant that you should have it. That's how much he cared.'

Matheson's eyes were sad. 'But you got him some money anyway?'

'Enough to enable him to stay in his home. Him and his cats.'

'Ah yes.'

'The whole business was quite complicated and the result of a long involved search, but my sponsor was a wealthy collector and he was willing to pay just to get a glimpse of the journal. He is an honourable man and had spent a lot of time and money seeking it out, so although I never let him see the real thing I felt it right that he should know of its contents. I took the liberty of giving him a copy.' Maurice rose from his seat. 'Wait there a moment.' He vanished indoors, and returned seconds later holding the book. He placed it on the table, carefully picking a shaded place. 'This is the real thing.'

They all looked at it. The wife spoke for the first time. 'It's big.'

'Nearly four hundred pages,' replied Maurice. 'Some two hundred entries. And it's been edited down from the original by her son Frank. Later Sir Francis Darwin.'

'Is it so important then?'

Maurice gazed at it for a moment. He did not wear spectacles any more. Frances had finally got him onto contact lenses, for which he was grateful. 'It depends on how you look at it, Mrs Matheson.'

'Call me Diana, please,' she said.

He nodded. 'Well, Diana—it has played a disproportionate part in my own life.' He threw a glance at Frances. 'It brought me my wife amongst other things.' She gave the slightest of smiles as she cut into the quiche. 'Apart from that, to anyone interested in old books, in science, or simply in historical memoirs, I would say it has relevance at the very least. To those who aren't, it's only of passing significance.'

The woman's smile had a hint of irony. 'As a housewife with three children and married to a man who works in high technology, would I find it interesting, do you think?'

Maurice turned to Frances. 'What would you say, Frances?'

Frances spoke to her in that gracious way that attractive older women reserve for attractive younger women. 'I've no doubt at all that you would.'

Diana nodded. 'Well then, I look forward to reading it.'

Her husband spoke. 'But you say there's a problem as to what to do with it?'

Maurice hesitated, and stared across the garden for a few seconds. 'Yes,' he said. 'As you know, your father has left the book to you for the reasons that the solicitors have explained. I persuaded them to let me retain custody of it until I could hand it to you. There's a moral problem with it, which I have to leave you to resolve. You see, the volume could be very valuable. It's one of only half a dozen or so printed copies, and it's been kept secret for well over a century. The reason it's been kept secret is that Emma Darwin wished it so, and the descendants have so far all respected those wishes.' He hesitated, seeking his words. 'However you are not a direct descendant of the family, and so to some extent you are not bound by the same obligations. The real question is twofold. Firstly, do you wish to capitalise on your legacy. And secondly, is the world entitled after all this time to know about it's contents.'

He paused. There was silence around the table. Then Matheson said, 'What does your rich collector think?'

'He thinks it should be published and released to humanity. He feels that, like other private journals which achieve significance after their author's death, it has too much historic importance to be locked away for ever.'

'And there's something about a secret postscript by Darwin himself?'

'Yes, but that's a whole other thing. No-one knows where that might be.'

Matheson nodded, and reflected again. He took a sip of wine and said, 'I'm a civil engineer as you know, Maurice. I'm currently working on a large desalination plant being constructed for the Victorian government in Australia. Australia has huge problems with its water. Parts of the country never have enough, other parts get far too much, far too suddenly. I have experience of similar environmental problems in other parts of the world.' He hesitated and glanced at his wife. 'In some ways this planet is in a rather desperate state.' He inclined his head. 'It is much talked about, but at present no-one is doing anything serious about it. The natural catastrophes seem to be becoming more frequent and more widespread— whether through human action or natural causes, who knows? But if the process continues it will eventually lead to famines, mass population upheavals, civil unrest. All of which our children and grand children will have to survive.' He glanced at Maurice. 'The real crisis may not affect my generation too much, but I have serious worries for future ones.' He paused and looked at the book. 'From what little I know the journal isn't going to throw any more light on the science of all that. But it sounds as if it has a lot to say about the human condition. In which case my attitude would be, every little helps.'

Maurice nodded. '*History is a race between education and catastrophe.*'

The other spread his hands. 'I'll read it and see what I feel then.'

'Yes, good,' said Maurice. 'And if you decide to publish, or indeed dispose of the book, then I have various contacts who might be of help.'

'I don't think I'll sell it. I might lend it to some museum or other.'

Maurice nodded again and smiled. 'That would be a generous decision.'

When they had left, he sat on his stone bench again and blew through his lips. 'Good,' he said, 'I'm glad to have that off my hands.'

She sat beside him. 'I quite liked them,' she said. 'I think it's in safe keeping.' There was silence for a moment. 'You know the boys are coming down this weekend?' she said.

'Oh, good.'

She threw him a glance. 'I think Daniel may bring his new girl friend. The first time he's brought anyone here. It must be quite serious.'

'Hm.' Pause. 'We've only three bedrooms. How will they sleep?'

'I'll leave it to them. There's the twin room for the boys and the double for her. If they want to change arrangements after lights out, that's up to them.'

He sighed. 'Life would be so much simpler if mating wasn't necessary for procreation.' His wife smiled and patted his knee. She rose and pulled a weed from the nearby flower bed. He looked critically up at the sky. 'Perfect conditions. I might take the boat out for an hour or so.'

'You do that. I'll stay and pick the raspberries.' She stopped by the seat, and looked at him quizzically. 'Do you think we did the right thing coming down here?'

'The right thing?'

'It is the back end of nowhere.'

'Of course we did.' Well it wasn't Innisfree, but it would do quite nicely.

'You're still a young man, you know.'

He reflected. 'I used to think London was the centre of the universe, and the book shop the source of all my creativity. Now I know it wasn't the shop at all. It's the books themselves. Seeking them out, reading them, corresponding about them. . . .' He pulled a rueful face. 'The odd thing is, I think I do better financially trading specialist things around the world than I ever did running the shop.'

'We could do with a few less of them in the house.'

'You're beginning to sound like Alice.'

She smiled again, then said, 'Is it only the books?'

'No, of course not. It's living. It's here. It's you.'

She kissed the top of his head, a bit bald now, and went indoors.

He turned his face up to the sun. 'Am I doing all right?' he murmured to Alice. He very rarely talked to her these days.

'Of course you are,' she said. 'She's good for you. Different to me of course, but came along in the nick of time. Don't you think you're doing all right?'

He nodded. 'Yes.' He gazed again at the distant sea. 'Yes, I think Charles D might say I've survived.'

Attached note: I and my siblings have taken the decision that this Addendum to my father's work shall be lodged in the archives of the Royal Society and that the contents shall not be disclosed or published without the unanimous agreement of all Members of the Society.

F.D. 1898

ADDENDUM

Homo sapiens is a strange species. By far the most intelligently advanced of all that inhabit the earth, yet by far the most perverse and consciously self destructive. Of extraordinary intellectual powers, yet prone to illogical prejudices, dogmas and superstitions. The only species to have developed an analytical and a moral sense, yet the one most subject to irrational drives, unnecessary cruelties and unreasoned fears. There has to be an explanation for this.

Over the years my exhaustive researches into many of the families, genera and species on the planet have convinced me of the one simple fact. Despite the persuasions of much of humanity, nothing is planned. Nothing is ordained. It is a matter of simple evidence that the universe operates in a way which is completely fortuitous. The earth is but one planet amongst innumerable planets which happens by chance to have the resources to support life. That life comes and goes with a fickleness and a ruthlessness that is total and disinterested. Whatever the biological form, it suffers plague and pestilence, contest and brutalism, deprivation and extermination, without respite and without structure. Whole generations die at a circumstance, entire species become extinct at a change in the weather, complete life forms disappear through the whim of a natural disaster. As I have, I hope, shown in my writings, natural selection is the ultimate decider in the great struggle for survival—one superior developed form superseding another, one better equipped species outliving another—each succeeding generation either extending its superiority through its inherited characteristics, or yielding to a still better endowed competitor. Extermination is a universal and brutal necessity. If it were not so, if all life were to proliferate unchallenged, then the earth would have suffocated through overcrowding millions of years ago.

This is a difficult circumstance for humans to comprehend. It is anathema to many. For they recognise only the beauty of nature and attribute this to the beneficence of the Almighty. But were they to look more closely they would observe that underneath nature is of necessity savage, merciless, dispassionate. It is a perpetual contest for survival. The ichneumon deposits its eggs to feed within the living bodies of other insects, the queen bee slaughters her own daughters as they are born for the preservation of her own community, one ant community destroys or enslaves another for the sake of its posterity. And of course man perishes in his thousands at the advent of a drought, the onslaught of a plague, or through the insanity of war. In nature justice has no sway, virtue is irrelevant, circumstance is all.

The very fact that man has become the dominant creature is, I believe, pure chance. It is probably due largely to the fortuitous fact that his ancestors developed dextrous fingers in order to find safety in the trees and probe there for fruit and other foods, which then enabled them to hold sticks and stones as weapons, and thence to fashion tools, and so begin thinking creatively. Had the first wolves developed fingers instead of claws, or birds become more adept with their own talons, then the lords of the earth might have been canine or had wings.

This is not a message easily accepted by many, perhaps the majority. That we are the product of simple circumstance. That we are here by accident—this is a concept inconceivable to all who have been conditioned by generations of earthly dominance, by centuries of religious teaching, and indeed by their own arrogance. But it is, I am convinced, a fact. Once it is understood all things become clear. The vicissitudes of fortune, the aberrations of behaviour, the injustices of ordinary existence. We are tempted, amongst the mysteries and the travails of life, to seek for explanations in the stars and in the unseen blowings of the wind. We desire above all things to believe in a strategy behind the turmoil, a guiding authority amongst the havoc. We crave the assurance of a benign paternal power from the first glimmers of awareness—a loving father, a wise school teacher, an infallible political leader, and ultimately an omnipotent god. I myself was brought up in that tradition and accepted it until well into adult life. However the more I developed my theory of natural selection the more I realised it was incompatible with such beliefs. I tried in my principle writings to accommodate the possibility of an Original Creator in order that too many readers should not be offended and so become distracted from my major argument. I would describe myself as an agnostic in such questions. I concur that the first origins of life or matter is a question which may never be proven, although even here one has to ask why a supreme authority would start such a process and then abandon it to mere anarchy. However it seems unequivocal to me that, whatever the initial spark, no such authority has since taken any hand in, or exerted any influence over what occurs in nature. One only has to observe the progress of life objectively to realise this is true. Does a divine power decide which hundred gnats a swallow shall snap up in its flight, at what moment a hawk will stoop upon that swallow? Does a supreme being determine that a good man shall be struck by lightning under a tree, causing his wife and children to be cast into the workhouse? Does God instigate the destruction of mass populations of species, having first created them? The growth and then decline of inferior genera, having first designed them? The agony of premature death by slaughter, starvation, or disease of the vast majority of organic beings through the ages, having supposedly brought them into life? I cannot accept such a concept. I listen to prelates preaching about the love of the Almighty, the power of his protection, the might of his omnipotence, and I see no atom of evidence of such in any circumstance of the observable world. Truly there is beauty, there is goodness, there is advancement, as well as savagery. But these are random and inconstant, due solely to the fortunes of the moment and to individual aspiration, not to any organised design.

Likewise the dreams of a heavenly afterlife. These are comforting no doubt to man in his tormented existence, but I do not see the reason. I cannot envisage the method. That we are put here to struggle and suffer and perish, only then to attain celestial eternity? It is surely a pointless preliminary to a supernatural sequel. Even more meaningless the notion that we suffer eternal perdition if we transgress here on earth. Why then allow random tragedy and barbarity to exist in the first place? Simply to challenge us? A divine entrance test? And if so what of those who die in infancy? Do they qualify for a place in heaven? The idea that God gave us Free Will precludes any function for God in the first place. Such reasoning has no logic, except that its promotion is a powerful means of instilling a moral conformity in the interests of the community.

Yet, if one puts aside these primitive concepts and considers dispassionately the principle of survival of the fittest, it becomes evident that this must be the remarkable and efficient tool by which the progress and development of Life is achieved. The simple fact that a chance variation in the emergence of a new generation can fortuitously equip that generation better for survival in a particular environment, and so lead by further procreation to an improved species, is so obvious and so logical, and furthermore is scientifically demonstrable. Thus it is that, over aeons of time and thousands of generations, the giraffe procured an ever longer neck for access to higher branches—although having the same number of vertebrae as an elephant; the rose developed ever brighter colours to attract fertilising insects—although plants fertilised by other methods such as the wind have no need of gaudy colours; the bat developed its flying abilities and extraordinary hearing system to enable it to go hunting under the safety of darkness—although it has similar eye and finger bone structure to other mammals. Natural selection is the means by which the first microbes crept from the sea to the land, the means by which the first flora took root, the first fauna drew breath. And the means by which the species of man has attained his extraordinary powers.

Those developed powers are so astonishing that he is in fact the first creature to have some hope of <u>controlling</u> his own future. The first organism to escape the ruthless process of natural selection and begin to make his own selections (as the farmer, the rose grower and the pigeon breeder already select). Dare I say it, it is <u>man</u> who is the supreme authority, on this planet at any rate. But only for as long as he utilises that authority for the ultimate benefit, else he too will go the way of all other extinct forms.

Of course man wishes—one might almost say needs—to have faith in a greater power. He requires such in order to make sense of a mystifying and capricious world. He has ingrained beliefs stemming from his primeval past, when the stars, the mountains, the seas were things of awesome mystery, his imagination endowing them with supernatural properties and divine occupation. And although he has now explored much of the mystery he carries these concepts still, buried deep in his psyche. And he passes the myths on to the infant in the cradle, as a means of reassuring the child that all will be well in a precarious existence.

Yet it seems to me strange that so many intelligent and educated persons should carry such beliefs into adult life. Curious that they should cling to an irrational conviction in the face of all the evidence—the myriad of conflicting ideologies, the lack of any true verification for any of them, the evident randomness and inequity of existence, even the wholesale oppression perpetrated throughout man's history in the name of a chosen deity. All this, one would think, should outweigh the resolute insistence on 'faith'. Yet still they pay homage to ancient prophets and supposed divinities, ignoring the questions as to why none such have succeeded in changing the general course of man's behaviour, or why their belated appearance should be necessary in a created universe in the first place.

One has to ask why this is. One has to wonder that this supposedly advanced species still clings to such groundless conceptions. Why do humans place reliance on external powers for which there are no proofs and no evidences? Why do they travel hundreds of miles to shrines with purported miraculous features in order to cure their infirmities, when the ordeal invariably proves ineffective and even in many cases fatal? Why do they create and congregate in the most magnificent constructions ever built in order to seek salvation from deities who patently exert no great effort on their welfare or survival? And above all, why do they act in defiance of all the moral codes supposedly imposed by these omnipotent authorities, and continue to behave with depravity in pursuit of spurious benefits?

The only explanation I can discover is that homo sapiens, notwithstanding his extraordinary accomplishments, is still at base a primitive animal. He is an undeveloped creature who, despite being able to design a steam engine or compose a symphony, is yet prey to primal urges and instincts. There is not so much discrepancy in this paradox as might be thought. One only has to consider the astonishing technical achievement behind the creation of a spider's web or a bee's honeycomb—two organisms which have the basest intellectual development, and both completely subject to the motivations of inherited instinct—to see how nature can achieve such contrast. In my writings on instinct in species I have described at length how my researches have led me to the conclusion that these inherited traits form one of the most powerful tools of evolution. Inherited instinct provides a modus for both the individual and the community, and the strongest instincts protect and enhance a species' existence, hence the examples of the ichneumon, the queen bee and the ant described above. So it is with humans. The instincts to conquer, to extend territory, to defile and terrorise opponents, to beget maximum progeny are all deeply embedded in the human psyche. As are the instincts to venerate and placate conceived superior powers or divinities. Inherited mythology is a powerful thing. And I have to accept that it has been necessary, perhaps essential, for humanity's wellbeing to maintain belief in an absolute authority and a final reward in heaven. Without such concepts how could we have survived the appalling vicissitudes of fortune? How could we have endured so cruel a life where little semblance of order or hope exists? In primitive times such faith is almost a condition of survival.

Nevertheless, as I have said, it is also true that man has now evolved from his early state, and is, compared to the other denizens of the earth, a much progressed creature. The instincts within him, acquired for his early survival and assurance, are mostly redundant. I would suggest that, in order to properly employ his newly developed dominance, he should by now be discarding them. It seems to me that, just as his savagery is no longer of use in a largely ordered world, so his superstitious inclinations are now a constraint on his awareness of reality. Indeed I would go further and say that a reliance on a supreme authority could well be a hindrance to man's progress, since it encourages him to place the burden of salvation on God's shoulders and not on his own. It exonerates him from responsibility.

Furthermore there is a liberation in forsaking such concepts. Once freed from the constraints of historical ideologies man will be able to explore morality for its own sake, to seek individual fulfilment objectively, to grow old with acceptance. Then his appreciation of the glories of the universe, his knowledge of the remarkable way it works and develops, his ability to exploit its limitless powers, will so far eclipse his innumerable visions of paradise and mystically ordained structures that he will wonder at his early innocence. He will appreciate his contribution to the whole gigantic pattern, as each plant contributes to the life of the forest around it, and thus be free of his need for lone benediction.

I would offer an alternative philosophy, albeit one that will no doubt earn me accusations of sacrilege. For me, it is the gradual progress of man, and far beyond man of the universe itself, through natural selection and towards an ultimate perfect self design, that is the only concept of heaven that is credible. One might say that God is the end, not the beginning.

I have been remarkably fortunate in my own life. Chance has been kind in my case. Despite my share of tragedies and afflictions, I have seen the marvels of the world, I have experienced the love of family and humanity, I have discovered a vocation that goes to the heart of existence. I know that life itself is the only thing that merits faith. Evolving life in all its extraordinary forms, the changing firmament in all its spectacular beauty, the infinite possibilities for future attainment, these are what justify worship.

The method of my own worship has been through biological research. Scientific exploration has been my fascination, my joy, and at times my demon. In that it is the only path reliably to discover and to exploit the truth, it is I believe man's destiny.

CD. 1859

Lightning Source UK Ltd.
Milton Keynes UK
UKOW05f1337030913

216451UK00001B/125/P